DEADHOUSE LANDING

www.**penguin**.co.uk

Also by Ian C. Esslemont

NIGHT OF KNIVES
RETURN OF THE CRIMSON GUARD
STONEWIELDER
ORB SCEPTRE THRONE
BLOOD AND BONE
ASSAIL
DANCER'S LAMENT

For more information on Ian C. Esslemont and his books,
see his website at www.malazanempire.com

DEADHOUSE LANDING

Path to Ascendancy
Book 2

Ian C. Esslemont

BANTAM PRESS

LONDON • TORONTO • SYDNEY • AUCKLAND • JOHANNESBURG

TRANSWORLD PUBLISHERS
61–63 Uxbridge Road, London W5 5SA
www.penguin.co.uk

Transworld is part of the Penguin Random House group of companies
whose addresses can be found at global.penguinrandomhouse.com

Penguin
Random House
UK

First published in Great Britain in 2017 by Bantam Press
an imprint of Transworld Publishers

A CIP catalogue record for this book
is available from the British Library.

ISBNs 9780593074732 (cased)
9780593074749 (tpb)

Typeset in 11/13pt Sabon by Falcon Oast Graphic Art Ltd.
Printed and bound by Clays Ltd, Bungay, Suffolk.

Penguin Random House is committed to a sustainable
future for our business, our readers and our planet. This book
is made from Forest Stewardship Council® certified paper.

1 3 5 7 9 10 8 6 4 2

For Simon Taylor

ACKNOWLEDGEMENTS

Once again I wish to thank A. P. Canavan for his insight, attention and discretion as a prereader and editor. Also, my gratitude to Nancy Webber for her sharp pencil and precise mind. And thanks as always to my agent Howard Morhaim for all his work on behalf of the World of Malaz.

Quon Tali

N

FALARI SEA

WICKAN PLAINS

COLONNUS SEA

ICE FIELDS

The GREAT FENN RANGE

FOREST FENN

NOM PURGE

POR

SETI

DAL HON PLAINS

FOREST HORN

BLOOR SENTRY SEA

KARTOOL ISLAND

REACHER'S OCEAN

MALAZ ISLAND

Malaz City

NAPAN ISLES

GENI

APIT SEA

THE HORN OCEAN

The Horn

DRIFT AVALLI

Baran
Hobal
Balstro
G'ris
Haljhen
Tool's
Nita
Davig
Athrans
Jurda
Unta
Drim
Larent
Yellows
Gust
Vure
Aythan
Carasin
Thade
Rath
Thade
Bloor
Telo
Estavn
Netor
Shedry
Soitar
Bris
Marl
Lages
Halas
Aska
Cawn
Ipras
Askra
Fenga
Boridl
Buldn
Traly
Then
Utto Kan.
Pryl
Laeth
Wal Tes
Wal Fend
Nap
Nex
Ijor
Fedal
Horan
Kyris
Largan
Bajin
Ero Lake
New Seti
Haran
En Krael
Li Heng
Idryb
Tellick
White Lake Seti
High Postern
Seti
Nadir
Bastial
Cutlis
Quan & Tali
Attic
Aireck
Byth
Garalt
Purage
Dash
Valanth
Ebond
Destry
Korn
Panys
Aralth

MALAZ CITY
Pre~Empire

N

1 Deadhouse
2 Hanged Man Inn
3 Back Street
4 Obo's Tower
5 Agayla's Shop
6 Riverwalk (N)
7 Riverwalk (S)
8 Malaz River (lesser channel)
9 Rampart Way
10 Smiley's
11 Golden Gyrfalcon

MALAZ BAY

Reefs

Reefs

Reefs

OLD LOOKOUT ISLAND

MUD ISLAND

WORM ISLAND

salt marsh Reefs

salt marsh

Mock's Hold

centre docks

Inside harbour

Old Point Keep

mourn

Tiller Autumn

Ridge Wall Ridge

Redcave River

Lightings

farms and pastures

Fist Road

Old Upper Estates

Raven Hill Park

Mossy Toot Park

Mouse Quarter

Vines

DRAMATIS PERSONAE

The New Arrivals
Wu   A mysterious mage
Dancer   A notorious assassin

The Napans
Lady Sureth   Exiled noblewoman of Nap
Cartheron   An ex-flank admiral
Urko   An ex-captain
Hawl   A mage of Ruse
Grinner   Lady Sureth's bodyguard
Choss   An ex-captain
Tocaras   An archer
Amiss   A sailor
Shrift   A swordswoman

Of Malaz Island
Mock   Ruler of Malaz, admiral, and marquis
Tattersail A mage of Malaz
Viv   A serving girl
Nedurian   A retired mage
Obo   A wizard of Malaz
Agayla   A sorceress of Malaz
Hess   A Malazan captain
Guran   A Malazan captain
Renish   A Malazan captain
Dujek   A marine
Jack   A marine

Of Kartool
Tallow   The Holy Invigilator of D'rek
Ithell   The Demidrek (a high priest)

Salleen	A high-ranking priestess
Tayschrenn	A high-ranking priest
Silla Leansath	A priestess
Koarsden Taneth	A priest
Feneresh	A priest

Others

Dassem Ultor	The Mortal Sword of Hood
Nara	A follower of Dassem
Lars Jindrift	An adventurer
Tarel	Newly installed king of Nap
Koreth	A Napan admiral
Clementh	A Napan officer
Horst Grethall	A caravan-master
Shear	A masked caravan guard
Geffen	A Malazan crime boss
Koro	A winged inhabitant of Shadow

Prologue

DARIYAL, CAPITAL CITY OF THE NAPAN ISLES, BURNED IN the night. From the heights of the harbour fortifications Cartheron Crust watched the flames swirl and dance and leap through the smoke. He followed that black plume as it billowed higher to obscure the bright silver eye of the waxing moon, and whispered to himself, 'So it all ends.' In fire, destruction and betrayal. Even the best laid plans.

He leaned forward to peer over the guano-stained edge of the battlements to the streets below, where bands of militia and partisans loyal to either side of this transfer of power hunted one another in the clash of running city-wide battle.

'Captain!' a voice called, and Cartheron glanced to his cordon of guards; a messenger had arrived. He waved forward the sweaty, soot-smeared woman.

She saluted. 'Sir! We've lost control of the north quarter.' Involuntarily, he glanced towards the arc of the harbour, and cursed inwardly. 'Sir . . . the mole . . .'

He nodded. 'Yes. I understand. Who are you with?'

'Captain Hawl, sir.'

'Very good.' He took a slow breath, tasted the smoke on his tongue, and, grimacing, thought, *It is now irrevocable.* 'My compliments to Captain Hawl. Have her withdraw. We will regroup at the agreed location.'

The young Napan's indigo features darkened even further as her lips clenched in disappointment. She saluted. 'I'm . . . sorry, sir.'

He waved her off. 'Go quickly.'

She ran. Cartheron turned to the stairs behind him that led to the top of a curtain tower. He drew off his helmet and dragged a

1

hand through his tangled sweaty hair. He let out a long low breath; now for the hard part. He started up the stairs.

When he reached the topmost landing he found her looking out across the city, her back to him, slim, ramrod straight, hands clasped behind her back, in a plain long cotton shirt and trousers. He cleared his throat into a fist and inclined his head. 'Princess Sureth . . .'

She turned and Crust found himself confronted once again by the hard wall of that flat gaze. Even now, he thought, with everything on the line, so damned . . . distant.

'Yes, captain?'

'We've lost control of the north quarter. Your brother no doubt intends to close the harbour at the mole. M'lady, we must withdraw or risk capture.'

Her dark gaze slid aside to the north and it occurred to him that no longer was he looking down at the tousled, mousy hair that she always kept so short; the princess was now nearly as tall as he. *Has the ruling Garell House strength, she has. And trains harder than any of us.*

If only her brother hadn't been so damned greedy . . .

She gave one slight nod. Her stony gaze returned to him. 'I see. And what of our vaunted circle of Napan councillors?'

Cartheron could not hold her eyes. He glanced aside. 'I'm sorry, m'lady. Tarel offered more.'

She set her hands over the stone parapet before her – hands he knew to be as hard as the stone itself. 'Councillor Amaron must have offered just as much on my behalf.'

Cartheron pulled his fingers through his beard. Gods! How to say this? 'Your demeanour. Your . . . ah, frankness . . . m'lady, has won you no friends on the council.'

She blew a harsh breath out her nose. 'I see. They prefer Tarel's shallow glad-handing and easy demeanour to my . . . what? Cartheron?'

He cleared his throat. Gods give him strength! She'd spoken truth to those fool councillors – that their policies were leading Nap into further decline . . . could he do any less? He drew a steeling breath. 'They preferred the lies that you chose not to give them.'

One corner of her thin lips twitched. 'I see. Sunk by my own mouth. You think I should have plied them with lies and flattery as well. You and Amaron.'

'It is as he has tried to teach you all these years. Statecraft, m'lady.'

Those hard lips drew down in a savage scowl. 'I refuse to play that game.'

Then you will lose! Cartheron steadied himself with another breath.

'But . . . I grant you that I must guard my mouth more closely in the future.'

One small victory, at the least. 'We must withdraw, m'lady. Sail today to fight tomorrow.'

A sad half-smile drifted across her pale blue features. 'That old sailors' saw. Napan to the core, Cartheron. Yes. Exile, then. Though it disgusts me.'

He motioned to the stairs and she nodded, preceding him.

He paused here, at the top of the tower, and his gaze returned to the smoke. Lit from below by the flames, it churned into the night sky. So be it. Exile. A new toss of the Twins' dice; nothing new to an experienced sea-raider. He turned to face the iron waters of the Strait of Storms and glimpsed there the thick clouds of a gathering namesake.

* * *

Nedurian tossed his line from the end of the Malaz City harbour wharf and sat back once more to let the day pass. Sometimes, when restlessness came over him, he wondered whether he'd been right to walk away from the battles, the long string of command tents and encampments and the challenge of matching another talent in the field. But usually, in the next instant, he remembered the pain, the terror, the fallen comrades, and all the damned loss and waste, and could not regret the decision he had made so long ago.

After these moments of weakness he would recall his new appointment and cast his awareness far out upon the waters of the Strait of Storms, watching for any similar restlessness there deep within those dark frigid waters. Then, come the dusk, he would wind up his line once more and make the long walk back to the city waterfront for a drink and a meal at the Oar and Anchor.

This evening, an old-timer among his fellows sitting on a bench greeted him. 'Fish don't like you today, Ned?'

3

He gestured with his rod back towards the wide black waters. 'I was lied to! Ain't no fish out there at all.'

The fellow guffawed. Another considered his pipe and suggested, 'I think he just plain scared them off.'

Nedurian thoughtfully drew a finger down his broken flattened nose and brushed the ridges of the scars that ran from his temple down to his chin. 'Now what makes you say that, ol' Renn?'

'You do know you have to put a hook on that, don't ya?' offered another fellow.

'One of those things? Hood, a fish stole my last long ago.'

The old-timers chuckled again. 'See you tonight?'

He ambled on up the wharf. 'I'll be there.'

He headed inland, up the slight grade of the waterfront district. Beyond the sun-greyed shake roofs rose the craggy wind-clawed cliffs of the escarpment with the stained granite stones of Mock's Hold perched above like a crow's nest.

He'd taken a room in town with an old widow who, out of decades of stubborn habit, still kept a watch for a sailor husband long past returning. At least he thought of her as old, even though he'd already seen more years than her in her grandmother's time. Years of warfare in which he'd sold his services to petty robber barons, bandit despots, the kings of Purge and Bloor, all the way up to the last dynasty of the Talian hegemony.

But no more. No more fighting and no more battle magery. He now lent his talents to a far more worthy cause.

He paused to set his elbows upon the mortared stone ledge of a bridge over one of the many river channels that cut through the town, built as it was on a boggy marsh, remembering his surprise upon retiring to this back-of-beyond island of Malaz to find talents here that could blast away any of the mightiest practitioners he'd duelled on the continent. All settled, or gathered, for one reason alone. One he'd been ignorant of though living all the while across a relatively narrow band of water. Oh, certainly, he knew all the myths and legends of the Riders, but to him they'd been only stories . . .

Something tickled his nose then and he raised his head, turning to the waterfront. What *was* that? Something . . . new. He cocked his head, cast his awareness outwards. He knew it was there but he couldn't pin it down. All he could sense was that there'd been a sudden shift in the wind.

4

He'd have dismissed the passing sensation as a mere shudder, or the distant echo of some far off plucking of the Warrens, but for one small thing. Far above, atop Mock's Hold, possibly the highest point of the island itself, stood an ancient weathervane hammered and chiselled into the form of a demon. And at that moment of heightened awareness he noticed it too had suddenly shifted to point directly to the east.

A coincidence? He tapped the fishing rod on his shoulder, considering. Best not to jump at every visiting talent who happened to pass through town. Even this misbegotten backwater. He'd wait and see.

Perhaps it would come to nothing.

Part One

Chapter 1

'THOSE CAWN MERCHANTS WERE FOOLS TO HAVE TURNED us down!' Wu assured Dancer from across their table in a waterfront dive in Malaz City.

'*You*,' Dancer corrected. 'They turned *you* down.'

Wu waved a hand airily to dismiss the point. 'Well, that still leaves them the fools in my little scenario.' He sipped his glass of watered wine. 'As to chasing us out of town . . . an obvious overreaction.'

Dancer leaned back, one brow arched. 'You threatened to curse them all to eternal torment.'

Wu appeared surprised. 'Did I? I quite forget – I've threatened to curse so many.' He lowered his voice conspiratorially, 'In any case, Malaz here suits our purpose even better. It is fortunate. The Twins favour our plans.'

Dancer sighed as he poked at his plate of boiled pork and barley; he'd quite lost his appetite recently. 'It was the first boat out we could jump.'

Wu opened his hands as if vindicated. 'Exactly! Oponn himself may as well have invited us aboard.'

Dancer clenched the edge of the table of sun-bleached slats and released it only after forcing himself to relax. *It's all right*, he assured himself. *It's only a setback. There are bound to be setbacks.* 'Plans,' he said. 'You mentioned plans.'

Wu shovelled up his plate of onions and beans, then spoke with lowered voice once more. 'Easier to control a small city and confined island such as this. An excellent first step.'

'First step to what?'

Wu opened his hands wide, his expression one of disbelief. 'Why . . . everything, of course.'

Dancer's answering scorn was interrupted by the slamming of a stoneware tankard to their table in the most curt manner possible. The servitor, a young woman whose skin showed the unique bluish hue of the Napans, stalked off without a backward glance. Dancer thought her the least gracious help he'd ever encountered.

In point of fact, she was the fourth Napan he'd seen in this run-down waterfront dive. Two were obvious hired muscle hanging about the entrance, while the third was a tall lad he'd glimpsed in the kitchens – another bouncer held in reserve. The nightly fights in this rat-hole must be ferocious.

'. . . and for this we need a base of operations,' Wu was saying. Dancer blinked, refocusing on him.

'I'm sorry? For what?'

Wu looked hurt and affronted. 'Why, our grand plan, of course!'

Dancer looked away, scanning the sturdy semi-subterranean common room more thoroughly. 'Oh, that. Right. Our try anything plan.' Stone walls; one main entrance strongly defended; slim windows; a single narrow back entrance. And he'd seen numerous windows on the second floor – good for covering fire. Quite the fortress.

Wu drummed his fingers on the tabletop, his expression sour. 'You don't seem to be taking this in quite the right spirit. If I may tell you my news . . . ?'

Still eyeing his surroundings, Dancer murmured, 'Be my guest.' He noted that the bouncers at the door were far from the typical over-sized beer-bloated souses that usually slouched at the doors of these low-class alehouses. They were obvious veterans, scarred and hardened, their narrowed gazes scanning the room and the street outside.

This was not your typical sailors' drinking establishment. In fact, everything about it shouted 'front'. And everyone in Quon Tali knew Malaz Island was nothing more than a pirates' nest; he wondered if he was looking at one of their bases.

Wu, he saw, was watching him, looking quite vexed. 'What?'

'Do you wish me to continue?'

'Certainly.' Dancer motioned to the Napan server who was now leaning against the wall next to the kitchen's entrance, examining her nails. The woman made a disgusted face and sauntered over.

'What is it?' she demanded.

He motioned to his plate. 'This food is atrocious.'

'Atrocious. Really. A plate of boiled pork. How atrocious could that be?'

Dancer invited her to take the plate away. 'Well, your cook managed it.'

The woman scooped up the plate and stalked to the kitchen entrance. 'Hey, Urko! There's a fellow out here taking issue with your cooking.'

A great basso voice thundered from the kitchens. '*Whaaat!*'

The doors burst open and out shot fully the biggest and scariest-looking Napan of the lot: monstrously wide, with the shoulders of a strangler, yet wearing a dirty leather apron. Dancer readied himself for a confrontation, but instead of facing him the man turned on the server, bellowing, 'I don't need these complaints! I didn't want to be the damned cook anyway. Make Choss the damned cook!'

'He's a better shipbuilder,' the woman calmly returned, leaning against a wall, her arms crossed.

The big fellow raised fists the size of hams to his head. 'Well . . . give the job to my brother then, dammit to Hood!'

'He's at sea.'

The gigantic cook sniffed his affront, grumbled, 'Trust *him* to find a decent job.'

The server pointed back to the kitchens and the huge fellow – Urko, apparently – clenched his thick leather apron in his fists until it creaked. He scowled at the woman then drew a hand down his face, snorting through his nostrils like a bull. 'Well . . . I got onion soup. Offer him that.' And he stomped back through the doors.

Dancer could only shake his head at the state of the hired help here. He supposed it was difficult to find quality labour on the island. He motioned to the door. 'Let's try another place.'

Wu gave a strange high laugh, almost nervous, and Dancer cocked an eye at him, suspicious. 'Change of management,' Wu explained, gesturing to encompass the establishment. 'Be patient.'

Whatever. Dancer tried a sip of the beer and found it far too watery. He made a sour face. 'You said that you had news?'

'Ah! Yes . . . news.' Wu fluttered his hands on the table, the wrinkled knotted hands of an ancient as the mage was still maintaining his appearance of an old man, but his motions were quick

11

and precise; not those of a doddering oldster. Dancer decided he'd have to coach him on that. 'So,' Wu continued, still brushing his hands across the tabletop, 'yes. News. Well . . . while you were out reconnoitring the waterfront, I happened to fall into conversation with the owner of this fine establishment . . .'

Seeing that this was going nowhere fast, Dancer forced himself to take another sip of the foul beer. 'Yes? And you killed him for gross incompetence?'

This raised a weak laugh that faded into a long drawn out coughing fit. 'Well, actually, no. I found that he was in a feverish hurry to sell . . .'

Dancer set down the tankard. *Oh, no. Tell me no.* 'What,' he began, calmly, 'have you done?'

Wu raised his hands. 'As I was saying – we need a base of operations for our plans. This location is ideal. Close to the waterfront, great for smuggling . . .'

Dancer pressed his palm to his forehead. *Mustn't lose it.* 'What,' he began again, through clenched teeth, 'have you done?'

Wu opened his hands wide. 'Our partnership has entered a new phase. We've gone into business together.'

Dancer somehow found himself on his feet, towering over Wu, his hands flat on the table. '*You bought this rat-hole?*'

Wu's dark ferret eyes darted left and right. 'So it would seem.'

Through his rage, Dancer sensed a presence close to him and snapped his gaze aside – it was the serving woman. *How did she get so close?*

But her sullen attention was on Wu, ignoring him. She flicked a piece of dirt from the table. 'You want to see your offices now?'

Wu brightened immediately. 'Why, that would be excellent! Thank you . . . ah . . .'

'Surly,' the woman supplied, with a tired curl of a lip.

'Ah, yes. Excellent. Thank you . . . Surly.'

She motioned to the stairs and Wu bustled off. His walking cane was now in his hand, tapping as he went. Dancer decided that the privacy of an office would be a better place for their discussion, in case he accidentally strangled the wretched fellow, and so he followed, but not before he noted the woman's hands: hardened and calloused. The hands of a servitor? No, not the cracked and reddened skin of washing and scouring. Rather, skin toughened and scarred. Hands like his.

The office stood over the common room and here he found Wu waving a cloud of dust from his face after pushing a heap of papers off a chair. The mage gave a nervous laugh. 'A quick whip-round and it'll be decent in no time.'

Dancer closed the door behind him and pressed his back to it. 'What have you done?'

Wu turned, blinking innocently. 'What? Why, acquired a property at a fantastic price!'

'Did you just spend all our remaining—' He snapped up a hand. 'Wait! I don't want to know. What I do want to know is why.'

'Hmmm?' Wu was now inspecting the desk, which was heaped high with garbage and plates of dried crusted food. He poked his walking stick at the mess. 'Why what?'

Dancer sighed, raised his suffering gaze to the ceiling. 'Why did you purchase this place?'

Wu blinked again. 'Ah, well, actually the price was a steal because the fellow thought the Napan employees were conspiring to kill him and take the business. Why he should think that I have no idea . . .' Dancer just glared until Wu's brows rose in understanding. 'Ah!' Swinging the walking stick, he brushed aside all the clutter on the desk, sending papers, glassware, tin plates and old candles crashing to the floor. Satisfied, he sat behind the expanse of wine-stained dark wood and gestured to the empty surface. 'There we are. You see? One must sweep aside the old before building anew.'

Dancer crossed his arms. *Okay.* 'Why here?'

'The moment I set foot on this island I felt it.' Wu raised his hands, brushing his thumbs and forefingers together. 'Shadow. It's close. This place has some sort of affinity.'

Dancer let his arms fall. 'So you say,' and he added, half muttering, 'if only to justify this stupid purchase.' He crossed to the one window. It overlooked a side street of ancient wood and stone buildings, all muted grey and dingy in a thin misting rain. He turned on Wu. 'But we're still only two. What's the plan?'

The lad was undaunted. He raised his hands once again. 'Why, as before. We take over the town.'

Great. As before . . . when we failed. Dancer drew breath to tear into the fool but silenced himself as he detected someone on the landing outside the door. A knock sounded. Wu cleared his throat and steepled his fingers across his stomach, arranging his features into a stern frown.

'Ah! Yes? Do come in.'

The door swung inward but no one entered. Intrigued, Dancer leaned forward to peer out. It was the serving woman, Surly. The young Napan was surveying the room before entering and Dancer smiled to himself: *More than a mere servitor. For certain.*

She took one step in – still not clearing the door – and eyed Wu as if she'd found a particularly annoying mess. 'Do you have staff of your own you'll be bringing in?'

Wu's tiny eyes darted right and left. 'Ah . . . no.'

'So, we'll be staying on, then?'

'For the foreseeable future.'

'Good.'

'Good?'

The young woman's expression twisted into even more of a scowl. 'Work's hard to come by on this damned island.'

Wu leaned forward to set his chin on a fist, cocking his head. 'I should think you and your, ah, piratical friends should easily find employment with any one of the crews that sail out of this island.'

The lips curled up into a humourless half-smile. 'Don't know much about the history between Nap and Malaz, do you?'

'You're rivals,' Dancer supplied. Surly gave him a reserved nod. 'You've fought for control of the southern seas for hundreds of years.'

'That's right. They won't have us. And in any case,' and she raised her chin, her gaze suddenly fierce, 'we work for ourselves.'

Pride, Dancer read in her every stern line. Ferocious pride. How did anyone come to such monumental arrogance? And he smiled inwardly. *Well . . . I should know.*

The girl made it clear she considered the interview over by backing away – not turning round, as anyone else might, but sliding one bare foot behind the other and edging her weight backwards. And Dancer smiled again, inwardly. One should not advertise one's training so openly.

Also studying the girl, one brow raised, Wu motioned to him. 'My, ah, partner, Dancer.'

Surly eyed him anew. He watched her gaze move from his face

to his hands, to his feet, a knowing amusement similar to his own growing in her dark eyes. 'Partner,' she said. 'I see.'

'So what brought you here, then?' Wu went on.

The amused light disappeared behind high, hard walls. 'Shipwreck in a storm. We are the few of . . . the crew who made it to shore.'

What had she been going to say just then, Dancer wondered. *My* crew, perhaps?

'I see . . . well, thank you.' Wu motioned her out.

The scowl returned but she withdrew, pulling the door shut as she left.

Dancer remained poised next to the window. He eyed the door, musing aloud, 'I heard of some sort of dispute among the royal family of Nap not long ago. A civil war. This lot might've backed the losing side. So they can't go back. They're stuck here.'

No answer came from Wu and Dancer turned: the lad was leaning back in the captain's-style chair, using his hands to cast shadow-images on the wall. Sensing Dancer's attention he glanced over, blinking. 'Sorry? You were saying something?'

Dancer gritted his teeth. 'Never mind. Let's talk about our plans.'

Wu thumped elbows to the desk and set his chin in his fists, frowning in hard thought. 'Yes. Our plans. No sense tackling one of the corsair captains here – the crew wouldn't follow us. I've never sailed. Mock rules from his Hold, but he probably doesn't care who runs the streets. So, for now, we limit our attention to the shore. The merchants and bosses who control the markets and warehouses.'

Dancer had pursed his lips, considering. 'What do you propose?'

Wu raised his head, smiling. 'Why, our forte, of course. Ambush and hijacking.'

Chapter 2

'Awake, awake, Mistress Jay!' Light blossomed and Sail winced, pulling the covers over her eyes. ''Tis late! What are you thinking, lolling about in bed?'

'All the rich ladies in Unta do it, Viv. It's good for the complexion. And it's not Jay. It's Sail.'

A poker rattled in the stone fireplace. 'Well, I'd think it's not good for the complexion. Makes the eyes puffy and all.'

'You know nothing, Viv.'

There came a huff and a sniff. 'Well . . . if Mistress *Sail* says so . . .'

Sail took the time to stretch. She arched her back, luxuriating in the soft smooth glide of clean cotton sheets – so unlike the coarse flea-infested rags of her youth. Her hand emerged from the layered covers to encounter the chill morning air of Malaz Island and she flinched, drawing her knees to her chest.

Gods, it was freezing! It was summer and it was freezing! How she hated this damned island. And trust Viv to start the fire late.

She dared poke her head from beneath the heaped quilts, and blinked at the light of mid-morning. 'Is the chamberpot ready?'

Viv, her supposed lady-in-waiting, though having seen a bare twelve summers, turned from where she knelt at the fireplace. She wrinkled her tiny freckled nose. 'Why do you have to use that smelly thing? Just use the privy like everyone else.'

Through clenched teeth Sail said, 'Because that's not what real ladies do.'

Viv rolled her eyes, then returned to rebuilding the fire. 'More work for us,' she grumbled.

'Don't forget who I am.'

'Oh, I ain't forgetting. You're in bed, not me.'

Sail gathered the duvet about herself and dragged it across the icy bare stone floor of the bedroom to the divider behind which lay the ceramic chamberpot. She crouched over it and eased her bladder in an embarrassingly loud hiss.

She wondered what the real ladies in Unta did about that. She shuffled from behind the divider. 'Now dress me.'

Viv sighed and straightened from the stone hearth, brushed errant strands of black hair from her snowy-pale forehead.

Well, Sail reflected, as least they'd progressed past comments like 'Can't you dress yourself?'

'The riding skirts,' she said.

Viv searched through the clothes chest. She grumbled, just loud enough, 'Ain't no horses on Malaz.'

Sail almost despaired. Couldn't this foolish child see what a benefit this was for her? She was learning an art she could market on the mainland. 'They're all the fashion, Viv.'

'Where?'

'What do you mean, where?' She waved impatiently. 'In the cities. Tali and Gris and Unta!'

'Do much riding in these cities, do they?'

Sail clenched her lips tight, hissed, 'Just bring them.'

Viv held out the layered thick skirts and Sail dared stretch an arm out of the duvet to take them. 'And the velvet long-sleeved blouse, and that woven Wickan vest.'

Viv blew hair from her face and returned to the chest. 'It's summer,' she said. 'Why not a sleeveless dress?'

Sail shuddered in her wrap. 'Summer here? What a joke. Bring the heeled shoes too. The black ones.'

'Yes, mistress.'

Sail drew on the skirts. 'Where's Mock?'

'Don't know.'

As always, the dislike in the girl's voice was obvious, and, as always, Sail chose to ignore it. She found the waist of the skirts too tight and realized she'd have to get Viv to let them out once again; she'd always been curvy, but perhaps there was a limit. 'Don't know?' She waved her off. 'Well, find out. And don't forget to air the bedding and send someone to empty the pot.'

Viv dropped the remaining clothes on the bed and flounced from the bedchamber. 'Yes, mistress.'

That's right, child. Mistress. I am mistress of this castle – and don't you forget it. She dressed hurriedly, tried to fluff up her tangled hair. The Deck of Dragons beckoned from the writing desk. It fairly burst with swirling potential this morning, but she'd already decided to find Mock. She turned away to the door.

Her search brought her down to the main floor of the keep. This consisted almost entirely of one large reception and banquet hall. Here Mock held court during long evening meals where he entertained his pirate – or, as they called themselves, *privateer* – captains. Privateers because they carried letters of marque and reprisal, penned by Mock himself, that allowed predation on all seagoing commerce during times of war. And war, of course, was constant.

Sail also knew that no state recognized the man's right to issue such letters. But this was of little concern to Mock, the self-styled Marquis of Malaz. A title no state acknowledged either. When any ruler was forced to speak of him, Sail knew he was usually referred to as 'that damned outlaw of Malaz Island'. And she was certain that in private their language was even less flattering.

She was at the bottom of the wide stairs that opened on to the main hall and thinking of heading to the kitchens for a late breakfast, when she caught sight of something that nearly made her trip and fall. She grasped hold of the stone balustrade and stared at the person who had just come in – *was that really* . . .

Aged, yet tall and lean, with an aristocratic air, her thick long mane of dark hair shot with streaks of grey – by all the daemons of her youth! It *was* her.

Sail stalked across the hall. She had to stop herself from pushing up her sleeves and raising her Thyr Warren as she went.

'Agayla!' she called. 'What are *you* doing here?'

The willow-thin woman turned, raising a brow, and Sail experienced that same old sensation of being looked down upon. Her teacher and mentor offered that too-familiar indulgent smile. 'Why, Jay, what a pleasure to see you. Still here, I see.'

'What do you mean, still here? Of course I'm still here! And it's Sail now,' she added, then hated how petulant that sounded.

Agayla shrugged. 'Well, one never knows the vicissitudes of nobility, does one? Especially the men.'

'I am mistress of this Hold, I'll have you know.'

'And where is your master?'

Sail stuttered, tongue-tied as always by her old teacher. She

18

cleared her throat and began again, '*Mock* is elsewhere. May I help you?' But Agayla had turned away and was now gesturing to the door, inviting in two burly workers who carried over their shoulders a large roll of cloth. 'And what is this?' Sail asked.

Agayla crossed her wiry arms. 'My commission, of course. A tapestry for the main hall.'

Great gods! I'm going to have to stare at her work over dinner? Sail collected herself, crossing her own arms. 'A commission? Truly? Your work will be a wonderful addition to *our* Hold.'

Agayla regarded her for a time, her lips compressed. 'Jay . . . why are you here? There are academies in Itko Kan that would take you in an instant. You are wasting your potential here.'

Sail let her arms fall. *A record. Back to the old argument in less than two minutes.* She turned away, sighing. 'Agayla – I will go to the mainland. But I will arrive as the Marquessa of Malaz.'

The old mage snorted her scorn. 'Meaningless titles. You can achieve far more than such pretty baubles.'

It took a strong effort to control herself, but Sail managed, swallowing her anger. 'Auntie, thank you for all that you have done for me. But with respect, it is no longer any of your business.'

The old woman's gaze narrowed, and Sail briefly recalled her youthful dread of this woman's temper. 'It is my business, Jay. Nurturing this island's talent is one of my duties – among others. And I would be negligent if I allowed a promising student to waste her time hanging on the arm of a cheap brigand.'

Sail felt her own expression harden into a frozen mask. She inclined her head in dismissal. 'You may hang your tapestry, weaver. Good day.' She turned her back and walked away.

She found him at the east wall battlements, overlooking the coast and the city harbourage just to the south. An older man, she well knew: grey at his temples, but still hale. Pirate admiral – marque – who had herded this unruly island of privateer captains for years. Fought two wars at sea against Nap and the kings of Itko Kan, and now wore a corset beneath his shirts and vest to maintain his lean figure. Mock, commander of the three men-o-war that ruled the southern seas: the *Intolerant*, the *Intemperate*, and the *Insufferable*.

Mock indeed.

He turned as she approached, smiling, and rather self-consciously brushing back his moustache. 'Tattersail, my Thyr witch. How are you today?'

She pressed up against him. 'Well. What brings you up here? Planning?'

He ran a hand down her waist to her rear and squeezed her there. 'Indeed. There is word of a convoy heading out of Cawn for Unta. We cannot let that pass us by without challenging it.' He kissed her brow. 'The captains would be very reassured if you would accompany them. Their fearsome battle-mage, Tattersail.'

'I'm sure the captains would be far more reassured if *you* accompanied them.'

He drew away, leaning both elbows on the stained limestone of a crenel. 'I wish I could. But you know the moment I leave the captains will raise their eyes to the empty Hold and wonder: *Why shouldn't I sit there?*' He chuckled then, letting out a long breath. 'Funny. Just like me. I wanted nothing more than to make this place my own. But now it's as though I'm a prisoner. Not daring to leave . . .'

This direction of talk made Sail strangely uncomfortable. She took his arm. 'You've gone on forays before.'

'Yes. When I was younger. But now, with every passing year, these new captains become ever bolder. Well . . .' He kissed her brow. 'Will you travel on board the *Insufferable* in my stead?'

'Of course I will.'

He squeezed her shoulders. 'Thank you, Sail. I rely upon you a great deal.'

And I will not let you down. You will see. 'When do we go?'

'In a few days. Lie in wait off the Vorian coast, yes?'

Sail nodded. Yes, that rugged mountainous coastline was a favourite hunting ground. 'And what of the Napans? Surely they will make a play for any convoy.'

Mock held out an arm, inviting her to take it, and started for the corner tower. 'Nap remains in disorder. It just may be Malaz's turn to rule the coasts. Then we will have them, Sail. All recognize Nap as an island nation – why not Malaz? Imagine that, yes? Mock, King of Malaz?'

Sail squeezed his arm tight. Yes. And Tattersail, Queen of Malaz.

Imagine that.

The deputation arrived outside his open threshold at dawn. All five knelt to one knee in the dust of the Street of Temples, awaiting his attention.

He let them sweat through the morning while he sat cross-legged before the sarcophagus that was his chosen altar, and prayed to his god. A god few prayed to, and then only in extreme need or exigency. A god ignored by most yet escaped by none in the end. Hood. The Grey God. The Dark Taker. The god of death itself.

In time he raised his head, straightening his back and setting his palms on his knees. Nara, who had been waiting just to one side, offered a wood platter bearing a light meal of yogurt, bread, and thin beer.

Bowing his thanks, he backed away from the altar and ate, sword across his lap, sitting on the stone threshold of what was once – and remained for all practical purposes – a mausoleum.

Through all this the five still did not raise their cowled heads.

Brushing his hands clean, he stepped out on to the street, and adjusted his sword at his hip. 'Yes?'

The foremost of the five inclined his hooded head even further, then straightened, head still bowed. Only the tip of an iron-grey beard showed beneath his hood. 'Lord Dassem. We come seeking a boon.'

'And you are?'

'We are chosen deputies of these lands' largest congregations of our lord the Grey Walker.'

'What of it?'

'Lord Dassem – a scourge has appeared in many of our cities. A sickness that spares none. Young, old. Poliel's visitations are known to us, of course, but this one's touch is death. Some name it Hood's Wrath. And so we come begging that you intercede with our lord. How have we transgressed? What have we done to earn his disfavour?'

'Why?'

The spokesman paused, glancing back to his fellows in obvious confusion. 'Well . . . so that we may avert this scourge. Turn his displeasure aside from us. The populace is becoming fearful and angered in many cities. There have been reprisals. Killings of devotees.'

Dassem shook his head. 'It is I who am angered that you should come to me. Angered and disappointed. You above all should know there is no turning aside Hood's hand. There can be no propitiation. No bribe or sacrifice can be made that will save anyone. There is no cheating death. It comes at its appointed time – sooner or later.'

The spokesman fluttered his hands in apology. 'Do not misunderstand. We seek no special favour for ourselves – we seek only for the safety of our flocks. Do you wish *his* worship to become repugnant in the eyes of so many? Blamed and denigrated? Outlawed, even?'

The rear delegate spoke up in a young man's voice. 'Everyone knows you came to Heng to challenge the Protectress's ban on *his* worship! And you broke the ban! You brought *his* message to Heng. Why abandon it elsewhere?'

Dassem continued to shake his head. 'I merely walked where my lord set my feet.'

'You refuse us, then?' the young delegate answered in rising anger.

The foremost lifted a hand for silence. 'Control yourself, brother Jaim.' He addressed Dassem. 'Lord, are you saying you will not address our master on our behalf?'

Dassem let out a long slow breath. 'I am saying it is pointless. What happens, must happen. There is no good or bad. Only what is necessary. Death. Ending. Destruction. Call it what you will. It is necessary in existence. Hood stands in that role because none other would. His is the face upon an inescapable truth of life. Some choose to hate him for it. They are foolish to do so.'

The spokesman bowed his cowled head once more. 'Your interpretation of the faith is a most harsh one, Lord Dassem. Harsh and rigid and unforgiving. I wish you luck with it, but fear you may come to regret such an inhuman stance.' He turned to his companions. 'Come. We must return to our brothers and sisters and endure as best we might.'

Four of the deputation moved to leave, but the fifth, the last, remained facing Dassem, who noted his fists within his loose sleeves clenched and white.

'Brother Jaim!' the spokesman called, a note of warning in his voice.

In one swirling motion Brother Jaim threw off his robes,

revealing a lean young man in leather armour, twinned longswords at his sides. He glared at Dassem. 'I say you refuse because you are false! You are not the true Sword. You are an impostor. I say you must prove yourself – *now*!'

Dassem turned a glance upon the other four. The greybeard, his hands crossed and hidden in his robes, bowed his acquiescence. 'So be it.'

Dassem tilted his head to Jaim. 'I accept, of course.'

Jaim drew his blades and passing Hengans backed away, some shouting their alarm. The main way emptied. Dassem slowly crossed to its dusty mid-point. 'We need not do this,' he called to Jaim.

'On the contrary – you must. You must prove yourself.'

He shook his head once again. 'Prove myself to you, you mean.'

'Anyone can claim a title,' Jaim answered, now beginning to circle.

Dassem drew his hand-and-a-half and struck a ready stance edge-on to the man. He shifted as the fellow circled, waiting, as Jaim was the challenger.

It came quickly in a flurry of blows which Dassem slipped and blocked. The swordsman was good, Dassem could admit. As he would have to be. Yet not inspired; or he was holding back for the moment. Dassem now shifted, circling as well.

All had become eerily silent on the Street of the Temples, normally a hub of murmured prayers, hawkers, and chants of devotion. The four deputies watched motionless. The way was choked off far up its length at both ends as Hengans gathered. Nara watched, frozen in the mausoleum's open entrance, a hand clutching her throat.

Dassem waited, husbanding his strength. Patience was one of his advantages. Many he'd fought became panicked the longer a duel dragged on. Or exhausted themselves in anxiety and constant tension. He remained relaxed, his shoulders and arms loose and fluid, and this alone often unnerved an opponent.

After his initial testing, Jaim also eased back into a similar waiting stance. Dassem offered him the slightest tilt of the head in acknowledgement. For as Jaim had been testing, he had been as well.

Now the strategy of the duel began. Weapon-masters are of

course correct when they insist that most fights end in the first few passes; this is common truth. Those that do not, however, become less battles of exchanges and more battles of will and insight. Those who excel in either typically emerge the victor. And Dassem excelled at both.

He watched, studying his opponent, as Jaim through narrowed eyes likewise studied him.

Weapon-masters are also correct in warning against watching one's opponent's feet, their weapons, or their eyes; all can and will be used in diversion, deceit, feint, and stratagem. This is truth as well. One must cultivate the whole, take in thousands of tiny hints, the slightest of movements, a brush or suggestion, building an image of the opponent until one can understand their thinking. Their strengths and their weaknesses. Until you know them intimately; only then can you defeat them.

Here Dassem excelled as well. Indeed, so sensitive was his awareness that, watching any blade, he could filter out the extraneous irrelevant shifts and movements until he could discern the very tiniest of vibrations transmitted from the palm of the bearer through the grip and up to the utter tip, and know the pulse rate of his opponent's very heart.

In a seemingly casual move, Jaim tried to disguise the forward shift of his centre of gravity. At the same instant his pulse rate jumped, and Dassem knew he was about to come at him not in a test or feint, but in a serious effort. He readied himself to counter-attack.

The man came on in a beautifully coordinated series of passes of both blades, and Dassem was saddened that he would have to end this confrontation in so final a manner. Both knew there could be no first-blood here, no quarter or yielding; this was, of course, a duel to the death.

He yielded, circling and waiting, and finally his opening came. It appeared in the overextension of Jaim's right foot. Dassem lashed out with his forward leg, striking the knee outwards, and Jaim, unbalanced, tumbled to that side as Dassem knew he would, his own blade already thrusting to take him through the heart as he fell.

Jaim struck the dirty cobbles of the road with Dassem already withdrawing his blade. He lay staring, a puzzled expression on his face, blinking at the sky as his fate registered in his mind. Then the puzzlement cleared and he nodded to Dassem, mouthing silently, *My apologies . . .*

Dassem saluted him, grip raised to his chin.

Three of the deputies converged on the body, collecting the swords, a waist-pouch, and other possessions. The fourth, the greybeard, bowed to Dassem. 'He was the best of us. None other could touch him.' He shook his cowled head in wonderment. 'Our apologies, Sword. But we had to be certain.'

'I offer no blame.'

'We shall return to our congregations and struggle to survive this plague as best we may. You, too, should prepare, Lord Dassem. I suspect Heng will not be spared.' And he bowed for the last time, gesturing his brothers away.

Dassem watched them go, then turned to Nara; she stood with her hand still clenched at her throat. 'Every time, I worry,' she breathed. 'Even though I know I should have faith – I cannot help it.'

He returned to sit cross-legged before the sarcophagus once more. 'I understand.' He looked up at her. 'Will you accept my training now?'

She shook her head. 'I do not want to hurt anyone.'

'But you may have to defend yourself.'

She winced and let her hand fall. 'Well, there is that . . .'

He nodded. 'Good. We'll use the open yards between the mausoleums.'

A voice called from the street, making Nara jump, 'Acolyte, or priest! Or champion. Or whatever it is you choose to call yourself! There's a body out here.'

Dassem sighed and rose. He urged Nara further back into the mausoleum and moved to its open threshold, squinting against the light.

A single man stood in the centre of the street. At first impression he resembled a dock labourer or farm worker, in ragged tunic and trousers, his hair a greying unkempt mop upon his scarred, uneven scalp. But in Dassem's vision he fairly glowed with power and potential.

One of the city mages who ruled Li Heng, named Ho.

Dassem stepped out on to the street. At least two others of the five city mages were probably present as well, hidden, watching from among the crowd.

'Do you wish my professional opinion on the matter?'

The man gave a toothy smile. 'Looks to me like your work.'

'How can you tell?'

The mage's meaty hands twitched at his sides and Dassem sensed the sizzling energies of an open Warren. 'Call it intuition,' he said.

Dassem slowly crossed his arms. 'I understand you'll need a witness.'

'We'll find one.'

'Let me know when you do.'

'We will. It'll be exile for you, soon enough.'

'Come back then.'

'We will.' And he nodded aside, presumably to one of his compatriots. A Dal Honese woman stepped out from among the crowd of onlookers, heavy and broad-hipped, with a wild mane of hair – Mara. She walked right in front of him, a hungry grin on her lips.

'See you later,' she said as she passed, winking.

Dassem watched them go, then returned to the mausoleum. He eyed Nara for a time, thinking. 'We should begin at once.'

'You don't, ah, *fear* them, do you?'

'No. But I did not come here for a war. They are the law here. People they want gone tend to disappear.' He thought of the mad Dal Hon mage and his friend who had unleashed such a riot last season. They disappeared. Surprising, that. The slim one – the way he moved, so deceptively quick and graceful – he would've been a dangerous opponent. He was surprised these city mages got the better of that one.

And they'd wanted him gone all this time as well. All they lacked was an excuse. No doubt they thought they had it now.

He knelt once more before the sarcophagus, bowing so low his brow pressed into the cold gritty stone floor. *Father Hood. Grant me strength. What shall come, shall come. Your hand falls on all without prejudice. Good, bad. Worthy, unworthy. Death is not a judgement – it is a necessity. Even these men and women, your priests, even they could not understand, or accept, your impartiality.*

He pressed his brow hard into the dusty grit. *So, is it I who am wrong?*

Tayschrenn walked the Street of the Icon-Carvers in the Septarch district of Kartool city. Passing through the crowds, he hardly noticed the citizens and cult penitents who dutifully bowed to him. His thoughts, as usual, were completely occupied by the continuing subtleties and twists in his chosen field of priestly study – namely the immanency of D'rek, the Worm of Autumn.

So it was that his fellow priest, Koarsden, had to take his arm and pull him back, warning, 'Look out there, Tay.'

Blinking, he now noticed among the rubbish littering the cobbles an emaciated, near-skeletal figure wrapped in dirty rags. A body so neglected-looking that one would have been certain it was a corpse. Sensing attention, the unfortunate turned cloudy, disease-blinded eyes his way and raised a quivering hand.

Knowing his duty, Tayschrenn mechanically took the hand, as fever-hot as a burning ember, all bones and snake-dry parchment skin, and muttered a quick, 'May D'rek embrace you.' He then stepped over the devotee and continued on his way.

'Sometimes I wonder on the motives of these petitioners,' Koarsden mused as they walked the rising street.

'He is winning great merit for his descendants.'

'True. But some, I suspect, come hoping to be cured.'

Tayschrenn knew of the debates surrounding this uncomfortable heresy within the cult. That there were those who were passed over by D'rek. In the end, among the highest rank of the priesthood, the Convene of All Temples, it was decided that the motives and mind of a god lie beyond mere mortal understanding. Such survivors were thus not officially condemned as heretics or apostates, but explained as cases of merit accrued by some ancestor, or as intervention by close relations already in the embrace of the Great Worm – most usually a dead child or parent of the afflicted.

Belatedly, he realized he was once more indulging in the vice Koarsden and others most often accused him of – over-analysing. He cleared his throat. 'Why bother to drag oneself here, then? D'rek's influence coils the world. One can just as easily reach the Worm from anywhere, can't one?'

Koarsden lifted one of his shaved brows, watching him sidelong. 'Careful, Tay. You may be the Demidrek's favourite, but your habit of posing uncomfortable questions has not gone unnoticed.'

Tayschrenn merely shrugged beneath his black robes. 'Facts cannot be wished away.'

After a time, Koarsden answered drily, 'Unfortunately, they can.' They continued in silence, then his friend shot an arm upwards. 'Saw one.'

Tayschrenn raised his gaze, blinking at the tall spires jutting above. 'Just a reflection of the sunlight on the mirror mosaic there.'

'No, no. It moved. They're up there, I tell you. Getting bolder too.'

'The habits of the island's spiders are no matter to us.'

Koarsden tilted his long, hound-like head. 'Well, some commoners say it is a sign of D'rek's displeasure.'

'Displeasure? Displeasure with whom?'

'Well . . . with us, of course.' And he offered his ever-ready smile.

Tayschrenn waved a hand. 'The superstitions of the ignorant are no concern of mine.'

Koarsden did not answer, but his lips pursed in censure of Tayschrenn's dismissiveness. Finally, he cleared his throat. 'Tay . . . there may come a time when even you will need to pay attention to the concerns of those around you.'

'I do not see why,' he answered, only half listening. He was, in truth, now scanning the towers for any further signs of Kartool's infamous poisonous spiders. After a long silence he glanced to his companion and noticed his bunched brows and sour expression. He asked, prompting, 'You said . . . ?'

'Nothing,' Koarsden sighed.

The way ahead was now jammed by a large party crossing the street. The crowd was festive, cheering and laughing, holding long banners aloft; children among them waved twisting black and red paper worms. Koarsden took his arm to stop him. 'The executions are on. We should stop in.'

Tayschrenn groaned and pulled onward. 'D'rek spare me.'

Koarsden would not release his arm. 'No, no. It would be good for you to show yourself. The Demidrek's right hand visiting the pits. Can't have your critics painting you as soft on enforcement of the Worm's will.'

He relented, allowing Koarsden to drag him along. *Critics? Why ever would I have critics?*

The execution pits occupied a central position in the city of Kartool. They were just that, pits, roughly circular, of greater and lesser size and capacity. Any visitor ignorant of the city's traditions could easily fall into even the smallest, as, indeed, some unfortunates had. These were no more than mere cylindrical depressions in the stone, as deep as a man and no wider than a man's shoulders, in which the guilty were chained upright to await D'rek's punishment. Said punishment arrived over time as more and more flesh-eating insects fell or were drawn into the pit, to feast upon the transgressor. Or not. For in such diverse fates was the will of D'rek revealed.

The largest execution pit was a circular depression a good four chains across. Tall stone walls surrounded it, together with steep amphitheatre seating rising behind. This was the Civic Pit, and here the two priests found gathered many of Kartool's citizens, gossiping and passing the time by betting on how long each of the condemned – man, woman or child – would last.

Tayschrenn and Koarsden climbed the rising cobbled walk. They were among the crowd, but not crowded, as their robes announced their calling and they were scrupulously avoided, lest offence be given.

They left behind the mundane citizens when they took a side ramp that led to the seating permanently reserved for the priesthood. Here the curving stone benches were almost entirely empty. A few elderly priests dotted the seating, looking like bedraggled crows awaiting a sick animal's death. A few noticed Tayschrenn and rose, bowing their respect for the red sash he wore cinched about his robes – the sash of the highest rank beneath the Demidrek.

He and Koarsden took their seats near the front. Across the pit floor of jagged stones and gravel, dotted by bones, the day's Overseer of Justice, an older priestess whose name he could not recall, also rose and bowed her shaved head. Tayschrenn acknowledged the bow.

The rising rows of stone benches gradually filled, and he was surprised by the size of the crowd; he wondered if today were a feast day or lunar observance of one of the minor titular gods subservient to D'rek, such as Poliel, Beru, Burn, or Hood. Koarsden had fallen into conversation with one of the elderly priests, and inwardly Tayschrenn shook his head. Typical of the man; he seemed somehow able to get along with everyone.

After the conversation ended, Tayschrenn murmured aside, 'Quite the crowd.'

Koarsden nodded. 'Indeed. I was just commenting to Reuthen here on that very fact, and he filled me in. Seems we have a special attraction today.'

'A murderer?'

'No. An interloper. A priestess of that meddling enchantress.'

Tayschrenn was quite surprised. 'Really? The Queen of Dreams? Proselytizing here? Rather impudent. Still . . .' and he put the tips of his fingers together and touched them to his chin, thinking. 'It does set one to wondering. How does one capture the priestess of a goddess who claims to be able to predict the future?'

Koarsden chuckled. 'Good question. The goddess is false, of course. Only in D'rek can one see daily demonstration of truth in the world. And that truth is the cycle of death, decay, and renewal. Rebirth and Return. Such is the balanced double face of D'rek. Destruction and Creation.'

'Well said!' one of the nearby hunched old priests put in, approvingly, then hawked up a mouthful of phlegm and spat aside.

Tayschrenn and Koarsden shared a wry smile and settled into a mutual silence. Their words were not as private as they'd hoped.

As the most minor of the punishments began – thieves having their hands eaten away before their eyes by the especially virulent grubs the priesthood bred – Tayschrenn reflected on the hoary old litany supplied by Koarsden. Yes, D'rek alone of the Elder faiths – and D'rek was among the most ancient – emphasized that enduring truth: that out of death came life, and that each was thus necessary to the other. The ill-advised worship of Hood came closest, but in the eyes of those who embraced the teachings of D'rek it represented at best a half-measure, or mistaken turn. A wrong path, if one would. Death was not an ending, nor a destination. Rather, it was a doorway. A doorway into transformation and service to the new generations to come. The merest glance to the world around should convince anyone of that. The leaves fell, but were renewed. Out of rot and decomposition emerged new life. Such was self-evident. So did D'rek bear two faces. The male of destruction and the female of fecundity.

A couple in chains were led into the pit. They were pelted with rubbish and rotten vegetables. These two must be divorcees. They had had the temerity to end their marriage and so naturally they must be put to death. For who knew how many future lives had been sacrificed by their selfishness? Any society or religion that valued birth and fertility must perforce denounce the separation of a mated couple as the worst of offences. Any who divorced had of course to be stoned to death. It would have been absurd to claim to value life without doing so.

After the punishments of these common offences the priestess overseeing the day's justice – Salleen, that was her name, Tayschrenn remembered – raised a hand for the final execution. A bound woman was led into the pit. Tayschrenn was surprised by her youth. She was bloodied and bruised, her clothes torn. Yet she held her chin high, proud without appearing disdainful.

He approved; after all, she was a priestess.

Salleen raised both arms for silence and the crowd quietened. She stood and crossed her arms, her hands disappearing within the folds of her black robes. 'Messinath of Purge,' she began, 'you have been found guilty of manifold crimes. Of encouraging apostasy. Of heresy. Of spreading religious lies and denying the truth of D'rek's message.' Salleen paused here and the crowd took their cue, booing and hurling refuse. This call and response struck Tayschrenn as amusing. The routine and predictability of all this public theatre was of course necessary – people had to know what their roles in society were, what was expected of them, and how to behave.

Salleen raised a hand once more for silence. 'Therefore you have been condemned to death. You are allowed last words – I advise you to use them to beg for D'rek's clemency.'

The young priestess of the Enchantress raised her chin further, talking a deep breath. 'Priests and priestesses of D'rek,' she began loudly, startling Tayschrenn, 'I am come to bring you warning. Change your ways or you shall suffer the consequences of your recklessness.'

Across the pits, Salleen met Tayschrenn's eye and he raised a brow in commentary. *Astonishing.*

'Otherwise,' the woman continued, her voice ringing throughout the amphitheatre, 'there shall be a time of reckoning. And you shall know D'rek's displeasure and punishment yourselves.'

Salleen surged to her feet, thrusting a finger. 'Further pitiable lies!' She shook her head in regret. 'We generously offer you a

31

chance to pray to D'rek, and instead you spout further profanation.' She threw her arm down. 'Let the punishment begin!'

Down at the pit level, behind the inner stone wall, a line of drummers took their cue and began hammering the fat kettle drums set on the bare ground before them. The muscular musicians were naked from the waist up, and a fine black filigree of tattooed scorpions, beetles, and centipedes covered their backs and arms. The insects seem to writhe as the drumming intensified.

Everyone waited, even the condemned priestess of the Queen of Dreams. She stood panting, glancing left and right as if searching for some executioner; this told Tayschrenn that she was indeed a stranger to the island. That she hadn't fainted or started begging for mercy showed the strength of her inner convictions and character.

A shame, really, that someone so strong should be so wrong-headed. But then, whom else would the cult have chosen for such a dangerous mission as proselytizing on the island of Kartool?

A ripple of anticipation ran through the crowd as a hissing noise reached the benches. It emanated from the holes in the pit floor; the condemned had noticed it as well, as she was now backing away from the nearest of these openings.

The hissing became a loud seething. The drummers now hammered with all their might. Up from the many holes came a boiling tide of writhing insects.

The priestess's mouth opened in a scream of utter horror that was inaudible beneath the coursing of millions of grating carapaces. A living flood that was now engulfing the pit.

Again, to her credit, she did not try to run, for there was nowhere to flee. She found the tallest of the cracked rocks and stepped up upon it; a promontory of perhaps no more than shin height. There she stood, weaving slightly, a pale island surrounded by a rising sea of ten million hungry mouths.

The carpet of vermin now covered the entire floor of the pit. Waves seemed to course through it as if it were searching, frustrated. Searching for something it knew to be present. Still it rose, deepening. Outliers of beetles and centipedes scuttled up the stone wall. Children armed with sticks ran back and forth, laughing, to flick them back into the mass beneath. Some they captured in tiny wicker baskets to keep as pets.

Eventually, some grubs or maggots climbed the rock the

condemned had retreated to and found her naked feet. The entire chitinous sea seemed to flinch. It pulled away from the edges of the pit, gathering towards the middle. The woman screamed again, soundlessly, as the rising flood washed over her feet. It covered her legs, climbing in a thick layer up beneath her skirts. She buckled in agony, mouthing something more, and toppled, to disappear beneath the foaming blanket.

The shapeless hump writhed for a time, struggling, then fell still. After a few moments it began to move – perhaps being dragged, or rolled – towards the nearest opening. While the crowd watched, silent and awed, the seething bulge slid over the edge and disappeared as if down a throat.

The flood of insects followed down the many pit openings like a draining ocean of foam, leaving the bare rock floor picked clean of every scrap of litter and thrown refuse. Of the condemned, there remained not one sign.

The crowd began to rise, heading for the exits. The oldsters in the priests' section hobbled to their feet. Some walked with the aid of twisted and polished wooden canes. A few helped others with hands under their arms. Koarsden stretched, shading his eyes to study the sun in the sky. 'That took longer than I thought it would.' He turned to Tayschrenn. 'Well . . . what do you say we find some lunch?'

* * *

Dancer did not think much of this so-called capital city of Malaz. Judging from its grim and derelict character the island itself must be dirt-poor indeed. Low, ancient stone buildings squatted like tombs in the cold rain, roofed in slate, grey shakes, or ceramic tiles. Most were too far apart to allow rooftop runs, except for the very city centre.

He and Wu stood pressed against one of these cold and damp stone walls under the cover of a roof's ledge while rain pattered down a night-time alley. To warm himself he crossed his arms beneath his cloak and gripped the baldrics over his chest.

'Damned cold rain,' he grumbled beneath his breath to Wu.

'It's the Storm Straits,' Wu answered, just as low. 'A very cold sea. Subaqueous abode, they say, of the daemon Stormriders.'

Dancer snorted at that. 'Children's stories.'

'Not so. We of southern Dal Hon know of them.' The mage straightened. 'Here they come.'

Dancer pulled a scarf up over his nose and mouth, shifted his grip to the cold damp iron of his throwing knives.

Two figures came tramping out of the gloom of the alleyway, side by side, hands hidden beneath their oiled sealskin cloaks. Holding loaded crossbows, point down, Dancer judged. Behind came a small woman in a similar cloak, and behind her two more guards.

Dancer stepped out to block the way, throwing blades drawn. The leading pair jerked to a halt, quite startled by his sudden appearance. Their cloaks bulged outwards as the crossbows rose.

Dancer pointed one dagger past them to the woman, who had also halted. 'Drop your shipment.' Droplets of rain, he noted, fell from the tip of his extended blade.

'Who the fuck are *you*?' one guard asked, incredulous.

Dancer ignored him. 'Drop the package,' he insisted. The woman's hands remained hidden beneath her cloak. Her eyes moved from Dancer to her guards and back. Her black hair was plastered flat to her skull by the rain. Silver earrings glimmered wet and bright in the dark.

'Is this, like, a dumbass hijack?' The guard's tone held a near-laughing note of utter disbelief.

'Just take him,' the woman hissed.

'Stupid bumpkin,' the guard sighed, and he and his partner shot from beneath their cloaks. In the same instant, Dancer dropped to the ground, rolled forward, and jammed his blades into their thighs. Both grunted their pain and went down to the wet cobbles, clutching their legs. Springing up, Dancer landed before the woman and slashed her cloak open to reveal sewn pouches hung about her shoulders. These he also slashed loose. The woman pulled a knife from the back of her belt but he grasped her wrist and twisted; the knife fell from her numb fingers. 'Your men require attention,' he told her.

'Get him, damn you!' she grated, glancing back over her shoulder, then froze; the guards behind her also lay prone on the cobbles. She glared murder at Dancer. 'You are dead right now.' He threw a piece of the slashed cloak over her head. 'We will find you and kill you.' He tied the cloth there like a hood and pushed her down. 'It's a damned small island!'

'Don't move till you count to fifty.'

'Bugger you!'

The pouches, he noted, were already gone. He jogged off up the alleyway. Behind, the woman was already up and tearing at the hood. He turned a corner, picking up his pace, and watched, impressed, as the murk of the shadows seemed to thicken all along his path. He wondered where the little fellow was; surely he wasn't capable of keeping up with him? Watching from his Warren, he decided. Tracing him somehow.

After taking a very long way round, checking that he was not being followed, he returned to the bar whose ridiculous name Wu had refused to change. Smiley's. Personally, he hated it. Yet everyone on the island knew it by that name and so he had little choice but to go along with the idiocy.

By this time it was close to dawn. He pushed open the heavy front door and shut it firmly behind him, locking it. Crossing the main common room he paused as a sound reached him.

He scanned the gloom of the murky room until he made out someone sitting at a table, a steaming hot drink before her. Their hostess, Surly. He let his hands fall from his baldrics. 'You're up early.'

'And you're out late.'

'My morning constitutional.'

'Or evening rendezvous.'

'Nothing for you to trouble yourself over.'

'True.' She rose, taking her cup with her, and came to stand before him, arms crossed and cup steaming between them. He was a little surprised, and again impressed, to find that she was almost exactly his height. 'Unless you're bringing trouble here,' she continued. 'Then I'd be upset. Because, you see, we've worked hard to find a place here and we wouldn't want it pulled out from under us.'

'"We" being you and your Napan friends.'

She took a sip of her tea, watching him over the brim of the cup. 'That's right. Do you have any idea how hard it is to be Napan here on Malaz? Of course you don't. Our two islands have warred for control of the seas for all history. No one will even give us a berth as a damned rower. It's a goddamned insult.'

He thought of his own youthful attempts to establish himself from Tali to Heng, and the stinging backhanded treatment he had received from everyone – except Wu. 'Don't complain to me about how tough it is, okay? Because you have no idea either.'

A corner of the woman's thin lips twitched upwards. 'Fine. Let's agree to disagree. Just be warned. Don't bring any trouble here. All right?'

'Just don't forget who works for who here, all right?'

She blew a plume of steam from her tea. 'Oh, I won't. How could I?'

'Fine.' He headed for the stairs, but, struck by an afterthought, he turned. 'Oh – and get that Urko fellow out of the kitchen, okay? He cooks about as well as a Wickan horseman.'

'Fine. Who should replace him?'

He started up the stairs. 'Who cares? Why don't you hire a real cook?' He added, grumbling, 'Maybe we'd actually get some real Hood-damned customers in here.'

Closing the door to the office he turned and stopped short, finding the room completely dark. 'Oh, please,' he complained, and light blossomed as the thick shadows retreated to reveal the desk lamp flame flickering and Wu seated behind it.

'Who were you talking to?' the mage demanded, hunched, his tiny ferret-like eyes darting.

'Our hostess, Surly.'

Wu straightened, lowering his hands. 'Oh. Well, never mind then.'

Dancer leaned back against the door and crossed his arms. 'Actually, there does seem to be more to her than meets the eye.'

Wu was rummaging behind the desk. He pulled up three canvas pouches and set them on the empty surface. Raising a finger, he added, 'As with us, my friend. As with us.'

Dancer pushed himself from the door, advancing. 'True.'

Wu examined the leather ties securing the pouches. 'Nothing special that I can see . . .'

'What of Warren-laid traps?'

Wu yanked his hands away. 'I don't detect anything . . . but not my field of expertise.' He offered one sack to Dancer, who raised his hands high.

'You're the mage.'

'You're the thief.'

'Not a thief,' Dancer corrected.

Wu drummed his fingers on the desk. 'Semantics.' He picked up one pouch and examined its tie. 'Fine. I'll have you know that I'm the one taking all the risk here.'

'If it's a Telas explosion, we'll both be consumed.'

Wu shrugged. 'Oh. In that case.' He pulled on the leather tie and it easily untwined. He upended the pouch. Small items individually wrapped in twists of parchment slid out on to the desk.

Both examined what looked like nothing more than a collection of sweets. Wu picked one up and studied it. 'Writing on the parchment. Some kind of code.'

'Seller and buyer?' Dancer suggested.

'Perhaps.'

Wu gently unfolded the parchment, revealing the small, hard object at its centre. Both craned forward, breaths held. Wu screwed up his eyes until only one was open. Dancer plucked the object from the wrap to examine it between thumb and forefinger. It was shaped like a pebble, oval, yet curled around itself with a narrow opening, white with tan stripes.

He refocused his puzzled gaze on Wu. 'It's a fucking seashell.'

Wu held out a hand. 'Let me see.' Dancer dropped it into his palm. Wu held it a hair's breadth from an eye. 'Damn. It really is a shell. Not one I know, either.'

Dancer threw himself from the desk. 'Who the Abyss cares what kind? What is this? A scam? Did you swap these out?'

Wu threw up his hands. 'Now, now. Let us examine the evidence here. Are these the pouches you saw?'

Dancer was pacing, cursing himself. *Took the wrong Hood-damned packages! Should've searched her!* He waved a hand. 'Yeah. Fine. Decoys. Hood-damned decoys. Fell for it like an amateur.'

Wu raised a finger. 'Not necessarily.' He juggled the shell in his hand. 'These look like a very rare type of shell. One that I have never before seen. And Dal Hon has a long coastline. Some tribes even use them—' He cut himself off, his thick brows rising.

'Well?' Dancer demanded.

Wu set the shell down and opened another wrap to reveal a near-identical shell. He drummed his fingers on the desk once more, deep in thought. Finally, he breathed, 'Well. This is awkward.'

Dancer paced. 'How so? What is it?'

Wu tapped his fingertips together. 'The problem is one of how to transport money – or value – on an island populated entirely by thieves and pirates.'

Dancer stopped pacing; faced him. 'So . . . these are just tokens? Tokens of value these merchants agree to honour because they have no value elsewhere?'

'For certain large exchanges, clearly.'

'No wonder that guard laughed . . . So, what do we do?'

'Change of tactics, obviously.'

'Yes. Forget about cornering the markets. We should switch to protection and extortion. Take control that way.'

Wu sighed. 'So much more messy. But, agreed.' He started repacking the shells. 'Why does everything have to be so damned difficult? That's what I want to know.'

Chapter 3

NEDURIAN WAS FISHING, AS USUAL. HIS LINE HUNG STRAIGHT down from the high wharf to the water. But for most of the morning he'd been far away, thinking of his last great duel – his dusk to dawn battle against the witch Jadeen in south Itko Kan. Because they were both Adepts of Rashan, the Warren of Dark, it had been a war of subtlety, countermoves, bluffs and feints, all woven in multiple layers . . . like a duel fought through folded night itself.

In the end, neither had managed to land a decisive blow. But he'd marked her, and she – and he touched a finger to the jagged scar that bisected his face – had marked him.

But he was in the twilight of his years, after all. In his youth she'd never have even got close. *Or so you tell yourself, old man,* he thought, snorting.

Shade where none should be brought him back to himself, and he peered up, blinking, at a scowling giant of a fellow standing over him. 'What do you want?' he asked, then shifted his attention to his line and gave it a shake.

'Geffen wants to see ya.'

Geffen, the blackmarketeer and enforcer who pretty much ran the island – under the auspices of Mock, of course.

'I don't owe him one damned copper sliver.'

'If you did, I wouldn't be asking so damned nice an' all.'

Nedurian considered. So far, he'd managed to stay clear of all the local gambling, loansharking, boozing and drug pits. His one weakness was women. And considering that he'd just been daydreaming about one of the most lethal females he'd known, perhaps it had been too long.

Not that he was sure he could perform anyway; it'd been a *damned* long time . . . 'What is it?'

The fellow's scowl of distaste deepened even further. 'Like Gef tells me. Just come along.'

'And if I tell you to go take a long walk on this short pier?'

The fellow snapped his fingers and four more toughs came slouching up the faded wooden slats. Nedurian knew he could handle them, of course. Easily. But then there'd be four more, and so on, and then he'd no longer be retired, would he? Sighing, he rose, dusted off the seat of his trousers, and gathered up his line.

The brawlers escorted him to Geffen's gambling house where it stood close to the waterfront. Its sign was that of a golden gyrfalcon – a play on the man's nickname. Of course, the place was nothing special compared to similar establishments on the mainland. Downright coarse and shabby, really, but enough to part these common raiders from their loot and shares.

He was guided up stairs to offices above. The first room held seven guards, and, after having his small belt-dagger taken away here, he was led further in. It seemed to him that Geffen, a cutthroat nasty enough to rise to the top of an island of cutthroats, was scared.

Within, the man himself stood leaning against a broad heavy table next to the room's one window. Two personal bodyguards stood at the door. One of these shut it on the rest of the lower-ranked toughs. These two then stood close to either side of Nedurian while their employer, Geffen, looked him up and down. He in turn studied the other man: lean – almost fevered lean – greying hair pulled back in a queue, face scarred by a multitude of small cuts. A knife-fighter of particularly grisly repute. And an experienced seagoing raider, as everyone on this cursed island was.

Geffen, meanwhile, was shaking his head. 'You don't look like much. But there're people who say you're a mage to be reckoned with.'

'People should keep their damned mouths shut.'

This brought a thin smile to the man's lips. He gestured to the table. 'Like you to take a look at something for me.'

'We haven't discussed my consulting fee yet.'

Geffen just gave a look that seemed to say *Now, now*. He flicked a leather wrap aside from something on the table. Nedurian crossed over, peered down. It was a dagger.

He leaned his hands on the table – careful to keep them far from the weapon – and bent closer. 'Nothing special. Typical knife.'

'Been trying to backtrack the last person to hold that,' Geffen said while Nedurian studied the blade. 'Half the island's wax-witches, sea-soothers, and warlocks have shambled through here for a peek. They all did the same thing: took one look, went pale as ghosts, turned and walked away.'

Nedurian stroked his chin. 'Really? I don't see anything unusual.'

'Take your time.'

It wasn't his speciality, but he raised his Warren for a look. He passed his hands over the blade, sensing for anything, and felt it immediately. This weapon had been exposed to powerful magics some time in the recent past. The lingering energies were clear. The aura, however, was also very odd. Like no Warren he'd ever seen before, in fact.

'Strange . . .' he murmured.

'A coupla' warlocks said that too,' Geffen offered. 'Before they bit their lips and fled.'

Nedurian frowned. He refined his probing, dug deeper in the lineaments of the traces, struggling to examine their character.

He found that it was something he *had* seen before. He'd encountered brief hints of it a few times, and always indirectly and cloaked. Most powerfully, though, a very long time ago.

It had been in his youth. He'd been newly appointed battle-magus commander attached to the Talian Eleventh Iron Legion then. One of the youngest ever. They'd been charged with pacifying the northern tribes of the forests on the border of Lake Ero and there they had met the gathered enemy. Late in the battle, down out of the Fenn Range came the wild-haired shaman who'd been stirring them all up, the Seti, the Fenn giants, the western Wickan tribals.

All the front line warlocks had fallen to the strange new Warren this fellow had thrown himself into with utter madness and abandon. Nedurian would never forget that terrifying battle. The moon itself seemed to darken at the wild man's command. The right flank collapsed when monstrous howling beasts came rampaging across the blasted and flattened forest. It was all he could do to deflect one of them at a distance.

That dawn the Eleventh retreated, ravaged and clawed. But not defeated. For along with all their many victims the daemons had consumed the shaman also, and soon enough the tribes fell back to bickering and raiding one another.

During the storms of black flame and attacks of rippling darkness that he and the shaman had exchanged, he'd glimpsed the character of that Warren and realized its name. It was a discipline mentioned in teachings, but which no sane practitioner ever pursued because of its wildly unstable, fractured, and unpredictable nature: the Warren of Shadow. Also called Meanas.

He returned his hands to the table and rested a good deal of his weight on them, thinking.

'The others went pale,' Geffen offered. 'But you just flushed all dark. What is it?'

'How did you come across this?'

Geffen pushed himself from the table. 'Ah.' He waved the two guards from the room. They hesitated, unwilling.

'You sure?' one grumbled.

'Yes I'm fucking sure! Now go!'

Both shot Nedurian murderous glares, but they stepped out and pulled the door shut behind them. Geffen poured himself a drink, then held out the ceramic decanter. 'Want some?'

'What is it?'

'Rice liquor from Itko Kan.'

'No thanks.' He scanned the various decanters and found what looked like red wine. He poured a glass and sipped – it was a passable Untan blend.

Geffen was now at his desk, idly poking through the mess of parchment sheets heaped there. He cleared his throat, saying, 'I woke up a few days ago with that thrust through the headboard of my bed. No one else knows it happened. Not even my guards.'

Nedurian blew out a breath. 'I see. So, a message.'

Geffen turned on him. 'Yes, a godsdamned message! But I'm not gonna roll over! I don't know who this guy thinks he is, but if he wants a fight I'll give it to him. Starting from now you're on the payroll. I want a secure perimeter and constant monitoring. We'll catch the bastard next time.'

Nedurian set down the wine. 'No.'

'What d'you mean, no?'

'Not for hire.'

42

Geffen frowned down at him. 'You scared of what you found on that blade? Well, don't be. Be more scared of me right now.'

'You're already embroiled in one fight, it seems. Don't start another.'

The tall wiry fellow eyed him sideways, then leaned back, crossing his arms. 'I see you still got a few teeth left in that scarred wolf's head of yours. Good for you.' He raised his chin, calling, 'Okay! C'mon back in!'

The door slammed open and the two bodyguards stepped in. Geffen threw a small pouch on to the table. 'Your fee. I might have work for you ahead.'

Nedurian eyed the pouch, then shrugged his shoulders and took it. 'You know where to find me.' He strolled out as casually as his prickling back would let him, and once on the street started deeper into town, circling a few blocks to make certain he wasn't being followed – not that he thought he would be – before heading for Agayla's.

She ran a modest spice shop in one of a long lane of anonymous terraced houses. Its sign was a strung sheaf of twigs, plus fresh garlands of various dried plants hung all over the thick oak door. He pushed it open and stepped inside.

The shop-front was a counter behind which stood rows of shelving choked by glass jars and wooden boxes. Standing rows of tiny wooden drawers covered the walls. Hanging down from the low rafters, and obscuring everything like a bizarre upturned forest, reached dried bunches of various plants, flowers, and woven braids of grasses.

From the room beyond came the rhythmic shush of a hand-worked loom. Nedurian cleared his throat. 'Agayla?'

The loom quietened. He could hear the woman's long skirts brushing the wooden floor as she approached. She entered, adjusting the tie of her thick bunched hair and pulling the mane forward over one shoulder as she came. He himself had seen near to two hundred years, but he knew he was the youngest of striplings compared to this sorceress. He inclined his head in greeting. 'Agayla.'

She reached out across the counter to take his hands; hers were warm, dry, and hard. 'Nedurian. What can I do for you?'

'I bring . . . disturbing news.'

She released his hands. 'I see . . . well, come in.' She lifted a portion of the counter for him and retreated to the rear. He followed. In the back room she motioned to a chair along one wall next to a small table. A massive homemade loom filled almost the entire room. She sat at the intricate mechanism of wooden slats and strung thread and pushed the sleeves of her dress up over her lean arms, then depressed the wide foot pedal. The twin leaves of strung thread spread apart with a loud shush.

He watched her work for a time, admiring the economy of her movements, the play of the musculature of her arms, and her swift nimble fingers.

'What is the news?' she asked.

'I'm fairly certain that someone's meddling in Meanas here on the island.'

The loom slapped to a halt. She held the shuttle in one fist, glaring his way. '*That's* what's been bothering me of late! I knew there was something . . .' She tossed the shuttle through the weave, shaking her head. 'On this island, of all places. The fool.' She raised her gaze to a narrow window high on one wall; her arms, hands and feet worked automatically for a while, shifting and plucking, as she cast her awareness elsewhere.

Eventually, her gaze shifted to him, sidelong. 'He's a sly one,' she murmured in grudging appreciation.

'I agree. I couldn't get a fix on him.'

'Perhaps he just wants to be left alone.'

'Sadly not. Worse is, he's making a play for Geffen's job.'

Agayla threw herself entirely from the loom to press her hands to her thighs in frustration. 'Blood and tar! That's the last thing we need right now. War for control of the streets.'

'Is there any chance Mock—'

'Mock cares nothing for whoever runs things in town so long as he gets his cut.'

'Thought so.'

She sighed, then returned her attention to her work. 'Well, we'll just have to keep an eye on things. If it gets out of hand, we'll put an end to it.'

He blew out a long breath. *Oh-kayyy* . . . 'And who is this "we"?'

'Obo and I.'

The name rocked Nedurian. *She can reach through to Obo?* Belatedly, he realized that his name wasn't on her list. *I don't even rate a mention in that company.*

'In the meantime you'll sniff round, yes? See if you can pin down our foolish friend.'

He nodded his assent.

Agayla returned to work and he returned to watching her. It occurred to him that the finished portion of this particular piece – carpet or tapestry, call it what you will – was very short indeed. He asked, 'Is this a new work?'

She nodded absently. 'Yes.'

'What's it about?'

'As always – what is to come.'

From the assurance of that simple comment he felt again the preternatural shiver that this woman raised on the nape of his neck. While no Ascendant herself, she was a potent agent to powers, said to be favoured not only by the Enchantress, but by Jhess the Weaver as well. Powers that he, even as an Adept, could only sense distantly.

He studied the colours of the thread gathered in a basket next to the loom: deep aquamarine blue, blood carmines, gleaming night-black, pewter greys, and sunset purples.

'The future looks dark,' he said.

Agayla merely pursed her thin lips colourless and bent to her work.

*　　*　　*

To Cartheron, everything on board the *Honest Avarice* was slack-ass and sloppy. But then, it was a Malazan raider. Not a Napan one. Twin-masted, the fore raked far forward, lean-beamed and shallow-draughted, she was damned fast; that he had to admit. But still . . . not Napan.

It was the night watch and they were anchored in a tiny cove on the Vorian coast. He kept to the stern deck, rearward of the mast. Here at least he had some peace; forward, it was another situation altogether. Constant elbows and thumps that had to be endured with gritted teeth. 'Watch it, Napan,' was the sneering refrain, or, 'Don't you Napans know how to sail?'

All this despite the fact that the ship's officers damn well knew he was here because of his unparalleled knowledge of the south coast. Well, expecting any fairness in the world was something he'd given up on as a child.

Even worse, this cove had been one of his family's favourite hiding-holes for generations, and now he had been forced to share it with these wretched Malazans. The western arm of the headland curved well over, its shore more than deep enough for this shallow corsair.

And not even one word of thanks from the captain, Bezil, a Bloorian renegade who seemed to think he was some sort of nobleman. Just a grunt, as of a job done to minimal satisfaction.

How he wished he could've swept over this ship with his old crew! But Lady Sureth, or Surly, as she called herself now, was right. Where would they find safe habourage? Certainly not on Nap, nor then Malaz. And they were wanted all along the coast. Set off for parts unknown? A deep-water journey across Reacher's Sea for the Seven Cities region, Genabackis, or legendary Jacuruku? Where they wouldn't know the shallows or the shoals?

No. Best to establish a base. Some safe harbour where they could refit and repair, resupply and even recruit. But it was galling. So damned galling having to stomach these puffed-up raiders. None of whom could stand against even the worst Napan crew, in his view.

Footsteps, and Griff, the old steersman, joined him at the rail. The wizened wiry fellow boasted so many tattoos on his bald scalp that it was now as blue as Cartheron's own native hue. He was puffing on a long-stemmed clay pipe, and he offered a nod of recognition that Cartheron answered with relief – some wisdom had been knocked into this one's skull, at least.

'Fine cosy berth you found for us,' Griff said round the stem of his pipe.

'Thank you.'

'Not long now.'

Cartheron nodded at that; the convoy was in fact overdue.

'Still . . . strange,' the taciturn fellow added in a billow of smoke.

Cartheron nodded again. It was odd that knowledge of the convoy should have been so widespread. 'Word sometimes gets out,' he murmured.

The steersman offered a noncommittal grunt. In the silence, waves slapped the planks of the vessel and cordage creaked overhead as the vessel rocked. Out beyond the cove in the open waters a storm was rising beneath fat clouds.

'What happened there on Nap anyway?' the old sailor asked.

Cartheron felt his back tense and his hands tighten on the wooden rail. He forced a shrug. 'Tarel usurped the throne.'

'Ah. And that princess. What of her?'

He let out a long hard breath. 'Died that night.'

'Found yourself on the losing side, hey?'

Cartheron didn't answer. He leaned more of his weight on the rail.

'Faugh,' the old sailor grunted. 'Land and politics – curse 'em both to Oponn. Leave it all behind, son. Best to be at sea in the clean air.'

'I hear you there, old-timer.'

The steersman regarded the dark foam-capped open waters beyond. 'A high sea.'

'Indeed. They may have lain up.'

'Too dangerous, I'd wager. The Vorians wouldn't allow a prize like that to pass.'

A cold chilling rain now came pelting down and Cartheron nodded his agreement with the old man's assessment. 'Probably running on a few scraps of cloth.'

Griff grunted.

'And the men-o-war?' Cartheron asked.

'Out in deeper waters, waiting.'

'Waiting to drive them towards the shore – and our waiting arms, hey?'

Griff eyed him, puzzled. 'Thought you knew the plan.'

'Bezil tells me nothing.'

Griff snorted a great cloud of smoke. 'Hunh! Too many years fighting you Napans, I suppose.'

'Probably thinks I'm a spy.'

'As they say: blood and tribe first. All others are enemy.'

Cartheron shook his head at the narrow-mindedness of it and rested his elbows on the railing.

Griff had returned to eyeing the rough moonlit whitecaps and now he stiffened, straining. 'See that, lad?'

Cartheron squinted. After a few moments he glimpsed it as well: a long thin dark line amid the waves, rising and falling. 'A longboat.'

'Scouting the shore.'

'Looking to pull in?'

The old man shook his tattooed bald head. 'No. Scouting the route. The cargo vessels should be following along.' He waved one of the night crew to him. 'Wake the captain. Silence rules, yes?'

The sailor nodded and padded off on bare feet.

Cartheron kept watch while the *Honest Avarice* came to life around him. All was readied in utter dark and silence. Though light and slim, the corsair packed an inordinately large crew of marines-cum-sailors. They were, in fact, its only cargo. Everyone fought; no one held back. Even Cartheron was expected to join in, though a hated Napan.

They lined the side, watching, while one by one, then in twos, the convoy of cargo vessels came plodding past like fat slow oxen, each showing minimal canvas to the intensifying storm.

Cartheron had to admire the skill of their navigators. To continue the run in such a blow; still, what options did they have, after all? And no doubt they'd made this trip many times before.

Lightning now joined in, the rain driving. In the brilliant flashes Cartheron glimpsed the vessels lit in silhouette. Amid their wide round contours he saw a new shape lancing through the waves and showing near full sail – lean and tall, like a scimitar, he recognized one of Mock's men-o-war.

Around him, the crew sent up a great bloodthirsty cheer.

'At 'em!' someone yelled.

Then came Bezil's great bellow. '*Not yet!* Wait for them to scatter! But,' he added, 'ready poles and sweeps!'

The crew jumped to the ready. Griff untied the tiller-arm. Cartheron helped him with it and the old man nodded his thanks.

With the sweeps working, and crewmen pushing off rocks, the *Honest Avarice* headed out into the centre of the cove's mouth. Now came the tricky, and potentially deadly, manoeuvre of turning and catching the driving wind without forcing the vessel on to the waiting rocks.

Griff's gaze was fixed on the foremast. There hands waited, gripping lines, their eyes on the old man. Glancing to the shore, he nodded, and the hands yanked the lines. The lateen fores'l rose and Griff fought to throw the rudder. The bows heaved over, the ship leaping and yawing. Then the old man's feet slipped on the wet deck and he stumbled. Startled, Cartheron caught the tiller, but in that instant the ship's prow swung dangerously towards shore. Cartheron slammed the arm over; the old man's timing would have been perfect, but now they were too far behind in the arc of their turn.

Sailors yelled their alarm; Bezil came storming up to the stern deck, glaring rage at Cartheron. Yet even he was not foolish enough to interfere as the sleek corsair yawed over, timbers groaning, and the wet rocks of the shore slid past seemingly within arm's reach.

They passed the small headland – all hands bracing for that terrifying judder and squeal of timber over rock – and slid onward, scudding the coast. Bezil relaxed, letting go of the hilt of his sword, but still glared just as murderously.

'Damned Napan! Trying to get us killed?'

Griff rose unsteadily, holding his head. 'No, captain. The lad saved us.'

'Saved us? Blasted near sank us!' Bezil jabbed a finger at Griff. 'Get us out to sea.'

'Have to gain some room and headway before we can turn into the wind.'

Bezil waved him on. 'Yes, yes. Just get it done.' He turned on Cartheron. 'You – stop interfering and ready your weapons. You're with the boarding crew.'

Cartheron gingerly relinquished the arm to Griff. 'Aye . . . captain.'

Bezil stamped off. The old man offered Cartheron a look of commiseration; the Napan could only shrug.

Griff singled out their target among the line of sluggish merchantmen and came closing in on the vessel from behind. Cartheron watched the action from among the assembled boarding crew. He caught intermittent glimpses of other lean wolf raiders darting in now upon the convoy. Jagged tongues of lightning lit Mock's three men-o-war out among the heaving waves as they engaged the escort of five barques.

The *Honest Avarice* was close enough now to steal the wind from their quarry and the vessel lost nearly all headway, rocking unsteadily in the rough contrary waves. Cartheron carried twinned long-knives, both broad parrying daggers, more blades at the rear of his belt, and two on a baldric across his chest. He was ready for a fight, but still he hoped to see the white flag climb the mainmast ahead. As a Napan privateer himself, he knew raiders could be notoriously murderous when their quarry failed to submit. It was perhaps their strongest weapon: fear and savagery at sea.

Ahead, on the taller deck of the merchantman, Cartheron glimpsed sailors readying for boarding. So, it would be a fight. Perhaps they counted on the rough sea to make a difference in the engagement.

Now that the *Honest Avarice* was almost upon their quarry, Bezil called out, 'Ready grapnels!'

As they came alongside, crewmen threw line after line across the slim gap. '*Heave!*' went the call. Lines went round bollards and even the masts as sailors pulled to bring them in closer. Some snapped under the strain. The sea churned between the vessels, shooting upwards and spraying all. Sailors on board the merchantman took pot shots with crossbows, but with both vessels rising and falling most went astray.

Now came the hard part. To his credit, Bezil set one booted foot up on the rail, a line in his hand. 'Up and at 'em!' he bellowed, and started climbing.

With an animal roar that momentarily drowned out the sea, the near-entire crew of the *Honest Avarice* followed.

Sailors on the merchantman now chopped frantically at the lines above. Cartheron surged up hand over hand, desperate to make it before his was cut.

He made the railing and rolled over to land on the rain-slick deck. The sailors had retreated from the side and gathered together round the companionways and cargo hatches, swords and knives readied.

'Yield!' Orwen, Bezil's first mate, shouted.

'Come and die, Malazan scum!' someone answered from among the crew.

Cartheron thought it damned odd that they should retreat from the side and be ready to fight on though clearly outnumbered. Usually most crews submitted rather than be slaughtered whole-sale. But Orwen waved the Malazans forward, charging, and calling, 'At 'em!'

Cartheron surged forward with the rest. He engaged a fellow armed with a shortsword, parried, edged the blade over, and thrust, only to feel his long-knife skitter, rebounding. Armour? There beneath the man's torn shirt gleamed iron. A cuirass! What in the Lad's name . . .

He shifted backwards, disengaging. *Bloody Abyss* . . .

Yells of surprise and alarm from the cargo hatches. 'Soldiers!' someone screamed.

The sailors laughed, parting, and from behind them surged forward armoured troopers bearing bucklers and helms who immediately began slashing on all sides.

Cartheron retreated frantically for the rail, parrying for his life. Chaos erupted as the soldiers broke out to take the deck. He caught sight of Bezil falling, run through. 'Trap!' the man bellowed, then gasped, 'Retreat.'

Cartheron locked blades with one soldier and kicked him backwards. Turning, he took hold of a line, waved all nearby to follow, and leapt overboard. He descended hand over hand until the knotted line shook, then suddenly he was falling with it.

The sea took him like a blow to the stomach. A shockingly cold punch, yet he held on to the line, and even continued to climb – though now through churning frigid darkness.

A trough in the waves allowed him one quick breath. He now hung suspended low from the side of the *Honest Avarice*. It had broken free of the merchantman, trailing countless lines, but wallowing without headway. Cartheron forced his numb hands and arms to move. A peak washed over him, tugging at him, but at last he reached the rail to roll over on to the slick deck.

Dazed, he glanced about at the chaos around him. Oil flames burned in the rain amidships. What few hands remained fought the canvas to keep the ship upright in the storm. He staggered to the stern, found Griff pinned upright to the tiller-arm, shot through by crossbow bolts, yet somehow still alive.

'I'll get us home, old man,' Cartheron whispered as he hugged the fellow to heave the rudder over.

'Closer to the wind,' the old man told him in a gasp, and he flashed bloodied teeth in a death's grin. 'She can take it.'

'Closer it is.' Cartheron looked to the canvas. 'Don't reef the mains'l!' he bellowed. 'Keep her taut!'

'Aye, aye,' came the faint wind-whipped answering call.

The continued ferocity of the lightning storm lit the men-o-war. They were surrounded now by merchantmen, like wolves amid a pack of leaping hounds. Cartheron frankly thought them lost until a lightning strike came sizzling down to blast right through one of the merchantmen, which burst into an expanding cloud of shattered timbers and flame.

He blinked, shielding his eyes from the conflagration.

Hugged to his chest, Griff chuckled, almost inaudibly. 'That's our lass,' he murmured, grinning through the blood.

'Who?' Another lightning strike blasted yet another vessel, leaving behind an after-image in Cartheron's vision of light escaping through every seam in its side before the timbers flew apart. 'Who?'

'Our Tattersail . . .' The man's head sank to his chest. 'She'll see them through . . .'

'That's one ferocious battle-mage you have there, old-timer . . . Griff?'

Cartheron peered at him; the man now hung limp, pinned to the arm. Yet Cartheron did not relinquish his grip, legs braced, a hand either side of the corpse.

A bloody marine bearing a number of slashes climbed to the stern deck. Leaning close, he yelled above the storm, 'Fire's out! We're hands short and you're taking us into deeper waters?'

Cartheron recognized the burly squat fellow from among the boarding crew. 'You fought your way clear of the trap?'

'Aye.'

'What's your name?'

'Call me Dujek.'

'Very well, Dujek. Lay on more canvas. I plan to get us home.'

The fellow roared a laugh. 'Might as well. I counted us dead a while back.' He stamped down to the midship deck, bellowing, 'Tighten the fores'l! Watch the sheets!'

Cartheron kept his weight on the tiller-arm and Griff's cooling body. The *Honest Avarice* responded like a leaping colt. They sped past a caravel closing to cut them off, its decks teeming with soldiers who shot salvo after salvo of arrows after them, all of which flew wide in the raging winds. Steadying the arm, Cartheron sent them deeper into the teeth of the storm.

* * *

At dusk, Dancer took to the streets to find Wu. He hadn't seen him all that day, which was quite unusual lately. It was overcast, as he was finding drearily normal for the island – even in the summer.

He was no mage and so couldn't track the fellow down, or sense his direction, or anything preternatural such as that. However, as they'd become partners he'd come to know him quite well – perhaps better than he'd prefer – and one thing he'd noticed was that when out for walks the mage had a strange affinity for a certain quarter of the old town, just behind the waterfront. He set out to survey that quarter and sure enough, he soon found him – standing right out in the open too, like a damned bloody fool. A troop of scruffy kids were watching from a little way down the cobbled street.

He had his walking stick out before him, hands planted on it as he rocked back and forth on his heels before the overgrown iron gate of an old house that commanded an unusually large area of wild and tangled grounds. Dancer came up beside him, hissed, 'You're in the damned open.'

The short fellow's brows rose and he peered up, blinking, as if coming back to himself from far away. 'Ah! Dancer. Excellent.' He pointed the stick at the house. 'There it is.'

Dancer paid the place scant attention, saying, 'You need to stay under cover.'

'They're hunting you, not me.'

'Don't be so certain. I still say that calling card was a mistake.'

'We can't go killing everyone.' He made shooing gestures with a hand. 'We need little people to order about. How can I delegate if there's no one to delegate to?'

'He's not the type to work for anyone.'

'We had to make the offer. Let it not be said that we did not observe the civilities. And in any case, he works for Mock, doesn't he?'

Dancer gritted his teeth. 'Well, sort of. He's on his guard now, that's for sure.'

'No matter.' He indicated the house again. 'I've found it.'

Dancer couldn't keep the irritation from his face and voice as he snapped, 'Found what?'

'The centre of the nest of power on this island.' His expression clouded. 'That is, if nests have centres . . . anyway, this house. Tell me . . . what do you see?'

Dancer cast the building a quick glance. 'Just a decrepit old stone house. It looks abandoned . . . but,' and he frowned, suddenly uneasy, 'it's not.'

'No? It's not? What do you sense?'

'As if someone's in there. Watching us.'

Wu was nodding to himself. 'Good. You are no mage, but your training has heightened your senses. You can tell this place shouldn't be meddled with.'

'It makes me feel . . . tense. Nervous.'

'That is an aura it is projecting. Camouflage. It does not want anyone approaching.'

'You talk as though it's alive.'

'Some scholars claim it is – in a manner perhaps incomprehensible to us.'

Dancer crossed his arms, scanned the surrounding dark streets, half obscured by the misting rain; the urchins were whispering among themselves, and staring. He felt even more exposed and uncomfortable. 'Hunh. So, why the interest?'

Wu said, with a strange grimness, 'I intend to gain entry to that structure.'

Dancer snorted a laugh. 'I've been getting into buildings all my life.'

'Not like this you haven't.'

'Well, you *have* ruined the sneaking-in approach – standing out here like some kind of frightened tinker.'

Wu raised a finger. 'True enough,' and he pushed open the wrought-iron gate, which squealed loudly. Down the street the street-urchins let out audible gasps of awe.

Dancer wanted to slap his brow. 'What are you doing?' he hissed. Strangely, he felt like an urchin himself, prodding some unfamiliar slumbering beast.

Wu waved him onward. 'Come. We'll knock. Simple process of elimination, yes?'

Dancer edged forward on to the walk of laid flags, all wet and overgrown by moss and lichens. Why was he following this fool into yet another uncertain situation? Could he not let him get the better of him? Was it rivalry? No. He took hold of the heaviest blades at his baldrics. Reluctantly, he was coming to the realization that he actually felt quite protective of the helpless fellow; as one must watch out for a halfwit younger brother.

Ahead, Wu was apparently approaching the front door with complete nonchalance; he was tapping his walking stick, humming tunelessly. The walk curved around mounds that dotted the large overgrown grounds. Squat, dead or near-dead trees brooded over these mounds, their branches empty of all leaves, black and gleaming wet. A low wall of heaped fieldstones enclosed the property.

Wu used the metal head of his walking stick to rap on the stout door.

Dancer stood behind, scanning the rear and the grounds. Something about the forsaken unkempt yard troubled him more than the house itself.

'Hello?' Wu called. 'Anyone there?' He reached out to take hold of the wrought-iron latch and pulled, to no effect.

Silence from the house, while the rain hissed and the sea, not so distant, rolled against the rocky shore and the city wharves. The impression the place gave Dancer was of a hunched brooding bulk. It was constructed of dressed stones, two-storeyed, with one side slightly taller in what might be a tower of sorts, but all that seemed a façade for something else, something deeper. For example, a few small deeply seated windows dotted the structure, but the glass was faceted and smoky, as if merely ornamental. The only analogue he could come up with was a cenotaph, or a monument, constructed of solid stone and built to resemble a manor house, yet empty.

Dancer wiped cold rain from his brow. 'Let's go. No one's home.'

'Someone *is* home,' Wu insisted. 'They're just ignoring us.' He stepped back from the wide slab of iron-blue slate that was the house's landing and shook his fist. 'Fine! I will be back! And you won't ignore me then – I swear!'

He turned to Dancer and adjusted his dripping wet coat. 'Let's go.'

'So long as you're done yelling at an empty house.'

Wu pointed both forefingers in emphasis, 'I am far from done, my friend!' He stamped off down the walk.

'Hey, mister!' a kid yelled from the street. The street-urchins now lined the fieldstone wall. Some were short enough to lean their elbows on it.

Wu halted. 'What?'

'Step out on to the grounds,' the tallest of them called, while his peers chortled and covered their mouths. The younger ones froze at this suggestion, their eyes huge.

'The grounds? Whatever for?'

Dancer waved an arm. 'Get lost, you damned brats.'

'G'wan,' the lad called, 'we double-dare you.'

Wu looked to the overcast sky in exasperation. 'Fine.' He stepped out among the dead knee-high grasses and weeds. 'There. You happy now?'

'Wow, he actually *is* that stupid,' the lad whispered to his friends in wonderment.

Dancer waved Wu onward. 'Stop showing off.' He started for the gate.

A slithering, hissing noise among the weeds spun Dancer round. Wu had heard it also, and was scanning the dense matted bracken, looking puzzled. All at once something yanked the mage off his feet and he sprawled, his arms flailing.

The kids stared, jaws agape, then all screamed and scattered into the dark.

Dancer was in the air, blades already out. He fell slashing only to find tough dry roots wrapped about Wu's ankle. He sawed them, but as soon as one parted two or three more took its place. Wu fumbled at the vines as well, but Dancer slapped his hands away and continued slashing even as both men were violently yanked through thorny brittle brush. He cast a quick glance ahead to see that they were being pulled directly towards the nearest mound – and that its heaped earth was steaming and roiling. Thicker roots now came snaking out of the dirt.

'Do your stuff,' he told Wu.

'Well,' the mage said, his voice tight with pain. 'This is rather embarrassing.'

Another yank and they slid forward until Wu's booted foot was up against the side of the mound. Dancer sawed and slashed frantically. '*Do something!*' he yelled.

'Can't. Shadows won't fool this . . .' The mage suddenly raised his head in obvious inspiration. He raised a finger.

Dancer pointed a blade. 'No! Don't you dare!'

Wu's foot sank into the steaming earth up to his shin. Fatter roots now emerged to twine round his thigh. Dancer noticed, distractedly, that no vines or roots were pulling at him.

'The only chance, I'm afraid.'

'No, not yet. We'll think of something.'

'Can't be helped . . .'

'No! Don't you fucking dare!'

Cold darkness swept over him and he shuddered. What seemed

like a storm of murk came whipping all about him and either it lifted him, or the earth fell, but he found himself falling in darkness. He hit hard, the breath punched from him, and rolled in dusty sandy earth.

He leapt to his feet, blades readied, turned a full circle. They were in some sort of desert and it was deep twilight. But then, it seemed to always be dusk in Shadow. He spotted Wu a short way off and stamped over to him.

'I can't believe you stranded us in Shadow again!'

Wu was holding his leg; his boot and trouser leg had been torn clean off. 'Well, it worked. Remember that. I think my ankle's broken.'

'Well, I'm not carrying you.'

Wu glanced about almost contentedly. 'Fine. I'll just rest here until my ankle's healed.'

Dancer pressed the cold pommels of his daggers to his brow and gave vent, stamping back and forth and kicking at the dust. 'Arghh! Goddammit!' He sheathed the blades savagely in his baldrics. 'Okay! Which way?'

Wu pointed, squinting. 'What is that?'

Dancer looked far off where the terrain climbed, but then realized that the mage meant closer in: there, a small dark object appeared to be hanging in the air. He wondered if it was a bird – but a bird that did not move? 'Don't know.'

'Let's have a look.'

Dancer took hold of Wu's arm, grumbling, 'Famous last words.'

He lifted the skinny fellow on to his back. He was a very light load. The dusty ground was quite flat, except where outcroppings of bulbous rocks rose suddenly, almost like islands.

'Those are old coral reefs,' Wu announced as they passed more of the curving buttes. Dancer grunted his disinterest.

Coming close to the object – or, rather, the ground beneath it – Dancer slowed his pace, staring. He set Wu down, hardly able to take his eyes from the thing.

Finally, Wu announced, rather nonplussed, 'It's a boat.'

Dancer nodded his agreement; it was indeed a boat. Round, or basket-shaped. A line descended from it to a net that hung just above them.

'I wonder what would happen if we—'

'No,' Dancer snapped. 'You've been caught once today. Isn't that enough?'

While they stood watching, the boat rocked and the line began to rise, taking the net with it. Once the net was pulled up out of sight, a paddle appeared and the unseen occupant slowly headed off.

Dancer scratched his head. 'Fishing in air?'

Hopping on one foot, Wu pointed ahead to where the ground rose. 'Not necessarily. See how we're in a broad deep valley here?' Dancer nodded. 'It could be that to our fisherman friend there's a lake here – like two different moments in time overlapping. Sort of like layers.'

Dancer grunted his understanding. 'But . . . why?'

Wu limped off with the aid of his stick. 'Perhaps it is a characteristic of Shadow. Many scholars agree that the realm, or dimension, or place – call it what you will – is shattered. Broken. Perhaps this is a consequence. Shards of moments overlapping. In any case,' and he pointed again, 'let's say hello to the locals, shall we?'

Dancer strolled, keeping pace. 'Too dangerous. We should just return.'

'Oh, come now. We're here anyway . . .'

Dancer took a deep steadying breath, said through clenched teeth, 'We need to get back.'

'Won't take but a moment.'

'The last time didn't go so smoothly . . .'

Wu raised a finger. 'Ah! But did you notice our transition in?'

'Yeah. We fell about a fathom.'

The Dal Hon mage looked crestfallen, his tangled brows crimping. 'I meant how easy it was. Progress! No ritual or preparation. We're getting to know each other better.'

'We?'

'Shadow and I.'

Dancer just rolled his eyes skyward. Then he noted drily, 'Your ankle seems to have recovered rather quickly.'

Wu paused, his shoulders hunching. 'Ah . . . yes. My amazing powers of recuperation, obviously.'

Dancer could not help but look to the sky once again.

They climbed a series of sloping hills. As they plodded along Dancer tried to put himself into the strange mindset that Wu was prattling on about. After thinking about it for a while he found he

58

could picture that they were currently climbing what the locals would think of as the gradient of a lake, or an inland sea.

Where the ground levelled out they found a camp of domed huts built of bent branches and rough hides. Boats of similar construction, but inverted, lined what Dancer imagined would be the shore. The locals, however, made him flinch to a halt and snatch at his weapons.

Daemons, they appeared to him: inhumanly tall, insectile, with black spiny fur and large faceted eyes. Wu, however, hobbled right up to the nearest. Dancer hissed warnings at him and tried to head him off, but he took no notice.

'Greetings,' he said. The local didn't seem to hear him, or simply ignored him as it squatted on its thin limbs, busy trimming branches. 'Hello?' he tried again. Now the creature raised his, or her, head. 'Could you tell us where we are?'

The local stood. Peering about wildly, it backed away, then ran deeper into the camp. Dancer approached Wu, weapons drawn. 'We should leave while we can.'

Wu raised one hand for patience then set both on his walking stick and rocked on his heels, waiting. Dancer found himself wondering whether it was the real stick, or just another shadow-copy, and decided that it really didn't matter. He now understood that looking for anything like the 'truth' was the wrong approach to take with the mage. And he wasn't sure that it really mattered to him any more, either.

The first local returned, but with an even larger one in tow. They were deep in animated discussion and Dancer didn't recognize anything of the language. Finally, the bigger one waved a chitinous limb, perhaps for silence, as he, or she, scanned the area.

'Can you even see me?' Wu tried.

The creature cocked its head, made further complicated gestures. The numerous pincers at its mouth worked and to his amazement, and unease, Dancer heard, 'Are there ghosts with us this day?'

Wu caught Dancer's eye. *Ghosts*, he mouthed.

'There are indeed,' he said.

The local spoke to its companion then returned its attention to Wu. 'Why are you here? Do you seek vengeance? Do you require propitiation?'

Wu's interest was visibly piqued as his brows rose. 'Propitiation?

What form would that take? Bright shiny stones perhaps?'

'No. That I should cut myself to release blood for you. Or vomit food.'

Wu's face wrinkled. 'Never mind the propitiation. We are just travelling through and would question you about yourselves and this region.'

'Ah. I am brood-mother Xethel. We are the—' What followed was a series of noises that Dancer couldn't possibly recreate. Wu flinched. 'We live here by the lake and fish and hunt. The world was created in such a way for us and we are content.'

Dancer peered at the desert that now surrounded him and arched a brow in silent commentary.

'Have you no enemies, then?' Wu asked.

'Well, there are the—' Xethel let loose another stream of high-pitched whistles and clacks. 'But they are far away. You may know them by the name they call themselves, the Tiste Edur.'

'We do indeed know of them,' Wu answered. 'They claim this land as their own.'

Xethel let loose a series of noises that Dancer guessed might be laughter. 'No. They are newcomers. This land is ancient and we have been here since it was created. And anyway, the land cannot belong to anyone. Surely it is the other way round? People belong to the land that nurtures them, yes?'

'I bow to your wisdom,' Wu answered. Studying his walking stick, he asked, 'We ghosts are common here, then?'

'Not so much in the past, but more now.'

Clearly intrigued, Wu answered, wonderingly, 'Really?'

A noise pulled at Dancer's awareness and he turned his head, concentrating. After a moment it came again across the dunes and he cursed. It was the distant baying of a hound.

Even Xethel turned her fur-covered head. 'You are trespassing and have raised the ire of the guardians. You should return to the gate.'

Now Wu's brows shot up. 'Gate? There is a gate?'

'You do not know of it?' She was backing away, making motions that they should follow.

'No. We are from . . . far away.'

'Then come, quickly.'

The baying was gathering in intensity, and held a new eager note. Dancer took Wu's arm and helped him along. Xethel led them up a tall dune and there, in the basin beyond, stood a structure very much at odds with its surroundings. Dancer helped Wu jog down the slope, keeping pace with Xethel.

It was a small arch of cut and dressed black basalt – built to endure the ages, obviously, but draped in wind-blown sand and dust now.

Xethel motioned to it. 'Go.'

Dancer released Wu's arm. He was no mage, but clearly this construct was no more than an ancient curiosity. He neither sensed nor saw any power or aura about it.

'It is closed,' Wu said in disappointment.

An unreadable emotion crossed Xethel's alien features. 'Are you blind? It is quite open. Many have used it.'

'In your time, perhaps.'

Xethel was weaving her long thin fingers together, perhaps in unease. 'Please do not think badly of me, but I must go.'

'But I have so many questions,' Wu said.

Xethel laughed again, though rather nervously this time. 'Then I name you *Amman-an-ash*. The One Who Would Know Everything.' She nodded in Dancer's direction. 'And you I name *Coth-tel-ish-ath*. The One Who Watches and Judges.'

The baying burst so close upon them that even Xethel winced, her bony shoulders hunching. 'Now,' Dancer snarled.

But Wu was eyeing the arch, a finger at his lips. 'Interesting. It looks to have been sealed from *this* side . . .'

'*Now!*'

The little mage rolled his eyes. 'Oh, very well.' He tucked the walking stick under his arm. 'Let's see if I can remember . . .'

Gravel clattered nearby and both men turned their heads. Atop the dune behind them stood a massive canine, nearly the size of a pony. It was short-haired, and dirty cream in hue. It stared down at them with an almost quizzical tilt of its wide head, as if confused as to why they weren't running.

Wu gaped. The walking stick fell to the dirt. 'On it,' he gasped. Dancer faced the creature and drew his heaviest fighting knives, though he had little hope of his chances. Xethel was backing away, peering round frantically, obviously sensing the beast, but not able to see it.

With a chuff like a bull's cough, the animal charged. Dancer had only one idea. A technique he'd heard of where one leapt over the

61

head of a beast and stabbed downwards. It needed momentum, so he immediately charged as well, pumping his arms, blades held in reverse grip. His footing was poor in the yielding sand, but there was nothing to be done about that. He watched the creature's head rising and falling as it hurtled towards him, drool flying from its maw and its bright eyes seeming to glow with bloodlust.

His sense of timing told him it was now or die and so he leapt, but everything turned and twisted in a strange way while he was in mid-air and he came down hard on wet sand that shushed beneath him. He gasped for breath. It was dark, and a cold wind was blowing, and on that wind he thought he heard a diminishing howl of daemonic frustration and rage.

He lay peering up at clouds and familiar stars peeping through their ragged gaps. Malaz. Coughing and splashing sounded nearby and he raised his head. Wu was attempting to rise in the surf while the waves splashed up to his chest. He came staggering over to stand brushing at his sodden clothes.

'There!' he announced. 'More reliable, yes?'

'You? Reliable?'

Wu extended a hand that he took to help pull himself up. Together, they headed for the bar. Water was dripping from Wu's sleeves and his boot squelched as he walked. 'You really charged that beast?' he said.

'Going to be torn to pieces anyway.'

Wu was nodding, hands now behind his back. 'True, true. There must be a way, though . . .' and he walked on in silent thought.

They pushed open the door to find the bar empty of customers but for three drunks. Surly was at the counter and a few of the Napan hands were cleaning up, sweeping and clearing tables.

'Where have you been?' Surly demanded from across the room. 'And you're getting the floor wet.'

'Went for a wash,' Wu answered.

'About time,' one of the Napan bouncers next to the door muttered under his breath. The one called Grinner.

Dancer hid his own grin, while Wu pretended he hadn't heard. He bustled across the floor, making for the stairs. 'I'll be in my office should I be needed.'

'Needed?' Surly murmured, leaning up against the counter, her arms crossed.

Following Wu, Dancer had just reached the stairs when the door smashed open and more people came charging in. He spun to see five men and one woman – and he recognized the woman. It was the diminutive, black-haired courier with the silver earrings.

She pointed straight at him, a blade in her gloved fist. 'Told you it was a small island! Get 'im!' Her men charged. Dancer whipped his knives from his baldrics and shifted to cover Wu.

In that instant all the Napans moved. Grinner, at the door, lashed out to punch the woman in the side of the head and Dancer saw her eyes roll white as she fell.

Three of the toughs came charging across the room. Two remained at the door. One thrust at Grinner but in such close quarters Grinner caught his arm with one hand, took hold of the man's belt with the other, lifted him overhead and smashed him down on a table. The other slashed at Choss, who slipped the cut and rammed his elbow into the man's throat: he fell, clutching his neck.

The lean Napan, Tocaras, swept up a chair and lobbed it at a scar-faced thug, dropping him. Shrift threw a heavy knife, pommel first, that bounced from the skull of another attacker, while Surly, leaping an entire table, struck the last in his side with one extended heel. Dancer heard the man's ribs breaking as he fell unconscious.

He lowered his blades, blinking in the sudden silence. *Damned impressive. Who* are *these Napans?*

The door to the kitchen was thrown open and the gigantic cook, Urko, emerged holding an unconscious man under each arm. 'What in Mael's name is going on?' he demanded.

Surly sent him a hand signal of some kind, said, 'It's handled.'

The man grunted, satisfied, then looked perplexed. 'Well, what do I do with these two?'

From over Dancer's shoulder, Wu supplied, 'Just set them out with the rest of the trash.'

Dancer saw the man cast a glance to their hostess, Surly, for confirmation. The woman nodded, and he grunted his compliance. Dancer looked at Wu, but the mage seemed oblivious of the finer points of the exchange; the fellow made little shooing gestures with his hands, said, 'I'll leave you to clean up then, shall I, Surly?'

The wiry woman rolled her eyes in disgust. Wu waved Dancer up the stairs. 'Let us discuss things.'

Dancer clenched his lips against saying anything there in front of everyone, sheathed his blades, and followed.

Inside the office he shut the door behind him and leaned against it. Wu was pacing back and forth tapping the tips of his fingers together, obviously very agitated.

'Did you see that?' Dancer demanded.

Wu turned on him, his tiny eyes glittering and bright. 'Yes! Amazing! I have the best henchmen ever!'

Dancer looked to the ceiling and crossed his arms, sighing. 'I don't think they're *your* henchmen.'

'Whatever. Chain of command, Dancer. Chain of command. Now we can set to work.'

'Work?'

'Yes. Tackling Geffen, of course. We have the personnel.'

Dancer blew out a breath. *This guy's miles ahead of the cart, let alone the horse.* 'Let's not rush over any cliff here . . .'

Looking vexed, Wu sat behind the desk. 'Then what would you suggest?'

Dancer motioned back behind his shoulder. 'I'll have a word.'

Wu raised his brows. 'Ah. Excellent idea. Take your time. I must think.'

'About what?'

The little fellow rested his elbows on the desk and set his chin on his fingertips. His eyes almost closed. 'About gates. And how to open them.'

Dancer pointed a warning. 'Just don't make any more trouble for us right now, okay?'

But the mage's wizened and wrinkled face was already dreamy. Dancer was tempted to give him a cuff and ask whether he'd heard, but shook his head instead.

Noise to his right spun him round, blades whipping free. The shells of nuts lay there on the floor, and more fell as he watched. He raised his gaze to the rafters and there sat the damned nacht, Wu's pet. He'd wondered where the blasted thing had got to lately.

As he eyed it, the little beast bared its sharp pale fangs at him then set to work gnawing on another walnut. He waved it off – eliciting an answering hiss – and left, pulling the door shut behind him.

Downstairs, all the attackers were gone and the mess was being cleaned up. He spotted Surly and deliberately crossed straight to

64

her, pulled up a chair and sat backwards on it, crossing his arms on the back.

She peered down at him for a short moment then nodded and waved off the other Napans, who'd suddenly appeared to crowd close. She sat opposite him and crossed her arms.

'Want a drink?' she offered.

He nodded.

Without taking her eyes from him she called out, 'Our best wine, Hawl. Two glasses.'

A moment later Hawl – burly and heavy-set where Surly was greyhound lean – set down two fine-stemmed glasses and a decanter of wine.

Surly poured, tasted the vintage, then set the glass down. She eyed him, her mouth set straight, thin, and hard. 'So,' she began, 'you're hijacking.'

'You questioned the toughs, hey?'

'Yeah.'

'Where're they now?'

'Being thrown off a pier.'

'What if they don't swim?'

The woman raised a brow to say she didn't give a damn. 'You should've approached us,' she said.

He snorted.

'I don't like you bringing trouble here.'

'Shut up. I'm talking to you – not the reverse.'

The rage that flared in the woman's eyes was informative. *Not used to such a tone, this one.*

It took her a while to unclench her teeth and control her breathing, and she remained quite flushed by the outrage that seethed within. She asked, terse, 'Why then are we even talking?'

'I have a proposal.'

Her gaze slid past his shoulder and he dared a glance over. Another of the Napan women, Amiss, young, wiry, and full of nervous energy, was peering out of the door. She nodded an all clear. He returned his gaze to Surly. 'You have perimeter guards out already?'

She gave a brief nod of assent.

'Good.' His tone was casual, but again he was impressed. He sipped the wine and nodded to her – at least it was Untan, he could tell that much. 'Where should I start? Captain, is it?' She lifted her shoulders, neither assent nor denial. 'So. A Napan raider crew. Wrecked on Malaz where no one would even cross the street to spit on you. Why not take passage to the mainland and return to Nap? Because you can't. Wrong side of the recent transition in power, hey?' Again the woman merely lifted her shoulders. She took a drink and he noted that this time she tossed back the entire glass. 'The deal is a ship,' he said.

The woman turned the glass in her hand. 'We'll get one,' she said, her tone low and fierce.

This time he lifted his shoulders. 'Maybe you will, maybe you won't. We promise one.'

'How can you possibly back up a promise like that?'

'Because . . .' and here he let out a long breath, as he was taking a huge gamble, 'the owner of this establishment happens to be a damned scary warlock.'

The woman's brows rose and she leaned forward, utterly incredulous. She raised a finger to point to the ceiling; mouthed silently, *What? Him?*

Dancer nodded.

She cocked her head, studying him, clearly trying to work out whether he was serious or insane. Finally, she broke out laughing aloud.

He allowed her to have her laugh, and after a time she cleared her throat and said, 'Bullshit.'

He tilted his head as if to say, *Have it your way*. 'What have you to lose? Give us a month and you'll have a ship.'

The woman was clearly restraining herself from laughing again. 'And in return? What do you want?'

'You work for us.'

'Only if the crew agrees.'

Dancer nodded again. 'Fair enough. Well . . .' He pushed himself from the table. 'Until then, everything stays the same, yes?'

Surly gave a little snort and shook her head, as if at his audacity, or her own gullibility. Since it wasn't outright refusal, he took it as agreement and returned upstairs. From where they sat about the room, the gaze of the remaining Napan crew followed him as he went.

Upstairs he found Wu still behind the desk, but leaning back with his feet up and his mouth open, sound asleep and snoring.

Dancer stifled a curse. Yet even as he watched from the door, the nacht creature, now squatting on the desk, pitched a shard of walnut shell towards Wu's open mouth.

It struck his nose and the little fellow grunted, snorting.

Dancer stepped up and waved the creature from the desk. It leapt to the rafters, chattering and giving vent to what sounded eerily like curses, while Dancer swiped the mage's feet from the desk.

Wu's eyes snapped open and he glared about in a momentary panic. Spotting Dancer, he relaxed, then frowned and brushed away the heap of walnut shells from his chest. 'Yes? What is it? I was thinking.'

'Is that what you call it?' He raised a hand, forestalling any answer. 'New order of business. Get us a ship. Immediately. We need one.'

Wu raised a brow, rather surprised. 'Really. A ship.' He leaned back once more, touched his fingertips together over his stomach. 'Hmm. An interesting challenge, that.'

'Is that you thinking again?'

Wu cast him a glare. 'I'll look into it.'

'Do so. We have to have one.'

Wu straightened his vest. 'The things I have to buy just to keep you happy . . .'

Chapter 4

DESPITE HOUSING CLOSE TO A THOUSAND ACOLYTES AND priests, the Great Hall of the Temple of D'rek on the island of Kartool was its characteristic silent self. And because Tayschrenn hated noise and its attendant commotion and disruption more than anything, he valued this calm and quiet devotion to duty very highly.

He was therefore quite annoyed when a murmuring buzz of whispers arose among the acolytes; it irked him so much that he opened his eyes and raised his head from where it rested upon the tips of his fingers to glance about for the source of the disturbance, frowning.

Silla, his neighbour at table, nudged him, whispering, 'There he is. The Invigilator, Tallow. Arrived last night. They say he hails from the Seven Cities region.'

Tayschrenn looked to the entrance. A priest in black robes trimmed with red was making his way up the central aisle to the top table. Tayschrenn's first impression was one of blunt raw power. Squat, bull-necked, his shaved bullet-head sun-darkened; the man fairly oozed authority and might.

He rested his chin on his fists, his elbows on the table. 'What is he doing here?' he mused.

Silla offered a knowing chuckle. 'Come to take the masters to task, they say. Talk is they've been lax.'

Tayschrenn studied the girl; like everyone's, her brows and scalp were shaved, and, like him, she wore the loose dark robes of a full priest. He frowned anew. 'According to whom?'

She gestured vaguely. 'Well, that is the word in the study halls.

Really, Tay, you should socialize more. Listen to what people are saying.'

'If they ever said anything worthwhile, I would.'

She raised one hairless brow. 'Well, thank you so much.'

The Invigilator took his place at the top table and the acolytes returned to their meals. The visiting authority, however, did not eat; his dark glittering eyes scanned the broad hall. His gaze met Tayschrenn's, and the priest was impressed by the prowess he sensed within this new master, far eclipsing that of the brethren at table with him.

Yet he did not immediately lower his gaze in deference, and chose instead to study that dense aura. For a fleeting instant he sensed within its heart a strange coloration that he'd detected in none other.

The Invigilator broke the connection, looking away to join his neighbour in low conversation. Frowning, Tayschrenn once more lowered his brow to his fingertips, thinking.

The quiet bass resounding of a gong signalled the end of the assigned mealtime and Tayschrenn glanced at his still full bowl. Somehow, he could not bring himself to eat. The crude physicality of the act nauseated him. It was of the flesh; all that he sought so dearly to slough from him and leave behind.

A group of acolytes stopped by the table, greeting Silla. 'Come to the common room, yes? We have free time.'

Silla extended a hand in invitation to Tayschrenn. 'Coming?'

'No, thank you.'

A younger male student made a face. 'Not the golden boy. Too good for us, no doubt.'

Tayschrenn looked at the lad, who was a few years behind him in his studies. He shook his head. 'No. It is just that I have no interest in what you spend your time talking about: your joking exchanges, your veiled flirting, your predictable teasing and meaningless gossip. It is all completely trivial and boring.'

The shocked expressions among the group surprised him. Silla urged them to go on ahead, saying, 'I'll catch up.' She glared down at her neighbour. 'It's called making friends, Tay.'

'None in that group are interested in establishing true friendships. They just seek to fill their empty hours with diversions and amusing nothings. I see no reason to try to entertain them, and nor do I find them in the least entertaining.'

Silla tilted her head, studying him as if seeing him anew. 'Tay . . . sometimes . . .' She sighed. 'I believe it's also called having fun. You might want to try it sometime.'

'As I said. I do not find it fun. In fact, I find it rather painful.'

She raised her gaze to the ceiling in despair. 'Dear D'rek! Why do I and Koarsden even try? Stew in your own juice, then; I'm off.'

Alone, he set his chin in his fists once more. Stewing? There were many mysteries among the disciplines of higher Warren manipulation that constantly preoccupied him, and now he was presented with this strange new coloration that the Invigilator had brought with him . . . was it a by-product of initiation into the higher cult echelons? A mystery he was not yet qualified to know? Yet he'd detected none of it among the temple's older priests.

And was all this stewing? He wasn't quite certain.

Perhaps he should take a walk. Walking always helped him think.

He pushed up from the table and set off for the deeper halls of the temple; wandering these solitary paths always eased his mind. Once or twice he believed he'd even found solace there in the darkness and felt all about him, for a privileged moment, the deep slow reverberating heartbeat of the Worm of Autumn itself.

The next morning Tayschrenn was meditating. He sat cross-legged on the cold stone floor of his cell, his hands up the wide sleeves of his robes for warmth. The only light came from a single narrow opening far up in one wall, through which wan daylight filtered down like a thin mist.

The frail wooden door was shut. Only now, in private, did he dare fully explore the furthest boundaries of his researches into the Warrens. For through his probings – and extraordinary endurance and prowess – he had advanced far into strange regions where Warren boundaries and definitions appeared to merge and meld. Here Thyr and Telas seemed to come together and touch upon even more fundamental, complex and distant realms that he recognized as not of human origin.

And Thyr, it appeared, was the best starting point for such researches. Unfortunately, Thyr was forbidden, as a tool of the meddling enchantress, the Queen of Dreams.

A knock brought his head up. He withdrew from his Warren,

cleared his throat to wet it and answered, rather irritated, 'Yes?'

A female acolyte spoke outside. 'You are summoned to the side of Ithell.'

'Very well.' He rose, rubbed feeling back into his legs, and headed for the quarters of the high priest, Demidrek Ithell.

He found the door open. The smoke of burning fragrant wood and incense wafted out in thick tendrils and scarves, but could not overcome the far more powerful and clinging miasma of long rotten flesh. The outer chamber was crowded by the usual cadre of healers, Dragons Deck readers, and other such consulting prestidigitators, some from lands very distant indeed. These Tayschrenn considered little more than minor talents, if not outright charlatans. But they were a comfort to the Demidrek in his illness and dotage, and so he simply ignored their presence.

He moved to pass through to the inner audience chamber, but before he could do so a woman caught his sleeve, her long sharp nails penetrating the weave of his robes to clench his upper arm. 'Tayschrenn, yes?' she said in accented Talian.

He frowned down at the short, dark-haired woman. 'Yes.'

'We should discuss the enhancing potential of certain drugs in Warren exploration.'

I would rather have iron spikes driven into my eyes, woman. Or, more accurately, into yours. 'Thank you – but I am awaited within.'

Leaning closer, she whispered, 'The Invigilator also waits within, and there is something about him that troubles me. You have seen it too, yes?'

'What is your name?'

'Lady Batevari, from far Darujhistan.'

He removed her clawed hand. 'Well, Lady. Your insights are interesting. Perhaps we could discuss them sometime in the future. Thank you.'

Her answering glare was ferocious. She tossed her head. 'Or perhaps not – as I do not appreciate having my time or effort wasted.'

He offered a thin smile as he turned away, dismissing her. *Ancient Ones! The lesser the skill, the greater the arrogance.*

The bedchamber was even more crowded than the outer room, as all the Demidrek's staff and assistants were gathered round his bed. A number had to shuffle aside to allow Tayschrenn to approach. On the opposite side stood the Invigilator, his bronzed, sweaty face floating in the murk like an oval mask.

One of the aides bent down to whisper in the Demidrek's ear. It had been more than a month since Tayschrenn had last seen Ithell, and he was shocked by the man's decline. He lay buried under the rich bedding. His arms resembled bones wrapped in parchment – the veins distended, a deep blue, near to black. The man's head seemed already a fleshless skull, the cheeks withered and sunken, the eyes bruised dark pits.

One emaciated arm rose and beckoned Tayschrenn closer. Obediently, he leaned over the bed, though the churning stink of rotting flesh was a near physical barrier. 'Tay,' the Demidrek's voice came as the barest of sour breaths, 'this is Invigilator Tallow. He has been sent to oversee the transition.' Tayschrenn inclined his head to the Invigilator. 'You will offer him every assistance.'

Tayschrenn nodded. 'Of course. But there will be no need. D'rek has more work for you, I am sure.'

Ithell's lips pulled back in a wry smile that resembled a death's rictus. He patted Tayschrenn's arm, his hand a bundle of hot dry bones. The arm fell and an exhalation rippled the ancient's chest, revealing the effort that just that small gesture took.

Tayschrenn straightened from what he was certain was a deathbed. The Invigilator, Tallow, gestured to the open door and he nodded in response. The two eased their way through the crush of gathered brothers and sisters come to pray for the Demidrek's soul.

In the main room Tayschrenn was quite amused to see the Darujhistani seeress, Batevari, pull away from the Invigilator as if the man carried some plague. Tallow ignored the woman; he gestured Tayschrenn forward. The priest dipped his head in assent and preceded him out into the hall.

For a time the two walked side by side down the darkened stone tunnel, hands clasped at their backs. Once they had some measure of privacy, the Invigilator cleared his throat.

'It is an honour to meet you, young Tayschrenn. Tales of your prowess and early accomplishments have reached even unto the synod.'

'The honour is all mine, Invigilator.'

'Ithill himself plucked you from the streets, I understand. Yes?'

'Indeed.'

'You grew up in the temple compound, then. A very strange upbringing for a child. I heard that your mastery of Telas exceeded the cult's teachers before you were ten. Is this so?'

'I have been self-directed in my studies for some time now.'

'You have, I understand, served as Ithill's secretary. Relieving him of the burden of administrative duties.'

'Indeed.'

'The committee of transition may call upon you, then.'

'I would serve however I may.'

Tallow stopped. 'Of the many qualified to take over the mantle of Demidrek,' he asked, 'to whom do you think the position ought to go?'

Tayschrenn shrugged. 'It is not for me to choose.'

The Invigilator stepped closer and Tayschrenn found himself pressed up against the cold damp wall. He was suddenly aware of how intimidating a physical presence the heavy-set, frowning man projected. 'Of course not. However . . . if you had to?'

'It would not be proper for me to name anyone.'

The man snorted. 'Because your name is among the candidates.' The man's thick fleshy lips drew down even further. 'Do not think me a fool, young Tayschrenn. You may have squirmed and politicked your way into the confidence of a doddering old man, but you carry no such favour with me. If I detect any evidence of efforts to influence or intimidate the committee I will not hesitate to act. Do I make myself clear?'

At that moment Tayschrenn held in his head the image of Koarsden howling in laughter at the idea of his ever conniving with or 'politicking' anyone. Yet all that was swept aside when he glimpsed once more in this man's theurgic aura something strange. A tinge he'd not witnessed in any other's – almost a discoloured moiling of power. So faint was it, and buried so deep within the core of the man's projecting energies, that he half imagined he'd mistaken it.

Forgetting everything, even their discussion, he frowned, quite puzzled, and searched for it once again.

Tallow's own gaze narrowed then and he pushed Tayschrenn away, adjusting his robes. He snapped, 'I will tolerate no interference,' and stalked away up the tunnel.

Tayschrenn watched him go; from this distance could not detect anything odd. Perhaps he had imagined it. In any case, it was clear

73

that the Invigilator did not want him interfering in the process of transition – though what form the other man imagined his interference might take he had no idea.

* * *

Dassem kicked the burning wrack from the doorway of the mausoleum, ducking, as he did so, the heaved cow manure, rocks, and burning brands. The besieging crowd shouted curses, waved fists, spat and damned him.

It was halfway through yet another night of attacks. He kept his face impassive as he nudged a flaming torch from the tossed broken wood. At least, he reflected, oil was expensive and rare. Otherwise he could find himself in a conflagration.

A louder note entered the shouted cursing – one of fear and surprise – and Dassem squinted through the smoke, ducking more rocks. He was certain it was no adherent of Hood, as he'd forbidden any street battles.

A huge dark silhouette reared above the crowd and people ran, shouting in sudden panic. As Dassem watched, the giant figure of Koroll, a city mage, swung his tall staff sideways, cutting a great swath through the crowd.

'Disperse!' the newcomer bellowed. 'By order of the Protectress!'

The ring of protesters scattered in all directions and quite quickly the Thelomen giant was alone among the wreckage and abandoned crackling torches. Alone but for a smaller version who came stepping over the guttering brands and kicking through the broken crates and rubbish. Ho.

There was something about this particular mage that disturbed Dassem more than any other. Hood, he sensed, did not approve of this one. Ho shook his head, his arms crossed. 'You're causing a disturbance, swordsman.'

'I am but a peaceful worshipper.'

'Your presence is a lightning rod for rage. Nothing generates fear and panic like a plague – and you're seen as its very author!'

'It is everywhere, you know that.'

Ho was shaking his head. 'Yes, yes. But tell that to someone who's just lost a loved one.'

Dassem rested a hand on the grip of his sword. 'Is this an eviction notice?'

'It is a summons. Shalmanat wishes to see you.'

He glanced back to the mausoleum. 'I cannot leave the temple unguarded.'

'Koroll will keep watch.' Ho turned to the Thelomen giant, peering up. 'Is that not so?'

Beneath the tangled forest of knotted and matted hair a wide grin split the giant's craggy tattooed features. 'I will indeed. Fear not, Hood's Mortal Sword.'

Dassem frowned, wondering whether to bother disputing the assumption that he was afraid, but the Thelomen's grin was so open and honest he chose not to argue. He inclined his head instead, in gratitude. 'My thanks.'

Ho swept an arm, inviting him onward. 'The Protectress awaits.'

With Ho at his side Dassem passed through gates and checkpoints unimpeded. The armies of Itko Kan had withdrawn long ago, and no outside threat currently menaced the city, but Shalmanat was maintaining strict martial law until all the damage from the recent siege could be repaired; it was not incidental that it also helped to maintain order in the face of the plague.

Dassem was surprised by the summons. Since crushing the army of Chulalorn the Third, the Protectress had been a virtual recluse. Few, if any, save her servants the city mages, had even seen her. Some claimed that she'd died in the firestorm she'd summoned and that the city mages were colluding to hide the fact. Others whispered that she was now horribly disfigured.

Ho led him to the main audience hall where Shalmanat had formerly heard petitions and dispensed justice – the city mages handled such duties now. It was dark and empty, only a few lamps burning in wall sconces. Ho stopped at the doors, gesturing for Dassem to go on without him. 'She would see you alone.'

Dassem paused. 'I am armed.'

Ho nodded. 'Yes.'

'You have not asked for my weapon.'

Ho lifted his chin to indicate the far end of the hall. 'She said you would never surrender it.'

Dassem shifted his shoulders, suddenly uncomfortable. 'That is true.'

'Very well then.'

'You would allow this?'

Ho nodded, indicating an appreciation of Dassem's point. He crossed his thick wrestler's arms. 'You claim to be Hood's Mortal Sword. Well, let me just say that should you strike Shalmanat down now it would merely prove that you most certainly are not.' And he smiled, motioning him forward.

Dassem wanted to strike that self-satisfied smile from the man's face, but had to content himself with shutting the door on him instead. He walked up the long hall of polished marble flags to the dais where Shalmanat waited, wrapped in a white cloth that shimmered in the half-light.

At the foot of the steps he knelt to one knee. 'Protectress.' Raising his head, he saw her answering nod.

'Mortal Sword. You honour me.'

'Not at all. I am your servant.'

'The reverse, I assure you. I sit before you as petitioner.'

He could not keep the reflexive wince from his features, his hands tightening to fists. 'Please. Protectress . . . do not do this.'

'I must. It is my duty. My city is threatened. I must do all in my power to avert this threat.'

He shook his head, gently. 'Please . . .'

Struggling, she tried to rise from the white marble throne. His breath caught as the wrap of silk slid free and revealed her bent form, all bones and strange angles. With her good arm she reached behind the throne to grasp a cane and with its aid she managed to get to her feet, but she remained hunched, as if crippled or ill.

Dassem's own heart laboured with her as she fought to descend from the dais.

'I have given my beauty. My youth. My grace, all in defence of this city, Sword,' she said through gritted teeth. 'What more would you force from me?'

He could not stop shaking his head. 'Please . . . do not do this.' She stood before him, tense from the effort, and it was all he could do not to fall at her feet. 'Please.'

'I beg you, Sword of Hood. Spare my city. Intercede with your god.'

'You do not understand . . . I cannot.'

'No? You demand more? It is true then, what they say – that one must give up one's humanity to become a mortal sword?'

She struggled to lower herself before him and this he could not endure; gently, he took her frail body in his arms and returned her to the dais. 'Is there nothing that can be done for you? No High Denul healings?'

'You know this was sacrifice,' she murmured. 'You understand sacrifice. It cannot be taken back – so do not change the subject.'

His voice almost cracked as he managed, 'I have no control over *him*.' He raised the wrap to hide her disfigurements, tucking her in. 'I am his servant, not the reverse.'

'Like me,' she answered. 'I serve the city. Then you must ask yourself, Sword. What price are you prepared to pay?'

He bowed his head to her. 'Like you. Any.'

She glanced to the far doors. 'Go then, damn you. The price you pay I fear will be no less.'

He bowed once more, honouring her, then backed away down the hall. Closing the door behind him, he turned to Ho, who stood waiting. 'She will have to show herself eventually.'

Ho nodded. 'I know. At Burn's Festival, perhaps. High at a parapet, possibly.'

'Do not underestimate these people. They will still want her, despite this.'

'I know – but she will not have it.' Ho turned to leave and for a time the two walked side by side in silence.

'Know you why she summoned me?' Dassem asked at length.

Ho nodded once more. 'Yes.'

'And you know my answer?'

'Yes.'

'And . . . ?'

The burly mage shrugged as they walked the empty streets. 'The effort had to be made. More important,' watching Dassem sidelong, 'what will you do now?'

Dassem chose to echo the mage's shrug. 'I serve. It is up to Hood.'

The city mage lowered his gaze, clearly dissatisfied with the answer. In silence, he walked Dassem through the streets to his temple-mausoleum, where Koroll lumbered to his feet from the threshold. The giant bowed his head. 'Sword.'

Ho moved on, but the giant paused, glancing back to the open stone portal of the mausoleum. 'I wish you luck, Sword,' he said, his voice low, and then he shambled off.

Dassem watched them go, then entered.

Nara lay where he had left her, and he knelt at her side. The fresh sheet he'd laid upon her was already soaked through across her chest, stomach and thighs. He dipped a cloth into a bowl of sweet water, squeezed it, and substituted it for the one on her brow – so warm to his palm. 'You spoke with Koroll?' he asked.

'We spoke,' she answered, swallowing. Beads of sweat ran from her temples into her gleaming wet hair. 'He said he'd met other mortal swords and that he thinks quite highly of you.'

Dassem allowed himself a quiet laugh. 'An unusual point of view.' He took up a crust of bread and dipped it in a cold broth, then brought it to her cracked lips.

She grimaced and turned her head away.

'You must eat.'

'I'm sorry,' she gasped.

'Sorry?'

'I know this is very . . . hard for you.'

He snorted his disagreement. 'I am not the one suffering here. You are.'

'You know what I mean.'

'Not at all. You are ill – you will recover. That is all there is.' She clenched her lips, saying no more. 'Sleep,' he told her, and rose.

He retreated to the very rear of the mausoleum, where the stone sarcophagus, the unofficial altar, resided. He eased himself down before it, cross-legged, hands on his thighs, and sat for some time, motionless.

Slowly, almost imperceptibly, as dawn's pink and gold light slid in through the doorway, his hands clenched into tight white fists.

*   *   *

After four more days at sea, the *Honest Avarice* dropped anchor in Malaz harbour. Cartheron expected that all those vessels that had survived the ambush would have arrived before them and so he scanned the harbour with a gauging eye. Losses, it appeared, were severest among the lighter class of vessels, the shallow-water sloops and galleys. All three of Mock's men-o-war had fought their way free, though the *Intolerant* and the *Insufferable* looked to have taken terrible punishment from the ambush, scoured by flame damage, sails all down for repairs, spars and railings shattered.

A launch approached. It bore the freebooter admiral himself, plus four of his picked captains. A rope ladder was lowered and he climbed aboard. He peered round at the damage the *Avarice* had suffered, then frowned, confused. 'Bezil?' he asked of the crew in general.

'Fallen,' one answered.

Mock nodded. He tapped his fingers on the silver pommel of the filigreed duelling sabre he always carried. 'Who captained?'

Several of the crew motioned to Cartheron where he leaned on the stern-deck railing. Mock beckoned him down.

'And you are?'

'Cartheron, admiral. Cartheron Crust.'

'You are not first mate. Nor quartermaster.'

'Common seaman, sir.'

'Took command in the fight, sir,' a sailor said. 'Steered us free.'

Mock nodded again, stroking his goatee. 'And took your time returning my ship. Thought perhaps the *Avarice* had gone a-roving.'

Cartheron indicated the thin crew. 'We were short on hands and sail and the sea was against us.'

Mock considered, eyeing the crew. After a moment, perhaps taking in the mood of the *Avarice*'s hands, he laughed, cuffing Cartheron's shoulder. 'Well done. You acted as any crewman ought. You have my gratitude.' He turned to one of his captains. 'Hess – take command.'

Hess bowed. 'As you order, sir.'

Cartheron noted a number of frowns and some grumbling among the crew. Dujek spoke up. 'A promotion, perhaps, admiral? For service.'

Mock turned to him. 'You desire a promotion?'

Dujek laughed and ran a hand over his scalp. 'Not for me, admiral. I'm no sailor. For the Napan. He saved the *Avarice*.'

'All the crew did their part, I'm sure.'

'A' course. I'm just sayin' . . .'

Mock returned his attention to Cartheron, now openly appraising. One of his captains leaned close, whispering, and he snapped, irritated. 'What? Speak up, man.'

This captain brushed his moustache – a long thick one similar in style to Mock's own. He indicated Cartheron. 'This one's part of that Napan crew causing all the trouble in town. There's fights every night with Geffen's people.'

Cartheron started. *Trouble? What's Sureth started?*

Mock scowled anew. 'And what is that to me, pray tell?'

The captain raised his brows, rather nonplussed. 'Well . . . I was just saying.'

Mock eyed Cartheron. 'Steersman, then. Well done, sailor.'

Cartheron bowed his head, accepting the promotion. A number of the crew raised a huzza in approval. Mock waved a negligent hand. 'Yes, yes. Dismissed.'

A launch took those on leave to shore. The first rotation included Cartheron and the man who had spoken up for him, Dujek. On the pier, curious, Cartheron asked, 'If you're no sailor, then what are you?'

The man's laugh was large and full-bellied. 'A fool, perhaps?' Cartheron smiled. 'Naw. A fighting man all my life. Soldier, mercenary, bodyguard, hiresword . . . marine, now.'

Cartheron nodded. 'Ah. See you when we're recalled, then.'

The marine saluted his farewell, laughing. 'Not too soon, I hope!'

Cartheron smiled again. 'True enough, friend. True enough.' He shouldered his kitbag and headed up the pier. As he neared the block containing the bar, Smiley's, he noticed a large number of toughs lounging about the street corners. Many nudged their companions and pointed him out. *Gods, what trouble has Sureth – Surly – got into now?*

Turning a corner, he found himself confronted by a gang of the ruffians. *Damn – I'm not ready for this.* They were showing no weapons, but he was certain they were armed. All he carried was his sailor's knife.

He dropped his kitbag to free his hands. 'What is it? Like to talk, but I'm late for a drink.'

'You Napans need to get your blue arses out of town,' one fellow drawled.

Cartheron shrugged. 'Fine by me. Buy us a berth.'

Another snarled, 'Let's just teach this one a—' He shut his mouth. As one, the gang backed away. Though a touch mystified, Cartheron drew his sailor's knife and crouched into a fighting stance; he knew something was going on behind him, but daren't turn his back on the gang in front.

He felt a presence at his shoulder and glanced over. A youth now stood at his side, though he'd had no inkling at all of anyone's approach. The lad was of middling height, very lean, with short dark hair. His hands rested crossed at his chest, inside his loose cloak.

'Who're you?' Cartheron demanded.

'One of your employers.'

'That would be old Jeregal.'

'Sold out and moved to warmer climes.'

The ruffians continued backing away. One pointed, mouthing, *Later.* Cartheron found himself alone with the newcomer among the wet cobbles and stained stone walls. He straightened, tucked his knife back into his belt. 'It appears they don't like you.'

The youth nodded. 'They've learned.' He gestured down the street. 'I'm here to escort you in.'

Escort? What in Mael's mercy is going on? He eyed the lad and the fellow nodded his understanding. 'Surly will explain,' he said.

Ahead, the shop-front of Smiley's was a battered, boarded-up derelict-looking mess of broken glass and strewn garbage. 'What's this?'

'An effort to put us out of business.'

'Urko's cooking must've got worse.'

A reluctant smile climbed the youth's thin lips and he inclined his head. 'I don't think that's possible.'

Cartheron pushed open the heavy door, noting at the same time the fresh blade hacks and burn scars that now marred its iron-bound planks. He found the common room empty but for members of the crew: Grinner, Amiss, and Lady Sureth, who was leaning up against the bar.

He turned to the lad, but he was gone. Frowning, he pulled the door shut behind him then crossed to Surly. 'What's going on?'

'We're embroiled in another war,' she supplied laconically. 'You been paid?'

'Not yet. A war? What kind of war?'

'The protection and extortion kind. Get paid – we need the money.'

He glanced about the empty common room. 'I'll say. Met a kid claiming to be one of our bosses.'

'He is.'

'Who are the rest?'

'One. Claims to be a mage. An obvious lunatic.'

'Great. Guess I'd better get my pay.'

'Yes. But not now. Got a job for you.'

'Do I have time to eat?'

Surly gestured to the kitchens. 'Help yourself.'

He ducked through to the kitchen area and found his brother leaning over a stone oven. 'Progress?' he called.

Urko glanced at him from under frowning brows. He straightened, crossed his thick arms over his stained apron. 'Damned scones won't rise.'

Cartheron leaned back against a stone-topped counter. 'Maybe it's your age. You know, as you get older . . .'

'Very funny.' Urko took a cast-iron skillet from a hook, held it in his hands. 'There's fighting almost every night 'gainst Geffen's boys 'n' girls and Sur— Surly won't let me out!'

'Geffen? We don't have the personnel for that.'

'Tell that to those two crazies. They've taken him on and we're in the middle.'

'That's stupid. Why did Surly go along with that?'

Urko hefted the heavy skillet. 'The deal is they get us a ship.'

'A ship.' Cartheron leaned forward. 'When all the ships and crews are controlled by Mock? That's horseshit. This is a bad deal.'

His brother grasped the pan and the handle of the skillet. His thick forearms flexed, cabling. 'I'll say,' he exhaled, hissing. 'She keeps me cooped up in here when I could tear down that fucker's entire building.' The blackened iron creaked, screeching, and the skillet folded completely in half. He tossed the wrecked object aside then stood looking rather embarrassed. 'Sorry.'

'Still,' Cartheron observed, peering about the kitchen, 'you got a nice set-up here. Indoor oven, enclosed fire pit.'

His brother brightened, nodding. 'That's true. Beats having to go outside in the damned rain.' Then he scowled, suddenly suspicious. He jabbed a meaty finger into Cartheron's chest. 'Don't you try to pacify me.'

Cartheron raised his hands. 'Wouldn't dare. Listen, I'll have a word, okay?'

Urko grunted his agreement. He lifted the lid from a large blackened kettle that hung over the fire. Steam billowed out. 'You do that.'

After a bowl of watery soup Cartheron went to find Surly. Their best mage, Hawl, was currently guarding the door. The woman was no beauty, with wide lumpy features and a thick build, yet she and Grinner somehow maintained a relationship that satisfied them both. 'Surly?' he asked her.

She raised her gaze to the ceiling. He nodded and headed for the stairs. Surly had taken the largest room on the second floor as her private quarters. Approaching the door he heard the shush of quick steps and the thump of blows. He was not alarmed; he knew the sound of her training.

He knocked and waited. After a few moments the door opened a crack and Lady Sureth peered out, her hair and light Napan-blue features gleaming with sweat, her taut chest rising and falling beneath a damp shirt.

Seeing him, she turned away, leaving the door open.

He entered, shutting the door behind him. Inside, the room stood nearly empty but for a thick training pillar at its centre, the hard blackwood beaten, scuffed and dented. The only hint that anyone lived here was bedding kicked up against one wall. Surly had returned to the tall training piece and was practising knife-hand strikes.

'I've been promoted to steersman,' he said.

'Good. We can use the money.'

He leaned back against a wall. 'I'll say. No one's downstairs.'

She glanced at him, her eyes gauging. Years of working together allowed her to ask directly: 'What is it?'

'Urko wants to know why we haven't torn Geffen's house down around him. I take it that's because you're trying for something a little more subtle.'

She switched to alternating right and left kicks at head height. Her bare feet snapped up with blurring speed, yet such was her control that each touched with the lightest of taps. 'We don't want Mock's attention,' she explained. 'We don't want these damned Malazans uniting against us. And . . . I'm waiting for a ship.'

He nodded to himself. 'Met one of these would-be bosses. Is he why you're training so hard?'

She cast him a dark look over one shoulder. 'Get better armed. You're on babysitting duty.'

He grimaced. 'Managed the soup, but I'll eat elsewhere if that's okay. Wait, babysitting? What do you mean?'

'Our employer who claims to be a mage has a habit of wandering off. We have to keep an eye on him.'

Cartheron straightened. 'Is he for real? Or is he just all talk?'

Surly paused in her strikes. He noticed her hands, loose at her sides, all red and bloodied. She tilted her head, considering. 'You know, I really have no idea. But if he can't deliver then we fall back to the old plan.'

He nodded. 'Grab the shop title and buy a ship.'

She sucked the blood from the side of one hand, studied the wound. 'He has a fortnight. Dismissed.'

Cartheron saluted. 'Aye, aye.'

He sat with Grinner and Hawl in the common room and caught up with the news. Back with his old friends he found himself once more being called Crust rather than Cartheron, while his brother was just plain Urko. He didn't know when or why it started, but it was probably simply easier to bellow 'Crust' in storms and battle. He learned that they'd gained control of a few warehouses and shop-fronts and that the main work was in protecting these from being raided or burned to the ground.

'There's not enough of us,' he complained to Hawl.

'Tell us about it,' she grunted, slumped in her chair.

He needn't have said anything. Her exhaustion showed in her dark sunken eyes and lank unwashed hair. Her hands, cracked and red-raw, restlessly tapped at the table and he watched them for a time, thinking, *Is that nerves?* 'Any local talent to worry about?' he asked.

That elicited a snort of disgust. 'No and yes. Geffen has no one – but there are some damned terrifying powers here on the island. They're not involved, but I can feel them none the less. My back won't stop itching.'

Grinner reached out and took her hands in one of his, stilling them. Hawl let out a long breath, her shoulders easing.

'And our mage employer? Is he for real?'

She nodded. 'Oh yes. He has access to *something* all right. Just what that is I don't know. Whatever it is, it's damned grating. I've felt his raised aspect a few times and let me tell you – for a mage it's like having needles hammered into your skull. It just ain't right. I even had a nosebleed one time.'

Cartheron picked up a fist of bread and tapped it to the table. Rock hard. He nodded to Hawl. 'Okay. What about Amaron and Noc? Any word?'

'Still in the grass,' Grinner answered in his soft voice – so jarring from someone so scarred and savage-looking. He looked to Hawl. 'But I don't think they're gonna find any support left on the island. I think the powers that be all consider it a done deal.'

Hawl nodded her sour agreement, and Cartheron had to go along with their assessment. Sureth could not hope for any funds or support from that quarter.

Grinner tilted his head and murmured, 'Speaking of our employer . . .'

Cartheron turned. A little gnome-like fellow had descended the stairs and was now on his way to the door. Dal Hon dark he was, wrinkled and grey-haired, though quite spritely in his quick walk, and dressed all in black, swinging a short walking stick.

'Where do you think you're going?' Cartheron called.

As if caught in some criminal act, the fellow froze in mid-step. He looked over, his grey caterpillar brows rising, 'Why . . . out for some fresh night air. Constitutional. Health. All that.'

Cartheron turned away. 'Not tonight. Tonight we sit tight. Night fogs are bad for your health, in any case.'

The next sound Cartheron heard was the heavy door creaking shut. Grinner, opposite, raised an eyebrow. 'You're up, Crust.'

Cartheron raised his gaze to the heavy, soot-blackened beams of the ceiling. 'Oh, for the love of all the sea gods . . .' He threw himself from the table, taking the fist of hard bread with him. Maybe he could bean a would-be attacker with it. At the door he snatched up a sheathed sword.

Outside, he would have lost the fellow in the gathering evening scarves of fog but for the tapping of his walking stick on the cobbles. He found him standing in front of a public shrine, leaning on the walking stick in quiet regard. He pointed to the shrine. 'And this is?'

Cartheron studied the statue. It was the stone figure of a woman crudely carved from the local granite. She stood with bare arms upraised, a large seashell in one hand, the other empty. Old faded scarves and garlands graced her shoulders while stubs of candles, burned incense, and other offerings littered the statue's base. He knew the figure well. She was missing the set of scales that she was supposed to hold in her right hand – corroded away, or taken, perhaps. With those scales she judged the worthiness of those at sea, and the likelihood of their return.

'Lady Nerrus. Goddess of the Shores. Calmer of storms and a patron goddess of sailors and fishers. Sister to Beru, Lord of Storms.'

The stick tapped again – perhaps his habit while in thought. 'This island has given much to the sea,' the old man mused.

'Yes – as has Nap.'

'Sea power,' the fellow half-murmured to himself; then, suddenly, he was off again and Cartheron was left standing alone with no idea in which direction he'd gone. He squinted into the mists, panicked; how could he have lost the bugger?

The tapping of the stick once more alerted him to the fellow's location – far down the street towards the waterfront. Cartheron hurried after him, wondering how the old codger could have got so far ahead.

He reached the wharves and peered right and left in a panic. Surly would have his balls . . . Then he saw him next to a pile of crates and bales, talking to a gang of labourers.

Cartheron came to his side in time to hear him saying, 'What ship, then, would you never serve on?'

The men and women were eyeing him as if he were a lunatic. One rose from lounging on the bales and confronted him. 'What do you mean, y'damned Dal Hon fool?'

Cartheron stepped up between them. 'Forgive my friend – he doesn't get out much.'

'I'll say. Who in Hood's name does he think he is?'

'Just a harmless old fool.'

A female stevedore gestured aside, observing, 'Well, your fool friend's wandered off.'

Cartheron turned, cursing. The mage – if indeed he was a mage – was now further along the wharf talking to a gang of kids. He jogged over to him and arrived just as a young lad was saying with a shrug, 'Sure, there're unpopular captains.'

Wu laughed indulgently and held up a copper Talian coin. 'Ship, I meant. Sailors are a superstitious lot. Worse even than soldiers. There must be an unlucky ship.'

A girl pushed forward. 'Oh, you mean the *Twisted*. No one will sign with it.' She reached for the coin but Wu pulled his hand away.

'And where is this unfortunate vessel? Is it with us now?'

The girl sneered her scorn. 'Didn't I just say no one would sign?

Sure it's here. Where it's been f'r years!' She pointed down the wharf.

Wu tossed her the coin. 'My thanks.'

One lad, who had been watching the mage with a strange intensity, now pointed. 'Ain't you the one who entered the Deadhouse yard?'

Wu nodded. 'Yes indeed.'

The gang of waterfront youths all stilled, their eyes growing huge. 'Well,' the lad continued, 'how'd you escape?'

Cartheron was aware then of a thickening of the evening murk about them. It was a sudden darkening, like the eclipses he'd known over the years. Shadows seemed to have gathered about them, especially the old man, who now appeared enveloped in a deepening shade. And out of the obscuring darkness he heard an eerie hollow voice whisper: 'Who said I did?'

The gang of youths gaped as one, then broke, scattering in all directions. He and his employer were suddenly alone and the darkness faded away – just as an eclipse might. Cartheron was then unsettled by a high childish giggle from the old Dal Hon mage. He composed himself to demand, 'And what was that all about? Scaring children?'

The old man fluttered a hand to wave aside his disapproval. 'Casting seeds, my friend. Merely casting seeds.' Then he was off again down the length of the wharf. Cartheron looked to the darkening half-overcast sky and followed, a hand on his cutlass.

The mage was standing among a tall collection of cargo and supplies in barrels and crates. As Cartheron approached he pointed the walking stick to the very far end of the wharf, where a lone vessel lay berthed, far from any of its fellows, as if the bearer of some sort of contagion. 'The *Twisted*,' Wu informed him.

Cartheron eyed the vessel. Narrow and high, three-masted; a modified coaster rig. Probably carrying mixed square and lanteen. Potentially fast, but also very obviously poorly maintained for some time. Wood at the railing was greying, paint was worn from the sides, which were stained by run-off from the fittings. The running rig hung loose, the ratlines torn in places. The hull was no doubt badly in need of scraping, if not rotten.

'It's a derelict hulk,' he told Wu, sneering.

'It has acquired that terrible affliction – the reputation of a cursed vessel. Everyone says so.'

87

Cartheron knew the damned fellow had deliberately piqued his interest but couldn't help following along and asking, 'Cursed? How?'

The little fellow fluttered a hand once more. 'Oh, a few unfortunate deaths during its last voyages. And a long failure in bringing in any prizes.' The mage flashed a crooked grin that he then forced from his lips, clearing his throat. 'Recently, however, it has been acquiring an even *worse* reputation.'

Cartheron wearily prompted him once again. 'Which is?'

'That it is haunted.' The fellow glanced about the shadowed alleyway between piled cargo and nodded to himself in a satisfied manner. 'And so . . . I must get to work.' To Cartheron's immense surprise – and unease – he began to fade away. 'Don't stay up for me.' And he was gone.

Cartheron cursed and searched among the barrels but could find no sign of the fellow. Surly would kill him for losing the codger! He turned to the ship, the *Twisted*, where it lay at berth. Well, at least he knew where he was – or claimed to be. He backed away into the narrow alley to sit on a barrel and crossed his arms, waiting and watching.

Some time later he started awake, disorientated, then remembered where he was and why, and sat back. It was night and something had woken him. He peered round but saw nothing strange in the darkness. At least the fogs were gone, he noted, now that the evening airs had stopped churning. The *Twisted* lay motionless – but not abandoned; its stern lantern was lit and a faint gold glow shone from one cabin's porthole.

A yell sounded then – an involuntary shout of surprise and alarm – and boots stomped along the wharf. A figure stormed past his hiding-place. All Cartheron had was a glimpse of an older gentleman, grey-bearded, his face as pale as snow, his eyes wild.

He sat back and eyed the *Twisted*, thinking. Did he really want to . . . No, he decided that he would definitely prefer not. And anyway, if this mage was as billed then he didn't seem to be in any danger of being clubbed by Geffen's men. He straightened, stretching, and headed back to Smiley's.

He had to take a few detours to avoid gangs of brawlers lounging at street corners near the bar, but eventually managed to slide in the front door. The place was empty but for members of the crew.

At the door, Shrift asked, 'Where's our would-be employer?'

'Working . . . I think.'

She was tall, a swordswoman who favoured heavy leather armour in battle, and now wore tanned hunting leathers. She sat back, crossing her arms. 'Doin' what?'

Cartheron eyed her. 'You scared of ghosts?'

The swordswoman scowled at such an idiotic question. 'Course. Who wouldn't be?'

'Then you don't want to know what he's doing.'

'Is he really some kinda mage?'

'I think so.' In fact, he now wondered whether the fellow was of the *worst* kind. That the old man truly was a mage seemed to trouble the swordswoman, so Cartheron added, 'At least he's on our side.'

Shrift didn't appear relieved. She slapped her side where her weapon usually rode. 'I don't understand why we don't just storm over there and put everyone to the sword.'

'Because then it would be war between us 'n' all the locals – and guess who would win?' Her tight mouth worked as she ground her teeth, but she subsided and leaned back on her stool. 'Slow and steady,' he told her, passing on.

He took a seat next to the fireplace and set to work building up the fire against the relentless damp. That accomplished, he leaned back to study his fellow crew on watch – Shrift and their tall lean archer, Tocaras. Neither looked happy sitting and staring out at the mist-cloaked streets.

Garrison duty, he reflected. Not our strength. No fighting man or woman's, frankly. Surly would have to be careful. Loyalty was one thing, but frustration and a perceived lack of success or advancement could erode even the strongest allegiance. Something had to give. And while he had complete confidence it wouldn't be any of them, still, he prayed, and hoped.

Chapter 5

TATTERSAIL LEANED HER FOREARMS ON THE GRITTY SALT-stained stone of a battlement crenel and considered the island's modest highlands to the north. Her loose hair blew about and she pushed it from her eyes. Overhead, gulls and cormorants hovered in the brisk wind, calling harshly. She watched their easy freedom for a time then lowered her gaze to the dun-brown hillocks of the Flint Plain. North, little more than a day's journey beyond the last Malazan headland, lay the continent. So close, yet, as they said, so far.

Something needed to be done if she and Mock were to come into their titles. And if he were too . . . how should she put it . . . too *content*, then it must fall to her. The question then, was just *what*.

And the answer that came to her mind was an old-fashioned expedition. A raid upon the mainland such as used to be organized in Mock's younger days and before. All in the honoured pirating tradition of Malaz.

That should remind them who controlled the seas, all their valuable shipping, and the entire coastline itself, and who was therefore owed the recognition and respect due to such a power. *That* would put the fear of gods into those quaking merchants in Cawn, the decadent aristocrats in Unta, and those damned snobbish Kanese.

She pressed a fist to the guano-streaked stone. Done. She'd settle it with Mock tonight.

A throat-clearing behind her brought her attention round to a guard. 'Yes?'

'A ship at the harbour mouth, m'lady.'

'So?'

'Lubben thought you'd be interested.'

Lubben – the hunchbacked castellan of the Hold. 'Very well.'

She crossed to the nearest overlook. Guano dotted the ancient stones of the walk and Tattersail found herself hating the damned old heap of rock. How she looked forward to getting off this gods-forsaken backwater for a proper manor in a real city like Unta or Tali!

The vessel was anchored as far out as could be managed. It was long and low, two-masted, tiny in the distance, yet she knew it instantly for what it was without even needing to be sure of its blue-tinted sails. 'What in all the seas is a Napan ship doing here?' she asked aloud.

The guard nearby wisely judged her question to be rhetorical. 'They've sent off a launch with a flag of truce,' he observed.

What was there to talk about, she wondered. 'Well, Lubben was right. I am interested. Keep an eye on them. Have a party ready as escort. I'll go tell Mock.'

The guard bowed and she swept off for the main keep.

She found him in their sleeping quarters. Oddly, though it was mid-day, he was in a state of undress, flushed and struggling with the ties of his corset. She hurried over and slapped his hands away to take the ties. 'What are you *doing*?' She yanked, fiercely.

He shrugged, embarrassed. 'The outfit simply was not right . . .' He gasped as the breath was squeezed out of him.

'So you've heard.'

'Heard what, my love?' She might have been mistaken, but his voice sounded slightly higher.

'Napans! Here, in the harbour! It may be an official delegation.'

Mock kept his arms wide while Tattersail tightened the many ties of the corset. He stroked his long moustache, thinking. 'A delegation . . . yes. This new king we've heard about. Official relations . . .' His usually narrowed dark eyes now widened, 'Or official recognition!'

He took her hands in his, urged her away. 'Summon that new girl, Viv. You meet them in the audience hall. *I* must dress properly.' He walked her to the door.

'Well, if you think it best.'

'Very good. This may be our first step towards all that we have wished for, my love.' He gave her a hurried kiss and shut the door behind her.

As she descended the stairs it occurred to her that the bed was a mess – it hadn't even been made yet! She would have to have stern words with Viv about that.

The delegation – and she assumed it was a delegation, as three was rather small for a raiding party – consisted of two men and a woman. One fellow was quite old, the emissary, she assumed, accompanied by two younger armoured guards. All three bore the bluish tinge to their skin that was the mark of natives of their isle. The emissary alone was allowed entrance to the hall.

Tattersail awaited him at the foot of Mock's raised wooden seat at the head of the top table.

The emissary came walking up. His heels struck loudly on the stone flags. To Tattersail's eyes the man did not look the part; too short, and pear-shaped. Inwardly she sighed, but they were dealing with Nap, after all. One mustn't get one's hopes up too high.

Halting at a respectful distance the emissary bowed, with a rather oily smirk. 'Admiral Koreth, at your service.'

She answered the bow, thinking that if this rat of a fellow was a real admiral of Nap then the isle must be overrun with them. 'Welcome, admiral. You honour us. Please accept our hospitality. For too long has our sister island been out of touch.'

The emissary stroked his goatee – which held streaks of grey – and nodded his grave agreement. 'And whom,' he began unctuously, 'do I have the honour of addressing?'

Tattersail struggled to keep her expression pleasant while she mentally berated herself for her awkwardness. 'My apologies, admiral. I am Tattersail, mistress of the Hold.'

The emissary's brows rose in appreciation. 'Ah! The formidable Tattersail. Your prowess is the talk of the entire southern seas.' And he bowed once more.

It occurred to her that this clearly inoffensive fellow might not have been such a foolish choice after all. 'You bring word from Tarel, the newly installed king of the Napan Isles?'

He bowed again. 'Indeed. And are you to speak for Mock, the oh so long-standing Admiral of Malaz?'

Tattersail struggled once more to keep her expression light. Her initial judgement had been the right one. *Admiral, is it? Fine. Be that way. No official exchanges with the mistress.* She returned his bow. 'He has been informed of your arrival and will be joining us soon.'

'Excellent.' The fellow made a show of studying his surroundings. 'So this is the Hold's main hall. It is so very . . . charmingly rustic.'

Fuck you too, you damned fat prick. She smiled, nodded her agreement. 'My thanks. That means a great deal, as you in Nap must surely know what you are speaking of.'

The emissary answered her smile in kind.

Tattersail could not help but follow his gaze as he peered about, and the tapestry across the way caught her eye. Agayla's new work. It was a portrait of the Hold, as seen from sea, at twilight. At least so it first appeared to her. Now, however, as she narrowed her gaze, the landscape seemed to darken. Ragged dark shapes like clouds threatened above. Their obscuring shadows seemed to crawl across the cliffs and the keep's great seaward walls.

She blinked – the emissary was talking. She smiled, panicking, and coughed against the back of her hand to gain time. *Damn Agayla! What does she mean by weaving such an ugly thing!* She gestured to a small side entrance. 'Perhaps I should go and see what matter is delaying Mock.'

Koreth's bow was so shallow as to hardly be worthy of the name. 'Indeed,' he answered thinly.

To her relief, the main doors swung open at that moment and Mock came sweeping in. He was wearing what she called his 'reckless' smile and sported his finest loose linen shirt, leather trousers and heeled shoes. He, of course, was armed, with his sabre at his side.

He threw out his arms in welcome, calling, 'Koreth! Is that you, you dog!'

The emissary bowed low. 'Admiral.'

Mock took him by the shoulders and looked him up and down. 'Look at you now. You captained the *Steadfast* at the siege of Bris, yes?'

The emissary blinked, startled, then flushed, obviously quite pleased. 'Yes, indeed. Though we saw little action.'

Mock laughed off the answer. 'You are too modest. That was a Napan victory to boast of!' He threw himself into his raised seat, slouched, his booted feet out straight before him. 'What can we in Malaz do for our friends and fellow sailors of Nap?'

Koreth blinked anew, quite thrown, and Tattersail hid a smile; this was the Mock she admired, always manoeuvring.

'Well . . .' the fellow began, perhaps rethinking his tack, 'King Tarel sends his greetings, of course. It is his hope that our two islands may now begin afresh – without the unfortunate rancour of the past.'

Mock slapped an armrest. 'I agree! This Tarel is wise indeed. An accord may be in order between him and me!' He gave Koreth a wink. 'This would free us up to eye the mainland, hm? Bris may be ripe for yet another sacking, yes?'

Koreth looked rather taken aback by such a direct proposal, but quickly mastered the reaction sufficiently to nod, smiling in apparent welcome of the prospect. 'A formal accord between us would be an excellent first step, admiral.'

'Excellent! Wine!' Mock called. 'A drink to seal our agreement!'

A young lad entered bearing a silver tray on which were set two tiny cut-crystal glasses and a carafe. Tattersail recognized their finest Grisian crystal, and reflected that it was fortunate they had two of the precious pieces.

Mock stepped down to pour, then raised his glass. 'To the prospect of a formal peace between Nap and Malaz. Brothers and sisters of the sea!'

Koreth answered the toast, emptying his glass, then carefully returned it to the tray. He cleared his throat. 'Any attacks, interceptions, or levying of fees on all Napan shipping and vessels should, of course, cease from this point onward.'

Mock returned to his seat, dangling his crystal glass. 'Of course. Pending ratification of the agreement.'

'Of course.'

'And likewise, of course.'

'Certainly.'

'Excellent. Then our ships are in line, as they say, yes? Will you not stay for dinner? We must celebrate our agreement!'

Koreth fluttered a hand. 'Sadly, I must turn down your hospitality, admiral. I must immediately bring this proposal to my king.'

Mock stood, nodding. He cuffed the shorter man's shoulders. 'Of course. We do not want any misunderstandings, hey?'

Koreth bowed. 'Until later, then, admiral.' He offered Tattersail a bow as well. 'M'lady.' Tattersail extended a hand, which he kissed. 'Admiral.'

The emissary turned as if to go, but Mock spoke. 'I have one small request to seal our agreement, sir.'

Koreth turned back, tilting his head. 'Yes?'

'These letters of accord between our two islands . . . they should all be headed: *From Tarel, King of Nap, by grace of the gods . . . to Mock, King of Malaz, by grace of the gods.*'

The emissary's eyelids fluttered in astonishment. For a time he was unable to respond, until he gasped, finally, 'I . . . shall put this to my king for his consideration, of course.'

'Excellent!' Mock answered, and raised a hand in farewell.

Koreth fairly ran from the hall and the doors swung shut.

Once the doors were firmly closed, Mock took Tattersail's hands and kissed them. 'We are halfway there, my love!'

But her gaze remained on the doors. 'You shouldn't have pushed so hard.'

He laughed and offered a wink. 'I asked for king but will settle for count.'

'It all relies upon how much Tarel wants us out of his way – what are his plans? Is he eyeing the mainland?'

Mock shrugged again. 'A small price to pay to be sure of his flank. His scrawl on a mere piece of paper.' He snatched up the carafe. 'We must celebrate this night!'

'I'll wait for Tarel's answer.'

'Don't worry. You always worry. But,' and he brushed her cheek, 'what would I do without my Tattersail?' He raised the carafe. 'Come! Let us celebrate.'

She watched him back away, arms wide, and shook her head – so like an eager boy. So . . . King of Malaz. That would make her . . . She lost her own grin. They weren't married. She would go from mistress of a pirate admiral to mistress of a king.

She felt her jaws tighten. They would have to have a talk, he and she.

* * *

Dancer pushed open the door to the office above Smiley's common room and paused on the threshold. It was empty – the fool had

95

wandered off again. Where to this time? Back to that eerie house? He strode in, examined the mess of papers on the desk: more of the fellow's sketches and enigmatic map-like drawings of lines and overlapping circles. The maps reminded him vaguely of astrological charts he'd glimpsed tacked up in the stalls of Dragons Deck readers.

Something crackled under his heeled shoes and he crouched to run a hand over the slats of the floor. Grit of some sort. He examined his hand, rubbing a thumb over the fingers. Sand. Fine sand. And – he sniffed – a faint lingering spice-like scent. Sweet. But with a bite, like mace.

Now he knew where Wu had disappeared to.

The fool. There was a good chance he may never see the lad again.

Someone on the stairs. He stilled. His hands went to the short wooden batons he carried for the moment; he wasn't killing anyone – yet.

It was the youngest of the Napan crew, the girl named Amiss. She halted in the narrow stairwell. 'Trouble in town.'

'All right.' He straightened, crossed the room and locked the door behind him.

Amiss tried to peer in past him. 'Where's . . . you know . . . the old man?'

Wu had yet to give his name to anyone, and Dancer suspected why – the vain idiot. 'He's off trying to gather more power to himself.' Which was technically true.

The girl's dark eyes widened in superstitious dread; Nap, it seemed, produced few mages other than those of Ruse. 'Oh.'

'So, what's the problem?'

She blinked, nodding, and invited him down the stairs. 'A shipment of liquor got past us and Geffen's boys are using it to reclaim the concession to the bars in town.'

They reached the common room, which was its typical near-empty self. Dancer set his hands on the batons shoved into his belt. 'Great. Who's free tonight?'

'Just me 'n' you.'

Not the best combination – two knifers. But that was not strictly true . . . on this island he was the heavy. He waved her onward. 'Fine. Let's go.'

She led the way out on to the night-gleaming wet cobbles.

Dancer paced along, hands on his batons. 'How'd they get hold of the shipment?'

She waved, disgusted. 'You kidding? Everyone on this island's a damned smuggler.'

He offered her a grin. 'Like Nap, I imagine.'

She snorted her agreement. 'Yeah. I guess so.'

He studied her sidelong: petite, with a pert nose and hair hacked so short it stood on end, like fur. A kid, really. Yet so serious all the time. 'How long have you been on Surly's crew?'

She looked quite startled, almost jumping. 'I've always been with m'— that is . . . a few years.'

It seemed to him that she'd been about to say, "m'lady". 'So . . . she's Napan aristocracy. I thought so.'

The girl scowled ferociously, her lips clamping tight.

'Fine. It's all right.' He peered about through a night mist that was too thin to be deemed rain. 'Which way?'

'They started with the best places and are working their way down the rungs.' She gestured. 'Let's try the waterfront dives.'

They headed down the gentle slope that led to the waterfront. Here all he could hear were the waves striking the shore and the distant creak and groan of the vessels at moorage. Then the light of a swinging lantern in an alley betrayed movement. He pointed Amiss to the roof of the neighbouring building and headed in.

He heard voices raised in argument and came upon the rear of a crowd of Geffen's thugs gathered at a door harassing a very frightened-looking fat fellow in a stained apron.

'Take it and pay us later, then,' a woman said, and he recognized their earringed friend.

The fellow, the proprietor no doubt, was wringing his hands in his apron. 'I'd really like to, really. But I'm all stocked up, you see. Got no room . . .' and he gave a laugh that was like a strangled titter.

'You'll take it anyway,' the woman snarled. 'Consider it an advance from Geffen. He'll collect later.'

The innkeeper laughed nervously again, almost wilting in sweat. 'I would! Really! But there's no room back here . . .'

The woman gestured to two of the muscle with her. 'We'll make some room.'

The two surged forward, only to rebound from a new figure

97

that had suddenly replaced the fat proprietor in the doorway. This one filled it like a solid wall.

'Out of the way, y'damned beersot,' the woman warned.

'No fighting in the bar,' the huge fellow rumbled in a voice like a thumped empty barrel. The woman snapped her fingers to urge the toughs forward once more. They straight-armed the huge figure only to rebound again as if having run into brick.

Dancer drew his batons and raised them to rest each on a shoulder. 'I have room in a warehouse I know,' he announced.

All heads turned his way. The woman emerged, having pushed her way through the crowd of street muscle. 'You again,' she sneered. 'Look at you – standing there bold as brass all alone. Time you were taught a lesson.' She snapped her fingers again to urge the hired thugs forward. The gang drew truncheons and other short clubs. Dancer counted twelve and he didn't wait for them to sort themselves out; he waded in immediately.

He smacked knees then skulls as the owners of the knees sank. He pressed forward, attacking. Incoming blows were blocked and returned with counters to elbows, knees and heads. Anywhere to inflict maximum damage with least effort. The ruffians fell before him while the woman retreated between them, her eyes growing ever more huge. The sharp crack of hardwood on bone echoed in the narrow brick channel of the alley.

The last of the twelve fell from multiple blows to the knees, stomach and skull to sprawl unconscious at the woman's feet. She stared now at Dancer in open disbelief. Behind him lay a carpet of thugs either out cold or clutching knees and heads and groaning in pain. 'Why are you here?' she breathed, awed despite herself. 'Why is someone like you wasting your time on this wretched island?'

'That's my business. Now I suggest your employer catch the next ship out.'

She shook her head. 'I know him. He won't.'

'Then we have a problem.'

Her hand strayed to the knife at her belt and he gave her a warning look; the hand slipped away. 'Yes,' she stammered, 'yes, we do.'

'What's your name?'

'Lee.'

'Lee? Really. Well, my name's Dancer. And I'm calling your boss out. Either he abandons all claims to any territory here in the city, or I'll come for him. Is that clear?'

She nodded, her jaws clenched tight.

'Very good.' He nodded that she could go. She backed away up a portion of the alley then turned and hurried away into the misting rain.

Dancer turned to the giant who still blocked the back door. 'What's your name?'

The man frowned down at him, looking puzzled, then announced, 'No fighting in the bar.'

Dancer raised a brow; *Right*. He called loudly through the door, 'The liquor's all yours. I'm sure you have room for free casks.' Then he picked his way between the fallen out on to the main street.

As he left the alley he heard the proprietor asking cautiously, 'Is it safe?'

Amiss joined him on the street, grinning. 'You were a big help,' he complained.

'They said you were good – but I didn't know you were *that* good.'

'Thanks . . . I think.'

'Teach me?'

He eyed her sidelong. 'Sure. But I don't think we'll have the time.'

'Planning on going somewhere?'

He laughed. 'I plan on all of us being damned busy.'

The girl was nearly skipping along over the puddles. 'We'll see. Maybe this Geffen fellow will finally get the message.'

Dancer had to shake his head. 'No. I'm gonna have to beat him unconscious and throw him on to a ship.'

'Why haven't you yet?'

He wiped the cold mist from his face. 'Because it's his organization we have to beat. Otherwise one of his lieutenants will just step up and we'll get nowhere.'

'Ah. I see.'

They were nearing Smiley's and he hurried his pace, pulling her along. If there was going to be an ambush, it would be here.

The door was thrown open and Shrift nodded them in. Dancer relaxed. He inclined his head in farewell to Amiss, then climbed the stairs.

He unlocked the door and checked within. Maybe . . . But the room was still empty. For a time he stood in the darkness regarding the desk. Wu shouldn't have gone alone. The damned fool needed him to keep him alive. What could he possibly have been thinking?

He pulled a chair over to the wall next to the door and sat, leaned back on the two rear legs to rest against the wall, and set his hands on the cold hilts of the thin daggers hidden at his waist, which he always kept there – just in case. He sat in silence, regarding the dark room while the rain hissed against the shuttered window, then let out a long breath and closed his eyes.

*

Nedurian sat on a bench eating an apple; it was a sunny day and he was enjoying the warmth. The usual old dogs sat about, trading their tired old lies and generally watching what little corner of the world this square in the market quarter of Malaz City offered. He was only half listening – he'd heard all their stories and opinions on everything twenty times over – but when the talk suddenly died down he raised his gaze to see what had arrested their attention and choked on the mouthful of apple. Agayla stood before him, hands on hips. A rich brocaded silk scarf was thrown round her neck, and her long hair blew loose about her like its own black silk banner.

'There you are!' she announced as if he were some truant lad. 'We're late. Hurry!' and she marched off, heading for the waterfront.

Quite bewildered, Nedurian rose, apple loose in his hand.

'One widow not enough for ya, Ned?' one of the old dogs offered.

Nedurian made a show of running a hand over his unkempt beard, and straightened his frayed collar. 'Can't help having what these gals want, boyo.'

The oldster shot a smirk to his companion. 'Yeah . . . obedience.' Both of them cackled, showing a remarkable lack of teeth.

Nedurian raised a warning finger. 'Careful there. The fish might find you tasty.'

The old fellow waved him away. 'Ach . . . they've had plenty a chances.'

Ned caught Agayla glaring at him from up the street. He hurried on.

The gallery of old dogs sent him off with hoots of laughter.

Pacing Agayla, he cast her a brief puzzled glance. What could be the trouble? He'd never spoken to her outside her shop – couldn't even remember *seeing* her outside her shop. Her pace was quick, and her long straight black hair whipped in the offshore winds.

'What's up?' he asked.

She ignored him and so he bit down on any further questions. She was leading the way to the crowded main docks where commercial vessels unloaded cargo and took on passengers for the day's journey to the mainland.

Here she scanned the crowds, raising herself on the toes of her shoes, biting her lip. If he didn't know better, he'd almost say she was anxious. And anything that would make this woman anxious was way out of his class.

'I don't see him,' she muttered, frustrated. 'He should be here by now.'

'Who?'

'Obo.'

He was rocked, though he managed to stop his mouth from hanging open. *Obo!* By all the gods and demons above and below. He'd only ever heard that name – and then only whispered by the most accomplished mages. They were going to meet him? Was that what this was about? Somehow he doubted it.

She waved him onward. 'Well, can't be helped. We'll just have to meet her ourselves.'

Ah. A woman. 'Who?' he asked. Again she ignored him. He ground his teeth against his annoyance as he followed her to the foot of the pier where the most recent vessel had moored. She crossed her arms, then uncrossed them and pulled back her hair, knotting it through itself, before pushing up her sleeves and crossing her arms once more over her thin breast.

She really is nervous, he realized, rather appalled that anyone or anything could elicit such a reaction in this magus.

'Who is it?' he asked out of the side of his mouth.

'Quiet. Keep your hands empty. And by all the gods, don't raise your Warren.'

'*What* is it?'

She hissed her annoyance. 'Think of this one as an Ascendant,' she snarled, tense and angry now.

Nedurian could only raise an eyebrow. Really. An Ascendant.

Then why in the Seven Realms were they even standing here?

He watched the crowd of passengers making their way down the pier. None appeared in any way remarkable. As he watched, however, the figure of a woman seemed to single itself out of all the surrounding people, or rather it was as if all the people faded into insignificance next to the weight and power of her presence – all others became somehow indistinct. Ghostly, even.

He'd never have given her another look had not Agayla fore-warned him. Wearing old travel-stained leathers, she appeared middle-aged, with plain unhandsome features and her hair short and mussed. A rural farmer's wife, or rustic trader, one might imagine her. Yet while she brushed shoulders with her fellow passengers, who passed her without notice, to his senses she appeared to be a lodestone of power.

The woman came before them and halted, a small bag of gear at one shoulder. Her dark gaze was all on Agayla, and for once Nedurian did not resent the exclusion. 'And you are?' she asked.

'Agayla.'

The woman's gaze moved past them and she nodded a greeting. 'Obo.'

Nedurian glanced behind, startled. There stood a short, gangly, pale old man, bald, with a liver-spotted pate and a wild ring of grey hair about his ears. *This* was the fierce and terrible Obo? He could've passed him on the bench this morning.

The fellow, Obo, sent him a glare, as if to say, *What're you looking at?* Nedurian quickly turned back.

'And what name are you travelling under now?' Agayla went on.

'Nightchill.'

'And what are your intentions? We want no provocations. The Riders have been quiescent of late.'

The woman's thin lips quirked as if at some hidden joke. 'Just research,' she said.

Agayla appeared to have regained her confidence as she was scowling now as usual. 'I hope so. You understand we'll be keeping an eye on you while you're here.'

'Of course.' The woman tilted her head in farewell and walked on.

Agayla turned to Obo. 'What could bring *her* here?' she hissed, sotto voce.

The fierce and terrible Obo shrugged his bony scarecrow shoulders. 'Don't know.'

'There's a fellow messing with Meanas here,' Nedurian offered.

Obo gave him a scornful appraisal up and down. 'And who'n the Abyss are you?'

* * *

Once he'd made up his mind, it took Dassem three nights of silent vigil at the altar before he mustered the necessary resolve and firmness of mind to clear his throat and speak. It was one of the most difficult decisions of his life to date, and in making it he felt that he'd betrayed everything he had come to believe about himself, and the world about him. Yet the girl was weakening daily; and his equivocation was solving nothing.

'My lord,' he began, sitting cross-legged, head bowed, his voice weak and hoarse, 'it pains me beyond all endurance to say this . . . but I must ask a boon.'

A long silence in the darkness answered his words. The night seemed to have swallowed them. The air about him turned very cold indeed. Then, a stirring, and a presence, one sour with disapproval, and even a tinge of frustration.

'Dassem Ultor,' came the faint breath. 'You too. And to think I had such great hopes for you.'

'Please, master. She is an innocent.'

Frustration verging into exasperation. 'You know that is irrelevant.'

Dassem bowed even further. 'Yes. I'm sorry. It just slipped out.'

'Then there is nothing more to discuss.'

He straightened, slightly. 'Unfortunately – there is.'

The skull on the ancient corpse atop the sarcophagus shifted, turning his way. 'Oh?'

Dassem straightened his back. 'Take me.'

'I'm sorry?'

'In her stead. Accept me. A life for a life.'

The skull turned away. 'I make no deals.'

'Then you have no Sword. I set it aside from here on.'

A dark laugh answered him. 'You would not dare.'

He was on his feet in an instant. 'It is done. In all these years I have made no requests, asked for nothing. Yet now that I ask for one boon you refuse me like a beggar at the door.'

The desiccated corpse edged itself up into a sitting position. 'You mortals are all beggars before my door.'

Dassem was nodding to himself. 'I know this. And so I go as a beggar.'

The skeleton hissed in a dry laugh, 'A rather arrogant beggar – you are nothing without your precious title.'

Dassem turned his back. 'We are done.' He threw a few personal items into a shoulder bag, plus two bags of coins – offerings to Hood – then, kneeling, he scooped up the girl in his arms, blankets and all. He headed for the entrance. She nestled against his chest like a hot coal.

'And where will you go?' came a thin shout.

He turned. 'The temple of the Enchantress. Perhaps *she* will honour my service.'

Sinew creaked as a withered hand gripped the edge of the sarcophagus. 'Very well. Perhaps there *is* something . . .'

He turned at the entrance. 'Yes?'

'She is dying, and, as I have made clear, there is nothing I can ever do about that. Yet there is one possibility . . .'

'Yes?'

'There are places where she could be taken. Where she may be laid to await a cure. Places where time passes . . . differently.'

'And the nearest?'

'Nearest? Well, the most accessible stands on an island to the south. The island of Malaz. It is called – and I do not joke – the Deadhouse.'

'I know *you* do not joke,' Dassem muttered. 'Very well. You pledge to withhold your hand until I should reach this place?'

'I shall . . . abide.'

He gave a curt nod. 'Very good. I leave immediately.' And he walked out through the gaping entrance.

Silence settled into place over the empty mausoleum. The only sounds were those of far off muted voices and the clatter of a few carts on neighbouring streets.

Then, a long low chuckle softly echoed about the stones. A dried hand of withered ligaments and bare bone rose to make a casting gesture as of tossing a dart into the distance, and the corpse collapsed into a cloud of dust, sinew and rotten cloth.

*

A kick woke Rebben to darkness and a godsawful taste in his mouth. He whipped out his knife only to have it slapped from his hand. He squinted, focusing on the fellow who had a handful of his shirt. He pawed at the hand. 'What in the fucking Abyss?'

The Dal Hon fellow shook him again. 'This boat leaves now.'

'No it godsdamned well doesn't.'

'Why not?'

The hand released him. He fell back against the riverboat's side and winced at the stab of pain in his back. 'Quarantine 'gainst the sickness. The river gates are all closed. No shipping up or down.'

The Dal Hon cursed softly, straightened from looming over him. 'Dammit . . . Very well. Sorry to trouble you.' A heavy coin fell against his chest and he clutched at it, touching his brow.

He waved the fellow off as he lightly stepped up to the dock, then raised the coin to the faint light. Now there's a turn – being assaulted in the night and *handed* money instead of having it taken? First time that ever happened to him. He froze upon catching the glint of gold and a stamped design unfamiliar to him. Just how old was this thing, anyway?

Dassem headed to the southern Outer Round gate, known as the Gate of the Mountains – a reference, perhaps, to distant Kanese highlands far to the south. He cradled Nara tight against his chest, wrapped in her blankets.

When he reached the vicinity of the gate he went to the nearest trading house and banged on the door. Eventually, it opened, and he faced a rotund bearded fellow in a long nightshirt who blinked at him, squinting, 'What in the Protectress's name d'you want?'

'I want transport. A cart or small wagon, preferably covered. And horses.'

The trader smacked his lips, drew a hand down through his thick beard. 'And this can't wait till morning?'

'No it cannot.'

The trader rolled his gaze to the ceiling. 'Why do I always get the winners? Fine. But let's see your coin – up front.'

Dassem handed over one of his small coin bags. The trader opened it then held it to the lamp next to the door. His brows shot up almost to his jumbled hair.

'Whatever you have,' Dassem said.

The fellow studied him, almost stunned, perhaps looking for

fresh blood on him from recent murders, then leaned forward to peer up and down the street as if expecting at any minute the crashing arrival of the city guard. Seeing and hearing nothing, he raised his shoulders in a shrug then stepped out and waved for Dassem to follow. 'This way.'

They crossed to a corral next door. Here, the trader pointed to a covered cart off in the shadows. Even in the dark, Dassem could see that it was painted a lurid red and gold. 'What is that?'

'An old dowager commissioned that for a pilgrimage to all Burn's holy sites on the road east. To earn merit, and to give thanks for all her grandsons.'

'So, you cannot sell it?'

'No. She died the day before she was due to leave. Now I'm stuck with it.'

Dassem studied the eye-wateringly ugly thing, then nodded. 'It is perfect. I will take it. I'll want two horses.'

The trader squeezed the leather bag in his grip. 'One'll do.'

'I want two.'

The trader's jaws worked, and then he sighed. 'Very well.'

'And throw in supplies – a cask of water. Forage for the horses.'

The fellow was nodding. 'I'll go wake the boys . . .'

It was light, but not yet dawn, when a brightly painted cart hauled by two horses came to the recently rebuilt southern Outer Round gate. The guards, half asleep, blinked at the startling sight. One nudged his companion, saying, 'Hey, Hurst . . . the carnival in town?'

Hurst rose, groaning and stamping his feet. 'Sure looks like it, Raf.' He leaned on the pole of his eight-foot tall halberd, muttered a bored, 'Gate's closed.'

The tall, lean Dal Hon leading the horses stepped up. 'Then open it.'

Hurst turned an amused glance to his companion, sniffed, and spat to the cobbles. 'Curfew. Order of the Protectress. Move along.'

'I intend to move along – to the south.'

Hurst cocked a brow. 'And how're you gonna do that?'

'Through this gate.'

The other guard, Raf, took out a pear and bit it; he offered

Hurst a wink. Hurst was nodding. 'All right. An' just how're you gonna get through the gate?'

'You're going to open it for me.'

Raf snorted a laugh, chewing.

Hurst offered his companion a knowing look, tapped a finger to his temple. 'Okay . . . An' why would I do that?'

The Dal Hon took a long hard breath, raised his own gaze to the purpling sky. 'Because I'm the Sword of Hood.'

'Really?' Hurst said, offering an exaggerated frown. 'C'n you prove it?'

Now the Dal Hon frowned, puzzled. 'Prove it? How?'

Hurst shrugged. 'I don't know . . . Kill something, maybe?'

Raf choked on his pear, laughing and snorting; he slapped his thigh, swallowing with difficulty. '*Kill something*,' he chortled. 'That's a good one.'

The Dal Hon lad looked from one to the other and sighed, his shoulders falling. He rubbed his forehead. 'I see,' he murmured aloud, as if speaking to himself. 'My mistake.' He rummaged at his belt and withdrew a small bag, opened it, and held out two coins that glinted gold in the rising light.

Hurst and his companion crowded forward, studied the coins, then withdrew, heads together. 'Whaddya think?' Hurst whispered.

'Two more.'

Hurst nodded. 'Right.' He returned to the lad. 'Two more.'

Sighing again, the lad pulled out two more coins. Hurst held out his hand and the lad let them fall into his palm. Hurst turned to Raf, but froze suddenly, setting his hands on his hips. 'Is that a breeze I'm feelin' there? Did you go 'n' leave the gate open again? Dammit, man. How many times do I have to tell you? Were you born in a barn or somethin'?'

Raf took one last bite of the pear then threw the core aside. 'Sorry there, Hurst. Guess I was distracted by the carnival and such – let's go have a look.'

The guards withdrew into the gate tunnel. Dassem took hold of the jesses of one horse and led it after them. When he reached the outer gate, one side of the huge double doors hung a touch ajar. He pushed the hulking great thing open further and led the cart on. The guards were standing outside.

'I am the Sword of Hood, you know,' Dassem told Hurst.

'Oh, sure. An' I'm the nephew of Burn.'

Dassem took breath to speak, only to realize that there really wasn't anything he could possibly say. He shut his mouth and moved on, shaking his head. The wooden wheels of the cart bumped and grated on the uneven cobbles.

Behind, at the gate, he heard Raf complain to his companion, 'You know, come to think of it, I *was* born in a barn.'

He turned his attention to the south and the much abused and littered road that led that way – the very road King Chulalorn's army marched up only to fall back upon last year, leaving behind the wreckage of shattered equipment, abandoned tools and weapons, and broken sandals.

Nara lay within the cart, hidden under its closed top of stiffened canvas, wrapped in blankets. She was still sweaty, but he was no longer worried that she would succumb to the fever, as the Grey Walker himself had assured him that he would withhold his hand until she was delivered to safety. Just what form this safety would take he had no idea. He had only the name.

Deadhouse.

Chapter 6

DANCER SAT AT A TABLE IN SMILEY'S, SHARPENING ALL HIS knives. It was morning and the place was quiet, but then it was always quiet. Amiss sat with him. She was leaning back in her chair, a heeled shoe against a table leg, rocking. Tea lay before him in a chipped stoneware cup, cold and forgotten. He was working on his seventh blade and had finished with the whetstone before moving on to his finer grit dry-stone. After finishing both edges to his satisfaction he polished them with a few final draws across leather, turning the knife absent-mindedly; he found it a very contemplative ritual.

Amiss eyed him for a time, then ventured, 'Don't worry. He'll show up.'

He drew down his mouth, shot her a glance. 'Who?'

'Your partner – he always shows up eventually.'

He tested the edge of the blade and sheathed it. 'Whatever. I'm not worried.'

'Course not. You're just grinding your blades down to nothing.'

'Don't you have duties or something?'

She stretched her long lean arms overhead, grinning at him. 'I'm off right now.'

He glowered, drew yet another thin blade from an ankle sheath, tested its edge and set to brushing it over the whetstone. 'What's the word on Geffen?'

'Withdrawn. Hunkered down. As if they're waiting for us to storm them in their stronghold.'

'Not likely,' Dancer answered without looking up.

'Funny. That's what Surly said: no need.'

He grunted at that.

'How 'bout those lessons you promised?'

He looked up. 'Like what?'

'Like close-in fighting.'

He shrugged, sheathed the knife. 'Sure. Out back, I suppose.'

Hawl entered, spotted him, and headed over. She looked as she always did: dishevelled, with tangled hair and tattered mud-smeared skirts. He wondered whether she ever washed or changed her clothes. Mages! The strangest sort. Still, Grinner didn't seem to mind.

'That ship,' she announced, 'the *Twisted*. It's up for sale. We're buying it, right? That's the plan?'

Amiss screwed up her face. 'That cursed scow?'

Dancer drew breath, only to realize that Wu wasn't here and that he didn't know what the damned fool intended. 'Yeah,' he managed, swallowing his fury. 'That's the plan.'

Both Hawl and Amiss asked, 'How?'

He made a vague gesture. 'Got funds hidden away. Listen, keep watch. Find out if there're any takers. Identify them. Yes?'

The mage's answering grin was knowing. 'Right. Can't have a bidding war, hey?' She went to the kitchen, no doubt to report to Surly.

Amiss was watching him expectantly. 'So? Where's all this coin? In your socks?'

He sat back, his jaws clenching, and ground out, 'It's coming . . .'

By time the evening arrived Dancer was fairly vibrating with frustration and annoyance. Where *was* the bastard? Didn't he understand that they had plans in motion? That he couldn't just take off like this, without talking to anyone?

Cold soup lay before him and he sat alone. The Napan crew seemed to be able to sense his dark mood and occupied other tables.

What were they to do? Kidnap the owner and force him to sign over the papers? Then what? A splash in the harbour, no doubt. But Dancer was no murderer. He was a killer, yes, but not a plain murderer. To his mind the difference was as vast as a chasm.

It was at that moment that the front door creaked open and Wu walked in. He was humming nonchalantly to himself and slapping sand and dust from his sleeves.

Dancer surged from his table. 'Where have you been?'

Wu froze in mid-stride, mouth open. He brought a hand to his chin. 'Well . . . I should think you'd know.'

Dancer waved that aside. 'Yes, yes. What I mean is, you've been gone for ages. Without word. Leaving the rest of us to manage. I had no idea when to expect you, or even if you'd come back at all!'

The lad's wrinkled old man brows rose. 'Why, Dancer – I had no idea you cared.'

The fury that this ridiculous fellow was able to raise in Dancer almost choked him. Through clenched teeth he ground out, 'We're *supposed* to be partners . . .'

From across the bar Grinner called, 'Could you two take your lovers' spat upstairs?'

Dancer shot the swordsman a glare, then gestured Wu to the stairs. The mage shrugged and headed up.

Shutting the office door, Dancer turned on him. 'Don't you *ever*—'

Wu shot a finger into the air with a grin that looked rather evil and maniacal on his wizened features, 'Progress, my friend! Great progress!'

Dancer stared, stunned for a moment. 'Really? Progress? How so?'

Wu brushed more dust from his dark jacket. He glanced round, spotted a carafe of water on the side table and took a long drink. Swallowing, he gasped, 'The gate. I think I may have it . . .'

Dancer eased into a ready stance, his shoulders falling. 'Really? It's open?'

The Dal Hon mage raised thumb and forefinger to his eye, a fraction apart. 'One smidgen from it.'

Dancer leaned back against the door, looked to the ceiling. 'So . . . it's not open.'

'It will be!' the mage insisted. He swallowed another mouthful, then waved a hand and started rummaging at the desk. 'That's why I came back. To get you. For the last stage.'

'So I'm supposed to be grateful?'

Wu was studying a handful of his notes and drawings. He peered up, blinking. 'Well, yes. But not just that. Together we've managed to overcome all obstacles to date. Your muscle and my brain!'

Dancer felt the hackles at his neck rising. 'You mean my muscle and brains and your . . . insanity.'

The little mage looked offended, and sniffed, 'I think not.' He pulled a satchel from beneath the desk and shoved a handful of the papers into it. 'We'll need food and water.'

Dancer raised a hand. 'Whoa. Food and water for what?'

'For the journey. Who knows what we will find?'

Dancer crossed his arms. 'No. Not tonight. You need to rest and we both need to prepare. In a few days. Okay?'

Wu hugged the satchel to his chest, his mouth agape in disbelief. 'What? A few days?'

'That gate's been there for what . . . a millennium? It's not going anywhere.'

'But . . .'

Dancer raised a warning finger. 'And no sneaking out without me!' The little mage thumped down into the chair, the satchel still clutched to his chest. 'Good. Oh, one last thing. Word's come that the *Twisted* is up for sale. What do we do? Do we have the funds?'

Wu nodded absently, pouting, his gaze on the cluttered desktop. 'Yes. I believe so. Arrange a meeting here tomorrow.'

'Good. I'll put Surly on it.'

Wu stirred, half-heartedly raising a finger. 'Be seen ordering her and the others around. It warms the locals' hearts to see the Napans being bossed about.'

Dancer nodded, thinking, *And I wonder how Surly will take that? Maybe she'll actually see the sense in it.* 'Okay. Tomorrow, then.' He nodded his goodbye and pulled the door shut behind him. He would have locked it if it had a lock on the outside. Shaking his head, he went to find Surly.

After making the arrangements, he thumped back down at his table. It was long into the night when he finished the last blade.

The next morning a knock at his door woke him. He wiped groggily at his face, called, 'Yes?'

'Noon,' a woman answered. Shrift. 'The owner says he'll come at noon.'

'Okay.' He dressed and went down to break his fast.

The Napan crew were already up and about, seeing to their assigned duties for the day: guarding various properties, showing

112

the flag on the streets, and generally letting everyone know who was in charge of the bars, warehouses and flop-houses they controlled.

After his meal of stewed barley, cheese, a wedge of bread, and an apple – a meal he selected very carefully, imagining that not even Urko could ruin it – he went upstairs and knocked on the office door. He waited, but no one answered. A flush of sudden rage took him by the throat and he threw open the door.

Wu was leaning back behind the desk, feet up, fingers twined over his chest, snoring. Dancer felt a twinge of guilt over his anger and gently closed the door behind him. He crossed to the side table and poured a glass of water, set it on the desk, and loudly cleared his throat.

Wu coughed, smacked his lips, and cracked open one eye.

Oddly, the wet snoring noise continued in the room. It seemed to be coming from overhead. Dancer slowly raised his gaze to the rafters above and there lay the hairy long-limbed nacht, pink mouth agape, fast asleep. He threw a wadded sheet of parchment at it and it coughed, smacked its lips, and cracked open one eye.

Dancer experienced an odd sensation of déjà vu.

Wu spotted the glass of water and drank it. He stretched, groaning – as did the nacht above – and drummed his fingers on the desk. 'So, what's the word?'

'Noon. He's coming at noon.'

'Excellent.'

Dancer sat on the edge of the desk. 'And . . . we *do* have the money, yes?'

'Oh, yes. After a fashion.'

He didn't like the sound of that, but refrained from questioning. He already knew the fellow didn't like to explain himself. 'Fine. You should eat.'

'Have Surly send up a meal.'

To that Dancer could only crook a brow. 'I don't think that would go over so well.'

Wu raised a finger into the air. 'Appearances, my friend. One must maintain appearances.'

Dancer straightened. 'Well, if you put it that way . . .' He headed to the door.

Behind, he heard Wu conspicuously clear his throat, and he turned back. 'Yes?'

The little fellow was twining his fingers together, his belly up against the desk. 'I've been thinking about what to call myself . . .'

Dancer nodded. 'I noticed.'

Wu gave a curt bob of his head. 'Indeed. Like you, I think I require a new working name. But in my case something grand, of course.'

Dancer clenched his lips tight and let out a hard breath. 'Like?'

'Well . . . something with the strong hard kay sound, like Keth, or Kell. Plus, the sinister and menacing vee sound, such as Val, or Veth, or Ved.'

Dancer looked to the ceiling. *Oh, good gods . . .*

Wu was oblivious, as usual. 'Like Vethkedell the . . . something or other. Murderous, maybe. Or Menacing.'

'No.'

Wu blinked, surprised. 'No? No to what?'

'To *that*. Something else with kell and ved.'

Wu's head shot up. 'What was that?'

'What was what?'

'There. What you just said. Kell . . . something.'

'Kell and ved.'

Wu snapped his fingers. 'That's it! Very well done, my friend.'

Dancer felt his brows crimping in confusion, and annoyance. *What in the Abyss just happened?* He gestured to the door. 'I'll have a meal sent up, then.'

Wu waved his hands impatiently. 'No, no. Not *now*. Have Surly deliver it during the negotiations.'

Dancer wanted to raise his fists to him, but refrained. He sighed instead in tired resignation. 'Fine. During the negotiations.' He opened the door. Wu leaned back, setting his dusty-heeled shoes on the desk, and knitted his hands over his stomach, a satisfied smile taking shape on his face. Dancer headed downstairs.

The owner arrived at noon. Dancer had Tocaras and Choss tail him from the vessel to make certain there would be no interference from Geffen and his boys. He was a veteran raider, grey-haired and grizzled. He entered the common room and stood peering round in the relative dark, uncertain whom to address. Dancer was waiting next to the door and he extended a hand to invite him upstairs. As he followed him up, it occurred to him that the owner looked just as worn down as his vessel. His eyes were bloodshot, red-rimmed and sunken, and his cheeks, which showed an unhealthy grey pallor, unshaven and drawn. He looked like a man who hadn't slept well in a very long time.

Dancer reached round him to open the office door, and Wu came out from behind the desk to invite him in.

'Kellanved,' Wu introduced himself, and Dancer blinked, startled.

'Durard,' the old fellow growled.

Wu – Kellanved? – motioned to a chair. 'Please, sit. Care for a drink?'

'Wouldn't say no to a glass,' the fellow answered, and sat with a weary sigh.

Wu – *Kellanved?* Dancer repeated to himself – looked to him. 'Would you be so kind?'

Dancer went to the side table to pour a glass of their best wine, which, if he was being honest, wasn't really all that good. Setting it before Durard, he went to sit over by the window and stretched out his legs.

Kellanved returned to the desk. 'Looking to put the sea behind you, yes?' he said.

Durard blinked at him, confused for a moment, then nodded. 'Ah, right. I suppose so.'

Dancer was repeating the strange new name to himself. Kellanved . . . what in the Abyss kind of name was that supposed to be? It didn't sound Dal Hon at all. And it sure didn't mean anything – he'd just made it up.

'Strange for someone to simply up and buy a ship, you know,' Durard was saying. 'Usually it's consortiums of merchants, or groups of owners. Like partners. Or cities, a' course.'

'Of course,' the mage answered, all soothing and agreeable. He motioned to Dancer. 'I do have a partner.' Durard glanced over and tilted his head in acknowledgement, then cleared his throat.

'So . . . how d'ya want to do this? Got letters of credit or such? Bullion?'

There came a knock at the door and Dancer rose to answer. It was Surly, carrying a tray with fruit, bread, and cheese. She gave Dancer a dark look and pushed past. At the desk she banged down the tray, gave Kellanved a look that could only be described as surly, and sauntered out.

'Ah, yes . . . well. Thank you, Surly.' Kellanved offered the food to Durard then tapped his fingers together, elbows on the desk. 'So, payment. Yes. Well, I *do* have something that I believe would serve here on the island. They are quite valuable – or so I'm told.'

He rummaged down under the desk and came up with a bag that he set on the desk. Dancer recognized it as one of the canvas pouches from the hijacking.

Durard leaned forward to peer in and his eyes fairly goggled as he saw what the bag held.

Wu – Kellanved – set down another pouch next to the first.

Durard's brows rose even higher.

Kellanved then set down the third and leaned back, clasping his hands before his chin. 'I do hope that this will cover the price.'

Durard's amazed gaze moved from the bags to Kellanved and back again. He coughed into a fist, stammering, 'Ah! Well . . . All three, you say?'

Kellanved nodded.

The captain slammed a hand to the desk. 'Done! You drive a hard bargain, friend!' He threw back the rest of his wine and raised the glass. 'Perhaps another . . . ?'

Dancer almost fell out of his chair. He glared bloody murder at Kellanved. Behind Durard, he mouthed, *What the Abyss!* and threw open his arms. Throughout the display the Dal Hon kept a stony face. Though seething, Dancer took the captain's glass. 'Certainly.'

Durard produced the paperwork from within his jacket. 'Have you a quill, then, old man?'

Kellanved blinked, uncertain; then realization came to him that it was he who was being addressed as 'old man' and he started, then searched about the desk for quill and ink. Finally, after much fumbling and drawer-banging, he produced a set.

'There you are,' Durard said, signing. 'The fine ship the *Twisted*. Serve you well, she will. Fast into the wind.'

Fast to the bottom, Dancer amended silently. Handing the captain his refilled glass, he reflected that Kellanved, now, was at least being consistent. *First he purchases a wreck of a bar; now he purchases a wreck of a ship.* The fool was resolutely grinding them into failure and penury.

Durard tossed back the wine and stood, then slipped the lightest pouch into a pocket within his jacket. The others would not fit and so he used the cut ties to hang them over a shoulder, snug down his side. He saluted Kellanved. 'Pleasure doing business with you, sir.'

Kellanved nodded benignly. 'All mine, I assure you. My thanks.'

Grinning, Durard sent Dancer a nod of farewell. Dancer showed him out. The fellow obviously left in a far better mood than when he'd entered; he was fairly chuckling. Dancer returned to the office and shut the door. The mage was munching on the cheese and bread. 'So,' Dancer began, 'Kellanved, is it?'

The lad swallowed. 'Yes – and many thanks.'

'What's it supposed to mean?'

Kellanved peered round, uncertain. 'Mean? It's just a name. A pseudonym. A veil to hide a thousand crimes; a rallying cry in battle; a curse on our terrified enemies; a—'

Dancer waved him short. 'I get the idea. But you just made it up!'

Kellanved sniffed. 'I gave you no such grief over your selection.'

Dancer waved his impatience again. 'Fine.' He poured himself a drink. 'So . . . you're determined to bankrupt us by throwing all our funds away.'

Kellanved leaned back, knitted his fingers before his chin. 'Those shells? Faugh! Useless to us. But the Napans . . . invaluable. And we must have a ship.'

'If you can call it that,' Dancer muttered into his glass.

'Come, come! These Napans are great sailors. They'll have it shipshape in no time at all. In two shakes of a lamb's tail.'

'Tell them that.'

'No, you will.' He slapped his hands together. 'Now I must prepare for tomorrow.'

Dancer set down the glass. Great – he got to deliver the happy news. 'Tomorrow then.'

Kellanved nodded absently, his thoughts already elsewhere.

*

Tattersail and Mock were having a private dinner in the hall; until recently such a thing was rather rare, as dinners were usually all-evening affairs where Mock and a raucous group of his select captains and officers would drink, trade stories, drink more, fight drunken duels, make up, and end up singing drinking songs long into the predawn light.

Tattersail would always excuse herself early from these gatherings and retire to their quarters. But even there sleep would be hard to come as the echoes of their laughter and cheers would reach even into the bedchamber.

And so she'd put her foot down with Mock that every so often they would sit together for a civilized meal – just the two of them. And as usual he'd complied, kissing her hand, murmuring, 'What would he do without his Tattersail?'

This evening, despite definite orders from Tattersail that they were not to be disturbed, a liveried servant pushed open one leaf of the double doors, slid within, and approached. Currently, the livery consisted of bright purple velvet with gold trim, Mock having been very impressed by such a combination flaunted by a visiting foreign dignitary from some backwater in Genabackis lands.

Mock drained his sixth or seventh glass of wine and gave Sail an apologetic shrug, as if to say: *Matters of state, my dear.* For her part, she wished he didn't drink so much. Especially as it did his performance no favours in bed.

Mock addressed the servant. 'Yes?'

The lad extended a tube of horn, sealed with a dollop of bright blue wax. 'Message from Nap, m'lord. Just arrived by cutter.'

Mock's brows shot up. 'Ah!' He yanked it from the lad and waved him off. He examined the seal, squinting, then showed it to Tattersail. 'See that? Kings get to do things like that. They have rings for it, you know.'

'Yes, Mock.'

He broke the seal and drew out a small scroll of fine creamy vellum. Struggling rather, as he was only marginally literate, he read the message it contained. Then he let out a great laugh, slapping the page, and regarded her, winking. 'There you go! Brother regent he calls me! He proposes a joint raid to seal our pact. A dawn raid on Cawn – at the equinox.'

Sail mentally did the maths. 'That's in four – no, five weeks' time.'

Mock nodded. 'He's obviously granting us time to refit and prepare.'

Yes, Sail reflected sourly – the emissary must have seen the sad state of the men-o-war. 'Do you trust him?' she asked.

Mock was pouring himself a fresh glass. 'Trust him? He's a king! He has to be good to his word. It's all reputation, you understand.'

'I understand *that*,' she answered, insulted. 'What I mean is . . . what if it's a trick? A ploy to draw you out.'

'A ploy?' He lowered the glass from his mouth, regarded her in the manner that irritated her so – as if she were a child. 'Tattersail, dear. You heard the stories of the civil war that raged across Nap. The capital burned. Entire fleets scuttled in defiance of his rule! He's weakened.' Mock threw out his arms expansively, as if aggrieved. 'He obviously can't pull off a raid like this alone and is proposing cooperation as a demonstration of faith. Plus,' and he tossed back his glass, 'he knows I want revenge on those damned Cawnese merchants.'

'Exactly . . .' Sail muttered. It still troubled her; and yet, did one not have to take risks to make any advances? And was she not considering a raid herself? 'Well,' she answered grudgingly, 'I would prefer it if it were us alone.'

Mock smoothed his long moustaches, grinning. 'Of course, dearest. And you will be there to keep any eye on them. Any sign of treachery and they're yours.'

She narrowed her gaze. 'And you as well, yes?'

The proposal seemed to have caught him unprepared. He sat back, threw an arm over the rear of his chair. 'Well . . . it will take all vessels and captains. There will be none to spare. And Tarel himself will not be accompanying his force, I assure you of that!'

'Then you will outshine him.'

The idea obviously pleased Mock. His smile grew, and he nodded, stroking his moustaches once more.

At that moment there came shouts from the doorway. Some sort of scuffle. Tattersail thought she heard something about not being put off.

Mock yelled down the length of the main hall in a very un-kinglike manner: 'What is it, dammit!'

One leaf of the double doors opened and the same liveried servant slipped in. With him came the shout, 'The puffed-up bastard better see me!'

Mock rolled his eyes. 'Is that you, Geffen?' He waved for the servant to admit him. The lad spoke to the guards and moments later a tall lean fellow was admitted, straightening his shirts and belt where weapons had obviously been yanked away.

Sail eyed the glowering fellow. So this was Geffen, Mock's man in town. She'd heard he'd been having trouble lately from a gang of Napans who were stranded there.

Mock refilled his glass, peered down at the man. 'What is it, Geffen,' he stated in a deliberately flat tone.

'Come to warn you.'

'Whatever for?'

'About these damned Napans—'

Mock cut him off. 'Not again. I've told you – if you can't handle things then that's your lookout.'

The scars that traced the fellow's face like a latticework grew white as his features darkened, and he glared near murder. Tattersail was almost tempted to raise her Warren.

'Not them,' he grated. 'The two they work for. One's a pro from the mainland. A trained killer. My boys can't handle him. The other's a godsdamned mage. And he's one scary practitioner. None of the local talent will go near him.'

Tattersail almost laughed aloud at that patent exaggeration.

Mock sipped his wine. 'So what is all this to me?'

'I can't tackle a mage. But you can.' He pointed to Tattersail. 'Send her down to blast them to Hood's teeth.'

Mock crooked a brow, grinning. 'Really?' He looked across to her. 'Tattersail, dear. Do I *send* you anywhere?'

She peered down at Geffen, making no effort to conceal her disgust. 'I *choose* to use my talents to support Mock. And I strike only ships. I don't murder people in the streets. Especially not on the say-so of some lowlife criminal.'

'Guess I'm just the wrong lowlife criminal, then. Listen, dearie, sailors die when those ships go down, don't fool yourself.' He returned his attention to Mock. 'If you won't help me, then I'll help myself. I'm sending word for a professional from the mainland. Someone to take them down. Just so you know. You brought this about.'

Mock waved him off. 'Hardly. And don't come back here again, Gef. I don't consort with your kind.'

'You don't shit gold, Mock. I knew you when you was a no-good backstabbing murderer yourself.'

Mock sent a pained smile to Tattersail. 'I'm a freebooter,' he answered. 'If I killed anyone it was on the high seas with swords crossed in battle.'

Geffen snorted his derision and turned on his heel.

'Nothing public!' Mock shouted after him down the hall. 'Don't scare off the merchants!'

Tattersail eyed him rather narrowly, and he cleared his throat, his mood obviously broken. He lifted the glass, saluting her, and downed the last of its contents. 'Well . . . preparations. We must refit the men-o-war.' He rose to his feet, unsteady. 'So, celebrations in honour of this pact, hm? I shall await you in my chambers, yes?'

She nodded, smiling. 'Yes. You go ahead, dearest. I'll join you shortly.'

He answered her smile, smoothing his moustaches, and headed to the stairs, staggering slightly. Tattersail knew that by the time she joined him he'd be dead asleep. She sat in silence, considering Geffen's harsh words. It was true, no doubt, that some sailors died when their vessels broke apart – but that was anyone's risk in joining battle. She'd never deliberately killed anyone. And it was something she didn't think she could ever bring herself to do.

She eyed her rosewater tea, cold now. Well, if all went as planned she wouldn't have to worry about such things again. She wouldn't have to get her hands dirty at all. There would be others to order about for that.

Brother regent, Tarel had named Mock, apparently. Hollow flattery? Then again, wasn't the story that the man had murdered his own sister to come to power?

She did not like that. No, not at all.

*   *   *

Tayschrenn walked the lightless tunnels of the deepness far beneath the Temple of D'rek's lowest halls. He walked with his powers raised to their utmost sizzling heights, his hands clasped firmly behind his back, barely aware of his surroundings, his senses cast far off in a maze of power conjunctions and interstices that wove and danced between the walls of the Warrens themselves. He did this offhandedly, though he'd heard that maintaining such a pitch of strength and focus was a feat rather difficult for other mages.

He knew such research was forbidden, touching as it did upon other Warrens – Thyr especially, but Rashan and others as well. He sensed underlying truths, however, and would pursue them wherever they may lead. And, recently, such hints had been drawing him ever closer to the half-forgotten ancient figure of K'rul.

So he walked the night-dark tunnels, sensing, briefly, the far deeper murmurations of Burn herself within D'riss, and the accompanying soothing rhythms of D'rek.

Starved of light, his eyes came to play tricks upon him, and so he was dismissive at first of one particular weaving spark of illumination as it seemed to draw near. Eventually, however, the spark resolved into a flickering golden flame and he was startled to realize that someone was holding it upright as they came.

He stopped, as did the newcomer. He studied the person as one might interrogate a mirage. Female, near his age, a far lower-ranked priestess unfamiliar to him, holding a torch and carrying a small iron box under one arm.

She bowed to him, murmuring, 'Tayschrenn.'

He answered the bow. 'Priestess.'

The resins and pitch of the torch popped and hissed between them, unnaturally loud in the utter silence. The torch he understood; and after a moment, the box as well. Many were the annual rituals and observations that the cult of D'rek was required to perform, and this box must be concerned with one such. Few knew the list of all the duties. Perhaps the box held an item that had to be replenished, or a scroll to be read in a certain location, or some offering to be made at a certain day and time. Or, some whispered, unmentionable food for *things* that had to be fed.

The priestess bowed again, murmured, 'My condolences,' and continued on her way.

He turned after her, his brows crimping. 'I'm sorry – did you say "condolences"?'

She stopped, turned as well. 'Oh. I am sorry. I thought you knew. Our guiding light, Lord Demidrek Ithell, passed on not two days ago.'

'Ah – I see. No, I did not know. Thank you for informing me.'

The priestess bowed again, then went away down the tunnel.

Tayschrenn watched the sputtering flame of her torch diminish into the distance, turn an unseen corner, and be swallowed by the dark. He searched his emotions. He knew that the man's death had been close, was inevitable, and that he should rejoice now that D'rek had taken him to her breast. Yet he was saddened. The man had been a kind spirit. Had shown him great generosity and patience. Had been the closest thing he could consider to a father, given that he possessed no memories of his life prior to his abandonment to the streets. Turning, he quickened his pace and headed to the nearest route up.

He found the main halls of the temple complex given over to the requisite mourning. Candles burned at every intersection and those ranked of the black all walked with cowls raised, heads bowed in prayer. Incantation and whispered songs of veneration murmured through the halls.

He headed for the Demidrek's private quarters to offer his services, should there be anything to be done.

Here he found his way barred by a lower-ranked priest, one Feneresh, of no particular talent save a rigid unimaginative devotion to the rules and procedural minutiae of the cult.

'Tayschrenn,' the younger man greeted him. 'What is your business?'

He was rather taken aback by the blunt words, but collected himself. 'I offer my services, of course, should they be required.'

The fellow inclined his shaven head in acknowledgement, his thin lips pursing. 'All is taken care of. You need not concern yourself.'

'I see. Well, may I kneel before our Demidrek and offer my prayers?'

'The remains have been removed for interment. You are free to pray before the icons of the Demidreks in the temple proper, of course.'

Tayschrenn tried to peer in past the shorter fellow to the private quarters beyond, but all was shrouded in darkness and low guttering candles. 'I see. Very well. My thanks, brother.'

'Of course. Glory be to D'rek.'

'Ah . . . yes.' He turned to go, but Feneresh cleared his throat and so he turned back. 'Yes?'

The priest pointed to his waist. 'Your honorary rank has been rescinded, of course.'

Tayschrenn frowned, confused for a moment, then realization came and he started. 'Oh! Of course.' He unwrapped the crimson sash and handed it over. Feneresh folded the cloth and tucked it away.

Tayschrenn bowed his farewell and turned to leave, but the

younger priest cleared his throat once more. He swung back, rather vexed now. 'What is it?'

Feneresh tapped a finger to his cowl. Tayschrenn frowned again, but suddenly understood and offered a stiff smile. He threw up his cowl and marched off.

Twice in his life Tayschrenn had experienced the terror of earthquakes when the very rock shook beneath one's feet and was revealed as unreliable, even deceptive. And as he walked the dim halls to his cell it struck him as odd that although this time the rock had not moved, he felt just as shaken. Just as in an earthquake, a blow had struck unlooked for and sudden, and he felt knocked sideways, strangely unsure of everything.

He needed to find his centre once more. He needed to meditate. Most of all, he needed to consider why his hands were fists hidden within his robes, why his pulse was a painful pressure at his temples and his breath short and laboured – and why he, a priest, was boiling with rage.

Three days later Tayschrenn was once more sitting in the Great Hall of the temple, a bowl of thin vegetable broth and a crust of dry bread before him. He'd studiously avoided the hall these last few days, but a General Assembly had been called and so he felt obliged to attend. The broad cavernous chamber was now more jammed than he had ever seen it.

An air of expectancy permeated the crowd, and whispered rumours of what was to come made the rounds. As a high-ranking priest, he'd been asked what he thought; his answer that such speculation was a waste of time as they'd know shortly had effectively silenced his interlocutors.

The benches were uncomfortably packed, but another newcomer was pressing in next to him and he felt a hand upon his arm. He looked up to see Silla. Sitting, she squeezed his hand. 'I'm sorry, Tay. I know you were very close to him.'

He nodded. 'Thank you.'

The murmuring and talk faded away as the Council of Elders filed into the hall. With them came Tallow, looking like a bull among a line of thin doddering storks and ragged dusty crows. His place near the centre of the front table troubled Tayschrenn. Normally, a visiting official or dignitary would be seated at one end.

Lukathera-amil rose to speak. She was Hengan, one of the dusty dishevelled crows. She was well liked, known affectionately as Luka among the lower ranks. She raised her arms for silence, though the hall was now utterly quiet.

'Kindred,' she began, her rough voice thin and dry, 'we are gathered here this eve to underscore and reaffirm one of the guiding principles of D'rek – that of continuity and reiteration. The eternal reprise and return of life and death.'

Her fellow elders banged upon the table in affirmation and the audience applauded – though quietly, and respectfully, as was proper.

Luka bowed her head for a time, then continued, 'Though we have lost one dear to our hearts, he is not gone. He is gathered to the breast of D'rek, and for this we must rejoice. We, each of us, may look forward to being reunited with him together with all of the righteous at the side of D'rek when our time, too, shall come.

'In this time of testing, we are blessed to have among us – due to the wisdom of the Synod of Temples – brother Tallow.' She motioned towards him and he rose, bowed, then sat down again. 'He has graciously agreed to serve as interim high priest and Demidrek until we, the Council, have chosen Ithell's successor.'

The assembly applauded again, respectfully. The elders of the Council joined the applause, their quavering hands soundlessly tapping.

Luka raised her arms once more. 'That is all. Now, let us bow our heads in prayer and thanksgiving.' She lowered her head.

Tayschrenn joined in, of course, but search as he might among his thoughts he could not find any single thing to be thankful for. He prayed instead for wisdom among the Council, for the idea of Tallow as temporary Demidrek troubled him. Why couldn't they simply have chosen someone and be done with it?

Later, during the meal, Silla whispered to him once more, 'You're not wearing your red?'

'It was taken from me.'

'Oh – I'm sorry.'

'It matters not.' He paused, considering, then asked, 'What do you think of this Tallow as temporary high priest?'

She frowned, as serious as ever regarding temple business. 'Well . . . it is good to have someone responsible in the interim. Things need to continue while the Council deliberates. And at least he's younger and vital, more energetic. He has made quite an impression here with his decisiveness.'

'Decisive. Well, I suppose he is that.'

Her gaze narrowed upon him. 'You are not so sanguine?'

He could not tell her of the man's words and actions in regard to himself, and so he merely shrugged. 'It makes me uneasy . . . an outsider taking charge of the temple.'

She looked at her own bowl of thin broth. 'He's hardly taking *charge*, Tay. It's a temporary posting only. And as to being an outsider – well, he's the Invigilator. A trained investigator of the cult.'

He smiled thinly, for her benefit. 'Of course.'

Chapter 7

WORD CAME TO DANCER VIA THE TALL AND RATHER DOUR Napan, Tocaras, that Kellanved was ready. He still had trouble using the fellow's new name, even though he was quite certain that Wu hadn't been the lad's real name to begin with, anyway, so it hardly mattered. He was almost ready himself. He wrapped the remainder of his equipment in leather, slipped it under a loose floorboard, then went up to the office.

The mage had a set of saddlebags over one shoulder, his walking stick planted before him. Dancer had armed himself with his best weapons and tools. His baldrics under his loose cloak hung heavy with sheathed blades. Rope and wire lay coiled about him, and he carried an emergency pouch of dried food and a goatskin of water.

Kellanved nodded. 'Very good. Let us go, then.'

A new thought occurred to Dancer and he raised a hand for a pause. 'One moment.' The Dal Hon mage, in his constant glamour of a wrinkled old man, sighed and tapped the walking stick on the floor.

Dancer returned downstairs. The burly swordsman Choss, one of Surly's lieutenants, sat at a table and Dancer asked, 'Surly?'

'Rear.'

Dancer crossed to the kitchen and pantries. He found her with the Crust brothers, taking stock. At least they claimed to be brothers; he could see no family resemblance beyond their blue skin. Cartheron was lean and short, while Urko was tall and as solid as an ox. Surly cast him one evaluative glance, raised a brow, and said, 'Going somewhere?'

'Exactly. You've noticed that W— Kellanved disappears sometimes.'

Surly did not appear pleased. 'So I've noticed.'

'Well, we're both going to be gone for a time. So you'll have to handle things until we return.'

She motioned the brothers out, waited for them to go, then crossed her arms, looking very like her name. 'Is there a time when we can expect you back?'

He considered this, wondering whether to tell her the truth, or to try to string her along with some not too distant date. But because he knew what he and Kellanved were facing, and held no misconceptions about their chances, he decided to be frank.

'I don't know. We may not come back at all.'

She raised a brow once again, perhaps impressed by his bluntness. 'I see. I'll keep that in mind.' She inclined her head, if not in gratitude, then perhaps in acknowledgement of the warning. 'Thank you.'

He answered her nod. 'Till later, then.'

'Yes. Later.'

He returned to the office to find Kellanved fighting with his pet nacht. The mage appeared to be attempting to force the monkey-like creature to perch on his shoulder, but the beast was on his back, had hold of the lad's short kinky hair and wouldn't let go. Round and round the desk they careered, Kellanved muttering curses under his breath, the creature baring its fangs in a grin.

'You ready?' Dancer asked.

Kellanved froze, then turned to face him, his features composed; the nacht, too, peering over his shoulder, suddenly looked innocent. 'Of course! What does it look like?'

'Like you're having some trouble with the help.'

'Nonsense!' He reached up and grasped the beast by the neck and yanked it from his back. 'Ha! Got you now.'

The creature reached to bite his arm and he let it fall, yanking his hands away. 'Now, now. Bad! Bad Demon.' The nacht clambered back up to the rafters, hissing what sounded eerily like laughter.

'I thought you were going to call it something else.'

'Many things come to mind, I assure you.'

'If you're finished?'

Kellanved sent the beast one last glare. 'Certainly.' He motioned Dancer closer. 'The shift should be smoother now.'

Dancer drew two blades and crouched into a ready stance. 'Very well.'

Scarves of murky darkness coalesced from the air about them, spinning and twisting, and for an instant his vision darkened. He blinked, squinting, weapons raised. Then a tilt in the surface sent him forward and something struck him a blow on the forehead. He staggered backwards in loose stones and gravel, falling.

The darkness slipped away. He lay on his back staring up at the leaden sky of Shadow. All about them stood a forest of tall cylinders, broken off at various heights.

Kellanved loomed into his vision, peering down, concerned. 'Sorry about that.'

Dancer jumped to his feet, rubbed the back of a hand to his forehead, slightly dizzy. 'It's fine. Never mind. What is this place? Ruins?'

'Of a kind. Take a look.'

Dancer examined the nearest column – it appeared to have been carved in the likeness of a tree, complete with scabs of bark. Yet the placement made no architectural sense. Towers rose everywhere, in no apparent straight lines.

Kellanved had started off across the hardscrabble rock pavement that lay between. Dancer followed, marvelling at the scale and insanity of the gargantuan site. 'Who would do this?' he asked. 'Do you know?'

'No one did,' the little mage answered, humming to himself once more and tapping his stick – a sure sign that he was pleased and at ease. 'What do they looked like?'

'They're made to look like trees. Perhaps these Edur we've heard of?'

'No. They *are* trees. I quite assure you.'

Walking between the countless trunks, Dancer couldn't quite bring himself to believe it. 'Real trees? Was it a curse? Who could possibly be so powerful? Anomandaris? Kilmandaros? Ancient K'rul?'

Kellanved waved his walking stick, chuckling. 'No, no. No one is that powerful – at least, so I hope and believe. No, scholars argue that this is natural. That if things are buried and remain inviolate for long enough, then they turn to stone.'

This made a kind of sense to Dancer. He grunted, saying, 'So, Burn's work then.'

Kellanved tilted his head to one side. 'Well. I *suppose* you could call it that.'

They passed through the boundary of the eerie silent forest to low dry hills, their tops carpeted in broken rock and brittle thorny brush. A heap of stones crowned a number of the rises – each a burial cairn, Kellanved explained. One had obviously been demolished, its stones scattered all down the hillside, and this one he approached. Dancer followed, wary, hands on blades.

The little mage stood staring down inside for a time, and, after scanning the surroundings, Dancer joined him.

The cairn held a half-revealed corpse. Tattered cloth and leather wrapped its bare white bones, the dry environment having preserved the coverings well. The bones looked nearly human to Dancer, though somewhat too robust. 'What are they?' he asked.

'Edur, I judge.'

'Did you . . .'

Kellanved shook his head. 'No.'

Dancer was relieved; not that he was overly superstitious. It just seemed . . . prudent . . . not to interfere in anything here until they understood the potential consequences.

A prickling brushed the back of his neck then, as of a faint awareness of *something*, and he spun, drawing his blades. There stood the man from the cairn – yet not him, less ragged in leathers, a spear straight at his side.

Kellanved turned, his brows rising, then bowed. 'Greetings.'

The man, or Edur – it was hard to tell since he was covered in dust and obviously dead – did not respond, and after a time Dancer sent Kellanved a questioning look. The mage signed for patience.

As if carried by the wind, or the brush of the sands over the stones, there came faint words. '*Disturb not the dead.*'

Kellanved bowed once more. 'We would not dream of it.' He waited for a response, tapping his fingertips together.

Once again, after a long silence: '*Disturb not the dead.*'

Now Kellanved sent Dancer a look of exasperation. He bowed his farewell to the figure and waved Dancer on.

Together they abandoned the hilltop, Dancer walking backwards, weapons still readied. He glanced away for a moment to make sure of his footing and when he looked back the figure was gone. 'A ghost?' he asked.

'We're all ghosts here. Shadows of pasts and futures.'

'I don't follow.'

'Emurlahn is broken, shattered. Perhaps one may think of it as a repository of all the shadows of everything past and future, now spilling over and jumbled.'

Dancer scratched his chin, thinking. Finally, he gave up. 'Sorry. Doesn't help one bit.'

Kellanved raised a brow at him. 'Really? I rather liked that one. Been working on it for a while.'

'Try again.'

'Critic.'

'Now, now. So, where's this gate?'

Kellanved raised the walking stick, pointing. 'Beyond those hills.'

'Couldn't you have got us a little closer, then?'

The mage eyed him for a time, as if wondering whether he was being serious or not. 'I don't *choose* where to appear, you know. Anyway, we have to make it there before—' He stopped himself.

'Before the hounds find us,' Dancer finished.

Wincing, Kellanved cast him a wary glance. 'Ah . . . yes. Before that.'

'Then we'd better hurry.'

They marched through the hills, passing more cairns and sand-choked scattered ruins. It struck Dancer that Shadow seemed nothing more than a gigantic mausoleum or trash heap of time and history. As if all the moments hidden by time in the world he'd left behind were all naked here, exposed and visible. Strangely enough, it made him rather sad to think of all that had been, or could have been.

He couldn't relax, however, and kept glancing back over his shoulder to a dark smear in the sky – a lazily flapping creature like no bird he knew of, which seemed to be following them, or, at the very least, going their way.

They passed between two hills to find the dark arch of the gateway ahead, still half buried in sand. To Dancer, the gnawed stones of its frame seemed weary beneath the weight of unknown ages upon it. Kellanved began rummaging in the saddlebags at his shoulder. Dancer peered round, waiting for the inevitable.

While Kellanved set to work, muttering to himself, or mouthing invocations, examining his drawings, and touching the stones in precise places, Dancer kept watch. Why, he wasn't certain, as there was nothing he could do in any case.

The Hood-blasted hounds remained a problem for them. Thinking about that, he probably should've brought a spear, like the one that ghost carried. He wanted to know Kellanved's ideas on their history and why they kept coming, but the fellow was busy. Were they guarding Shadow? Or were they just damned hungry?

The first thing that happened was that the flying thing came circling down to land on a nearby hilltop. Like a bat it was; dark, with broad leathery wings. But bore a long pointed beak more like a pelican. Dancer watched it and it watched them.

Then the distant baying reached him.

He switched to his set of heaviest parrying blades and readied himself, crouching. This was it. The confrontation he'd been dreading, and hoping he wouldn't really have to see through. To his surprise he found his mouth dry and his palms damp; no human opponent had ever raised such a reaction in him. Perhaps it was this damn waiting.

All he could do was to try to defend Kellanved to give the mage time to open the gate. Once it was open, they'd be gone.

'How's it going?' he asked over his shoulder.

Kellanved was too engrossed even to answer.

He edged forward a half-pace, shifting his feet into the sands for better footing. The creature on the hilltop seemed to settle down on to its haunches, perhaps to watch the show.

Bastard.

A dark brown hound appeared on another hilltop. Scars matted its short-haired hide and its eyes blazed a glacier blue. Spotting them, it let go another of the howls that so shook and froze its quarry. Then it came charging down the slope in a flurry of kicked-up sands.

Dancer knew there was no way he could counter such a charge, except for dodging. And that would leave Kellanved undefended.

There was nothing for it. He knelt even lower, leaning forward, blades held straight out before him.

Light burst over his shoulder and a sudden thrust of power pushed him a good two paces forward. The beast veered off, slamming to a halt, warily eyeing not Dancer, but something behind him. Dancer straightened, backing up. A deep thrumming of power now vibrated the sands beneath his feet and he called over it, 'Open?'

'Ah . . . nearly,' came the hesitant answer.

Oh, for the love of Oponn!

The beast had recovered from its surprise and was now edging forward, though still wary. Clearly it did not want to go bursting through a gate.

Dancer wove his blades, slashing at it, trying to force it back. Its haunches, he noted, came up almost to his own shoulders. It snapped at his blades as he slashed, but only half-heartedly; its attention, he noted, was fixed past his shoulder, on the gate beyond.

It was almost as if the creature was . . . fearful? No, not of the gate itself – of what might come through it.

Without taking his gaze from the massive beast, he called over his shoulder, 'Kellanved! Perhaps this thing was sealed for a reason . . . Maybe we shouldn't—'

'Ha! Got it!'

A blossoming of power pushed Dancer from behind like a giant's hand. The gigantic beast also flinched, snarling, down upon its forepaws. Dancer found himself eye to eye with the titanic thing. Its gaze was hot and lusting, but held more than just blind animal instinct; he thought he saw intelligence within the eyes. A kind of reasoning and cunning. Just what *were* these things?

A hand took hold of his collar, drew him backwards. He retreated, on guard, but the hound did not press its advantage; it appeared content to allow them to go – so long as they were leaving.

Plain guardians then? Set upon the borders? Or just fiercely territorial? Would he ever understand this mystery?

'This way,' Kellanved shouted. His words were almost drowned out by the steady deep waterfall thrumming. Dancer dared one quick glimpse over his shoulder and saw that the gate was indeed active now: its centre was cloudy, opaque. He could no longer see through it.

'What now?' he shouted back.

'We, ah, jump through, I suppose.'

'You don't know?' he yelled. 'You're supposed to be the expert!'

'Well, I've never done anything like this before, have I!'

133

Dancer noted the hound's sky-blue eyes narrowing, its haunches lowering and tightening. It seemed that with no monster worthy of its respect emerging from the gate it was running out of patience.

'You go now,' he called. 'I'll cover.'

'Oh fine! Send me through first!'

Irritated beyond belief, Dancer almost turned his back on the crouched beast. '*Would you just go through now!*'

'Well, if you're going to be like that about it,' Kellanved sniffed.

The beast's rear claws now clenched at the sands for purchase. Dancer spun, saw Kellanved standing with hand on chin still studying the arch, and summarily planted a boot to his rear and pushed him through.

The mage's yelp of surprise and protest was cut off as he disappeared within the clouded milky opaqueness.

Dancer leapt after him even as he heard the jarring clash of teeth closing upon the air just behind.

*

The beast remained crouched before the gate for a time, jaws upon its forepaws, patient and waiting. Eventually, however, with nothing forthcoming, it lost interest – or another summoning beckoned – and it loped off across the hills, howling.

Watching from its hilltop, the night-dark creature threw open its broad wings and took flight. It wafted over the sullen feature-less skies of Shadow, scudding low across the landscape, until it found what it sought: a lone figure marking a solitary path through the barrens.

It landed before the scarecrow-thin walker, who came to a halt. To all appearances it resembled an ambulatory corpse. Mummified leather-like skin clung to wind- and sun-greyed bone peeping out behind rusted and tattered ancient armour. A single weapon hung at its waist, rusted and blunted.

The desiccated corpse tilted its eyeless face to regard the flying creature. After a time it asked in a breathless whisper, 'Yes?'

'Those poachers have returned,' the bat-like thing hissed, somehow conveying disapproval and impatience. 'They escaped the hounds.'

'So?'

It hopped on its tiny clawed feet, clearly agitated. 'They

are meddling! They have opened a gate into the Scarred Lands.'

'That is outside my purview.'

The creature fairly leapt into the air. '*What?* Purview? They trespass! Vandalize! Fall upon them and rend them bone from bone!'

'No.'

'No? It is what you do. None have defeated you! Exult in your supremacy, Edgewalker!'

'You have no idea what it is I do, Koro.'

'Faugh! Your passivity is infuriating! If you will not act then at least set Telorast and Curdle upon them.'

'No.'

'No?' the creature fairly squawked. 'No? Why ever not?'

'Because I do not want them eaten. Not yet, in any case.'

Koro hopped in animated circles. 'Bah! Do you guard or not?'

'I do – in my own manner.'

'Infuriating!' And Koro leapt into the air.

'Do not interfere,' the skeletal figure called after it. 'Save at my order.'

The creature flapped away, though its torn membranous wings did not appear in any way adequate to keep it aloft.

The desiccated corpse, Edgewalker, regarded the flat umber horizon in the direction of the gate to the Scarred Lands. It adjusted the hang of the sheathed sword at its side, dust sifting from the cracked leather belt, and continued its slow limping walk.

*

Dancer fell into what felt like a heap of ash. Sooty black dust that marked him like charcoal. To one side Kellanved sat coughing. Dancer stood and faced the gate, weapons raised.

'It will not pursue us,' Kellanved said, his voice hoarse.

'Why not?'

'I believe because it has not been summoned.'

'We didn't summon them before.'

Kellanved slapped the dust from his chest and sleeves. 'Oh, we did! By invoking Shadow.'

Dancer eased his stance. 'Ah. I see.' He turned a full circle. Gentle rolling hills all round, bare, wind-blown, with scarves of ash and dust masking the distances. 'Another garden spot you've managed to find for us. Why couldn't it be an orchard, or a vineyard?'

135

Kellanved tapped his walking stick in the dirt. 'Don't blame me. All this is the legacy of ancient war, violence, and curses.' He nodded to himself as he examined the blasted hillsides. 'Yes. Curses. They linger even now.'

'Are we safe?'

The little mage blinked, distracted. 'What? Safe? Oh yes. Provided nothing from the period that produced this desolation should find us.' He pointed his stick. 'This way, I believe.'

Dancer set off with him, though every direction appeared the same. 'How can you tell?'

Kellanved pointed. 'I sense something over there. Some sort of disruption. Something perhaps impinging into the Warren here.'

Dancer shoved his blades home in his baldrics. 'Well, let's hope it's not too much of a disruption.'

They walked on. Dancer had no idea how much time passed, or how far they'd travelled. All the landscape ran together into one indistinguishable wasteland of blackened earth and blowing ash and dust. It left a taste of acrid smoke in his mouth, stung his eyes, and tricked his ears with faint ghostly brushings and moans.

He wondered if the place was haunted and decided it probably was.

After a time something changed ahead; some sort of haze blurred the distant hillsides, as of a dust storm. It appeared to be heading their way, like a moving curtain of darkness.

The two men slowed, then halted. 'What is it?' Dancer asked.

'I do not know – but it isn't natural, I assure you of that.'

'Nothing here is natural.' He drew out a handkerchief and tied it over his lower face.

Kellanved watched, amused. 'It is not that sort of storm. It is like a storm among Warrens. We must be passing over a bizarre region.' Dancer glimpsed the faint rippling about him that betrayed his raised Warren.

Dust and sand now buffeted them and the Dal Hon frowned. 'This isn't normal.'

Dancer turned his back to the wind. 'Of course it isn't!'

Kellanved shielded his eyes. 'No. I mean it should be one or the other. Magical or natural – not both.'

'Both?'

'Yes. I—' He broke off, raised his hands to his face and stared at them. He looked to Dancer, his eyes huge with dread. 'Oh no . . .'

'What is it?' Dancer studied his own hands: dust coated them, a fine rust-red powder.

The little mage let out a wordless cry and staggered off into the shifting curtains of sand. Dancer chased after him, calling, 'What is it?'

Lightning crackled like enormous releases of static sparks. Shadows whipped about like wind-tossed scraps. Dancer glimpsed Kellanved at the centre of this weird storm. The mage was spinning, his arms thrown wide, and he appeared to be slowly rising. The tatters of shadow seemed to be either emerging from him or eating into him; Dancer couldn't tell which. 'What is it?' he yelled again, desperate.

A voice called from behind and Dancer spun; a stocky figure was advancing through the dust storm, one arm over his face, the other pointing past Dancer. 'Knock him out!' he bellowed. 'Take him down before he kills us all!'

Dancer charged Kellanved, drawing a heavy knife as he did so. The lad had risen so far Dancer had to leap to reach him; he swung, blade reversed, and smacked him across the back of the head. Kellanved fell in a heap, unconscious. Dancer pressed a hand to his neck – alive, but weak.

The winds began to drop. The choking sand and fine ochre-red dust came sifting down in great long hissing banners. Seven figures emerged from the murk, all with crossbows aimed. The man who had called to Dancer closed, drawing a rag from his face; he was sunburned and grimy, in dusty, scuffed, much-repaired leather armour. Dancer drew two weapons and stood over Kellanved.

'Alive, eh?' the newcomer grunted. 'Might as well finish him. Trust me, it would be a mercy.'

'What happened?'

The fellow pointed to Kellanved. 'He's a mage, hey? Had his Warren raised, right? Any fool knows better than to step on to the Otataral Desert with their Warren up. His mind's gone now. Best just to slit his throat.'

'Touch him and I'll kill you.'

The fellow considered Dancer for a time. 'Fine. But I ain't carrying him.' He gestured. 'This way.'

Dancer picked Kellanved up in his arms and headed in the indicated direction. The crossbowmen surrounded him while the spokesman followed. 'Where are we?' Dancer asked over his shoulder.

'I done just told you. The Otataral Desert.'

'Where's that?'

'Land of the Seven Holy Cities. Hearda that?'

'Yes, I've heard of it.' From what Dancer could remember of the rough geography he had been taught, the lands of the Seven Holy Cities lay far to the north of the Falari archipelago, which itself lay north of Quon Tali. They had somehow wandered – or been brought – very far indeed. He wondered how on earth they would ever return; especially if Kellanved's mind had been destroyed.

The party crossed several steep dunes, passed between cliffs of bare layered rock, and emerged on to a plateau hardpan. Ahead stood a ragged palisade of standing logs. 'What's this?' Dancer asked, rather disappointed.

'Welcome to Skullcup mine,' the guide announced, indicating a heavy gate set in the palisade.

'Really? What do you mine?'

The fellow's cracked lips crooked. 'A rare ore.'

The gate opened and Dancer was escorted through. He saw now that the palisade was huge, encompassing a large open-face pit. Far down at the base of the sloping sides, cave tunnels led off into darkness. Huts and barracks stood between the palisade and the pit edge.

'Do your friend a favour and leave him here,' his guide said. 'We'll give him a decent burial.'

'No. What's your name, anyway?'

'Call me Puller. Now, put your friend down and hand over all your gear.'

Dancer set Kellanved down and straightened, his hands loose at his sides. 'And if I don't?'

Puller glanced to the surrounding crossbowmen. 'Then we stick you fulla bolts and take it anyway.'

Dancer tilted his head to acknowledge the logic in that. He began unbuckling his baldrics. It broke his heart to have to hand over all his weapons, but he told himself he'd have them all back in a few days – when he escaped.

Having dropped all his own gear, he set to handing over Kellanved's. The saddlebags were gone already, lost in the storm. The men collected the gear, then Puller motioned him towards a narrow dirt ramp that ran down into the pit below. Dancer picked up Kellanved and headed down.

Before he reached the bottom a crowd had gathered at the base of the ramp. They were a ragged, malnourished bunch of older men and women; Dancer judged that he could take them all down if push came to shove.

One squat, muscular fellow pushed to the front. He jerked a thumb at Kellanved. 'What happened to him?'

'Had his Warren up when he landed here.'

Every man and woman facing Dancer winced. This fellow shook his bald sun-darkened head. 'Best to let him go, lad. Ain't no hope.'

'I'll keep watch over him. If you don't mind.'

The squat fellow rubbed a hand over his sweaty pate. 'Well, truth is, we do mind. We're labour here. Everyone has to make their quota in ore. No quota, no food. Understand?'

'I'll make it for both of us.'

The man snorted. 'No need to ruin your health. He'll be dead in a few days, I guarantee it. Or he'll awaken with no mind at all.'

'That's my problem.'

The man's already slit eyes narrowed. 'See that it remains so. What's your name?'

'Dancer.' The fellow snorted his disbelief. 'Yours?'

The man gave a hungry, almost brutal grin. 'Call me Hairlock.'

Dancer glanced at the man's bald head, and snorted in turn. Then he hefted Kellanved, asking, 'Is there a hut or a cave we can use?'

The gathered men and women wandered off, too beaten down and starved to manage any sustained curiosity. Hairlock pointed to a wall of the pit where shallow alcoves had been carved from the soft rock, some of which were closed off by hanging flaps of tattered cloth. Dancer cast one last glance back up the ramp, thinking: *Sorry, Surly*, and made for the line of caves.

*   *   *

Cartheron, Surly, Urko and Shrift stood in a line at the edge of a pier and studied the *Twisted*. Seeing it up close, Cartheron was even more horrified by the ship's dilapidated state. Barnacles clung in a thick layer along the waterline.

'Look at this,' Urko announced. 'Proof that shit really does float.'

'It's not so bad,' Shrift objected.

'How so?'

'It's floating.'

Surly looked to Cartheron; he noted that she was being careful to mask her own reaction. 'You're in charge. I want it hauled up and repaired.'

Cartheron rubbed the back of his neck, almost wincing at the mountain of work ahead. 'We'll have to replace rotten planks, recaulk, recoat the hull, repair the decking, replace all the canvas . . . where's the coin going to come from for all that work?'

'We'll squeeze it out of our holdings.'

That will take some squeezing, Cartheron reflected. 'There could be trouble.'

'I don't care. This is our ticket off this wretched island. Fix it.'

'All right . . . I'll see about getting it hauled up.'

She turned to his brother. 'Urko, you and Shrift stand guard here day and night. I don't want anyone interfering.'

Urko grunted his assent. 'Well, they sure as the Abyss ain't gonna set fire to it.'

'See that they don't.' Surly walked off and Cartheron followed just far enough for some privacy.

'Any word from our erstwhile employers?'

She halted. 'No.'

'Any idea when they're comin' back?'

'No.' She hesitated, her thin lips compressed. Finally, she let out a breath, saying, 'They might not come back at all.'

Cartheron raised an eyebrow. 'Really? What in the world're they doing?'

'Judging from them? Either murdering someone or stealing something.'

Cartheron cleared his throat. 'Ah. I see. So, what do we do?'

'Just continue on and ignore them.'

He rubbed the back of his neck once more. 'Well, okay. But how do we know whether—'

'It doesn't matter,' she cut in. 'Just do what you have to do.' And she left him.

He watched her go and slowly shook his head. Everyone else might be relaxing their attitude towards rank now that they were so far from the Napan palace, but, understandably, it was much harder for her. He returned to his brother who was still studying the vessel, hand on chin.

'I don't want to be seen on this piece of crap,' Urko finally announced.

'Wear a hat,' Shrift suggested.

'We'll need a team of horses to haul this up,' Cartheron said neutrally.

'No horses on this island,' Urko grumbled.

'Donkeys, then. Or asses.'

'Plenty of them about.'

Shrift choked out a laugh then leapt round, drawing her sword and eyeing the piled cargo behind them.

Urko and Cartheron shifted, wary. 'What is it?' Urko asked.

'Thought I heard something . . .' She edged towards the heaped barrels, rope-tied bales of provender, and great wide-bellied baskets woven of sisal. 'In here!' she yelled, kicking a barrel.

A hairy creature exploded from the barrel, making Shrift scream in surprise. Urko cursed, ducking, and Cartheron flinched away. The thing bounded to the side of the pier and in an instant was up and over the side of the *Twisted*.

'What was *that*?' Shrift gasped, a hand at her throat.

'No idea,' Urko supplied; then he studied her. 'Did you just actually scream?'

'Shut up! It surprised me, okay?'

Cartheron was scratching his chin. 'I think I saw that beast hanging round our employer's quarters.'

Shrift's eyes widened. 'You mean like a familiar? A daemon of some kind?'

'Maybe.'

The woman pulled up an amulet that was hanging round her neck and pressed it to her forehead in a warding gesture against evil and ill-luck.

Urko just snorted. 'Looks like our employer's claimed his property.'

Privately, Cartheron agreed. 'Let's keep up the story that it's haunted – that'll keep everyone away.'

'But it is haunted,' Shrift said.

Cartheron rubbed his forehead in exasperation. 'I told you . . .'

She was shaking her head, her hand gripping and regripping

the worn leather handle of her longsword. 'No way – that ship's cursed. Plain as day.'

He threw out his arms. 'Fine. Whatever. Doesn't matter.'

'Matters to me,' Shrift muttered under her breath. Urko nodded his agreement.

Cartheron waved them off. 'Let's go. I have to find some asses – other than you two.'

Walking ahead of them, he heard Urko say to Shrift, 'Lots of asses on this island.'

'I'll say,' she answered. 'They've overrun the place.'

* * *

The island of Seven Ruins south of the peninsula that arched from the horn of the continent of Genabackis didn't have a permanent settlement in the usual sense. Its one town wasn't truly a functioning community; just a collection of huts and shacks atop cliffs above a set of piers which serviced the deep-water harbour that was the real reason anyone ever stopped at Seven Ruins.

Which was widely known to be the second most haunted island in the region.

Lars Jindrift was sitting in the one open tavern, Funal's the Full Sail, when the stranger entered. He heard him before he entered: he didn't walk like any other resident or visitor to the island. His footsteps were slow, heavy, and firm, quite unlike the drunken stagger or wary beaten-down shuffle of most of those who found their way here.

Such as himself. Though it was all the fault of that laughing minx. How was he to know she'd survive like that? She shouldn't have been out alone; it was all her damned fault for trying to yell for help – and for leading him on, of course.

This newcomer, however, trod the dry boards with firm and heavy conviction. When he entered everyone looked up: everyone being Lars; the innkeep, Funal; seven crew members from the three corsair vessels that happened to be laying over for repairs and supplies; and the notorious murderer, Shorty Bower.

The stranger – a great novelty on Seven Ruins Island in itself – was an old man with a lean face ravaged by age and scars. His hair and beard were long and ragged, and iron-grey. Even his eyes shone a sort of pale pewter. But most arresting was his habit; from some ancient hoard or pit the fellow had got hold of the most archaic armour imaginable. A long coat of fine-mesh mail covered him, dragging in ragged ends to the floor, where armoured boots peeped out. The cuffs likewise draped down over his wiry age-crooked hands.

A ridiculously huge two-handed chunk of iron at his side completed the costume.

Everyone stared at the apparition.

Lars was wondering: *Where'd he come from?* No other vessel had dropped anchor in days.

The fellow studied the room and everyone present, then looked to Funal and mimed raising a drink to his mouth. Funal blinked as he recovered from his astonishment and drew a stoneware mug of ale. The fellow's face almost lost its scowl as he drank it down. He handed the mug back to Funal, and, in a clash of rustling mail and articulating iron boots, he approached the main table where most of the sailors were seated. They all peered up at him, curious.

'I require transportation off this island,' he said in a thick, strange accent.

The corsairs exchanged amused glances. One cleared his throat, sitting back, 'We're not a ferry service, old man.'

'I will pay.'

The corsair's lips twisted up in a half-sneer. 'As I said – we are not for hire.'

The newcomer dug at his belt and came away with a leather pouch, which he held out over the table and upended. A glittering cascade of flashing rubies, emeralds and sapphires fell bouncing and clattering across the table in a display of the greatest treasure hoard Lars had ever seen or expected to see. Everyone in the alehouse stared, completely frozen, open-mouthed, enthralled.

'All this goes to the vessel which transports me,' said the man.

Torreth, of the *Bright Spear*, slid his narrowed gaze over to Grace of the *Striker*, who dropped a hand down to the horn-handled knife at her belt.

Patch of the *Tempest* suddenly swept a hand across the table in an effort to snatch up a swath of the gems. Dim of the *Striker* slammed a knife through Patch's hand, pinning it to the table. Grace slashed at Torreth but he blocked her arm then grasped her throat. Patch yanked the blade from his hand and thrust at Dim who threw himself back so violently that he toppled backwards. Stinkfoot of the *Bright Spear* kicked him in the head.

Meanwhile, Shorty Bower, being a wanted murderer, had obviously reasoned that the stranger must be filthy rich and so leapt on to his back and attempted to draw a knife across his throat. The stranger somehow snapped up a hand to block the slash, grasped Bower's arm, and in a display of astonishing strength tossed him across the room.

The table was kicked over, gems flying in a glittering rain, and the corsairs fell into a free-for-all, fists pummelling and knives slashing. Behind the bar, Funal, rightly blaming the stranger for the disturbance – or perhaps reasoning like Bower that he was damned rich – raised a crossbow and shot him.

The bolt glanced from the fine-mail coat; the stranger grunted, was knocked back a half-step, then closed on Funal, grasped his head, and slammed him face first down against the bar. Funal slid from sight behind the bar, leaving behind a bright red smear of blood.

Bower had somehow produced a long curved sword honed down to a sickle, what some might call a falchion, and came at the man, screaming. He was not notorious for nothing.

The fellow drew the comically huge two-handed blade at his side and proceeded to somehow parry Bower's frenzy of slashing, thrusting attacks. Lars was amazed that the man could move the gigantic bar of iron so deftly; but perhaps the widely spaced hands on its long grip gave him the leverage necessary.

Of the corsairs, Grace of the *Striker* and Tampoor of the *Tempest* now circled one another. Both bled from countless minor wounds; both panted, exhausted.

The stranger flicked his heavy blade in such a way that it drove Bower's falchion aside, then thrust. The archaic weapon actually held a point, and a good third of the iron was driven through the murderer's torso and out his back. Shorty fell to his knees. The man raised an armoured boot to his chest and pushed to yank the blade free.

Tampoor had a hand pressed to his neck, bright blood flowing between his fingers and down his forearm to drip from his elbow. He was slowing, every breath a gurgle. Grace stalked him, switching her blade from hand to hand as she closed, backing him into a corner. Trapped, his back up against a wall, he snarled a wet 'Damn you!' and lunged. Grace blocked his weak slash and thrust her blade home in his chest. He fell and she bent over him.

Lars stepped up behind Grace and, two-handed, slammed his long-knife into her back. She sagged on to Tampoor.

The stranger was cleaning his blade on Bower's clothes. Lars fell to his hands and knees and set to snatching up the gems. Wounded corsairs clutched at him for help but he slapped their weak efforts aside.

'With what vessel do you serve, sailor?' the stranger asked.

Lars thought quickly. 'With none at this time, lord. But I will negotiate with any of your choosing for passage. Which do you wish?'

'The most seaworthy.'

Lars rolled Torreth over to get at the gems beneath him. The man grasped at him with bloodied hands, but he pushed him aside. 'Ah, that would be the *Tempest*, lord.'

'Very good. You will secure passage for me.'

'At once.'

The fellow's armoured boots stamped the floorboards as he headed to the door. Lars scrambled round the bar, stepped over the dying Funal, and snatched up his cashbox. 'Coming, lord!' he called. Running, he caught up with the stranger and gestured ahead. 'This way.'

'I know the way,' the man answered, sounding amused.

Strangely, as they walked, Lars noted that the track of the fellow's incoming footsteps did not trace a route up from the waterfront as he had assumed. Rather, the distinctive trail led down from the island heights, which was strange as the only things up there were the ruins for which the island was named. There, so legend had it, had lain the capital and cenotaph of the ancient warlord who had terrorized all south Genabackis centuries ago. This island had been his fortress stronghold, and the ferocious cataclysms of those wars had given birth to the much-storied martial orders of Elingarth.

Far below, down the switchback trail that climbed the shore cliffs, lay the three corsair vessels anchored in the deep blue waters of the sheltered natural harbour.

'And where are you headed, great lord?' Lars asked, thinking of the astounding wealth now nestled down his shirt, hard and now warmed against his stomach. 'Elingarth? Darujhistan?'

145

The man lifted his lean, knife-sharp profile to the sky and frowned even harder behind his iron-grey moustache and long ragged beard. 'West,' he judged, eyeing that direction. 'Something happened in the west.'

Lars scampered along behind the man. 'Ah, yes, m'lord. And . . . your name?'

The fellow glanced back and stood still for some time, making Lars extremely uncomfortable with his eerie dead-eyed stare. Finally, he ground out, 'My name is Kallor. Does this mean anything to you?'

Lars shook his head. 'No, m'lord. Should it?'

The man slowly turned his head away and continued onward down the narrow rocky path. After a while, Lars heard him mutter, as if to himself, 'Time is the most merciless destroyer of all.'

Part Two

Chapter 8

THE RINGING CLASH OF A HAMMER AGAINST METAL THAT WAS the mine's alarm woke Dancer. He opened his eyes to harsh golden sunlight and lay for a time, already exhausted, his body aching, but eventually he had to rise as the heat of the coming day had already plastered his shirt to his chest. He swung his legs down from the stone ledge and checked on Kellanved.

The mage still slept, or lay insensate or lost in a coma; which of these, he wasn't certain. For days now no movement had stirred the lad's limbs, though his chest did rise and fall, if only as faintly as a bird's flutter. Dancer occasionally made an effort to remember him as someone of his own age, but this was becoming nearly impossible as even now the mage's seemingly permanent illusion of decrepitude remained. Everyone in the mine thought of him as a weakened ancient, and thus expected him to die; but Dancer knew otherwise and counted on the resiliency of youth to pull him through.

He took a gourd from the wall, unstoppered it, and gently poured a few drops of the precious water on to the lad's lips. The moisture disappeared, but was it even worth it? He was not allowed to draw an extra ration for Kellanved as the mage had done no work as yet. Dancer stoppered the gourd and pushed aside the ragged hanging of their alcove; the smothering promise of the day's heat almost drove him to his knees, yet he held on to the hacked stone, steadying himself. He glanced back to his insensate partner. How long could he possibly maintain this?

Yet if their positions were reversed, how long would he wish Kellanved to hope and to try?

For as long as was humanly possible. And infuriating as

Kellanved was, he had to grudgingly admit, with some surprise, that he was the best friend he had ever had. Perhaps the only, barring Illara.

He would not be the one to fail the partnership. And there was self-interest to consider as well, of course. If even half what he suspected the little mage was capable of came to pass, it could be well worth the investment.

Steeling himself, he set out to make it through another day. At this time in the morning the open pit of Skullcup was still mostly in shadow, yet this did nothing to spare its prisoners the heat of the surrounding desert. He headed to the barricaded hut that was the guard shack. Here he'd receive the day's work chit – a sliver of copper. No chit, no morning meal.

A line had already gathered. Dancer studied his fellow inmates. Seven Cities natives mostly; lean, not as tall as he, dark-haired, and tending towards a dark gold in hue as the sun beat down mercilessly in this place. Most, he understood, were condemned petty criminals, together with a smattering of transported mages and apostate priests. Some few were purely political prisoners, while he and a smattering of other outlanders were the contingent of trespassing foreigners.

An old woman with long scraggly dusty hair was in the line ahead of him and on impulse he asked, 'What did you do to deserve this?'

She glanced back, rather startled at being addressed, and then scowled. 'Nothing! This is all Yath's doing! I should be Holy Faladah! My interpretation of the Seven Holies is no less legitimate than theirs.' Then she pointedly turned her back on him – uninterested in foreigners, it would seem.

When he reached the barred window the chit was slid across to him and he then headed for the kitchen tents. The stabbing desert sun seemed to hammer his head and shoulders as he crossed the open ground and already sweat dripped down his back. To one side of the pit here lay pens of chickens and goats. Next to these were the night-soil gardens. Tending these were the soft assignments usually handed over to the eldest or most infirm of the inmates. Greybeards leaned on rakes and hoes, studying him with tired eyes as he passed, for he was an unusual exception among the population here. He had seen a third of the years of most; a fifth of some.

In this section of the pits a gleaming turquoise pool lapped up against the sheer north cliffs, and though everyone was as dry as a desert snake none touched that water, not even the animals. It lay glistening and unearthly clear, a constant invitation to parched throats and yearning stomachs, but undrinkable. For the water's eerie clarity betrayed its true character – alkaline death.

At the kitchen tents he received a clay bowl, a glop of mush, and a piece of rock-hard bread. Sometimes there was boiled meat, fish or sea-turtle, but word was the turtles were becoming more and more scarce.

He ate crouched in what slivers of shade he could find, then joined the line forming up in pairs for the day's assignments. When he reached the guards at the front of the line he was handed a long-handled hammer and his shoulders fell. The sledge again. Swinging the damned thing was killing him.

'Sorry, lad,' a gravelly voice croaked beside him, and he glanced over to see the squat and blunt-featured mage, Hairlock. Sweat already ran in rivulets down the man's bronzed bullet head.

The guard handed Hairlock a copper chisel and urged them along with a nod. Hairlock led the way up the maze of tunnels. Once they were far from the guards, he slowed, saying, 'No change in your friend's condition, hey?'

'No.'

Hairlock grunted his understanding. They walked the tight constricted tunnels until they reached the face of one side channel. Here the mage set the chisel to the rock and Dancer swung the sledge sideways – the tunnel was too low to allow an overhead swing.

Between ringing, deafening blows, Hairlock said, 'He won't recover, you know.'

Dancer, his teeth clenched with effort, answered, 'We'll see.'

'It's the dust. His mind, or spirit – what some call his kha – is disassociated. Lost. He's wandering the Warrens now as a ghost.'

'How does it work?'

'The dust?'

'Yes.'

'Well, no one knows for sure. It deadens magic. Suffocates it.'

A skinny grey-bearded elder who had been filling a woven basket with rock now straightened and approached them. 'Think of water,' he said.

151

Dancer hefted the sledge, thought of his own dusty-dry throat and croaked, 'I'd rather not.'

The fellow smiled indulgently. 'Water flows freely, yes? But when it freezes it holds its shape – understand? Some think the ore does this – freezes magic. Or metal. Molten it flows. Until it hardens. Otataral hardens it.'

'Thanks for the lecture, Eth'en,' Hairlock said, rolling his eyes.

Eth'en raised a bushy grey brow. 'This is an entire field of study, I'll have you know.'

Hairlock waved him away. 'Of that I have no damned doubt.'

The oldster picked up his basket and shuffled off. Hairlock watched him go. 'Scholars,' he sneered, derisive.

Dancer returned to hammering. After a few more blows, he asked, 'What is this place, then?'

The squat mage shrugged. 'Just a money-making enterprise. Privately held.'

'Not a prison?'

The mage eyed him for a time. 'Not as such. The Falari pirates who run it take whoever they're paid to hide away.'

'Like scholars and malcontents?'

A wide frog-like smile split the mage's face. 'Yeah. Kinda like that. Took two Holy Falah and one of the Seven City champions to bring me down. This is the only place that can hold people like me.'

'Mages.'

Hairlock grunted his agreement.

'A prison of mages.'

'And politicals 'n' thieves. 'Cept for the odd duck – like you.'

Dancer hefted the sledge over the crouching mage. 'Like me?'

Hairlock grinned up at him, revealing his greying rotten teeth. 'Been watching ya. This place can't hold you. Ain't built to. I figure your friend won't last much longer and you'll leave once he's gone.'

'So?'

'Take me with you.'

Dancer leaned on the sledge. 'Why should I do that?'

'You want to get off the island, don't ya?' He glanced about to make certain they were alone. 'I know where there're boats hidden.'

Dancer shook his head, disappointed. 'There are no boats here.

The supply boats arrive with food and water then leave with the ore, and that's that.'

'So the guards say. But I've been here a long time and I've heard things.'

Dancer returned to breaking rock. 'Such as?' he asked between blows.

'These islands, they're clan lands. Right now the Dosii claim them out of Dosin Pali. Every once in a while one of the Holy Falah gets his panties in a twist over the damned foreigners here and so they whip up their followers into delousing, if you know what I mean.' Dancer nodded his understanding. 'That's why they keep boats hidden nearby.'

'Okay. So why aren't you gone yet?'

'Can't do it m'self. Can't climb any wall. Can't sneak up on any guard. But you . . .' and he winked, grinning his ugly frog-grin, 'something of a speciality of yours, I'm guessing.'

Dancer said nothing. He continued hammering, though his arms burned as if afire. 'I won't go without my partner.'

Hairlock grunted, nodding. 'I c'n wait. Won't be long.'

The rest of the day Dancer worked in silence. When the dusk gongs sounded the end of shift, he shuffled back up the tunnels, deposited his sledge, and was given a new chit for the second meal.

He ate this in the alcove. His shoulders and arms twitched and he could barely raise his hand to his mouth. He kept a smear of the glop for Kellanved. This he pushed through the lad's lips, not knowing if he was swallowing or not. In the murk of the evening it appeared to him that the mage's form held a strange translucency, as if he were but an image, or shadow, of himself. He squinted, reaching out; touched the rough solid cloth of the lad's chest. He shook his head and collapsed on his own ledge to take the fitful rest of the exhausted and hungry.

A fist tapping on the rock nearby roused him. He raised his head. 'Yes?'

'Greetings. It is I, Eth'en. May I enter?'

Dancer swung his feet down. It was dark and desert-chill now; he draped his single blanket over his shoulders. 'Come in.'

The hanging cloth was brushed aside and the old fellow from the tunnels stepped through. 'Good evening. Pardon this intrusion. I was wondering if I might examine your friend?'

153

Dancer could not see why not. 'Go ahead. You know what you're looking at?'

'Indeed I do. I am of the Tano. A Spiritwalker – does this mean anything to you?'

Dancer shrugged. 'No.'

A wry smile touched the elder's lips. 'Thank you. You are a rebuke to the vain. You are quite right. There is no reason at all why you should know what it means.'

He turned his attention to Kellanved and Dancer saw his face change; his brows rose, surprised, and he withdrew his outstretched hand, as if wary. He raised his gaze and Dancer saw wonder in his yellowed bloodshot eyes. 'Please tell me . . . what were the circumstances of your friend's, ah, arrival here?'

Dancer explained.

Eth'en nodded. 'Yes. And this Warren – Rashan, I should guess?'

'No. Meanas.'

The Tano actually appeared shocked. He said, after a time, 'The Broken Realm. That is very unusual. So, he was walking you in through Shadow.'

Dancer considered, then shook his head. 'Not . . . really. We passed through a gate in Shadow.'

The Spiritwalker hissed out a breath and sat on one of the stone ledges. 'A *third* Realm? Describe it, please.'

Dancer shrugged again. 'It was dark and lifeless. Fields of ash – as if some sort of firestorm had passed through consuming everything.'

The elder pressed a hand to his forehead. 'The Moaning Plains?' he murmured wonderingly. He regarded Kellanved for a time. 'So . . . his spirit was stretched out across three Realms: ours, Shadow, and what some name the Scar. And then the Otataral took him . . .'

Eth'en sat back, raised his gaze to Dancer. 'There is a ritual we have among us Tano – a deadly test. If one is willing to risk one's essence, one's mind, one may walk out into the Otataral Desert and sing – summoning our version of the Warrens – and embrace the transformative powers of this ore. It is near suicide. But those few who return . . . they return *changed*. Able to do things none other can . . .' He looked away, his gaze far off. 'It lies at the root of our powers, you know. Our Spiritwalking.' He inclined his head

154

to Kellanved. 'They say delving into Meanas drives one insane. If your friend had already hardened his mind against its peculiarities, then when the Otataral struck . . . there is a chance.' He spread his hands.

'I see. Thank you.'

The elder rose, grunting, lifted the hanging, and turned. 'Do not abandon him. Even if you think him dead. There is a chance.'

Dancer nodded. He sat and stretched out his legs as if settling in for a long wait. 'We'll see.'

* * *

Horst Grethall, caravan-master, and merchant out of Ryns, of Itko Kan lands, was uncharacteristically optimistic this day as he watched the congregation of wagons and carts take shape at a traditional assembling field south of Li Heng.

Now that that city was once again open for business, goods from the west, specifically finer Quon and Tali products, were trickling in. And this was excellent for business, as the southern markets were screaming for Talian leatherwork, filigreed silver, and Quon liquors. So if all the pieces came together in their proper time, his might be one of the first of the larger caravans to arrive in Itko Kan bearing a supply of these oh so desirable goods.

And not only this; he also had reason to be optimistic regarding his security during the month-long journey south – regardless of rumoured bands of renegades from the dead king Chulalorn's shattered and beaten army, and opportunistic border raiders from Dal Hon – for he had acquired the services of the most sought-after caravanserai guard and fighting champion. She was a strange one, everyone agreed, but her reputation and skills were unimpeachable.

So he was in an almost cheerful mood as he walked the borders of the assembling field, seeking out old acquaintances and answering queries from his sons regarding marching orders, complaints, and disputes over fees. Veterans of his earlier crossings north and south across Kan lands wondered at this vision of a cheerful, near-carefree Horst, and they hoped he had not taken up smoking rustleaf, or d'bayang poppy.

It was near the end of the day when his youngest son came to

155

him with a report of one last wagon petitioning to join the caravan.

Horst waved the boy away. 'We're fat enough. That's why we're leaving tomorrow.'

'This fellow is quite insistent . . . and he looks like a competent swordsman.'

Horst shook his head. 'I have guards enough. I'm not running a charity for out of work soldiers.'

Sevall opened his hands. 'Well – he said he'll just follow along anyway . . .'

Horst stopped his walking inspection of the line, turned to his son and set his fists on his hips. He felt the heat of temper pushing up from his stomach. 'For the love of . . .' Then he reconsidered. He'd turned away three extended families hoping to travel south under the protection of his caravan: pale some of them had been, sweaty, with obvious fevers among the kids. Plague.

He knew they'd be quarantined before being allowed entry to Kan, but there was no sense inviting the damned sickness into the caravan before it even started. He and his were safe – he carried a poultice round his neck blessed at the waters of the Temple of Poliel – but strong hands were needed to lead all the wagons. He sighed. 'Fine. Let's have a look.' Sevall led him to the rear.

It was a garish red and gold oversized cart pulled by two horses – both of which looked healthy and well cared for, which was encouraging.

A single fellow stood before it in plain linen trousers and a long hanging shirt, his massed black hair unbound and loose, a long-sword at his side. And he was Dal Hon, or at least half so; this was not encouraging to Horst, who was only used to seeing Dal Honese at the opposite end of their hook-swords. He crossed his arms and looked the young fellow up and down.

'You wish to join?'

The youth inclined his head in a measured nod. 'I do.'

Horst gestured to the painted cart. 'What's this? The smallest bordello on the continent?'

'It is my grandmother. She intended a pilgrimage, but age has caught up with her and it is her last wish to be buried with her lineage on Malaz.'

Horst grunted at that; he'd seen many such aunts and dowagers on the pilgrimage trails. He pointed to the north. 'Why not take a riverboat? It's far quicker.'

The fellow shook his head. 'She has a dread of water.'

Now Horst frowned. 'Well . . . I'm sorry to be the one to give you the news, but Malaz is an island.'

A slight rise and fall of the fellow's enviably wide and muscular shoulders. 'A flagon of wine might be the answer to that.'

'It's the answer to all kinds of things,' Horst muttered. He nodded. 'Fine. But even if you can fight you still have to pay the shared protection fee – understood?'

'Agreed.'

'And my security chief has the last say.' He turned to Sevall. 'Get Shear.'

Sevall ran to summon her.

They waited. When Shear drew close Horst did not have to turn to look for it was obvious in the surprised expression and fixed attention of the newcomer. When he felt her at his side he turned to look up her slim lean figure to her tightly braided auburn hair, and of course the strange affectation of the brightly painted half-mask that covered her eyes.

Those eyes, mostly hidden behind the mask, were fixed upon the lad. Horst gestured to him. 'This fellow wishes to join his cart to the line. You demand approval of all additions. What do you say?'

She approached the newcomer, who, to his credit, did not laugh, or shrink, or give ground to this odd woman. In point of fact it was Horst who found himself becoming uneasy as Shear closed upon the young fellow until the two were nearly touching. Never had he seen anyone endure the strange outlander's gaze for so long – not even he, and he was her employer.

He was also struck by how similar the two appeared; both in loose unadorned trousers and shirts, both wiry and lean, he with a simple utilitarian longsword at his side, she with twinned equally plain and functional swords at hers.

After a rather uncomfortably long time Shear turned away, without lowering her gaze, and returned to Horst. As she passed, she gave the slightest nod of assent, and Horst found himself releasing a breath he wasn't aware he'd been holding. He clapped his hands together, rubbing them. 'Very good. We leave tomorrow. Your name?'

'Dassem, sir.'

'Sir? What do I look like? A damned Bloorian fop? That's Horst. Caravan-master to you. Your cart will bring up the rear.'

If the young lad was resentful of the order of march he did not show it; he remained oddly calm, tranquil beyond his years. Again Horst was struck by an odd similarity with the outlander swordswoman, Shear. She too projected a strange serenity – even when cutting outlaws in half.

* * *

The slight creak of the opening door woke Tayschrenn. His cell was the utter black of any subterranean unlit cave, yet his eyes, like the eyes of all those sworn to D'rek, could penetrate the gloom.

Recognizing the figure now slowly closing the unlockable door behind her, he said, wryly, 'This in an infraction of the rules, Silla.'

She turned, finger to her mouth. 'Shh! Quiet.' She sat next to him on the rope cot. 'You should go tomorrow,' she whispered. 'Tell no one. Just leave. Find a distant temple – any would welcome an adept of your rank.'

He smiled, quite amused. 'Whatever for?'

She peered round. The open fear in her eyes sobered him. 'Have you not been paying attention?'

'Attention to what?'

She raised her open hands, exasperated. 'To the questionings! The arrests! The disappearances.'

He shrugged. 'It is normal for any new regime to see to its security.'

Silla lowered her voice even further, fierce. 'All those being taken were close to Ithell. Don't you see it? He is working his way up to you!'

'Who?'

She squeezed her hands between her legs, lowering her head. 'Tallow – or his people.'

'Yet you welcomed him.'

'I did not expect this. He is the Invigilator! An authority in the cult . . .' She struggled to find the words, threw out her hands in frustration. 'Why? Why this? It isn't necessary!'

158

Tayschrenn dared to rest a hand on her shoulder. 'Perhaps it *is* cult business. Perhaps he is following his duty. Do not worry. I have nothing to fear. I've done nothing wrong.'

The look she gave him was one of incredible pity. 'Oh, Tay. You are so naïve. This is not about doing right or wrong, or following rules. This is about power.'

Feeling rather stung, he removed his hand. 'I happen to know a thing or two about power.'

She took his hand, squeezed it. 'Yes. I've heard all the stories. That when they awoke you to the Warrens the entire island shook. That all the elders combined could not master you even as a child. None dispute your might. What I am talking about is a different kind of power. Political power. Rulership. You are a threat to those in power now. Promise me you will go . . . please.'

He shook his head. 'No. I will not flee. That would be tantamount to an admission of guilt. I have done nothing wrong. I welcome any questioning. I will be exonerated.'

Her sad look remained. 'Oh, Tay . . . you think you cannot be touched. But you can. One day you'll see.' She pulled her hand away and he was surprised by how cold his own quickly felt. At the door she paused, whispering, 'I hope it will not break you when it happens.'

Two days later they came for him.

It was the middle of the night when four of the Invigilator's deputized special proctors came to his door to escort him to the courts. He offered them no resistance. They led him through empty, little-used tunnels and it soon became apparent that they were not taking him to the open general assembly hall, but to private chambers.

They sat him in a chair at the centre of an empty room lit by a few sullen candles and then withdrew. He assumed he was supposed to be nervous, his mind racing regarding what this was all about, growing more frantic as each moment passed, creating all sorts of fantastical scenarios of accusation and guilt. He waited instead with hands clasped and eyes shut, meditating.

After some time footsteps announced a visitor. He opened his eyes to see Tallow himself in the flickering gold candlelight and somehow he was not surprised in the least. The man wore a pained, saddened expression, and held his hands clasped behind his back.

'Tayschrenn . . .' The Invigilator sounded weary and regretful.

'Yes?' he interrupted, making an effort to appear especially attentive.

Tallow's thick lips compressed tightly for a moment before he continued, 'I want you to know that I personally do not wish to follow through with what has been ordered, but I am powerless before the will of the investigative council . . .'

'And these are?'

The heavy-set priest blinked, frowning. 'These are who?'

'The council. Which priests and priestesses are these?'

Tallow shook his gleaming bullet-shaped head. 'Tayschrenn . . . I am disappointed. Recriminations against the court will not help you now. It is too late for such games.'

'Games?' Tayschrenn repeated, one brow arched.

'Indeed. During questionings troubling facts and accusations regarding you have arisen. These all require further investigation. It is my unhappy duty to see to this.'

'Questioning . . . torture, you mean.'

'Determined interrogation,' Tallow corrected.

'And these accusations are?'

Tallow raised a hand. 'All in good time. More facts must be gathered. We must be thorough. Until then, please consider yourself under a sort of unofficial house arrest. More isolated quarters will be provided where you should reflect upon your past behaviour. Follow the proctors and please – do not cause any trouble.'

Tayschrenn understood that Tallow very much hoped he would cause trouble. Insubordination would make the man's job so very much easier. He decided, then, not to make any protest at all – not that he'd planned to in any case.

Tallow motioned and the four proctors emerged from the gloom. They now held staves and one pointed aside, inviting Tayschrenn that way. He rose, saying to Tallow, 'Until we meet in the temple courts for my hearing, then.'

A sideways humourless smile climbed the priest's lips, and of all that had unfolded or been said that evening, that smile was the only thing that made Tayschrenn uneasy. 'Until then.'

His new 'quarters' proved to be a cell close to the shore. So close in fact from the evidence of salt saints and damp that waves must splash in through its barred window during high tides. The proctors waved him in and closed the door, and he heard a lock being shut.

This must be one of the very few lockable rooms in the entire temple complex.

He sat on the cold stone ledge, its blankets rotting and stiff with dried salt. The flimsy door and simple lock were no barrier to him, and the sea beckoned as the waves came surging against the rocks just beneath.

They expect me to run, he realized, almost in disbelief. They *wanted* him to run. This cell was designed to lure him into fleeing. So close; so simple. And that would make Tallow's job so very easy, wouldn't it. Admission of guilt to any and all false accusations.

Well, he would not make Tallow's life easier.

He could outwait them, and endure anything they might invent. In his researches into the Warrens he'd stood before the vast emptiness of the Abyss itself, and faced entities that would blast the minds of any or all of these so-called masters.

There was nothing they could do to unnerve *him*.

No indeed. It would be they who would regret these actions. He would see to it.

And so he drew his sandalled feet up from the damp stone floor and crossed them, set his hands on his knees and settled into a course of deep meditation – to wait, to cleanse his mind – and to prepare.

* * *

A handful of the crew of the *Tempest* crouched together deep in the ship's hold and talked murder.

'Why sail onward?' asked Hela. 'He's one man, and rich! Let's toss him overboard and be on our way!'

'West, he says,' hissed Gudun. 'Like it's a stroll across the Deep. It's all the cap'n could do to convince him to head up the coast. I say we get rid a' him.'

'The isle of the Seguleh is close,' mused the mate, Wess. 'We could maroon him there.'

All broke out in gales of laughter at that suggestion. A bottle made the rounds.

'Then it's decided?' urged Hela. 'We take him down?'

Young Renalt of March raised a slim dagger, growling, 'Aye.'

Wess slapped the dagger aside. 'He wears a mail coat, y'fool.

161

How many crossbows 'n' such do we have in the armoury?'

'Enough,' answered Gudun, the quartermaster. 'And the cap'n?' he asked Wess.

'She'll go along or she'll be next.'

'What does Bonecutter Jute say?' Renalt asked of the group, and he gestured to where a grey-haired old man lay back against the planks, his eyes shut, a bottle clutched to his chest.

'Who cares what that old winesack has to say?' Hela snarled, but, glancing about, she saw frowns and uncertainty at her words among all those gathered and so she threw an arm out, inviting, 'Fine!'

Renalt jostled the old man's shoulder but it was not enough to rouse him. He cuffed him harder and the fellow snorted, smacking his lips, and blinking into wakefulness. 'More wine,' he croaked. Renalt tapped the bottle at his chest and he grunted, surprised and pleased, and took a swig.

'We're moving 'gainst this stranger,' said Renalt. 'What say you?'

The old man leaned forward, peered right and left, and cleared his throat. He raised a hand, finger poised, and said, 'Who?'

Hela blew out an angry breath. 'Our passenger, y'damned useless old soak!'

Bonecutter Jute nodded then, knowingly, and took another quick swig. He squinted up one eye and pressed the raised finger to his chin, thoughtfully.

The crowd waited silent and still while the old man considered. Finally, he unscrewed his eye and said, frowning, 'Who?'

All groaned their dismissal of the fellow; many suggested where he could put that damned finger of his. Wess eyed those gathered and told Gudun: 'Open the armoury.'

The crowd broke up, but Renalt remained with Bonecutter Jute. 'What is it?' he asked the old man. 'You're always soused, but not this bad.'

The oldster hugged the bottle like a floating timber in a storm. His eyes remained resolutely squinted shut. After a time, Renalt gave up and followed the others. Alone, Bonecutter Jute let out a long breath and raised the bottle. When nothing emerged from its mouth he frowned anew and returned to hugging it. Little beady eyes gleamed in the dark around him as rats came edging out of hiding. He whispered to them: 'I drink when I'm afeared. And I'm greatly afeared o' something.'

162

Above decks, Lars quickly opened the door to the ship's main cabin – the captain's, which the stranger had taken as his own – and locked it behind him. He immediately began coughing and blinking in a thick miasma of sweet-smelling fumes.

'Is there a fire, m'lord?' he gasped, rubbing his eyes.

'No,' came a low hoarse answer through the dense scarves of smoke. 'No fire. Why do you disturb me?'

He remembered his panic. 'The crew! They're coming for you – us! I was listening! We must get the captain behind us. Perhaps with his support we can turn some of the crew . . .'

A ghostly shape emerged from the smoke: the stranger adjusting his mail coat and hitching up his long leather weapon belt. Lars felt a strange shiver of preternatural fear at the sight, as if he were witnessing the visitation of some hungry revenant, or ancient spirit.

The stranger, Kallor, picked up a burning smudge, or candle – the source of the dense fumes – and extinguished it with his fingers. He set it aside, saying, 'That won't be necessary.' He asked, conversationally, while adjusting the set of his archaic, two-handed sword, 'What minimal crew – in your opinion – is necessary for the handling of this vessel?'

Lars blinked at the fellow. Had he gone mad? He stammered, 'Some forty, I should think, m'lord.'

The stranger raised his iron-grey brows in surprise. 'Forty? Really? You do not think that is an excessive number?' He stepped up to the door and Lars shifted out of his way; he grasped the latch, and turned to Lars. 'We could get by with twenty, do you not think? Now, let us go and face our assailants, yes?'

Lars could only swallow, utterly terrified. 'I will remain here and guard your possessions, if you do not mind?' He meant the man's riches, which he imagined must be hidden somewhere in the cabin.

'Suit yourself,' the fellow answered, shrugging, and he opened the door on to the darkness of the night and strode out, his armoured boots clanking on the wood decking.

Lars shut and locked the door behind him to stand panting, his mind racing: what to do, what to do? How could he ingratiate himself with the crew? Hang back and deliver the last blow to this Kallor's back and thereby win some credit? Or should he find and hide the riches? No, not that – they would only torture him to discover them then do away with him. He rocked in place, his hands at his own throat. How could he survive this? There must be a way!

Then he decided: side with the crew – it was the only possibility. He pressed an ear to the thin planks of the door, waiting for his chance. He heard voices in muted conversation: the lazy delivery of the stranger and the tense clipped demands of the crew's spokesman: the mate, no doubt.

An ear-shattering scream threw him away from the door and on to his back. The thump of multiple crossbows releasing punched the air. More screams – these now tinged with terror – and the stranger's armoured boots clomping as he marched about the deck. Panicked thumping of bare feet drummed the decking as well. Someone pounded the door, screaming, '*He's killing us all!*'

A length of bare iron punched through the door's planks, red-smeared, and withdrew with an ear-tearing screech. Whoever had been spitted on it sagged to the base of the door. The armoured boots clomped onward, slow and steady. Lars pushed open the door, shoving the corpse aside; was he too late already?

Outside, the deck was a heaving horror of sloshing blood and gore. Bodies rolled from side to side as the *Tempest* lolled, unmanned. A chill wash of watered blood and other fluids splashed over Lars' hands and knees as he crawled. Of the stranger he saw no sign; his hunt must have taken him below decks.

One sailor, female, sat back against the mizzen, a line firmly wrapped about one arm. She was alive, but slouched red with blood from a savage slash across her face down to white bone.

Another sailor sat against the side, hands pressed to his own face where blood streamed down his forearms to run into his lap.

He's marking them, the thought came to Lars. Marking the spared.

A new figure emerged from the companionway, tottering, unsteady. It was the *Tempest*'s old bonecutter and sometime sea-mage, whose name he couldn't recall. The old fellow walked hugging a jug to his chest, the wind whipping his long beard and grey hair. Seemingly oblivious of the charnel wreckage all about, he came stepping over corpses to pass close by.

Pausing, the oldster peered down at him, blinking his rheumy eyes. 'Ancient evil has returned,' he announced, and crossed to the side where, to Lars' disbelief and horror, he threw himself straight over the rail to disappear head over heels.

Lars wasn't certain, but he might have passed out for a moment after that. When he next looked up the stranger's gore-smeared armoured boots faced him and he raised his gaze up the long hanging mail coat, gleaming with others' blood, to the man himself, regarding him somewhat quizzically with his grey dead eyes.

The stranger cleaned his long blade by wiping it across the back of Lars' shirt. 'You can sail?' he asked.

Lars nodded frantically. 'Oh yes! Most certainly, lord.'

'Good. Join the others. All hands will be needed now, yes?'

Lars could not stop his manic nodding. 'Oh yes, lord.'

The stranger, Kallor, gestured to the sailor leaning up against the side, commanding him to approach. Blinking, near unconscious with pain and shock, the fellow levered himself up and shuffled to them through the wash of blood-stained water.

'You are mine,' the stranger told him. 'The Marked. Clean up the vessel then set course due west.' The sailor nodded miserably, both hands pressed to the savage gash across his face. 'Oh,' Kallor added, 'and do not toss the bodies over the side. The way is long and supplies are short. You may have need of them.' And he laughed, low and long, as he clomped his way to the cabin and shut the door behind him.

A cold rain began to fall from high clouds and Lars stood feeling the chill drops run down his face. He was beginning to wish that he hadn't taken those gems.

Chapter 9

THE TIME HAD FINALLY COME FOR HER TO VISIT HER . . . WELL . . . distant cousins. So far she'd avoided it, staying out of the city and keeping to the hillsides. Her needs were few: a small fire, a blanket against the chill. But she could delay no longer, even though the very idea of such a confrontation troubled her like few others. And so Nightchill steeled herself and walked down into the city of Malaz, heading for the waterfront.

She would have to be very careful; any escalation here could engulf the entire area in a conflagration of power that would scour the island down to the bare bones of its rock. Of course her . . . *cousins* had every reason to be suspicious of her approach. Over the ages they'd been attacked countless times by powers seeking the might, and the secrets, that they guarded.

Walking the empty rainy cobbled streets she reflected upon the many theories that had been suggested regarding their mysterious . . . withdrawal.

Some said they'd foreseen something; some event or arising so terrifying that they determined they needed to prepare for it. Others suggested mere greed: pig-headed hoarding of the most selfish kind. Of the true reason even she, one of their few remaining relations, had no idea.

They had withdrawn, turned within, and now none had any understanding of their motives or goals. For if the Azathani were regarded as strange and alien by the humans they now walked among, the Azath structures constituted an order far beyond even them.

She reached the marker in the physical world that denoted the edge of this one's chosen influence – a mere low wall of piled fieldstones – and paused, readying herself for the test to come. A test and a trial. For though she might be considered one of the mighty today, who knew how many of her fellows constituted this structure? Two? Or perhaps as many as ten?

She knew that should she be taken she might never escape, even in all remaining time. But she also knew that they took only those whom they deemed potential threats, those who they judged sought to take something from them. Such was not her intention. She wished only to speak with them – should they so choose.

Steeling herself, she pushed open the small gate and entered the unkempt grounds. Far underground – or so it appeared in this physical reality – figures writhed, imprisoned. Many reached out to her, imploring, begging her aid, but she was under no illusion; they sought to take her and restore themselves with her essence.

She walked the clear path to the front entrance and stood upon the wide iron-grey landing of a single broad sheet of slate. Then, respecting the conceit the Azath employed, she knocked upon the door.

Silence. Beyond the sizzling ropes of energy that kept so many enchained within the grounds, and their cries and curses, there rose the beating of the nearby surf, the waves murmuring against the stony shores, and beyond that, eerily, far out to sea past the Straits, came the crackling and booming of mountains of ice.

She shook herself, unsettled by the vision – was this a message from her brethren? Or mere chance? What was she to make of it? She brushed a hand across the thick planks of the door and sensed the guardian just behind, waiting. A mighty one, tensed, eager almost, waiting for her to raise her aspect against the house.

But she declined. She withdrew her hand. *Very well. Silent you have been over the ages, and silent you remain. Pursue your own ends and remain suspicious of others. It is earned. So many have sought to rip your secrets and your power from you. I will not.*

She waited a moment longer but heard nothing; no one or thing called to her, and so she turned away. Her back prickled all the way back up the walk.

Two figures awaited her outside the gate as she approached. The foremost was a huge bull of a fellow standing with a long spear tall at his side. The second was a short wiry fellow with his gaze all scrunched up, squinting at her.

167

'She is not taken,' this one informed his giant companion, who grunted, crossing his arms.

She opened the gate and faced them, asking calmly, 'You would dispute my passage?'

The squinting one gave her a hard look out of the side of one bloodshot eye, then started, surprised, and promptly fell to one knee. He pulled his companion down with him by tugging on the man's trousers. 'Forgive us, m'lady,' he murmured.

'There is nothing to forgive – you are fulfilling your duties. But I am no threat.'

'As we see.' He rose, bowing. 'The House made no move against you . . . ?' he said, inviting an explanation.

'I kept to the path and did not stray.'

'Even so . . .'

She shrugged. 'It acts for its own reasons, does it not?'

'Indeed it does,' the man agreed, bowing again. 'Indeed it does.'

*

The two men – both known Malazan street toughs – sat propped up against one of the gigantic logs that supported the *Twisted*'s hull where it squatted on the shore. Cartheron passed a hand before their wild staring eyes and neither reacted. He looked at his brother.

'What happened?'

Urko rubbed the bristles over his chin and cheeks and let out a long breath. 'Don't know. Choss found them this way. I think they tried to do some mischief to the ship last night. Maybe start a fire or something.'

Cartheron leaned down to one and asked loudly, 'What happened?'

The wild rolling eyes lit for an instant upon his. The man mumbled, half-slurred, 'The thing . . . the terrible thing . . .'

'That's all they say,' Urko grunted, hand at his chin.

'Hunh. Can they walk?'

'Dunno.' Urko grabbed one's arm and pulled him upright. He stood, weaving only slightly.

'It . . .' the man whispered to Urko, the word fraught with some unknown meaning.

'Right. The thing.' He pulled the other upright.

Together the two now peered round, wringing their hands. Their gazes roved upwards and they started, staring. Both pointed up at the hull curving above and both screamed, utterly terrified, 'The *thing*!' And both bolted across the mud and scattered lumber of the strand, climbed the lip of a dilapidated boardwalk, and disappeared.

Cartheron looked at his brother then both examined the *Twisted*. Cartheron put his fist to his chin. 'You don't suppose that little bugger . . .'

Urko peered up as if searching the ship's side for any sign of a certain hairy beast, then shook his head. 'Naw. Couldn't be.'

Both scratched their chins, then edged away from the rearing hull of the *Twisted*. Clearing his throat, Cartheron asked, 'Do we have enough timber for planking?'

'No.'

'Enough rope?'

'Gods, no.'

'Do we at least have enough canvas?'

'Course not.'

Cartheron glared at his brother. 'Then what, pray tell, *have* we enough of – if anything?'

'Asses,' Urko supplied, taking a crisp bite of apple. 'Got plenty of them. Up to our asses in asses.'

'No kidding,' Cartheron muttered beneath his breath. 'Okay. So, why the shortage? Is it money?'

Urko shook his head, chewing. 'Naw. It's Mock – he's claimed everything for the refitting of *his* boats.'

Cartheron kicked up a clot of mud. 'Hood take it. Fine. I guess we'll just have to fall back on the usual.'

His brother sighed. 'Right. We steal it.'

A new figure came heading over from the boardwalk and it took a moment for Cartheron to recognize the man: the marine from the *Avarice*, Dujek. He motioned to his brother to indicate that the man was a friend. 'I didn't do it,' he called to Dujek, 'whatever it is.'

Dujek gave an answering grin. 'How can you say that? The kid looks just like you!'

Urko elbowed him. 'Quick work.'

Cartheron gave him a glare. 'Very funny. Dujek, Urko.' Both nodded. 'What can I do for ya?'

The marine rubbed a hand over his prematurely retreating hair, clearly a touch uncomfortable. 'Well, it ain't me. It's this new captain, Hess. He's hoppin' mad. Wants you on the *Avarice*.'

'He's got plenty of hands. What does he need with me?'

'Don't know. But he's in a temper.'

Cartheron looked to the sky. 'For the love of Poliel . . .'

'I thought you resigned that berth,' Urko said. 'We've got the *Twisted*.'

Cartheron scratched his head, thinking. 'Surly says we need the prize shares. The *Twisted*'s going nowhere right now.'

'But with—' His brother stopped himself, eyeing Dujek.

The marine took the hint and touched his brow. 'See you on the *Avarice*?'

Cartheron gave the man a nod. 'Yeah. See you there.'

The burly marine headed off; Cartheron turned to his brother. 'So?'

'Well, with the jokers gone we can push off, right?'

The jokers – their erstwhile bosses. It had been more than a fortnight now with no reappearance. It was looking as though Surly was right; they'd failed in whatever scheme they'd been attempting. He nodded again. 'So?'

'So, me 'n' the crew, we've been talking. We think Falari's the answer.'

'I think you'll find that the Falarans pretty much have that sewn up.'

'We Napans can hold our own against them Falaran sailors!'

Cartheron raised his hands in surrender. 'Yes, yes. I mean, you know what everyone says – that the Falarans have Mael himself in their pocket. That no invasion of the peninsula has ever succeeded.'

His brother had spotted a stone in the mud and picked it up, and was now rubbing it, squinting at it through one eye. 'Well . . . it won't be no *invasion*. We'd just sneak in, all quiet like.'

Cartheron threw up his hands. 'Fine. Whatever. It's a thought. But in the meantime we need to get the *Twisted* fitted. Okay? So get on it. I have to go.' Urko popped the stone into his mouth and rolled it around there, then pulled it out and squinted at it anew. Cartheron felt his habitual impatience with his brother souring his stomach like acid. 'Right?' he asked.

Urko peered up, blinking. 'Yeah. Fine.' He waved him away.

Cartheron stormed off. *Gonna drive me to drink, he is.*

He found the *Avarice* a storm of activity, the deck piled high with lumber and nearly all hands busy helping the ship's full-time carpenter. Cartheron gritted his teeth, thinking what they could accomplish on the *Twisted* with a tenth of the equipment. He searched among the crew for the captain only to find him in his cabin, his booted feet up on a table. He saluted. 'Reporting for duty.'

Hess set down his glass of wine and looked him up and down, smoothing his long moustache. 'About damned time. The *Avarice* is your vessel, understood? I want you here sunup till sundown.'

'You have plenty of crew. I don't see what I—'

'Look over the rudder.'

'I'm sure the ship's carpenter is more familiar—'

'Hold yourself available for consultation, *steersman*.'

Cartheron clenched his lips against any comment, gave a curt nod. 'Very well, captain.'

Hess waved him off. 'You have your duties, sailor.'

Cartheron headed out to find Keren, the ship's carpenter.

Keren, known affectionately among all the crews as Fat Keren, as she possessed fine curves that all the male and some of the female sailors appreciated, was a damned fine carpenter. She just shook her head, hands on her wide hips. 'Got all the help I need, Cartheron.'

'And the rudder?'

'Wood's fine. Joins and tendons are tight. Tiller's worn but strong. All fine. Got worse problems elsewhere,' and she nodded aloft to the shrouds.

'Then why . . .'

Keren peered about right and left, then lowered her voice, 'Tryin' get your goat, is all.'

'Why?'

'Got the confidence of the crew, don't ya? Something he ain't got. Can't have any rivals, hey?'

Cartheron just looked to the sky. 'Oh, for the love of Beru.'

She gave a broad wink. 'Hey – light duties. What's to complain?'

He sighed. 'Right. Thanks, Keren,' and he wandered off.

After two days of slouching about on the *Avarice* with no assigned duties, he went back to see Hess. He was left waiting all afternoon until the captain emerged from his cabin. Cartheron saluted, and Hess eyed him, his displeasure obvious. 'What is it, sailor?'

'Duties all completed, captain. Permission to see to private obligations.'

'Permission denied, sailor.'

Cartheron refused to stand down. 'May I ask why, captain?'

Hess turned away. 'You serve at my pleasure, sailor. That should be clear.'

Cartheron closed his eyes, thinking, *Oh, to the Abyss with Surly's command to keep the post.* 'Then as a free raider I resign my berth.'

Hess stopped short; he turned round and closed, staring down at him – Cartheron was not a particularly tall man. 'You resign,' he said. Behind his moustache a one-sided smile climbed his lips. 'Is that so. Good. I've been hoping you'd do that. Resignation accepted.' He pointed to the side. 'Now get your damned Napan ass off my ship.'

'Gladly.' Cartheron headed for the gangway. On his way he caught sight of Dujek, who was frowning and rubbing the back of his neck.

Now for Surly.

The woman to whom he had sworn his unswerving loyalty was furious. She paced the rough planks of the common room floor, jabbed a finger into her palm with each point: 'You know we're in dire need of funds and you quit the *Avarice*?' The finger jabbed and Cartheron winced. 'We've sunk everything we have into the *Twisted*!' Jab, wince.

'Sunk is right,' muttered Grinner from where he sat on a stool next to the door. The finger swung to him. 'Shut the Abyss up or you're next.' Grinner looked to the street, whistling silently. Across the room Tocaras fought to stifle a laugh.

'Surly . . .' Cartheron began, trying to keep his voice as reasonable as he could.

'Quiet. I'm not finished. You know I was counting on the shares from your position on the *Avarice*.'

'Yes, but—'

The door opened and Shrift rushed in. 'There's a gang hanging around the Front Street cloth warehouse . . .' Her voice dropped away as she took in the thick atmosphere of the room.

Surly rounded on her. 'So? Take care of it.'

Shrift's dark brows rose. 'Okaaay.' She cuffed Grinner and he grunted, straightening. He checked his belted knives, and the two bowed out.

Surly swung her attention back to Cartheron and set her fists on her narrow hips. She studied him, her eyes slit, and he knew her well enough to wonder: *What's she thinking now?*

'You've left me no choice,' she said, nodding to herself as though she had reached some sort of decision. 'We'll have to do it.'

'Ah . . . do what?'

'Take the *Twisted* out.'

Choss, who had been silently taking all this in at the bar, nearly fell off his stool. 'You're joking! It isn't ready.'

She gave him a scowl. 'What can be ready for the raid?'

'You mean the one in two weeks? The secret one that the whole island knows about?'

Surly just stared. 'Yes. *That* one.'

He steadied himself on the stool, considering. 'Well . . . if I focused on the hull I could finish there – but that's all! The canvas is all old, the lines are worn and rotten in places, and of course the—'

She raised a hand to silence the litany. 'It'll float. Fine.'

'I wouldn't trust the rigging even in a moderate blow.'

'We'll manage.' She turned on Cartheron. 'There. We're going.'

He rubbed the back of his neck. 'Mock won't allow it.'

She returned to her pacing. 'What can he do? We're free raiders like everyone else. The vessel is ours. He can't stop us.'

Cartheron went to the bar to pour himself a tankard of weak beer and sent Choss a glare. The man scratched his chin for a moment, thinking. 'We don't have the crew,' he produced.

'Send out the word.'

'None will join with us Napans,' said Cartheron.

'Do it anyway.'

Choss gave Cartheron a shrug. Cartheron sighed, turned to put his back to the bar, and sipped his beer. 'Fine. We'll put out the word.'

Surly gave a curt nod and stopped pacing. She brushed her

hands together. 'Very well. I guess we're done.' She pointed to Choss. 'What're you doing here? Get to work.'

Tocaras let out a muffled laugh; Choss straightened from his stool and regarded him. 'What're you laughing at? You're comin' with me.'

Tocaras stood as well. 'Did I tell you I hate the sea?'

'Every damned day.' Choss looked to Cartheron. 'You too. Finish your beer.'

'Hey! I just finished a full day on the *Avarice*.'

'In which you did fuck all.' Choss motioned him onward. 'Now c'mon. It's time to do some actual work.'

Cartheron downed his beer and wiped his mouth. 'Wonderful. I hate this job.'

*　*　*

By Dancer's reckoning it had been close to a month and he was beginning to wonder if perhaps enough was enough. The lad was wasting away before his eyes and there hadn't been much of him to begin with. He looked parched and pinched and wrinkled and that wasn't just the glamour of his frail oldster façade: he was beginning to fit the part.

As he limped back to the cave from yet another exhausting day breaking rock in the mines Dancer wondered what he could do: pull him along on a kind of sledge? Carry him? Make that mage, Hairlock, share the carrying? Maybe the Falari had a donkey or a mule up there with them. That would solve the problem. He'd have to ask around.

He pulled aside the tattered cloth hanging and froze, staring: Kellanved's ledge was empty.

Those Hood-damned sons-a-bitches.

Though ragged from the day's work, he headed for the dirt ramp that led up to ground level. Even before he reached the top he started yelling: 'Where is he! What've you done with him, damn you!'

The Falari guards stared down at him, appearing rather confused.

'Where's Puller?' Dancer yelled. 'Get Puller!'

The guards exchanged looks, then one laughed. 'You don't go round demanding things, y'damned fool.'

'Fine, then,' Dancer snarled under his breath. 'I'll just come up there, shall I?'

'Wait!' a gruff voice shouted behind and he turned; it was Hairlock puffing up after him. 'What're you doing?'

A crossbow bolt slammed into the dirt between Dancer and Hairlock. Both slowly raised their gazes to the top of the ramp. Puller was there, flanked by two female Falari guards, both holding crossbows.

'Now let's just calm down here,' Puller called out. He pointed at Dancer. 'You. What's this all about, then?'

'My friend – the one I came in with – the mage taken by Otataral – he's gone!'

'Well, it's about time,' Puller said. 'You tellin' me that feller was still alive?'

Dancer cut a hand through the air. 'No. I mean, yes, he was. But he's gone now. Disappeared. What have you done with him!'

Puller raised his open hands. 'Hey, we ain't touched no rotten body, I can tell you that.'

'Then where is he?'

'Damned if I know.' Puller waved them away. 'Now fuck off. Both a' ya.'

Hairlock urged Dancer back down the ramp. 'We'll get to the bottom of this, lad. Don't you worry. I'll ask around.'

A crowd of inmates had gathered at the foot of the ramp. Just before they reached them, Dancer slipped an arm around Hairlock's neck and jabbed a thumb deep into his neck, up against his carotid artery. His mouth next to the man's ear, he whispered, 'Did you take him?'

'No,' the man gasped, his eyes bulging and his face reddening to deep crimson. *Please* . . . he mouthed, his breath gone.

The crowd parted and Eth'en now stood before them. 'He may still be here,' the old scholar said. Dancer released Hairlock, who collapsed to the earth, gasping for breath, hands at his neck.

'Show me,' he said.

Eth'en led him back to his dwelling. Hairlock followed, limping, massaging his neck. 'I still sense him,' Eth'en explained.

'Through the Otataral?' Hairlock growled, his voice even more hoarse. 'That's impossible.'

Eth'en glanced back to him. 'You know only of the refined finished product. It does suppress magic. But here we move through the raw ore. It is different. It can do other things. It can . . . transform . . . change those who would dare manipulate the Warrens in its presence. We Spiritwalkers have been experimenting with this for ages.'

Hairlock grunted, impressed. 'Well . . . he ain't no Spiritwalker.'

'Exactly. It is possible that he has set out on such a journey completely unprepared, unguided, and only now is beginning to master this new path.'

Dancer thrust aside the rotten cloth hanging revealing the empty ledge. He felt strangely disappointed, as if he'd fully expected to see the fool sitting up and laughing at them. 'He's still not here.'

'Yet I sense his life force, his spirit. He is not dead. I am certain of it.'

Dancer faced him; his fists yearned to grip cold sharp iron. 'So what do we do?'

'We wait. If he masters his new . . . condition . . . he should return soon.'

Dancer stared off across the empty main pit, the purpling night sky above. Scarves of sand blew through the heated air, rising, as if the naked earth was exhaling. 'I've waited too long as it is.'

'Just a few more days, I should think.'

After a time he gave a curt bob of assent. 'Very well. A few days.' He regarded Hairlock critically. 'You say you know where the boats are?' The squat mage nodded. 'They'd better be there – for your sake.'

Hairlock swallowed, wincing.

Three days later something woke Dancer from a restless sleep; he quickly glanced to Kellanved's ledge but it was still empty so he laid his head back down. He wondered, then, what had disturbed him.

Sands hissed, shifting and blowing. The hanging billowed and snapped in a sudden gust. Dancer leapt to his feet and pulled it aside; the night was thick with billowing dust – he couldn't even see across the pit.

So. It must be now. He looked to the empty ledge: *Sorry, friend, but this is too good to pass up.*

He drew on the leather straps of two skins of water he'd been saving and set out across the wide pit. He tied a rag over his nose and mouth as he went.

Inmates were out running about in some sort of panic, staring at the churning sands. Dancer grasped the arm of one, yelling, 'What is it? Why are you out?'

'Can't you sense it?' the oldster answered. 'This is no normal storm!'

I've heard that before, Dancer thought, and he peered about. *Kellanved! Yet where? Should I return to the cave?*

Hairlock emerged from the swirling umber sands. 'No time like the present, lad!' he shouted above the howling winds.

Dancer waved him close. 'Yes, I know. Find Eth'en!'

The mage's wide thick mouth turned down even more than usual, dismissive. 'Faugh! Never mind him! Now's our chance.'

Dancer shook his head. 'This storm. I think it's *him*.'

'Him who?'

Dancer started off for his alcove. Hairlock followed; they found Eth'en there. Even as Dancer closed, the old scholar was nodding.

'It is him,' he called.

Dancer swept an arm to the cave. 'But he's not here!'

Eth'en pointed to the ramp. 'Up there, to the south. That is the focus of the disturbance.' Dancer moved to go but the Spiritwalker touched his arm and leaned in close. 'You must remove him!' he shouted. 'It seems this land does not like what your friend is becoming. The entire island will rise against him!'

'Becoming? What do you mean?'

Eth'en waved them off. 'I do not know. Something more – if he lives.'

'Come with us!'

'No. I must remain. But thanks. Now go!'

Hairlock was already halfway up the ramp. Dancer nodded farewell to the Spiritwalker and followed, all the while keeping an eye out for any guards, but none emerged from the billowing eddies of sands. They hurried to the gate in the palisade and Dancer set to unlatching the fat crossbar. He succeeded in releasing one of the tall leaves and pulled, and the two men slid out. 'Which way?' the mage shouted.

Dancer peered round, his gaze shielded from the scouring winds. 'I don't know!' Then he heard something: distorted yells and the thump of crossbows releasing. He pointed the way.

They came upon the rear of a skirmish line of guards spread out across the grounds south of the encampment. They appeared to be stalking something, half with swords bared, half firing crossbows into the skirling storm of dust and golden sands.

Dancer snatched up a rock and struck down the nearest while the burly mage took another from behind and wrenched his neck clear round. Dancer took up the guard's cheap shortsword and charged down the line; Hairlock advanced on the next, his arms out like an experienced grappler.

Dancer did not know how many of them he struck down but eventually a shout went up – some sort of recall – and the guards backed away, giving ground. He let them go, regretting that he hadn't come across Puller.

He set to searching, shielding his gaze against the stinging sands. After a time he spotted a dark blotch against the umber and sere rocky ground. It was Kellanved, his black vest and shirtings tattered and torn, smeared in ashes and dirt. He turned him over, searched his face. He still wore the aspect of a grey-haired ancient.

'Kellanved!'

The lad appeared to be awake but was staring off at nothing. Yet he frowned then, and blinked, as if troubled, or searching after something. 'Yes,' he half-mouthed, and nodded. 'Kellanved . . . now.'

Hairlock appeared from the blowing sands, bloodied and bruised, his hands caked in sand that clung wet and dripping with blood. 'Let's go,' he growled.

'Lower your Warren!' Dancer shouted to Kellanved.

'I don't think I can,' the lad answered, sounding genuinely bewildered – and even a touch frightened.

'Dammit to Hood!' Dancer picked him up and ran.

They jogged. Hairlock covered the rear, giving directions. The storm seemed to lose strength over time as Kellanved was now deliberately trying to limit his own power, but it did not entirely fall away, and it appeared to be moving with them.

The desert coast came into view, the ocean sparkling beneath the night sky, which, bizarrely, stretched clear and bright with stars. Hairlock pointed to the west and led them through the night to a narrow cove where, at a heap of rock, he began digging in the sand. Dancer set Kellanved down and joined in.

After some searching, Hairlock exposed the tall prow of a buried boat, very narrow, constructed of horizontal planks, with a single step for a mast, which itself was missing. They found paddles buried within and eventually they had it empty enough to yank it free of its pit.

Kellanved then called from the night, 'Ah . . . I seem to be in trouble . . .'

Hairlock started dragging the boat down to the strand while Dancer staggered, exhausted, over to where Kellanved lay.

He found the mage half sunk in the sand. 'What in the Abyss . . . ?' He threw himself down and frantically started digging.

'It has me,' Kellanved hissed in pain.

'What does? Some thing?'

'No. The island. It's what it *does*.'

'Quit babbling – we'll have you out.' He dug down deep, then pulled, but couldn't get him free.

'Pull!' Kellanved gasped. 'It has me!'

Realizing that something very terrifying was happening to his friend, Dancer slipped his arms under the lad's, adjusted his footing, and yanked, straightening his legs with all his might.

Kellanved yelled his pain, writhing and puffing.

They fell backwards, Kellanved on top.

Hairlock appeared, peering down at them, frowning his impatience. 'Let's go,' he urged. 'This is no time to be lying about.'

Both Dancer and Kellanved nodded. Dancer helped his friend limp down to the surf and the waiting boat.

They paddled all night and through the next day. After that they took turns. By day the sun pounded down mercilessly. Dancer's lips cracked so severely he could taste his blood with every swallow. Hairlock sweated so badly he was the first to faint from dehydration. Kellanved simply sat back with his shirt held up over his head, dozing. Dancer tried to follow his example but kept starting awake as the narrow boat rocked in the waves.

He lost count of the days after seven – or perhaps eight, he wasn't certain. In any case one day he found himself blinking up at a new face: a concerned fellow, deeply tanned, with a scraggy beard, peering down at him. Moisture wet his lips and he swallowed, grateful if pained by its passage down his throat.

When he next awoke he saw that he was aboard a fishing vessel, along with Kellanved and Hairlock. One of the crew passed by and handed him a waterskin. He took it with a nod of gratitude.

179

'Who are you?' the fellow asked in an odd accent.

'Our ship went down,' Dancer said, his voice hardly recognizable even to himself, so hoarse was it.

'Is that so?' the fellow said, nodding sagely. 'And you three such obvious sailors.'

'Where do you sail from?' Dancer asked – eager to change the subject.

'Delanss. In the Falari archipelago.'

'We will pay for passage.'

The fellow gave a small motion as if to say: *It's of no matter.* 'We are all men of the sea here. We understand.' He patted Dancer's shoulder. 'Say no more about it.'

Dancer managed to take his hand and squeeze it. 'You have our gratitude.' In answer the fisherman pressed the waterskin into his fingers.

In the days that followed the seven Falari fishermen were repaid in laughter at the antics of their guests. Over and over the three heaved up buckets of seawater and emptied them over one another – all to the great amusement of the crew. They scoured their skin, their hair, their ears. They scrounged the oldest and most torn clothes the crew could spare and threw their own clothes overboard. Many of the fishermen tapped fingers to their temples and shook their heads, thinking it a shame that the sun had seared their guests' minds.

After four days of painful scouring, his skin raw and red, his hair hacked short and scraped clean, Dancer took a borrowed knife and sat back against the side, scraping any remaining dirt and grime from beneath his nails. Kellanved was leaning over the side, one nostril blocked, snorting his nose clear. Coughing, he hawked up a mouthful of phlegm and spat into the waves. 'Tonight, I think,' he informed Dancer.

'Good. We've been away too long.'

Hairlock was sitting on a heap of old rope, his rags no more than a tattered shirt and shorts; the squat, burly mage looked like an ogre that had eaten a child and now wore its clothes. He had one foot up across the opposite knee and was scouring the sole with a stone.

'Tonight,' Dancer called to him.

The man grunted, scraping his foot, fiercely intent.

'Come with us, yes?'

The man set his foot down, wincing. 'No,' he growled. 'I have unfinished business in Seven Cities.'

'People to track down, you mean,' Dancer clarified.

The mage nodded, quite unconcerned. 'That's right.'

'Well . . . if we succeed at getting out of here, look us up in Malaz.'

The man's wide mouth turned down in puzzlement. 'Where?'

'Malaz. It's an island south of Quon Tali.'

Hairlock grunted, unimpressed, and turned to scouring his other foot.

Later, when the majority of the crew had bedded down among the ropes and duffels and heaped canvas that crowded the open boat, Dancer and Kellanved met Hairlock at the bows. They shook hands with the Seven Cities mage and then Dancer looked at his partner. 'Well?'

Kellanved let out an anxious breath. 'Yes. Well, here goes.'

Dancer felt that prickling of his hairs and skin that marked an active Warren. He waved a farewell to the one lone fisherman who was regarding them with his brows clenched in puzzlement where he leaned on the side-mounted tiller . . . and lost his footing as things changed.

He stumbled among dry dusty ash and dust that rose in clouds into the air about him. Coughing, he waved it away. 'Kellanved?'

'Yes.' The lad sounded very weak.

He found him lying amid the dust, curled into a ball, arms wrapped around his head. 'That really hurt,' he said through clenched teeth.

'Too soon?'

A nod. 'Yes. Too soon.'

'Sorry.' Dancer gently lifted him on to his back, his arms hanging down over his shoulders. 'I'll carry you, then. Which way?'

Kellanved raised an arm to point and Dancer set off in that direction. 'Quite comfortable now, are we?' he asked.

'Oh yes, quite.'

Dancer rolled his eyes to the ash-laden sky. 'Wonderful.'

* * *

Dassem walked at the very rear of the caravan. He knew many would resent the position, thinking it the worst, the least safe, and the place where one must choke on the kicked-up dust of all ahead. Probably most would feel that way, yet he did not. He was not afraid; he did not yearn for a central position, snug in the middle of the herd and safe from attack. As to the dust – the winds were contrary, blowing mostly across the line of march, and so the nuisance was not constant. And he'd tied a rag across his nose and mouth in any case.

He usually walked next to the horses. If he wanted a break he would sit up on the front of the small cart. Sometimes, when Nara was lucid, they would talk. Small talk, mostly, of the adherents she'd got to know in Heng. Of small kindnesses or stinging injustices; the typical inadvertent or unthinking acts that carry such great weight and importance among youths.

At times the caravan guard, Shear, would pause in her circuits of the straggling line of wagons and carts to walk with him for a time. She would nod and he would nod in return. But not one word had she ever yet spoken to him, and so he'd responded in kind.

It was not until they'd passed the halfway point of the long road south – the first full moon of the march, in fact – that the first incident occurred. On this day the long line of wagons ground to a halt very early. At first he thought of trouble on the road ahead, a broken axle or a lost child perhaps, but then his gaze went to the tall hills to either side, the dense tree cover that ran right down to the rutted dusty traders' track, and he raised his gaze to the sky, sighing. He walked behind his cart and crossed his arms, waiting.

Shortly thereafter four very ragged individuals, two male and two female, emerged from the brush. One fellow carried a curved blade that was spotted with rust, one woman a long thin rapier; the other two held readied crossbows.

'Just stand still and no one will get hurt,' the woman with the rapier told him.

Dassem waited, his arms crossed.

The four kept glancing up the line then back to him, then away towards the lead wagons again. Two were frowning now.

'You're wondering where your friends are,' Dassem said.

'Shut up!' the fellow with the crossbow snarled. The heavy

weapon was drooping in his thin arms; he looked as if he'd not had a good solid meal in a long time. Of the four only the swordsman wore any armour, and this a hauberk of large over-lapping iron scales riveted to thick leather old enough to be an artefact from his grandfather's hegemony wars, which it probably was.

'See them?' the woman with the crossbow asked him.

'Shut up, Ahla.'

'I have a feeling that they won't be showing up,' Dassem said.

'Enough from you!' the crossbowman snarled, his hands tightening on the weapon. Dassem shifted sideways, putting the swordsman between them. Even as the crossbowman swore, Dassem kicked the swordsman backwards into him then shifted sideways again, putting them between him and the woman who was swinging her crossbow over to track him. He twisted the swordsman's wrist, holding the weapon aside, then snapped up the crossbow to smack the spokesman in the face; he went down mewling in pain.

The woman with the rapier displayed good form; she lunged to impale but he was faster, sidestepping with the swordsman, who was pulling on the blade to release it. Dassem allowed the man to pull but directed the movement upwards, pushing, adding to the force, and the man butted himself in the face with the iron pommel. His knees gave and he went down.

The duellist thrust again and he spun, closing, and took her arm, bending the wrist backwards. Gasping, she released the blade, which he then raised up under her chin. She rose to her toes and he held her before him and marched for the woman with the crossbow. She retreated, searching for a clear shot, but he closed quickly and reached out to swat her trigger bar with his free hand.

The bolt disappeared harmlessly into the brush.

He faced the two women with the rapier and motioned away to the hillside. The women gritted their teeth, furious, but they grasped the arms of their limp compatriots and dragged them off into the bushes.

A few moments later Shear appeared, her small painted half-mask at her face, her swords sheathed at her sides. She halted, frozen for an instant, her hands twitching, then she rested them on her grips. She studied the much trampled dirt and mud of the track. Slowly, her unreadable shielded gaze rose to him.

He gave a small shrug. 'We are ready to move on, perhaps?' he asked. She said nothing, her head tilting ever so slightly to one side, and marched off.

It took a while, but eventually the caravan got moving once more.

Two days later he was walking next to his horses when Shear came down the line of the rumbling carts and wagons. She carried two long staves, one under an arm, the other in a hand. The one in her hand she threw as she came and Dassem caught it.

He sighted down it; fairly straight. He flexed it. Not too dry – still holding a degree of suppleness. It was, not coincidentally, the length of a sword.

As they walked along Shear sighted down her wooden stave then drew out a short knife and started shaving off small strips.

Dassem went to the cart, found a knife, and started on his.

They passed the day shaping the pieces. Neither spoke.

Towards the end of the march Dassem gathered up a handful of sand and used it in his fists to roughen up the grip of his piece. He noticed Shear doing the same with hers.

Then she held it in a two-handed grip, the length of one fist between her hands, and tried a few experimental overhead cuts. She looked at him and he nodded. She gave the smallest slight inclination of agreement then headed off for the front of the caravan.

He spent most of the next day practising with his new training bokken.

That night he crouched next to his small campfire, boiling a pot of pigs' trotters that a trader's wife had offered him. He had a few wild potatoes to add and was trimming them when Shear emerged from the dark. She carried only her own wooden bokken, thrust through her belt, and two unlit torches.

He took the pot off the fire, dropped the potatoes in, and set it aside for later, then thrust his bokken through his belt. Next, he looked in on Nara; as usual at this time, she had fallen into that strange spell or suspended state that Hood had set upon her, and so he let the canvas fall and tied it off.

Shear tossed him one of the torches, which he lit from his fire, and they walked off into the woods. And still neither had said a word to the other.

They found a relatively clear meadow among the woods, bright and monochrome silver under the moon. Dassem set his torch at one edge; Shear hers at the other. They then set to sweeping down the taller grasses and weeds. Satisfied, they faced one another and bowed.

Shear struck a ready stance, her body held slightly sideways, her right foot forward; he mirrored her. Watching her, he found the alien conceit of the painted half-mask distracting. He wasn't used to facing masked opponents; it disguised the eyes. Yet eyes can lie, and so he mentally dismissed the detail.

They touched bokkens, pressing in ever more strongly until the wooden blades slid apart. Dassem adjusted his footing on the dirt and didn't like what he felt. He raised a hand for a pause. Shear slid backwards out of the kill zone, beyond the length of his weapon. He knelt and tightened the lacing on one moccasin. Shear swished her blade through the grasses, waiting.

Satisfied, he straightened, ready. She began edging in by sliding one foot forward at a time, and then their blades met with a sharp clack that echoed about the meadow. They met again, rebounding with staccato cracks that steadily picked up pace, ever quickening, until the clatter became a noise that rose and fell like a steady waterfall of thrumming.

After this long slow increase of probing – itself a basic testing that nine out of ten of his opponents failed – Dassem slid back and offered a nod of acknowledgement. Instead of answering the nod, Shear snapped her blade in a lightning cut that set him on the back foot and she kept on pressing, forcing him to retreat across his half of the meadow.

Before running up against the brush Dassem managed to circle round until she was the one held against the forest edge. At this she disengaged and offered a small acknowledging nod of her own. Dassem wanted to salute but dared not raise his weapon out of position. He slid backwards to the centre and awaited her there. She followed, swinging her arms, stretching, and rolling her shoulders.

They pressed blades together once more and began again.

Only when the moon set below the tree-line and it became quite dark did Dassem raise a hand to call a halt. It had been his best testing in years and he was sweating, though he was careful to maintain even breaths – as his teacher had lectured

185

him, never allow your opponent to see your breathing change.

Shear straightened, and touched her splintered bokken to her brow. He answered the salute and noticed how sweat gleamed on her bare arms, chin, and neck, although her breaths also appeared completely even.

She tucked the bokken up under an arm, and said, 'Perhaps next time you'll really try.' Then she walked away.

He stood for a time in the quiet of the meadow, surrounded by the trampled flat grasses, the stars gleaming overhead, and he allowed himself one deep breath. The night air chilled his back where his shirt clung to him.

Feeling a faint wind brushing through nearby branches, he cocked his head, thinking, and it occurred to him that, indeed, it *had* been a long time since he'd actually had to try.

* * *

Lee – whose given name was Leeopo Mulliner, though she'd die before ever revealing *that* – had a good thing going running Geffen's street toughs. For five years now she'd worked organizing and managing operations all across this damned dreary island of Malaz.

It had been a sweet arrangement. These stupid sailors went off risking drowning in an accident (something she'd never put herself in the way of) or death in a raid (something else she saw no percentage in), only to bring loot back to Malaz that they exchanged for coin (of which Geffen got his cut) in order to spend it in Geffen's taverns, brothels, and flop-houses until they found themselves destitute once more and eyeing the sea for yet another raid, whereupon the whole milking operation began again.

A lucrative system for him and for her. Until *they* showed up. The damned Napans and their cut-throat employer – the one with the old madman in tow. Why in all creation was someone like *him* wasting his time in the back of beyond on this island when he could be taking fat contracts in Unta or Cawn? It just wasn't the way things were supposed to be done.

It wasn't damned fair, that's what it was.

So now she was standing on the public pier with Gef, waiting for some major player killer from the mainland. A knifer all Gef's contacts swore by. A hireling whose price would damn well nearly clean them out.

Again, it wasn't damned fair. But they'd driven them to it. Left them no choice. Whatever would come, it was *their* damned fault.

She shifted her weight from foot to foot, unhappy with the errand, and rubbed her right silver earring. These were the one extravagance she allowed herself: Falari silver crafted into the shape of birds – hummingbirds, in point of fact.

She noted Geffen eyeing her fidgeting, and he gave her a scowl of his own impatience. 'Look,' he said. 'This guy's top talent. Worked all over – even Genabackis. You heard a' Genabackis?'

'No.'

'Well. Word is he's also an Adept of Dark. Rashan. So you watch your attitude. Okay?'

She looked away, rolling her eyes to the sky. *Whatever*. Probably just a fucking waste of time and money.

The tramp two-master nudged the pier. Hands threw lines, and a gangway was wrangled into place. Passengers began disembarking. Lee crossed her arms and let out a long breath. It wasn't a large crowd this eve, workers and petty merchants mostly. Carrying their bundles and bags, they parted round Gef and her until it seemed that no one was left.

She cast a questioning look to Gef and when she glanced back there he was right before them, making her start slightly, despite her scepticism. Small and skinny he was, almost painfully so; short midnight-black hair standing in all directions; and wearing the typical black trousers and black cotton shirt that were so clichéd they almost made her laugh – until she caught his expression and the sneer in her throat turned to a swallow.

Unnerving, his eyes. Like a reptile's, watchful yet somehow dead. And a knowing smile, predatory, that seemed to take great pleasure from the shiver that his gaze scraped up her spine. She cleared her throat.

'Let's go,' he said, motioning up the pier.

Geffen looked him up and down, his own scepticism obvious. 'This is all you got?'

The lad raised a bag he carried in one hand. It was slim, not even long enough to carry a sword. 'This is all I need.'

Geffen invited him onward. Lee walked alongside.

'Kinda young to have acquired such a reputation,' Gef said.

'Are you reconsidering?' the lad asked, and his unnerving smile widened as he asked. 'Because it would upset me to have come all this way for nothing.'

'No, no. Just . . . wondering.'

'Let's say I earned it.'

'Sure, sure.'

'Where?' Lee asked.

The lazy-lidded eyes shifted to her, looked her up and down with an undisguised contempt that made her clench her fists. 'Elsewhere.'

'No kidding. Where elsewhere?'

The smile grew, pulling back from tiny, sharp, white teeth. 'The Falaran peninsula most recently. I tracked down a fellow there who claimed a very important kill that wasn't his.'

'What kill?'

'A king.'

'So you killed him because he lied about the kill?'

'No, I killed him because he lied about who he was.'

They reached the base of the pier and here Geffen halted and set his fists on his hips. He stood blocking the way of an old bearded fellow in worn trousers and jacket, carrying a fishing rod. After a moment Lee recognized the oldster as the mage who had refused to work for them.

'What're you doing here?' Geffen demanded.

The old guy hefted the rod, but his gaze was fixed upon the newcomer. 'Fishing,' he said.

'Kinda late in the day.'

'You never know.'

Geffen waved him away. He passed them, yet still couldn't keep his eyes from the lad. For his part, the lad simply smiled back – the smile seeming to hint at some darkly amusing secret known only to the two of them.

They started up the cobbled way to Geffen's gambling house and tavern. Her steps, she noticed, had sounded from the pier's planks and now against the stone cobbles – but this lad's soft dark leather shoes appeared to make no sound at all.

'Your communication contained the name "Dancer",' the fellow said suddenly. 'I want to know – is that right?'

'Yeah, that's the name,' Geffen told him. 'Why?'

'Good.'

Lee showed an arched brow to the crime boss. *Fine, be that way.*

Geffen cleared his throat, looking uncomfortable. 'You can room at my place. Is that, ah, acceptable?'

'Certainly,' the fellow answered, all magnanimous, as if doing them a favour.

Lee clenched her teeth till they ached. 'So, what d'we call you?' she asked, rather brusquely.

'Cowl,' he said, smiling again. 'You can call me Cowl.'

Lee let out a snort and looked to the roiling overcast sky. *Oh, please! Is that supposed to be scary or something? What a fucking joke.*

Chapter 10

THE *TWISTED* SLID DOWN ITS GREASED TRACK OF LOGS WITH a shriek of wood on wood that made Cartheron want to cringe. It crashed into the harbour raising a spray that misted high enough for him to have to brush droplets from his face. Even so, he couldn't keep a satisfied smile from his lips – until he gasped as a hard elbow dug into his side.

He sent a glare to his brother, who was grinning and pointing. 'See that? Ain't she the prettiest thing?'

'Pretty? You said she was the ugliest wreck you'd ever seen.'

'*What?* I ain't never said no such thing!' Urko motioned again to the rocking, black-tarred hulk. 'Put the fear o' Hood into everyone, she will.'

'That's for sure,' Cartheron muttered darkly.

It wasn't that she looked particularly fearsome, he reflected. Neglected, perhaps. It was more her reputation, spread in waterfront taverns and sailors' bars all across the islands south of Quon Tali. A tale of men lost at sea, ill-timed storms, and bad luck all round. That last bit was the important part; men and women at sea were superstitious, and bad luck, like an illness, was something to be shunned. Not that he was some hick, or that he carried a charm to Nerrus round his neck.

Amiss ambled over, hands tucked up under her armpits, and nodded to him. 'Recruits, Crust.'

Cartheron pointed his brother to the vessel – 'Get to work' – then followed Amiss to where a line of five men and three women waited – none of whom were Napan, of course. One of the men he recognized immediately: the burly marine from the *Avarice*, Dujek.

He beckoned the fellow to him, laughing. 'What're you doing here, man?'

Looking a touch embarrassed, Dujek shook his hand. 'Hess is a jumped-up popinjay who couldn't handle a boat in a tub. When I heard you was captaining the *Twisted* here, I quit my letters.'

'Well, you're more than welcome.' He turned to the first of the women. 'And you are?'

'Autumn.'

Cartheron looked the slim young woman – still a girl, in truth – up and down. 'You a sailor?'

'Yessir.'

'Seen action?'

'Yessir.'

Cartheron didn't think that likely, but held his peace. 'Where do you hail from?'

'Purge.'

'Mock's short on crew – why aren't you signed?'

Dujek leaned in, saying, 'Took down one o' Mock's officers, she did. Crashed a chair over him for his straying hands.'

'Ah. Fine.' Cartheron moved on to the third recruit, a battle-scarred woman older and far bigger than Autumn. 'Name?'

'Glory.'

'Glory . . . really.' He knew it wasn't her real name, but that was to be expected. Most in this trade took on new names; a new name for a new life. 'You a sailor?'

The woman curled her lips in the way one who considered oneself superior to her company would. 'No, sir. More a fighter.'

He nodded. 'Very good.'

The next was very obviously an experienced sailor in tarred canvas trousers, sun-blackened and barefoot. 'Name?'

'Torbal, sir.'

'Why aren't you signed?'

The man's mouth turned down in distaste and he spat aside. 'Don't like Mock's way o' dispensing rank . . . sir.'

Cartheron nodded. 'I understand.' The next recruit was a female version of Torbal. 'Name?'

'Clena, sir.'

'What's your story?'

'I'm with Torbal, sir.'

Cartheron nodded again. The next recruit was a skinny kid, a boy. 'What's your name?'

'Orthan.'

'You look too young, lad.'

The youth's hands clenched to fists at his sides. 'Please take me on.'

'Why?'

'Two summers ago Gef's bastards beat my brother senseless. Ain't been the same in the head since. Can't hardly even remember his own name. Broke Mam's heart. Please take me on.'

Cartheron nodded. 'I see. All right, lad.' He came to the next to last recruit, a grizzled old veteran. 'Name?'

'Brendan, sor.'

'Long in the tooth, aren't you?'

The oldster smiled, revealing four yellowed and worn teeth. 'Know the *Twisted* of old, I do. Grew grey together we did over the years, you could say.'

Cartheron couldn't help but eye the fellow a little uncertainly. 'Really? You served on board her and now you're willing to return?' Then he had a thought and asked, 'All those stories of losing half the crew to the plague, all those sailors lost overboard or maimed in accidents, failing to take a prize in years – are they all just tall tales then?'

Grinning, the old man offered him a wink. 'Naw. They're true.'

Cartheron blinked, a touch nonplussed; personally, he'd half counted on that's being the case. 'Ah . . . well . . .'

'Naw. It's just that I'm of the opinion that runs of luck, good or bad, that's all just nonsense.' He scratched his scraggly beard and winked again. 'And maybe it's time for the luck to turn, anyway.'

Cartheron answered with a half-grin. 'I see. Then you are more than welcome.' Nodding a farewell, he continued on to the last recruit. He was a tall young fellow with a swordsman's wide shoulders. Dujek leaned in to say, 'I take credit for this one – recruited him myself. Been through the old Talian officers' academy at Unta.'

Cartheron looked the fellow up and down, impressed. 'So. An officer?'

The young man shook his head. 'No, sir. Didn't graduate.'

'Why not?'

'Killed a fellow student in a duel.'

Cartheron frowned as he considered this. 'I thought such things were sanctioned. An occupational hazard, you might say.'

'They are. But the student was of an Untan noble family and his father is a regent of the academy.'

Cartheron's brows rose as he understood. 'Ah. Put a price on your head, hey? And what have you been doing since then? A veteran, I assume?'

'Yes, sir. Some army work, some hire-swording.'

'What's your name, then?' he asked, knowing he'd get a pseudonym.

'Jack, sir.'

'Just Jack?'

The fellow looked quite uncomfortable and Cartheron felt for him – no need to embarrass him. 'Fine. More of a marine, safe to say then. Yes?'

The fellow actually saluted, saying smartly, 'Yessir.'

Cartheron waved them all in. 'Okay. Get to work. I'll write up the papers tonight.' He watched while Choss set them to work, thinking, gods, an island-wide recruitment and this is all who'd dare show. Malcontents and those spurned by Mock. They were still grossly under-crewed. If he were a superstitious fellow he'd almost say it reeked of bad luck . . . but he wasn't. He raised and kissed the amulet round his neck.

*

It was the overcast and rainy predawn of the day of departure and the entire Malazan fleet of forty-two raiders was finishing its last details and readying to quit the harbour.

All save one. The flagship of the fleet. Mock's own *Insufferable*.

Tattersail paced the wet deck, fuming. Where was the fool? Yes, he'd been out all night 'celebrating' with his favoured captains – all of whom had since reported for duty and were busy preparing their vessels for departure. *He'd* not shown up since!

Where was he! She shot yet another searing glare to Marsh, the mate, who ducked his head – almost guiltily, it seemed to her. Guilty? Why guilty?

'All is ready?' she demanded.

'Yes, ma'am.'

'And the rest of the fleet?'

'Waiting on the *Insufferable*, ma'am.'

She bit at her lip, seething. Should they depart without him? That would be absurd. A fleet without its admiral. They had no choice but to wait.

Moments later, a small carriage came rattling down one of the narrow cobbled lanes that led off the waterfront wharves. It clattered to a halt before the *Insufferable*'s waiting gangway and the door was kicked open.

Out unlimbered Mock, wincing and holding his head. He waved a farewell to someone within and tottered up the gangway, gripping its rope guide for purchase.

'Cast off!' he called the instant he set foot on the wet decking, and winced again, a hand cradling his forehead.

Tattersail pounced on him. 'Where were you!'

The pirate admiral blanched, hunching. 'Not so loud, my dear.' To Marsh: 'How's the wind?'

'Thin. But we'll manage.'

'Very well. Raise more sail if necessary.'

'Aye, aye.'

'And who was that?' Tattersail demanded.

Mock's brows clenched as if he were puzzled, then he waved airily. 'Just an old friend, dearest. That's all.' He slipped an arm round her waist. 'Come, let us retire to our quarters. My head is pounding fit to kill me.'

'Why didn't you return to the Hold?'

'Because I knew we'd be travelling together, yes? Now, come. I am sorely in need of your soothing hands.'

Tattersail steered him towards the cabin door. 'You fool. You're not young any more, you know.'

'I know, I know.' He leaned more of his weight on her and she was glad to accept it.

The *Insufferable* eased from its mooring as its sails bellied and the tide drew it into the bay.

Later that day, at sea, Tattersail walked the rocking deck. To either side and behind, the full fleet of the raiding island of Malaz slammed the waves under full sail; the *Intolerable* and the *Insolent* flanked her, the core of the strike force, while beyond stretched captured merchant caravels, galleasses, fat barques armed now with siege catapults and onagers, and even low open longboats, oared and under sail, captured from foreign travellers.

She nodded to Marsh, pleased with their passage so far. Soon they would make sighting of the mainland and head for the prearranged rendezvous off Point Spear, east of Cawn, before entering the Bight of Cawn as dawn rose and with the tide behind them.

All was going to plan – provided the damned Napans showed.

She glanced behind, far to the south, and thought she glimpsed something there amid the iron-grey waves – a dark blotch or smear. She motioned Marsh to her.

'What's that, there?' She pointed.

He shaded his gaze, frowning. 'I see nothing, ma'am.'

'Something's there. Get a man up top.'

'Probably just a laggard falling behind.'

'I don't like the look of it.'

'No need to worry yourself, ma'am.'

She eyed the man and raised one brow. 'Your sea-mage orders it.'

Marsh pulled a hand down his unshaven jaws, swallowing hard. He nodded, said, 'Yes, Tattersail,' and stomped off, yelling, 'Get Olan up top, right quick!'

Moments later a lean young lad went shimmying up the mizzen to where the very top swayed sickeningly with every wave and there he clutched the slim pole like a monkey, legs wrapped round it, peering to the south.

After surveying the waves for a time he shouted down: 'Can't believe it!'

'What, lad?' Marsh called up. 'What can't ya believe?'

'Damme! 'Tis the *Twisted*!'

Marsh turned to gaze at Tattersail in wonder. 'I can't believe they got that scow under sail.'

Tattersail crossed her arms, gazing south. She nodded to herself. 'Looks like we're going to be joined by all kinds of Napans.' She went to give the news to Mock.

The admiral was in their cabin, head clutched in his hands, a glass of wine before him. Tattersail braced herself with a hand on a beam of the low ceiling as the ship rocked in the waves.

Mock massaged his temples. 'Why are you telling me this?' he asked, his voice pained.

'Just thought you ought to know.'

'That ship is a wreck. It was legend decades ago. They'll just fall further and further behind. It matters not.' He looked up, blinking and pale, and it struck Tattersail that this vaunted pirate was, of all things, seasick. Or perhaps just hung-over.

'And how are we doing?' he asked, swallowing and grimacing at what he tasted.

'We've made the arc to avoid Napan waters and should make the rendezvous at Cawn in plenty of time.'

'Excellent.' He lowered his head once more. Tattersail thought she heard a groan.

She hesitated, but decided to broach the subject that was worrying her. 'Mock . . . about this raid . . . perhaps we should hold a few ships back.'

'Whatever for?'

'In case Tarel tries something. Betrays us.'

Leaning back, he waved a dismissal. 'Why would he do that? And in the face of a successful raid . . . sacrifice all that loot? No.' He opened his hands. 'Listen, Sail dear. I'm certain he wants the riches of Cawn as much as we do.'

She couldn't argue with that, though misgivings remained. She shook her head. 'I still don't like it.'

'Don't worry, child. We'll keep a close eye on young King Tarel, never fear.'

She almost felt embarrassed: of course they would be keeping an eye on things! What was she thinking, imagining these experienced raiders wouldn't be careful? She gave a nod, smiling, 'Of course, Mock. Do you need anything? Soup?'

The admiral paled, waved a negative, gasped, 'No, nothing. And Sail, not a word to anyone about . . . this. Yes?'

She took one of his hands, found it cold and shaking and slick with sweat. 'Of course, dearest. Not a word.'

*

Lee was in the main room of the Golden Gyrfalcon when the man himself came down to confront their new hired knife.

It was long overdue; for more than a week the lazy ass had done nothing but slouch around, eat Geffen's food, and take long ambling walks about town. Lee wondered why the boss had tolerated the situation for so long.

Geffen came to the table and stood there, hands on hips, glaring down at the young fellow where he sat peeling a boiled egg.

'I'm not paying you to rest,' he growled.

The lad continued peeling the shell from the egg – something in the way he did this with his slim fingertips made Lee feel vaguely sick.

'What are you waiting for?' Geffen prompted again.

The lad took a tiny bite out of the egg. 'He's not here on the island, is he?' He reached for the salt.

'Who's not?'

'Our man . . . Dancer.'

Geffen's hands clenched to fists at his waist – perhaps to avoid grasping the knives thrust through his belt. 'Who cares? His people are. Take them out, it'll weaken him.'

The skinny lad frowned at his egg as if the salt hadn't improved it. He set it down and picked up his tea. 'There's only one name on the contract, Geffen.'

'I don't fucking care, you damned prick! I hired your services—' He stopped himself, flinching slightly as the lad surged to his feet.

Lee was impressed to note that Cowl, as he fancied himself, didn't spill one drop from the full cup as he stood. He finished the tea and set the glass down. 'You hired me for one kill, and one kill only. Now, if you don't mind, I'm going out for some air.' And he ambled to the door.

Geffen stood fairly trembling with suppressed fury. With his glare he urged Lee out after the bastard; shrugging, she rose and headed to the door.

Walking after the fellow, she wondered why Gef bothered having her shadow him at all. After all, his strolls about town always brought him to the same damned place – coincidentally the one place Lee really did not want to linger. As a longtime resident of Malaz, she found it nearly as disturbing as the natives did. The local haunted house. Almost every city had something like it.

In this case an old stone house in a tangled neglected property close by the waterfront.

And so she found him here, a hand on his chin, regarding the selfsame abandoned dwelling. She made no secret of her approach; she knew he knew she'd been following him – she had to admit he was at least *that* good.

She leaned on the low stone wall, her head turned to him, away from the building itself, which gave her a headache whenever she looked its way. 'Thinking of house-buying?' she asked.

The lad actually smiled – a thin lipless slash. He raised his chin to indicate the place. 'What do you see?' he asked.

She refused to glance over. 'I'd rather not.'

He nodded his understanding, crossed his arms, let out a long thoughtful breath. 'When I arrived here and found that our man worked with a Dal Hon mage I knew I had the right target this time. He's the one.'

Lee was surprised that the fellow was actually opening up, and so she pressed, 'Why do you want him?'

He lifted his thin shoulders in a shrug. 'Reputation. It's all about reputation. I've worked hard to establish a name as the best at what I do. But as of last year all I hear is the name Dancer.'

'So . . . what'd he do?'

'He killed King Chulalorn the Third.'

Lee couldn't help herself – she blurted, 'Bullshit!' But the lad was nodding quite seriously. 'No fucking way! He musta bin guarded by an entire army of Nightblades and fifty trained Sword-Dancers!'

The lad looked quite irritated. 'I'm familiar with the story.'

'Sorry. So, if that's true, what's he doing here? He could cash in so huge on that. I mean, any king or ruler from Quon to Gris would pay just to buy him off.'

'Exactly. Now we get to the nub of the matter. Why here?' The lad crossed his arms and took hold of his chin once more. 'This is what has been bothering me all this time. Until now.' He pointed one long pale finger to the house. 'Now I know.'

Lee forgot herself and glanced where the finger pointed; the strangeness that assaulted her vision there made her wince and she quickly looked away. 'Why? What's there?'

'You're not a mage, are you? Have you any talent in that regard at all?'

She shook her head – she'd always secretly regretted that lack. 'No. Nothing.'

'Yet even you feel it. Power. There is power there and it is warning you to keep away.'

'Okay, so there's power there. So what?'

'Our friend and his ancient mage sponsor are going to make a try for it. Many have, you know. Over the centuries.'

'Many? You mean it's been looted?'

The slim youth ran a hand through his short hair and shook his head. His frail-seeming skin was so pale Lee could see the blue tracings of his veins beneath. 'No. All failed.'

'What killed them?'

The youth shook his head again. 'Oh, no. Most of them are still alive.' He pointed to the grounds. 'They lie imprisoned below. The structure is holding them there – perhaps using their might to defend itself.'

Lee's flesh shivered in revulsion at the idea. Perhaps this is what she sensed, and what repelled – or terrified – everyone about the place.

'So you're saying it would snatch me?'

That condescending smile returned but Lee let it pass. 'Not you. Unless you attacked it, I suppose. No. Not you. Me. It would like to get its claws on me. I can sense it now, you know . . . trying to reach for me . . .' The youth's voice trailed off as if he'd been struck by an idea and he nodded to himself, his brows crimping. 'You know – it would be a kind of immortality. You wouldn't die. It wouldn't let you.'

Lee shivered again, but not because of the house – because of this youth standing next to her.

The lad tapped a knuckle on the top fieldstone of the enclosing wall. 'Well. We'll see. If he doesn't return, then I'll just have to catch up with him elsewhere.' And he ambled off, whistling tunelessly to himself.

Lee remained behind for a time, still shivering, yet perhaps this time with the wet chill of the island. It now seemed to her that perhaps Gef had made a mistake in sending for this odd fellow; that they were caught up in something far beyond the usual mere scuffle of street-gangs. Something far more deadly, and rather frightful.

She decided then that Gef be damned. She'd keep her head down in the future – especially in any fight involving someone who made her skin crawl the way this one did.

*　*　*

Locked in his unofficial prison, Tayschrenn did not bother to keep track of the mundane passage of days. He was intent upon his meditation, and this, when he achieved total focus, was by definition timeless. And so it was something of a surprise when some strangeness drew him back to himself. He blinked, centring himself upon the here and now, and he found two of Tallow's cult proctors standing by the open door to his cell, their staves just lowering from prodding him.

He nodded and slowly straightened on his numb tingling legs. The proctors pointed the way, directing him by a roundabout route through unused narrow tunnels to a closed door that he recognized as a side way into the inner temple audience chamber.

So. The trial would be held here in the secret precinct rather than the open main temple. The audience would be kept to a minimum, all high-ranked cult functionaries. Tallow had stacked the deck as thoroughly as possible.

No matter. He was innocent of any wrongdoing; that truth would prove undeniable.

They waited, one guard behind, the other before him at the door. Presently, the small door was opened. The priestess who opened it was a red-robed court custodian – a Fang of D'rek – who carried one small curved blade only, but this was more than enough to enforce order, for its sheath was sealed in wax and the blade saturated in a scorpion's venom so potent that just being a Fang was the most deadly position in the cult, from accidental poisonings alone.

The hatchet-faced woman gestured him in. Only now did a tinge of unease brush his spine as it occurred to him that court sentences were sometimes served in a rather summary manner, and usually by the Fangs of D'rek. He entered, squinting momentarily, as the audience hall was very dark. Deliberately so, of course. The bench behind the heavy basalt table held seven judges – seven high-ranked priests. Tallow sat at the centre, the position of the Demidrek, and seeing this Tayschrenn could not keep a frown from his face. Before the court stood one priest whom Tayschrenn was surprised to recognize as Feneresh – he had not thought him sufficiently high in rank to be involved at this level. Similarly, he remembered two on the court as being far too low to be serving as magistrates. None were particular friends of his, nor allies of Ithell, while two, Salleen and Allatch, stood as longtime rivals of the former Demidrek. Tallow must have promoted these mid-echelon priests and priestesses within the last month. That sickening feeling returned to him in strength. He had not even considered the possibility of such a thorough winnowing of the ranks. Tallow had been very busy indeed.

He peered round the hall and made out a small audience, very small given the charges and – he presumed – the importance of the case. Feneresh gestured to him and announced to the court, 'The accused.' And from his pompous and self-satisfied smile, the loathsome fellow was obviously in his element.

The trial, Tayschrenn was surprised to see, had been in session for some time. Feneresh, acting as the prosecution, had already made his opening statement and now called upon a series of lesser priests and priestesses to answer questions regarding the accused. Tayschrenn could only lift one brow in silent commentary as he heard himself described variously as unfriendly, dismissive, cold, unfeeling, aloof, conceited, vain, ruthlessly ambitious, self-seeking, self-obsessed, deceitful, manipulative, and careerist.

He only frowned at the last few; these he'd certainly take issue with. He drew breath and addressed the court, speaking over Feneresh as he droned on. 'All very well . . . but flaws of character are no crime.'

Feneresh threw his arms up in exasperation as if to say: *See? What have I said?*

Tallow, he noted, remained unmoved, his thick arms crossed. It was Salleen who leaned forward, fingers tapping the stone slab table before the court. Old Salleen, whose official role was overseeing cult discipline – such as at the Pits. 'Of course,' she agreed. She directed a cold glance to Feneresh. 'You do have complaints of a material kind?'

Feneresh bowed. 'Of course, ma'am. Merely laying the groundwork.' He waved to another of the Fangs of D'rek. 'Bring forth the priest Imarish Laccon.'

Inwardly, Tayschrenn winced. By the Great Worm's Fate, *that* one was still rattling around? He would have nothing good to say.

The Fang brought forward an elderly, emaciated priest whose fringe of grey hair stood in all directions as if he'd just emerged from a windstorm. His rheumy reddened eyes darted about the temple until they latched on to Tayschrenn. He pointed, and began nodding fiercely. 'Yes, yes,' he croaked in his hoarse crow's voice. 'That's the one. That's the slimy dissembler. The trickster.'

Feneresh was waving his hands for silence. 'Please! For the court: what is your accusation?'

The priest drew himself up as straight as he could. He pressed a knotted hand to his chest. 'For near two decades I was assistant to dear old Ithell. You all know that. I wore the red sash and was proud to be of service!' He shot a bent finger to Tayschrenn. 'Then this one came along. Spreading lies about me, undermining my authority. Through his tricks and dissembling he wheedled his way into Ithell's confidence. He turned Ithell against me . . . the man I dedicated my life to . . . and he stole my position!'

Tayschrenn could not help shaking his head. The old man had never really recovered from being asked to step aside. But he'd been half blind, and so very forgetful; indeed, Ithell had been of the opinion that his mind had been going, and that was over four years ago.

Feneresh clasped his hands at his back and, lowering his voice, asked, 'What . . . tricks . . . exactly are we speaking of?'

The oldster nodded eagerly, the pointing finger quivering. 'He stole documents and hid them – important cult communications – and blamed me! He forged fake notes, records and inventories – signed them in my name! All to make me look bad . . .' the old man's wet lips started to shake and he was blinking uncontrollably, 'incompetent even . . . when I was just serving a great man! Broke my heart, the bastard.'

Tayschrenn knew he should stop shaking his head, but he could not. It was obvious that all the man's resentment and bitterness at being set aside had settled upon his head. As to the missing documents, and the error-ridden records, yes, he had called Ithell's attention to the oversights – duty had compelled him. And now Laccon had obviously deteriorated mentally even further; surely this must be obvious to all.

'He even . . . even . . .' Laccon wavered, swallowing hard and peering about as if lost.

'Yes?' Feneresh urged. 'He did what? You can tell us – you need not fear him.'

Fear me? Tayschrenn sent a beseeching glance to Salleen – please! The man was leading the witness to elaborate.

The man wet his lips. 'He even . . . even boasted about how he'd be the next Demidrek!' Hugging himself, nearly shrieking, he added: 'He said that he'd get rid of Ithell too!'

Quite a few of the audience gasped audibly at this revelation. Tayschrenn blurted a scoffing 'Oh, come now!' and instantly regretted the outburst. Six of the judges cast him glares, while Tallow kept his eyes lowered. Feneresh held both hands out towards Tayschrenn as if inviting all to examine him as if he were some sort of specimen, and murmured just loud enough to carry about the temple: 'Quite remorseful, I see . . .'

Furious with the ridiculous proceedings – and more with himself – Tayschrenn clenched his teeth until their grinding chattered about his skull. He'd played into Feneresh's oily hands. Yet Laccon's infirmity and absent-mindedness had been known to many here. Surely they must see his accusations as the phantasms of a weakened mind. Tayschrenn glanced to the gallery, and while he'd never been one to exchange pleasantries or nods of greeting with the many who crowded the temple halls, it unnerved him now to see open loathing in the eyes of some gathered there.

Had he been labouring under the delusion that abstract ideals such as justice or truth had anything to do with these proceedings he would have been even more outraged and affronted. Yet – naively perhaps – he found that he could not entirely set aside the belief that *some* element of reason and logic must apply. And so he cast Salleen a glare and called out, challenging: 'Where is the evidence?'

The old priestess actually nodded her bird-like shaven head and looked to Feneresh. 'Have you any more witnesses to call?'

Feneresh bowed. 'Just two, Magistrate.'

'Proceed, then.'

Feneresh turned to one of the Fangs of D'rek. 'Bring forth the priest Koarsden Taneth.'

Tayschrenn's breath actually caught. D'rek's mercy . . . what on earth could they want with Koarsden? He looked at Tallow, but the fellow was still sitting with his eyes downcast, hands clasped before him, thumbs tapping. The Invigilator had yet to speak, but Tayschrenn knew him to be the true architect of all this – and a masterful one at that.

Koarsden was dragged forward by one of the Fangs. The tall and always composed priest looked far from dignified now. He was sweating, his usually immaculate robes dishevelled, and though Tayschrenn sought his gaze his friend would not meet his eyes. His heart clenched. *Oh, Koarsden . . . not you too.* He found his own eyes stinging, and looked away, blinking.

'Koarsden Taneth,' Feneresh began, 'you know the accused?'

Koarsden nodded, then coughed into a fist, murmuring, 'Yes.'

'Would you describe yourself as his friend – in as much as this overly proud and disdainful man could be said to have any friends at all?'

Still unable to look at Tayschrenn, Koarsden nodded again, then added, weakly, 'Yes.'

'Would you say the accused and the honoured former Demidrek Ithell were close?'

Koarsden frowned, but nodded, 'Yes. I would say so.'

'And yet, was he present when Ithell was gathered up by D'rek?'

Koarsden shook his head. 'No. He was not.'

Feneresh was looking at the judges as he went on, 'Is it not true that in fact several days passed before the accused even bothered to enquire after the welfare of his great friend and mentor?'

Koarsden bit his lip, frowning again, but nodded. 'Yes. It had been a few days, but—'

'Thank you!' Feneresh cut in. 'And tell me, after Ithell's passing, did you detect any expression of mourning or grief from the accused?'

Now Koarsden was blinking, and it seemed to Tayschrenn that the man was holding back tears. 'No. He displayed none – yet everyone is different in—'

'Just answer the question!' Feneresh shouted. 'Now . . . think carefully about this. In your discussions with him, what was the accused's opinion of the appointment of Invigilator Tallow as temporary Demidrek?'

Koarsden had turned his face away from Tayschrenn – as if he could not bear to risk a glance; his hands were fists at his sides. 'He . . . disapproved . . .'

'Disapproved?'

'He thought it . . . wrong.'

'Wrong? I see. Who, then, did he think should have been appointed?'

Koarsden cleared his throat and swallowed hard, as if choking. 'Someone . . . someone from within the temple, I imagine.'

'And who would this have been, pray tell?'

Now the young priest leaned his head back, blinking rapidly. He took a shuddering breath as if steeling himself, and said, 'Himself, I think.'

Tayschrenn had to suppress a groan. He knew the terrible pressure that could be brought to bear upon anyone – the threats, the promises, the physical and emotional torture – but he'd hoped that Koarsden would have somehow resisted it all, somehow held out. Shouldn't he have? He wondered, then, whether he had ever really understood people at all.

Feneresh was nodding slowly and deliberately – for the benefit of the court. 'Yes. Thank you.' He waved Koarsden away. 'You may go. And thank you for your service to this investigation. I realize it must have been difficult for you.'

Koarsden turned to go, but at the last instant paused as if he would turn back, perhaps to look at Tayschrenn at last, and Tayschrenn steeled himself not to reveal the surprising hurt that clenched his heart. Yet Koarsden's will, or intent, faltered, and he could not bring himself to raise his gaze all the way. His shoulders fell, and he exited by the small side door.

Now Feneresh addressed the court once more, calling his last witness, and saying a name that Tayschrenn could not believe he heard. He flinched as if stabbed, and realized that all the torment he'd endured to this point was but the shallowest preface to what was about to come.

For Feneresh had called Silla Leansath.

She came on the arm of one of the Fangs of D'rek. Indeed, it appeared that the court custodian was supporting her as he drew her forward. She walked listlessly, her arms at her sides hidden beneath her long robes. She looked unwell to Tayschrenn, thin and drawn, her long hair clinging sweaty and unwashed to her skull.

Unlike Koarsden, she looked directly at him – yet not. No recognition glimmered in her dark eyes. No emotion whatsoever animated them. He thought it was as if she were asleep, or profoundly withdrawn.

'Silla Leansath,' Feneresh began, 'do you recognize the accused?'

'Yes,' she answered, her voice flat and dull.

'You are a close friend of the accused?'

'Yes.'

'Perhaps even the closest?'

Silla licked her lips, murmured, 'Yes.'

'So close,' Feneresh said, turning to address the entire court, 'that you met in his quarters many times late after hours, in defiance of all rules?'

She swayed, blinking, but nodded, and said, 'Yes.'

'And during those long, ah, conversations, what did the accused say to you regarding the arrival and installation of Invigilator Tallow?'

'He . . .' Silla paused, licked her lips, then continued, 'he was . . . furious. He thought he should've been named the next Demidrek.'

Tayschrenn would have thought he was dreaming were she not standing before him staring him directly in the eye, unblinking, as if mesmerized.

Feneresh nodded his understanding. 'I see. And what of the passing of his mentor, Ithell? What private demonstrations of mourning did you witness? What confessions of loss and heartbreak?'

She drew a heavy breath, moved to raise an arm as if to wipe her face but hurriedly lowered it before it emerged from the loose folds of her robes. 'I saw none such. He seemed . . . indifferent to the man's death.'

Tayschrenn could only stare; was this some imposter? An illusion? Yet no sorcery could possibly be enacted here – all would sense it. It was she.

Silla . . . what have they done to you? What had *he* done to her? Was she not standing here because of him? Because of his selfishness? His pride in refusing to flee? His mind seemed to wallow and capsize as he tried to make sense of what he was hearing, what was unfolding before his eyes.

Feneresh shook his head as if appalled. And he sighed heavily, as if greatly saddened. 'I see. And do you know what the accused was doing during his long errands so far beneath the temple?'

Silla swayed, blinking once more, then righted herself. 'Yes.'

'And?' Feneresh prompted.

'He was searching for any ancient poison, or weapon, or curse to use against Invigilator Tallow.'

The gallery gasped as one, both in outrage and in dread, for the precincts beneath the temple had long been put aside as the depository of all things most holy – and therefore most dangerous in the hands of an assassin.

Here Tayschrenn could have objected, for this was all supposition. Yet he could not speak, could hardly even move. It was as if he'd been struck senseless by the fact of Silla's standing here, now, witnessing against him.

'And how could you possibly know this?' Feneresh was asking. 'Is this mere speculation on your part?'

She licked her lips and took a steadying breath before enunciating, clearly and strongly: 'Because he told me so himself.'

Feneresh's brows shot up as he scanned the judges and the gallery. Tayschrenn jerked forward. He wanted to rush to her, to hold her, to apologize, to let her know he understood, then froze as a blade pressed his side.

'Move again and die,' the Fang next to him breathed.

'He told you?' Feneresh echoed with an exaggerated incredulity. 'How could this be so? Why did you not immediately inform the cult disciplinary body?'

Silla nodded at this and Tayschrenn screamed inwardly – *Rote!* Couldn't everyone see that it was all rehearsed? Then his shoulders slumped as he understood that of course it all was, and the magistrates knew it. They would not have dragged him out until everything had been prepared.

All carefully arranged beforehand. Theatre. Just theatre. Arranged for the express purpose of discrediting him.

He pulled his gaze from Silla in order to look at his true accuser here, and found him sitting with eyes still downcast, mouth pursed, fingers tapping; the very picture of the saddened and disappointed patriarch. How he burned to smash the man with all his force! Yet the blade still pushed against his robes – the slightest cut and he would be dead.

He forced himself to relax – and then he almost laughed aloud. Some strange, fey mood took him. What foolishness! All to dispose of a political rival within the ranks of the priesthood!

Indeed, he had to stop himself from actually saluting his enemy right then and there.

Silla answered, flatly, 'Because he threatened to kill me if I spoke one word of this.'

And Feneresh was nodding to the court in his exaggerated and outraged way. 'Of course,' he murmured. 'Well, your ordeal is at an end, child. You no longer need fear this monster among us.' He waved to the Fang and Silla was escorted from the court.

Tayschrenn wanted to call out as she went, but suppressed the urge, not wanting to risk possibly making things even worse for her. What he felt now was shame; shame that he hadn't given enough thought in the past to what was to come.

And to think he'd thought himself smart. A smart fellow. He raised his eyes to the ornate carved ceiling above and almost laughed again.

Really, he should be grateful. Tallow and the priesthood had taught him a great deal just now: in particular his complete blindness to the depth of human self-interest and duplicity. It was limitless, and never again would he assume otherwise.

A rather meaningless resolution, given the short time left to him.

Feneresh faced the judges and bowed. He announced, 'The prosecution rests, revered ones.'

Salleen nodded, then eyed Tayschrenn the way a crow might examine an extremely old and unpromising carcass. 'Accused,' she called, 'have you anything to say in your defence?'

He stared, almost bemused, considering it. Could he possibly have anything to say to this court? This ridiculous farce? Why say anything? There was frankly nothing that would sway any one of these men and women. So why bother? Why play through this pathetic pantomime that was human interaction?

He crossed his arms and shook his head, making an open show of his contempt. 'No. Nothing.'

Salleen nodded as if expecting such. 'Very well. The court will confer.'

The judges leaned to one another, whispering a few words. Tallow, Tayshcrenn noted, remained silent for the moment. Salleen took in the opinions of the others then leaned to the Invigilator. They whispered briefly and Salleen nodded her wrinkled shaven head. She returned her attention to the chamber and tapped a knuckle for silence against the basalt slab of the table before her.

Tayschrenn kept his arms crossed. Death was, after all, death. There was really nothing he could do at this point.

'Accused,' Salleen began, and Tayschrenn realized that even his name was in the process of being systematically erased, 'we have heard much testimony regarding your character and opinions, and we are agreed that its conclusions are disturbing. However,' and she cleared her throat into a fist, 'no direct evidence of wrongdoing or culpability has been presented, and so in the estimation of this court your guilt remains unresolved.' She regarded him critically, and idly tapped her crooked fingers on the polished stone surface before her. 'The burden of determining your sentence, then, falls to me, and the lack of conclusive proof drives me to offer the final decision to Holy D'rek. Therefore, it is my decision that you be presented to the Great One's judgement at the Civic Pit on the Feast of the Sun's Turn, in . . .' she bent her head to confer with another judge, 'in half a moon's time.' She rapped a knuckle to the stone slab in final punctuation, and added, 'May D'rek have mercy upon your soul.'

The judges pushed back their chairs; the gallery of witnesses started up a loud murmuring and whispering. Meanwhile, Tayschrenn watched Tallow, and was rewarded by the faintest crooking of his lips as he rose; this couldn't have gone any better for the new Demidrek, he realized. A rival eliminated and his hands completely clean of any perceived conniving or manoeuvring.

Likewise priestess Salleen: a death sentence levelled and all responsibility for said death sidestepped. An admirably bureaucratic solution to a thorny problem. He almost tipped his head to her in acknowledgement of the deft handling of such an unwanted and potentially damaging duty.

Two of the Fangs of D'rek now flanked him; the female gestured, beckoning him back to the small side door by which he'd entered. He nodded to indicate his cooperation yet hesitated, casting one last glance around for Silla – was she still present? Perhaps not, as he saw no sign of her amid the rising gallery of witnesses.

The guard urged him on with a hand at the small of his back. 'Don't make me use the blade,' she whispered.

Coming to himself, he blinked, nodding again. Feeling utterly numb, strangely disassociated from himself and the chambers, he allowed the two custodians to usher him from the court.

Chapter 11

A GHOSTLY PREDAWN LIGHT REVEALED THE WATERS SOUTH of Cawn empty of any approaching vessels and Tattersail found herself cursing the Napans for their tardiness, just as she'd fumed at Mock for his belated arrival yesterday.

Where were the blue-skinned bastards? Why weren't they here? Now she wondered whether she'd properly understood the arrangements. Perhaps they, or Tarel, had got the wrong night. But the equinox – who could misunderstand that? She went to find Mock.

Since they'd been anchored for a few hours close to shore in a sheltered cove just outside the Bight of Cawn, the admiral had regained his sea-legs. She found him walking the *Insufferable*'s deck, trading stories and greetings among the crew, reminiscing about one of the last engagements he'd participated in. It might have just been her mood, but it seemed to her that the freebooters were only half paying attention – the way one might endure a grandparent's favourite story or lecture.

When she motioned for his attention the men and women quickly melted away. The admiral stroked his long moustache, eyeing her, looking pleased with himself.

'Where *are* they?' she hissed, trying to keep her voice low. 'We can't delay much longer if we wish to arrive with the dawn.'

Mock shrugged expansively, quite unconcerned. He raised his voice, speaking to all within earshot. 'If the Napans renege because they have no stomach for a fight then that's all the better, hey boys? More loot for us!'

Cheers answered this, but to Tattersail they did not sound as enthusiastic as they might have. Keeping her voice low, she answered, 'I don't like it. We should withdraw.'

Mock almost laughed. 'Withdraw? We're in position. Cawn is ours!'

She refused to give up her misgivings. 'But why—'

He came close, and in the way that so infuriated her motioned for her silence by pressing a finger to her lips. When he invited her to accompany him to their cabin, she bit down on her outrage and followed, fuming silently.

Within, she drew breath to damn him for treating her like a child, but before she could speak he turned on her, saying, 'Do not unnerve the crew before battle, please.'

She blinked, quite taken aback. 'Well . . .'

'It could cost us lives – perhaps even the victory.'

'Well, yes, but I'm worried—'

'We're all anxious, my love.'

'Let me finish, damn you!'

Mock pulled away, his brows rising, then he stroked his moustache, nodding. 'Very well. My apologies.'

Still angry, Tattersail struggled to order her thoughts. 'The Napans aren't here. Why? What is Tarel planning? What is his strategy here?'

The admiral's nodding gathered strength and conviction as he took her shoulders, smiling. 'Ah, my Tattersail. Cunning lass. Doing your job. But do not worry. You think this is deliberate?' He pinched her chin between his thumb and fingers. 'There are a thousand reasons to explain why they have been delayed – or withdrawn. Poor sea conditions. Strong headwinds.' He pulled away to pace the cabin. 'Perhaps Tarel was embarrassed by the small number of vessels he could muster; perhaps he didn't wish to reveal that to me; perhaps—'

'Perhaps he is burning Malaz City even as we speak.'

Mock froze in his pacing, then spun on his heels to face her. 'Ah. I . . . hadn't thought of that.' He returned to stroking his moustache, pacing again. 'Yet, I think not. Our fleet remains. Upon discovering this we would naturally retaliate. Why invite that so soon after the burning of half of Dariyal? And his fleet is weaker than ours.'

'Exactly. There is something in this throw of the bones. I feel it.'

But Mock was shaking his head. 'You see treachery where mere incompetence or back luck would suffice. I am sorry – but I am not convinced.'

'But—'

He was shaking his head. 'Thank you, Sail. Thank you for your thoughts . . . but we are committed. Stay wary and observant, I value that. But now is the time to act.' He kissed her brow then pulled open the cabin door.

Tattersail could only raise her fisted hands in the air in mute fury, then follow. Mock signalled Earnolth, his steersman, who hailed from some benighted land called Perish. The huge fellow gave an eager nod. 'Raise canvas!' he bellowed, and heaved over the tiller-arm.

The *Insufferable* yawed as the mains caught the wind and bellied. Quickly, the surrounding vessels followed suit. They carved wakes as they swung round, gaining headway. A sick feeling clawed at Tattersail's stomach as she watched these preparations. Within hours they'd sight the harbour and Cawn; then she would know whether she was wrong to let her fears get the better of her, or whether she would face her strongest challenge to date.

She clenched the railing amidships, waiting and watching.

Later, as dawn touched the coastline to the north, her first view of the harbour made her wince for her foolish words. All appeared normal. No warships patrolled the waters in readiness. The harbour walls did not bristle with defenders and cocked catapults or onagers. The Malazan fleet appeared to have found their prey unprepared.

Marsh, the first mate, ordered the attack flags raised and the surrounding vessels answered the signal. He then bellowed, 'Ready landing parties!' The raiders – all those sailors who could be spared from manning the *Insufferable* – now crowded the deck. They strapped on extra armour and weapons. Tattersail, for her part, would remain with the vessel. Mock, she noted, was nowhere to be seen and she thought that negligent.

She was about to search for him when a shout went up from aloft that froze her in place: 'Sails to the south!' was the call, and she turned, her heart sinking with dread. *Oh, please, Oponn no . . .*

'What colour?' she yelled.

'Blue! Napans!"

212

Shit! She stormed for the cabin. Within, she found Mock with two hands on the cut-crystal decanter of wine at his mouth. 'Put that down!' she yelled.

The admiral spluttered, coughing and dribbling wine down his front. He wiped his mouth with a satin sleeve. 'What is it . . . dearest?'

'The Napans – they're behind us!'

Mock nodded, satisfied. 'Well, here at last. As they promised.'

'No. You don't understand. They're *behind* us.' He smoothed his moustaches and the gesture infuriated Tattersail more than ever. '*Behind!*'

He headed for the door, inviting her to accompany him. 'They're late. Wherever else would they be?'

'But . . .'

'Do not worry yourself, darling.' He pushed open the cabin door and stood blinking in the harsh light of the dawn, as if stunned. Tattersail pointed south, insistent, and the admiral nodded, shading his gaze. 'Yes, dearest.' He squinted. 'You see, there's nothing . . .' His voice trailed off with a note of confusion.

Tattersail peered as well; the brightening saffron light now painted a long broad line of sails that crossed the mouth of the bay from side to side. She stared, and her heart sank in disbelief. *By the gods – they're blockading the bay!*

She clenched Mock's arm in a furious grip. 'They have us in their jaws!'

A distant crash sounded then, as of the release of some titanic mechanism, and a fiery projectile flew from the harbour defences – a burning tarred bomb. Tattersail watched, helpless, while it climbed skyward in a parabolic arc that brought it down to strike the prow of a galley, shearing it off cleanly by the force of its impact alone.

'Tarel's betrayed us,' she grated.

The admiral appeared to have mastered himself as he drew a hand down his moustaches, scowling. 'Quite obviously, dearest.' He gestured to Marsh. 'Strike the attack! Raise the retreat!' Marsh ran to convey the orders. Mock strode to the great blond giant that was Earnolth. 'Bring us round tight. We'll break through and hold the opening.'

The hulking fellow picked up a line and began lashing himself to the tiller-arm, rumbling a laugh as he did so.

Tattersail clenched the railing and called upon her Thyr Warren. She felt it igniting the air about her. *Betraying bastards*. She'll send them all to the Abyss.

*

Cartheron was halfway into the job of rearranging the rigging on the foremast mains'l when Hawl came to his side. 'Be entering the bay soon,' she called, and he nodded in a distracted way. Whoever had set up this north-shore-style rigging had done them no favours. He preferred a tighter cinch. Less prone to slippage.

He spared a glance north to the distant shoreline – gods, they were far behind! And the sun was rising. They were hours from Cawn. What was the point now?

Choss came past carrying fresh line for repairs. He dropped the coil to stare at Cartheron's work.

'What have you done?' the man said, outraged.

Cartheron gestured to the rigging. 'Fixed it proper.'

'*Proper?*' The burly fellow set to redoing Cartheron's work. 'I had it all arranged just the way I like.'

'North-shore style is too loose.' He raised a hand to intervene but Choss knocked it aside.

'You mind your own station, Crust. I'm in charge here.'

Cartheron backed away, his hands raised. 'Okay, okay!' He shook his head. The problem with the *Twisted* right now was far too many captains and not enough crew.

'Smoke to the north!' Hawl called from the bows. Cartheron squinted that way. He raised a hand against the oblique rays of the dawn. He couldn't see any hint of smoke, but he trusted her Warren-enhanced senses.

'You see!' he called to everyone in general. 'The attack's started already! There'll be nothing left for us!'

'Get on it then,' Hawl answered, and Cartheron shook his head again. *Too many damned captains*. He hurried to the stern, to old Brendan at the tiller. Crossing the deck, he took in the sails, their deep bellies, the angle of the vessel, and the surge of the waves, and nodded to himself. 'A touch easy . . .' he murmured to the sailing master.

Brendan offered a wink. 'Nothing's chasing us yet.'

Cartheron quirked a smile. 'True enough, old-timer. True enough.'

The *Twisted* held north. Again Cartheron wondered what was happening back in Malaz; how Lady Sureth – Surly – was doing practically unguarded.

When she announced she wouldn't be accompanying them on board the *Twisted*, there'd been a near mutiny. They all shouted at once that they simply wouldn't go without her. Finally, after much mutual silent glaring, she allowed that perhaps Urko could remain to guard her. But that hadn't been enough for Cartheron. He'd also left Shrift, Amiss and Tocaras. Grinner wanted to stay as well, declaring that he'd dedicated his sword to Lady Sureth's service and his place was by her side.

He couldn't understand why Surly had refused to come. Yet that wasn't entirely true; he knew she was up to something. Some scheme. Geffen would no doubt try something in their absence – perhaps she planned to pick off some of his hired toughs. He wouldn't put anything like that past her. After all, she'd come within a hair's breadth of the throne of Nap. She certainly wasn't going to let some second-rate criminal stand in her way.

Now he could make out the smoke to the north drifting across the waters – and quite a lot if it too. He hoped the Malazans weren't burning down the entire city.

They rounded a rocky headland that guarded the mouth of the bay and he simply stared, completely dumbfounded by what confronted them. A full-blown naval engagement completely clogged the waters. Ships danced about each other. Some foundered, locked together in combat. Some lay half over, men clinging to their hulls; a few coasted helplessly, engulfed in raging flames.

Even as he watched, a salvo of flaming projectiles came arching from the Cawn harbour defences to slam into the jammed bay. Shattered wood flew skyward where a few hit targets, both Malazan and Napan, the Cawnese not being too particular at this point.

In the instant it took Cartheron to take in the engagement he grasped how Tarel's fleet was seeking to drive the Malazans into the Cawnese defences, while the Malazans had turned upon their ambushers and were trying to outfight them ship to ship.

Without pausing in his scanning of the battle he yelled to Brendan, though the man stood right next to him, 'Break off!' The sailing master threw over the tiller and the *Twisted* yawed mightily. Even as they turned, another of the clashing vessels burst into flames.

'Blue sails!' Torbal yelled from high on the mains, unnecessarily, for more than half the vessels choking the bay carried them – the full Napan fleet must be present.

As an ex-flank admiral in that very fleet, Cartheron stared, utterly fascinated, yet appalled by the carnage – the two largest privateer navies of the southern seas locked in a death-embrace. Who would emerge the victor? Part of him cheered his old command, yet he also could not help but damn the bastard Tarel's efforts to abject failure.

And standing there at the stern in full view for that unthinking moment was his undoing. It happened even as realization dawned; the *Twisted*'s arc brought it sweeping past the rearmost of the Napan fleet – an aged galleass he knew as the *Just Cause*. He also knew its captain quite well, Regen Leath the Fat.

And standing there at the railing of the *Just Cause*, staring back at Cartheron, stood Regen in his generous flesh. Across the waters mutual recognition lit both their eyes, and the man's mouth opened in a great exaggerated O, followed by the bellow, too distant to be heard: '*YOU!*'

Only now – too late, by far too late – did Cartheron duck down from sight. *Shit!* Shit, shit! Dammit to Hood! He turned to Brendan. 'We have to turn back.'

The man gaped at him as if he were a lunatic. 'Turn back, sir?'

'We need to take that galleass!'

Dujek was within earshot and he slid along the railing to close with Cartheron. 'What's this, captain? Turn round?'

'We have to take that galleass.'

The officer Jack, who was always alongside Dujek, saluted. 'With respect, sir. If we engage that vessel its sister-ships will swing round and we'll be overrun. We'd never escape. Also, that's a troop carrier. There must be over two hundred soldiers on board.'

'He's got a tactical point,' said Dujek.

Cartheron pressed a fist to his forehead. '*Dammit!* Fine! Full sails southerly.'

'Prudent,' Brendan put in, laconically. ''Cause it's pursuing.'

'*What?*' Cartheron almost jumped up to look but caught himself in time. Still, did it really matter now? He stayed crouched anyway, bracing himself at the stern railing. 'We can outrun a damned over-burdened galleass,' he growled.

Brendan said nothing, while Choss, who also was crouched at the stern, blew out a breath. 'Oh, come now!' Cartheron chided them. 'It's not like we're some damned Cawnese trader scow.'

'Well,' Choss allowed, 'we're not Cawnese . . .'

Cartheron waved him off impatiently. He turned to Brendan. 'Get us out of here.'

The old sailing master grinned and bellowed, 'Raise all jibs!'

Cartheron winced at this order, but didn't countermand it; so far he'd avoided the jibs as he wasn't completely confident of the ancient original bowsprit and booms. Hunched, he crossed to the starboard rail and peered over. The galleass *was* breaking off to give chase.

And he knew they simply could not allow themselves to be caught. That was certain. An old galleass, he thought to himself. At least they stood a chance. She couldn't throw up any more canvas than they. But Mael's breath, they were slow. So slow. And two old buntlines had snapped under the strain just getting here . . . He returned to Brendan, said, '*Now* someone's chasing us.'

The old sailing master laughed, revealing half-empty gums. 'Yes indeed. But it's a stern chase and we got us a good lead.' His smile fell away. 'That is, if everything holds.'

Cartheron stroked his chin, almost wincing. 'Bless Mael. Provided.'

Brendan pushed them far closer into the wind than Cartheron would have ever dared. He cleared his throat, almost ready to object, but swallowed the comment, reflecting, *Dammit, the man's the sailing master and I put him there – so I should just put up and shut up.*

He glanced back to the galleass, its huge square mains straining; they *were* putting open sea between them. If everything on this bucket would just hold.

*

Black choking smoke of burning tar, wood and oil half-obscured the bay. Ships seemed to emerge right before Tattersail's eyes and

217

it was all she could do to deflect countless attempted rammings and grapplings. Another Napan galley coursed too close to the *Insufferable* and she seized the Ruse mage in her Thyr powers, gasping, 'Strafe those oarsmen!'

The detachment of archers with her released as one in a sweep of the boards; the galley fell behind, chaos on her decks.

'Port!' came a yell from the lookout and she turned away to that side; sailors called amid the floating wreckage and pools of burning oil, but there was no time. The tall bronze-capped ram of an archaic trireme came darting like a loosed shaft out of the smoke and manoeuvring vessels of battle.

Reaching out with her Warren she threw all restraint aside and raked the entire deck with a storm of flames. The vessel lurched as every oarsman now writhed, oars forgotten, to leap howling into the waves.

She stood panting and saw the archers, who had been cheering her before, now eyeing her with something like dread. She pointed their gazes to the bay. Awful, yes, but this was battle – *this* was where she could exult in her powers, and tested them to their depths.

She raised her Warren as a gyring storm about her and whipped aside yet another effort to rake the *Insufferable*'s deck, sending the salvos of crossbow bolts wide into the littered waters of the bay. She then picked her way across the wreckage of a fallen mizzen lower yard, its rigging and canvas a tangled heap, to climb to the sterncastle where Mock and his flagmen were furiously sending orders ship to ship.

'Have the *Fancy* and the *Hound* heave off,' Mock was telling a flagger. 'They're bunching up.' He stood with his legs wide, hands tucked into his belt at his back. Now that battle had been engaged he had somehow come back into his own. Gone was the unsteadiness and world-weariness – the man was now grinning behind his moustache, calm, almost eerily cheery.

'We're clear!' she called to him. 'We should disengage!'

She was certain he must have heard but he did not answer. Instead, he turned to the mid-decks, shouting, 'Take another run at the *Sapphire*, would you, Marsh? She's lining up rather obligingly ahead.'

'Aye, aye,' the mate answered.

The *Sapphire*, Tarel's flagship. They'd been taking runs at each

218

other all through the engagement, with no decisive blow landed as yet.

She was angry, yet couldn't help reflecting that this was the man who two years ago had charmed her all through that first long raiding run eastward round the coast, when they'd sat down with greased Wickan traders to unload their massive takings.

'We should disengage!' she repeated, pressing.

He offered a wink. 'One more run, dearest . . .'

She shook his arm. 'No! We've lost the *Intolerant*, and the *Intemperate* is dead in the water. We're all that's left to guard the retreat.' The admiral frowned. She wondered whether, fixated as he'd been upon destroying Napan vessels, he hadn't been aware of these setbacks. She made a last appeal. 'Think of what's left of the fleet.'

He nodded then, smoothing a hand down his moustaches. 'Good for you, Sail. Yes, very well.' He turned to amidships, calling, 'Marsh! Raise the retreat! We're disengaging.'

Marsh halted in mid-step, blinking his confusion; then he shrugged, and, raising his chin to the highest tops'l, yelled, 'Raise the retreat!'

'Aye, aye,' came a faint and distant answer.

Mock took Tattersail's shoulders, facing her close. 'Can you drag the *Intemperate* along behind us?'

She could not help but glance to the huge flaming conflagration that currently was the *Intemperate*. 'But it's afire . . .'

'Exactly.'

'Ah. Well . . . I'll try.'

He squeezed her shoulders. 'Very good.' He turned to the mid-decks. 'Marsh! Did I not order to disengage? Sails! Where's our canvas?'

'On it, cap'n.'

Mock turned back to Tattersail. 'Sweep a hole open with the *Intemperate*, won't you, dearest?'

'They have the best Ruse mages on the seas,' she warned.

'Ah, but you're not attacking *their* vessels, are you?'

She could not help but shake her head at that, almost smiling. 'You canny bastard. Very well.' She prepared herself mentally, blocking everything out; everyone now knew not to bother speaking to her. She reached out to the *Intemperate*, grasping hold

219

as best she could, and held it as the *Insufferable* now pulled away beneath her. The mass of the great man-o-war fought her at first, but once it swung round and started moving it almost cooperated as she sent it veering towards the nearest Napan galleon now moving to intercept. The *Sapphire*, for its part, had decorously arced away, signal flags waving furiously as her captain sought to reorder the Napan lines.

Once it became clear that it was under threat from a blazing bonfire the size of a small town block, the captain of the pursuing galleon broke off the attack and swung clear. All Malazan vessels currently free to manoeuvre now turned away from the engagement and raised all the sail they possessed.

Straining, gasping for breath and almost fainting with the effort as her vision darkened, Tattersail sent the *Intemperate* wherever she could to discourage pursuit.

Thankfully, the Ruse sea-mages present among the Napan vessels declined to raise their Warrens against her directly; it seemed they were too busy deflecting the *Intemperate* whenever it veered too closely to any one of their ships.

Between the *Insufferable*'s massed barrages and the threat of the conflagration that was the *Intemperate*, the surviving Malazan vessels worked to free themselves of the closing jaws of the Cawnese defences and the Napan fleet.

*

League after league of empty sea passed beneath the *Twisted*'s freshly tarred hull. Their lead on the *Just Cause* widened. Choss now came to Cartheron's side. A worried frown crimped the big man's thick brows. He cleared his throat, hesitant, saying, 'You realize you're leading them straight to Malaz . . .'

Cartheron closed his eyes, nodding. *Yes, yes.* 'I'd hoped to have lost them by now.'

The soldier – an ex-Napan colonel – raised his brows. 'Well . . . ?'

Cartheron sighed, turned to Brendan. 'Sou'-east.'

The sailing master eased a wary breath between clenched lips. 'We'll lose headway.'

Cartheron shot Choss a told-you-so look; the man answered with a shrug that said they had no choice in the matter.

South to sou'-east, Cartheron reflected. This could suggest a curving retreat for distant Kartool. Let them chew on that – if they could shake them.

The *Twisted* groaned and creaked about them now in far heavier swells. A crossing to Kartool was no timid strike for Malaz; deep ocean lay before them where waves could build taller than their masts.

Cartheron cast a wary eye to their stern; the *Just Cause* pursued, her Napan-blue sails peeping just above the white-capped crests. If they could pull ahead far enough to lose sight of her, then they could strike a more southerly course . . .

The explosive crack of wood yanked his gaze to the bows in time to watch the jibs collapsing in a heap of canvas and shattered wood, shrouding the bow. A scream sounded. He ran to join the marines, who were already digging through the wreckage.

They pulled Clena clear. She lay cradling her arm, panting her pain. Hawl gently examined it. 'Broken,' she told Cartheron.

'What was it?' he asked. Hawl shook her head; she didn't know.

'Get those sails up!' Brendan barked from the stern.

Cartheron shot a glance to the rear. They were losing priceless headway. There was only one thing for it . . . He turned to Hawl.

She sensed his regard and raised her eyes to him. Her jaws worked as she slid her dark gaze to the stern. 'If they have a sea-mage . . .' she warned him.

Cartheron shared her worry. The *Just Cause* might have a Napan sea-mage, in which case he or she might know Hawl, or recognize her Warren-aspect.

He gave her a curt nod. 'Do it.'

She straightened from Clena. 'Very well. Let no one interfere. This could get messy.' She headed for the mid-deck, pushing up her sleeves as she went.

Cartheron glanced about; Dujek and Jack were organizing the marines into teams on tackle they'd thrown up to raise the two intact jib spars.

Torbal came to him. He held an old wooden cat-block in his hands. 'Was it a boom?' Cartheron asked. The sailor just handed over the block, which came apart in Cartheron's hands – split.

'Is it rotten?' the sailor asked; his gaze was on the near-unconscious Clena.

Cartheron examined the split then shook his head. 'No. Just old and worn. Should've been replaced before we set out. I'm so very sorry . . .' The sailor just shrugged. 'Get her below decks.'

He turned to Hawl; she'd positioned herself at the base of the main-mast, facing forward, her skirts arranged over her crossed legs. Cartheron would've nodded his encouragement, but the woman was already far into raising Ruse – her open-eyed stare held that unseeing thousand-yard gaze.

The vessel lurched beneath everyone's feet; it was as if the hull had scraped over a sandbar, and Hawl cursed, biting her lip and drawing blood. 'There's some kind of powerful spirit on board,' she gasped through clenched lips.

'That nacht thing – the mage's familiar.'

Hawl's teeth were set. 'Or the other way round. Damned strong bastard.'

'Is it—' Hawl snapped up a hand for silence and Cartheron swallowed all questions. The raised hand slowly clenched to a fist, whitening, then relaxed and fell, trembling.

Hawl eased out her breath. 'There. It was resisting . . . but it has stood aside. Good thing too – I'd hate to think of what it could do.'

'What's the damned thing *doing* here?' Cartheron asked.

'Under orders to make sure we don't just take off with the ship, is my guess.'

'Oh, come now,' Cartheron scoffed.

Hawl simply waved him off. 'I'm busy.'

Cartheron offered a mock salute and backed away to join Brendan. He asked, 'What's the last sighting?'

'Closing,' the sailing master offered laconically.

'The repairs?'

Brendan raised his chin to examine the bows, then shook his head in despair. 'Looks like a damned fire in a cathouse.'

'Too many marines and not enough sailors.'

'They know their stuff,' Brendan demurred, 'they're just not a crew yet.'

Cartheron understood. It took months and months of training to settle into an organized disciplined crew where everyone worked to the same rhythms.

The main jib creaked upwards on makeshift tackle. It caught the wind and tautened. The workers sought to tie it off.

The *Twisted* charged forward then, rocking Cartheron

backwards, and he knew it wasn't the jib; his glance shot to Hawl. Their sea-witch was leaning forward as if pushing headlong into a storm. Her arms were out, her hands clawed as if pulling on something, heaving it towards her, and he knew just what that was.

The *Twisted* lurched again, surging up the slope of an oncoming swell. When the vessel took the white-capped crest Cartheron scanned the northern horizon and cursed – he'd caught a glimpse of blue sail.

'As long as you can!' he yelled to Hawl, hoping she could hear him through her concentration.

'Due south,' he told Brendan.

'Aye, aye.'

Jack came to Cartheron's side; the young man was rubbing a chin that to Cartheron looked new to stubble. 'What is it?' Cartheron asked.

'That troop carrier is no deep-water vessel . . . *and* she's low in the water . . .'

Cartheron nodded. ''S true.'

'She may wallow in these high seas.'

Cartheron snorted. 'So might we.'

'Regardless, perhaps we should lead them onwards.' He offered up a smile that was almost sly. 'Perhaps it's time for a run to Genabackis . . .'

Cartheron laughed and slapped him on the back. 'Remind me not to try to match strategies with you, Jack.' He shook his head. 'I'll think about it. But let's just try to lose them first.'

The youth touched his brow in a half-salute and ducked away. Cartheron watched him go. *Jack* – too bland a name for a smart fellow like that. Have to come up with something better.

He stood with Brendan, ready to lend a hand at the tiller as the *Twisted* clawed its way up monstrous swells, pitched forward, then slid down precipitous slopes as long as hillsides. The water took on an iron-grey darkness and the spray bit his face like daggers of ice.

'Strait o' Storms dead ahead,' Brendan muttered in low warning.

'I know,' he answered, just as low. 'I know.'

'Would rather take on our Napan friend back there.'

Cartheron nodded his agreement. When they broached a crest

he searched the waves behind again and this time saw no sign of the *Just Cause* against the vast expanse of angry foam-webbed waters. Had they given up the chase?

Glancing ahead, he felt a chill take him as he glimpsed a line of darkness against the southerly horizon. Lightning flashes lit it from below like the fitful fires of a siege army. The Strait of Storms – home of the daemon Riders who haunted its frigid waters.

'Easterly, sailing master,' he murmured to Brendan.

'Aye, aye,' the old sailor answered with undisguised relief.

He now looked to Hawl; he'd go to her, perhaps take her hand to offer any help he could, but he had no wish to distract her. She was still upright in any case, her arms still outstretched, hands clawing the air.

Choss, who had been overseeing the repairs at the bows, now came to Cartheron's side. Leaning close he set his mouth to Cartheron's ear and and whispered, 'Ice glaze on the bowsprit.'

'Easterly, please, Brendan,' Cartheron warned.

'She's slow to come round, isn't she?' the man answered through clenched lips.

Cartheron studied the winds. Damn if they weren't against them for an easterly course. They'd have to claw for every league.

He now wondered whether he'd just traded a leap into the Abyss for Hood's bony hand.

'Keep an eye on it,' he told Choss. 'Have the crew strike it off as it thickens.'

The burly officer nodded, his face grim. 'Been a long time since we've dared tempt the Stormriders . . .'

'Just sneaking past, old friend. Sneakin' past quiet as mice.'

The fellow snorted a dour laugh and ran a hand over his brush-cut hair. 'Hunh. Let's hope they see it that way . . .' He headed forward.

Cartheron repeated, 'Quiet as mice.' He eyed the thickening black cliff of thunderheads that loomed before them and shuddered as the chill wind buffeted his face. Years ago he'd been part of an expedition north, to Falari, transporting liberated goods too identifiable to be sold anywhere on the Quon mainland. That journey had taken him past the coastline of the Fenn Mountains. There they'd passed monstrous tongues of ice that descended the slopes and slipped down into the steep bays like serpents. Icy winds had buffeted them then, too. *But now it is summer in this region! And a chill great enough to dominate this entire strait comes off these alien Stormriders alone.*

He touched a hand to the railing, now glistening with delicate hoarfrost. *Don't pay us no mind, my frigid friends . . .*

Chapter 12

LEE SAT IN THE COMMON ROOM OF THE GOLDEN GYRFALCON. It was crowded now to bursting with Geffen's toughs, plus a score of new hires, and she felt distinctly uncomfortable. Geffen had talked through his plan with her, of course, but she still couldn't shake her dismay at the outlay of such a massive hiring; every out of work would-be street-thug and worthless dock-front layabout on the island must be crammed into the common room.

She wondered on the scale of the riot should it come out that they didn't have the coin to pay half those present.

Geffen himself paced before the broad cobblestone fireplace, eyeing his gathered force, impatient.

'Everyone here?' he demanded.

She scanned the crowd. 'Near enough. I called for everyone.'

He gave a curt nod. 'Good.'

She couldn't help it. Her gaze drifted to the slim dark figure sitting alone despite the crowd, leaning back, arms crossed and hands tucked up beneath his armpits, that mordant smile on his lips as if he knew what was going to happen – and that it would all end in disaster. She yanked her gaze away.

Geffen raised his arms for silence. 'Okay! Everyone! You all know the fleet left this morning. Mock and most of his captains are gone – including most of the damned Napans.'

'Going to finally burn that bar down, Gef?' someone called from the crowd.

'Mock doesn't want property damage,' Lee snapped. 'Bad for business.'

Geffen gestured for silence. 'That bitch has earned it right enough. But that's just for openers.' He raised an arm, pointing towards the ceiling. 'Why mess around with the small timers when the Hold is empty?'

Though he'd let her in on the scale of his plan, Lee couldn't help letting out an awed breath. *Gods be damned . . . he's actually going to go through with it.* In the stunned silence she sensed the implications of Geffen's words settling in.

'Why should the captains listen to you?' someone called out, breaking the long silence.

Good question.

Geffen nodded, acknowledging the concern, then opened his arms wide. 'Because we're inside and they're out! Possession is nine-tenths of the law, my friend.'

Good answer.

'And the Napans?' someone else asked.

'We'll settle that score tonight. Then the Hold.'

Lee frowned, thinking. Why bother with the Napans at all? But then, if they couldn't handle even *that* feud then they sure didn't belong in the Hold. And so she nodded, sending Geffen her approval.

He nodded back, winking, and threw his arms wide. 'Tonight.' He gestured to her. 'Lee, take whoever you need.'

The crowd broke up, everyone preparing for the coming assault. The doors were barred and guarded against any word's getting out and the cellar store room doors were thrown open – the doors to the armoury hidden below. Geffen crossed the room, the savage narrow slit of his mouth set. Some hireswords stopped him to swear their loyalty; he acknowledged them, then pushed onward. Lee saw where he was headed and joined him.

The two stood staring down at the foreign knifer, Cowl, alone at his table. The young man was mutely clapping, offering his ironic applause. 'All hail the possible new ruler of Malaz,' he said. 'But I think you're forgetting one thing – what about his pet mage?'

Geffen lifted his bony narrow shoulders, unconcerned. 'I think she might like to know what lover boy's been up to all these years.' Then he waved the subject aside, scowling with undisguised distaste. 'Things have changed. I no longer require your services – wretched as they have proved to be. Our contract is void.'

The lad pressed his hands flat against the tabletop, dropped his sardonic smile. 'That would be ill advised. Drag me here only to dismiss me?' He shook his head at the magnitude of the mistake.

Lee was feeling the confidence of the company of some fifty toughs and hireswords; she leaned over the table and jerked a thumb to the door. 'Pack your stupid little bag and get your useless arse out of here.'

She did not know what to expect, but it wasn't the sudden laugh and the hands thrown up in mock surrender. 'Fine,' he said, 'I should be mad but I'm not. Because I'm grateful to you. If you hadn't brought me here then I wouldn't have found the real potential hidden on this wretched island. Power just waiting for someone daring enough and strong enough to take it.'

Geffen waved him down, as if he wasn't worth his time. *'I'm* taking it, arsehole.' He marched off.

Cowl watched him go, murmuring, 'I'm not talking about the Hold, fool.'

Lee hesitated. 'The house, you mean . . . you gonna try to enter it?'

The mage's gaze remained aside, following Geffen. 'Someone will, and soon. It's in the air. It's why powers are gathering here. It's like a lodestone.'

'What do you mean . . . powers?'

The young mage made shooing gestures with his hands. 'Go away, little bird. This does not concern you. But, by way of advice, I suggest you keep your head down.'

Lee waved him off as Geffen had done and turned to the jammed room. 'All right!' she shouted, 'Went, Quilla, Donner – pick five men each. You're with me.' She headed for the door. 'Let's go.'

She hated to rush, but they had to strike quickly before word got to the Napans. That gal in charge, the servitor Surly, struck Lee as canny; she might have taken the precaution of buying an informant among their hirelings, so they had to act now.

They closed on the waterfont and Smiley's bar. She sent Went ahead with his team to move in from the rear once they heard the rest entering at the front. She motioned Quilla forward, half mouthing, 'Take the door.'

'No lookouts,' one of the hired knife-fighters observed, sounding uneasy.

Quilla's boys kicked the door open and charged in. Lee waited, tensed, with Donner and his team. The crash of breaking furniture and crockery sounded from within, but no clash of blades or bodies. She edged in the doorway; the common room was dark and empty. Quilla came down the stairs, shaking her head. 'Gone. All gone. 'Cept for one,' and she gestured to the bar.

Lee crossed to where a young woman lay atop the counter, legs straight, hands crossed on her chest: Amiss, the youngest of the Napan crew.

She set her hands on her hips. *What in Mael's name . . . ?* Tentatively, she reached out to raise one shoulder and there she found the wound – stabbed in the back through to the heart, one expert thrust. Without taking her eyes from the corpse she asked, 'Gef put out any kill orders?'

'Not one,' Quilla answered. 'In fact, we was definitely told no bloodshed – for now.'

Lee nodded at her lieutenant's words. 'That's what I thought.' She let the shoulder fall – stiffening, yes, but still a touch warm. Must've been within the evening.

'We burn the place now?' Donner asked, eager.

Lee had to restrain herself from cuffing the hulking fellow. 'No, we don't burn it! It's ours now, innit? They've run off.' She backed away from the bar, nodded to Quilla, 'Hold the building,' then went upstairs.

The empty office was a mess of papers, most of them covered in shadowy drawings of obscure landscapes and mysterious charts of some kind involving multiple overlapping circles marked with hen-scratchings of dates and places; Lee couldn't make head or tail of it all. Other than that, the place was a mess: drawers pulled out and upturned in a quick search for valuables, broken glass and bits and pieces on the floor. Every step was a grating crackle of shards. After one last scan of the shabby place she returned to the main common room and waved her people to follow.

Outside, she raised a hand to shade her gaze against the spitting rain. Someone was stirring up a blood-feud, and she thought she knew who. The damned little smirking shit.

She squinted north, up to the black silhouette that was the Hold. Dark now; no watchfires. Was Geffen there already . . . and just where had the damned Napans fled to?

She spat aside, swearing, and motioned everyone onward. 'C'mon, y'damned useless layabouts – we're for the Hold!'

*

229

They jogged up the twists and turns of the steep Rampart Way up the cliff to the Hold, losing steam about halfway and labouring up the rest of the distance through the chill rain, only to be greeted by the hunchbacked gatekeeper Lubben, sitting under the stone arch of the entry tunnel, a lantern on an iron hook next to him. The old fellow was leaning back and drinking from a pewter flask.

'Is Geffen within?' Lee demanded of the old souse, brushing the cold wetness from her face.

The grey-haired fellow screwed up one bloodshot eye to squint at her. 'Aye.'

'Any Napans show up here?'

He shook his long hound's head. 'No.'

'Fine.' She motioned to Went. 'You stay here and watch the gate with your boys.'

'Not necessary,' Lubben objected, but lazily, without even stirring in his chair.

Lee dismissed him with a wave and headed onward into the dark and empty bailey. She crossed the wet cobbles to the doors to the main keep and found them ajar. Donner, next to her, had his light crossbow readied and she took it from him and motioned for him to push open the stained iron-bound door. This he did, then jumped back while she stepped in, crossbow raised.

She faced a long main hall, empty, but lit brightly from far within by what must be a roaring fire. Donner and his toughs readied their knives and clubs. Fresh wet mud marred the field-stone flags. She crept inward, a finger on the crossbow's tiller-bar.

Raucous laughter sounded from beyond; a godsdamned celebration. She crept up to the end of the hall and leaned into the room, sighting down the crossbow stock, then let the weapon fall.

The main audience chamber was crowded with Geffen's toughs. They'd cracked open kegs and were now at the long tables carousing. Sighting her, a number cheered and waved her in.

'What in the Abyss is this?' she snarled, and cuffed away a proffered tumbler of wine.

'We won, didn't we?' Two-ton answered, laughing loudly.

'Won?' Lee said, scowling. 'Won what?'

Their biggest enforcer lifted his thick shoulders. 'Well . . . the fight, a' course.'

'Not that there was much a' one,' Leath put in, and tossed back her glass. 'Mock's boys just put up their weapons and walked away.'

'Said they wouldn't die for him,' offered a new hiresword whose name she couldn't remember. 'The cowards.'

'I'd say they just made a sensible calculation,' Lee answered, and she took up a glass to sniff the wine, found it excellent. She sipped it and was amazed by how fine it truly was. She ruefully considered the jugs of godsawful plonk she'd been consuming all her life.

The new hiresword, a waterfront layabout by the look of his tattered canvas pants and tarred hair, frowned up at her, irritated by her answer. 'What d'you mean, calculation?'

'I mean they calculated that when Mock comes back you'll be doing it instead.'

The hireling swore and knocked the glass from her hand. 'I'll be doing no such thing, you damned bitch – and who in the Abyss are you anyway?'

With her other hand she raised the crossbow and jammed its business end into his chest until she could feel it grating against his ribs. 'I'm your boss, dim-wit.' She eyed Two-ton. 'Where's Geffen?'

The giant fellow had thrown up his hands and now he mutely pointed upwards. She raised the crossbow to rest it on her shoulder, snatched up the wine, and headed for the wide stone staircase. 'Thanks.'

She couldn't find Geffen immediately, but the occasional noise of overturning furniture or crashing ceramics on the fourth floor eventually led her to him. She tracked him down to one of the many bedrooms. He was tossing the place, and she leaned against the doorjamb, crossbow cradled at her chest, and enquired, sweetly, 'Whatcha doing?'

Geffen started, bent over as he was to inspect beneath a large armoire of some dark exotic wood. He straightened to his considerable lean height. 'What the fuck does it look like?'

'Searching for enemy dust-bunnies?'

He ignored her comment. 'He's got to have a stash hidden here somewhere.'

'You ain't gonna find it. Not like this.'

'Thank you for your support. So, what happened at the bar?'

She shrugged. 'They ran off. No one there 'cept the youngest – that girl – dead. Knifed in the back. Did you order that?'

To her immense frustration, her boss was hardly listening; he was studying the woodwork of the ceiling, frowning. 'No.'

'No? Well, she's dead.'

He shrugged his bony shoulders. 'So? She's dead.'

Lee finished the wine, shaking her head. 'So they're gonna think you ordered it. That it's a blood-feud now.'

He lowered his gaze, the frown deepening into a dark scowl of anger. 'I've taken the Hold and you're whining about a few Napans?' He waved her off. 'Get down there and sort out the lads and lasses. Do your job.'

She raised the crossbow to her shoulder, almost gaping at the fellow. Taken the Hold? So what? *Keeping* it was what worried her.

But he'd already dismissed her and was now running his hands along the room's rich wooden panelling, searching, no doubt, for some hidden cavity or latch. She pushed away from the jamb, shaking her head, and turned back to the circular stairs down to the third floor. If Geffen didn't have an answer for that pet mage then this was going to be the shortest occupancy in history.

On the way down, she stopped. She could hear voices. Geffen talking with someone. Carefully, she crept back up the curve of the stairs and ducked into the first side room to listen. Yes, definitely. He was talking to someone. A woman.

Gently, she pressed the tip of the crossbow to the stone-flagged floor, set her weight on the iron lever until it cocked, then raised the weapon and adjusted the quarrel in its channel. Taking a steadying breath, she started up the hall.

The voices led her to a meeting chamber. Stairs to an over-hanging balcony led off from the side, and she padded up them. Slowly, she edged forward until she could see over the edge of the balcony, and down the runnel of the raised weapon.

With some satisfaction – and no small relief – she saw that it was that damned Napan bitch, Surly.

She and Geffen were facing off.

Well . . . we have no time for this. She sighted on the woman's back and slipped her fingers over the weapon's trigger tiller to squeeze.

A cold blade pressed itself to her neck and a voice whispered from behind, close and wet in one ear, 'That wouldn't be fair, would it?'

The fucking knifer, Cowl.

He whispered, 'Drop it.'

She eased her fingers from the tiller, lowered the weapon. 'Why?' she answered, just as faint.

'I want to see what she can do, of course.'

'No – why kill the girl?'

'What girl?'

'The Napan scout.'

'I have no idea what you're talking about – ah!'

Lee knew he was lying but didn't answer as Geffen and the woman, Surly, were finished talking and he'd drawn his knives. Surly, for her part, faced him unarmed, striking some sort of ready stance, one leg ahead of the other, side on.

A grunt of appreciation sounded from the lad behind as he seemed to recognize what she was doing. He rested his chin on her shoulder and whispered in her ear, 'Now let's see how good she really is.'

Damn stupid is what she is, Lee thought. Geffen was a ferocious knife-fighter; had climbed through the ranks of the freebooters on his skills. She didn't think the woman stood a chance.

Geffen obviously thought so too, as he came on swirling and spinning, switching grips and slashing high and low. Yet somehow the woman managed to slip all attacks, blocking with hands and feet and counter-punching, driving him backwards to a wall where he rebounded, spat up a mouthful of blood, snarled and raised his razor-slim blades once more.

Cowl grunted. 'Good . . .'

Geffen kicked a table at Surly that she somehow leapt, bringing a heel down on his shoulder. Even from the balcony Lee heard the snap of bone. Yet he slashed at her as she spun away and both staggered backwards, Geffen's left arm hanging limp, his collar-bone broken certainly, while the woman's side was opened up in a long cut from shoulder blade to hip that now gushed blood down her leg, smearing her bare foot.

Yet she pressed forward, hands raised in loose fists. She left behind wet red footprints as she came.

Again Cowl grunted his approval.

The blade slipped from Geffen's limp left hand. He turned

233

sideways, facing her with his right, slashing in a blur of attacks. These the woman somehow blocked, her arms twisting until she suddenly had his good arm locked between hers. She bent it backwards until a snap resounded – his elbow – and he snarled his agony. Then one of her hands shot up under his chin and he stiffened, his eyes growing huge and wide.

She pulled backwards, releasing him, and he fell to his side, dead. She stood regarding his corpse for a time, then limped from the chamber, leaving a path of bright wet footprints behind.

Cowl whispered into Lee's ear: 'Still think you could've taken her?'

Lee grated through clenched teeth, 'No.'

'That's right,' Cowl affirmed, so damned smugly, his warm lips touching her ear, 'and yet *she* works for my boy Dancer. Think on that, darling.' And he drew away from her, chuckling. She spun, but he was already gone.

Fucking mages. She lifted the crossbow, checked to make certain of the quarrel, and headed for the stairs. In the main hall she paused for an instant, considering for a moment whether to follow the woman, but decided against it; even wounded, that was an opponent she didn't want. She headed down. *Now I have to find a way to pay off half these parasites without turning them against me.*

At the top of the wide main staircase she set her fingers to her lips and let go a shriek of a whistle. All the gabbling halted below.

'Geffen's dead,' she announced. 'Mock left behind some hidden guards and they did for him.'

After a stunned silence, some smartass called back, 'How do we know that?'

'Go check for yourself,' she invited. 'He's on the fourth floor.'

The fellow answered, 'How do we know you didn't do him?'

Lee hefted the crossbow and thought about skewering the fellow right then and there, but refrained. After all, there was a chance she might miss, and that would be it for her. She sighed, openly showing how little she really cared. 'Well . . . I guess you don't. We're pulling out.'

Two-ton's thick brows rose comically. 'Pullin' out? But we own the place.'

She cut a hand through the air. 'No! Mock still owns this place.

234

And even if he dies out at sea his captains will fight among themselves to claim it. There's no way they'll put up with us squatting in their way. So pack up.'

Two-ton peered round. 'Pack up? Pack up what?'

She showed them all a big grin. 'Everything not nailed down.'

*

Nedurian was sitting at his usual table in the dark, low-ceilinged bar that was Coop's Hanged Man inn – something of a local hangout for ex-pats, refugees, and those otherwise wanting a low profile – when in came two of the Napan crew from Smiley's and sat down in an empty booth. One was the giant hulking fellow, and he was supporting the other bar's serving-woman, who was wrapped in a rain-darkened cloak.

Nedurian had been keeping a close eye on Smiley's for some time now. He'd narrowed down the epicentre of the bizarre turbulence among the Warrens to its location and believed that the mage who'd bought the place was their practitioner of Meanas. He'd even managed to question old Durard on the sale of the *Twisted* before he'd left town and the fellow's description of the encounter meshed well with earlier accounts of this Dal Hon mage, especially the wild and disturbing tales out of Li Heng.

There was also the sale of the *Twisted* itself. Not a particularly impressive ship; quite the opposite, in fact. Yet known throughout the southern seas. And certainly not for its prowess in battle; for the dark name of its curse. Ill-luck, deaths of crew and prior owners, capture, ransom, plague, storm, and lack of any prizes at all made it a pariah to sailors in all ports.

Then there were the tales of its current haunting.

Only someone insane would buy that vessel. Or someone who believed that everyone made their own luck. Someone daring enough, or insane enough, to try his luck with Meanas.

So he'd been watching Smiley's – even becoming something of a regular – and knew that the woman, Surly, was much more than a mere servitor. He also knew what was transpiring this very night, now that Mock had gone away.

He picked up his mug and crossed to the booth, sitting down uninvited. The big fellow glared murder at that, his massive hands clenching, but the woman sent him a sharp look and he eased back in the bench seat, which creaked and groaned beneath him.

235

Nedurian noted that more than rain darkened the cloak wrapping the Napan woman, who appeared greyer than usual, and sheathed in sweat. So he made a cast hoping for a bite, saying, 'Did you get him?'

The woman eyed him warily – he knew she recognized him from Smiley's. 'And you are?' she answered, her voice tight and clenched.

He shrugged. 'A retired mage. Geffen was no friend of mine. So I ask again – did you get him?'

'No idea what you're talking about.'

Fat Coop came over to the table, rubbing his hands in his apron. 'What can I get you?' he asked.

'Wine,' said the woman weakly.

'Beer,' said the fellow – Urko, Nedurian believed his name to be.

Coop gave Nedurian a nod, saying, 'Good to see you. I'll get you your usual.'

Once Coop had left the table, Nedurian shrugged again. 'Fine. Be that way. But I'm sympathetic. I've been watching you, and I think that what you need is a mage cadre.'

The big fellow pulled a hand down his face to wipe away the rain. 'A what?'

The woman took a sharp breath, sagging into the booth. 'He means mages who are integrated with squads or crews, like in the old days among the imperial Talian legions.'

Nedurian gave her a nod. 'Showing a lot of book-learning for a servitor.'

The woman's smile was brittle with pain as she sat holding her side. 'I've just heard all the old stories, of course.'

His answering smile was equally sincere. 'Of course.'

'So?' she asked. 'What do you want?'

He opened his arms. 'Employment, naturally.'

She shook her head. 'We don't need another mage.'

Coop passed by and set down a tumbler of brandy before Nedurian. He turned it in his hands. 'Oh, yes. You have two. One is of Ruse. Excellent at sea, but limited on land. The other is . . . well, of questionable usefulness.'

Now her eyes narrowed and the front of disinterest hardened into a mask. 'I'm not hiring right now.'

The front door opened, sending the candle and lamp flames

236

flickering. It was another of the Napan crew, a tall, mast-thin fellow whom Nedurian knew to be named Tocaras.

This one crossed to the table and bent to whisper in Surly's ear. She nodded and moved to rise, carefully. 'Thanks for your offer,' she told Nedurian by way of dismissal. Together, the three exited.

He gave them a while, then rose and headed for the door. A cleared throat behind brought him up short. It was Coop at the table, who motioned to the glasses. 'On me,' Nedurian told him.

He felt eyes on him then, steady and level. He glanced over to see two of the long-standing regulars here, one a wiry drunkard named Faro and the other a giant of a fellow who sometimes served as a sort of unofficial bouncer when he was sober enough. He gave them a nod, which Faro answered in a strangely measured way.

Shrugging off the fellow's gaze, Nedurian ambled out on to the wet night-time street. He was in no hurry; after all, he knew where the Napans were headed. When he reached the block containing Smiley's he was rewarded by the noise of a scuffle and the crash of a door. He paused, leaning against a neighbour's shop-front, and watched while street-toughs came rocketing out of the door one by one to crash to the gleaming cobbles. Groaning, they picked themselves up, dragged their compatriots up off the ground, and limped away.

Nedurian smiled to himself in the dark and gave them a while, then pushed off, thinking, *Well . . . nothing has ever been gained by timidity.*

He pushed open the door to find himself facing one of the Napan crew, the tallest, Tocaras, longsword bared. 'Not now,' the fellow said, his face grim. Nedurian peered in past him to see another of the crew, Grinner, cleaning the counter.

'You're closed?'

Tocaras nodded, almost as if he couldn't trust himself to speak. 'Aye. Closed.'

The servitor and Urko emerged from the rear, the giant fellow still half supporting her. 'Who is it?' she called.

'That mage, Nedurian,' Tocaras answered over his shoulder.

'Let him in.'

Grinner and Shrift were slowly righting chairs and sweeping up broken crockery. They eyed him, suddenly rather hostile. He sat at the table nearest the door. Surly herself sat on a high stool at the bar, still wrapped in a cloak. She nodded the big one, Urko, to him. The fellow lumbered over, frowning. 'Uh . . . what d'you want?'

'Like I said. Employment.'

Urko glanced back to Surly. She tilted her head, her gaze hardening. 'You know who runs this place?'

A loaded question: he was tempted to say 'you' but decided she was testing his honesty and so he nodded. 'Yeah. Some Dal Hon mage, and a fellow who looks handy with a knife. But I haven't seen them lately.'

She nodded in turn, satisfied. 'Well, they're abroad. Could be back any time, though. So remember that.'

'All right.' *Interesting – she's using them as a threat to keep the hirelings in line. Are they really so scary? Well, that's what I'm here to find out.* 'I consider myself forewarned.'

'Do so. Now, why us? Why not the other lot? We're outnumbered, you know.'

He inclined his head at the justness of the question. 'Been watching for some time now. The other lot, they're a gang. But you're a crew.' He raised a finger. 'That's a very important difference.'

She was eyeing him steadily. After a few moments she pursed her thin hard lips as if to say, *Good enough*. Her gaze fell to the bar's counter then seemed to shy away; she regarded him anew. 'Can you heal?'

He shrugged. 'I know the basics. Both mundane and magical.'

She leaned back and waved to Grinner, who was standing as if quivering with some sort of rage – as if he wanted to knife someone, anyone, and even he'd do. 'Let's go upstairs. Mage, you have yourself a patient.'

*   *   *

Dancer squinted through a hanging haze of dust to a horizon of jagged canyons and flat isolated buttes and despaired. He stood at the crumbling edge of a ridge and resolved not to continue any further in this ridiculous exploration of Shadow. He crossed his arms as Kellanved came puffing up behind.

'We could wander like this for ever,' he announced, not turning round.

'Indeed, the Realm is ours to discover,' Kellanved answered, sounding very pleased with himself.

Dancer resisted looking to the pewter sky. 'I mean this is useless. We should return.'

'*Useless?* When every turn reveals new knowledge? Every vista a revelation of discovery?'

This time Dancer did look up.

The walking stick appeared, thrusting out past Dancer's side. 'What is that?' Dancer narrowed his gaze to the right. A tall mount? 'There is a strange light there – we should investigate.'

Dancer uncrossed his arms, let out a long-suffering breath. 'Very well. But after that we return, yes?'

Kellanved brushed past him, waving a hand. 'Yes, yes.' He shuffled down the slope rather awkwardly to the ravine below, setting off great rattling slides of rocks and shale.

Dancer followed, his gaze on the ridge-lines and the deeper murk of the boulders littering the valley below. He knew that the hounds would find them again anyway and that Kellanved would be forced to shift them like wind-blown leaves across Shadow regardless of their plans.

After meandering through a maze of steep and narrow canyons they glimpsed a horizon ahead, seemingly oddly close. It hung like a sky-to-ground curtain of shifting silvery grey, shot through by glimmerings of light, like sparks or motes.

Kellanved halted, planting the walking stick in front of him, hands atop it. As Dancer closed, his companion gestured to a turn in the canyon, and announced, as if he'd just created the panorama, 'Behold . . .'

Dancer peered over and grunted, astonished. The canyon allowed a direct approach to their objective, revealed now through the thinning dust not as a dark mount or pinnacle, but as a hulking construction like a fortress of dark rock, tilted near sideways along the slope of a butte, and apparently half sunk in the curtain of hanging silver light.

Of all the sights Shadow had revealed as yet, Dancer had to admit this was the most impressive. 'What is it?' he breathed aloud.

'I do not know,' Kellanved answered. 'But I must find out.' And he set off at a quick scuttle.

Cursing, Dancer hurried after the little fellow, who could move quite fast when he wished to. He drew his blades, hissing, 'We can't just march right up.'

'And why ever not?'

'There might be guards, occupants.'

'Nonsense. It is long abandoned.'

'You don't know that. How do you know that?'

The wiry mage started climbing the fan of broken rock and detritus that spread down from the nearest leaning walls of the immense structure. He threw a finger into the air, saying, 'I surmised.'

Dancer was tiring of the fellow's posturing. 'Surmised? From what? There is no evidence.'

Halting, Kellanved gestured ahead to the great hulking construct, then opened his arms wide. 'As I thought,' he announced, 'a Sky Fortress of the K'Chain Che'Malle.'

Dancer was not surprised; he'd already suspected as much. Studying the great broken edifice, its exposed galleries, floors, and cracked walls, he imagined in his mind's eye the enormous object crashing into the hillside to break apart and slide to its present tilted resting place. Yet what of this strange glittering curtain that blocked their view of half the remains? 'And this barrier?' he asked Kellanved.

The hunched, falsely old mage was already scrambling up the slope of shattered rock and gravel. He waved his walking stick as he held forth. 'As we know, Kurald Emurlahn – the Elder Warren of Shadow – was broken apart in great wars. That barrier must be one such border – an edge of this shard of Emurlahn.'

Dancer nodded to himself. 'So . . . we could pass through there into another Realm?'

'Very possibly so, yes.'

As far as Dancer could see they were alone, yet somehow he could not bring himself to sheathe his blades. 'Well, perhaps we've seen enough, then. We know it's here. We could return another time.'

Kellanved paused – probably to catch his breath. 'Nonsense!' he puffed. 'So close to who knows how many astounding discoveries?' He eyed Dancer anew, cleared his throat. 'Ah, you wouldn't happen to have any water left, would you?'

Sighing, Dancer tucked his blades away and passed over their last waterskin.

They clambered up the shattered lip of a broad room, an enclosed space as large as the great domed audience chamber of Li Heng. Rusted hulking machines covered in dust and broken rock littered the room. Those not fixed to the floor had slid down to rest in a jumbled heap at the lowest point. Dancer had no idea as to what their purpose might have been. In fact, he felt rather like a mouse poking his nose into an abandoned house and staring up at the enormous human-sized furniture. An overly inquisitive mouse at that. The fine hair on his forearms and the back of his neck prickled with a strange dread.

'Kellanved,' he began, 'I don't like—'

The distant brassy baying of a hound interrupted him.

'The barrier, I should think,' Kellanved announced, and took off at a run.

They lowered themselves down open canted floors where a great crack ran through the edifice. It overlooked the silvery grey curtain barrier and they were making their way down to the littered base far below where the gap disappeared into the strange glittering wall, beyond which nothing could be seen.

The baying drew nearer, echoing now from the surrounding walls, ceilings and floors. 'Shift us now,' Dancer called.

'No time,' Kellanved answered, panting and short of breath. Then he skidded to a halt amid a great collected heap of sand and dust, pointing. '*That* again!'

Dancer reflexively snapped a hand to a blade, but unnecessarily, as far across the great gap a familiar squarish, canted object was rising into the empty air.

Kellanved pointed, 'Ah, our old friend from before – taking off to leave us to our fate again!'

Dancer urged the mage onward. 'Never mind that little reptile. We can't stop.'

The mage awkwardly shuffled and half leapt down a heap of fallen rock. 'This must be its base,' he offered.

'Just keep going. We can't . . .' Dancer trailed off as it became clear there was something wrong with the flying fragment's trajectory as it skidded low across the ruins, heading directly for the tall soaring main section of the fortress. The smaller piece wobbled, perhaps as the creature within struggled to adjust its course, but to no great effect.

'It's going to . . .' Kellanved began, only to trail off as well.

The fragment crashed into a wall, shattering into bricks and shards, and Dancer thought he caught a glimpse of the lizard-like beast as it fell. An alien gurgled wail sounded across the great gap.

'Damn,' Kellanved said. 'I've wanted to examine that flying thing ever since we first came to Shadow.'

Dancer decided that this was not the time to comment on the man's lack of sympathy, opting instead to push him onward, down towards the base of the greyish, silvery curtain.

Another ear-punishing howl sounded and Dancer flinched; two of them. He launched himself past Kellanved, rushing pell-mell down the slope of loose broken rock and gravel. 'I will scout ahead!'

He was almost at the barrier – which remained utterly opaque, even at this close distance – when something hit him in the back. He spun, blades whipping out. Kellanved's walking stick lay at his feet. The mage himself came puffing and gasping after, waving his arms, his mouth moving soundlessly as he fought to say something.

'We have no time!' Dancer snarled, and turned for the barrier.

'*Stop!*' Kellanved exploded, panting, bent over, hands on his knees. 'Stop!'

'I'll just take a look.'

The mage waved his hands in a wild negative. 'No . . . mustn't.'

'*What?* What is it?'

Kellanved reached him and took hold of his shoulder – perhaps to support himself more than to hold him back. 'Grey,' he panted. 'Glitterings. Not barrier . . . edge.'

'Yes. To another Realm.'

The mage shook his half-bald, wrinkled head. 'No. Nothing. Chaos.'

A long eager hunting howl snapped Dancer's gaze to the north. *They have our fresh scent.* He shook Kellanved. 'What do you mean? Can we go or not?'

'There is nowhere to go *to*,' the mage answered, gaining a snarl of impatience from Dancer. 'This shard of Emurlahn is being consumed by Chaos. Eaten. Eroded.' He pointed to the shimmering, slowly wavering curtain. 'That is the edge of the nothingness between Realms.'

Dancer threw his arms up. 'Shift us away then. Quickly.'

The wizened fellow pressed a finger to his lips, squinting. 'There may be interference this close to the edge of Chaos. It may not be safe.'

'Fine!' Dancer thrust the man's walking stick into his arms, took him by the collar and began marching him off across the rubble. 'Start now.'

Kellanved wriggled, struggling to free himself. 'This is not conducive to the high arts of thaumaturgy, I'll have you know!'

'Neither is sliding down the gullet of a hound.'

The fellow's tiny ferret eyes shifted left and right. 'Well . . . you have a point. I will begin.'

'Do so!' *And if we ever get out of this it will be a miracle.* Dancer realized this was probably the third or fourth time he'd told himself this.

*   *   *

Lars Jindrift had always thought his lot in life unjust; he'd never had the breaks and everyone had always been against him. It wasn't his fault that that damned girl had struggled out the ground and come staggering into town to denounce him! How was he to know she'd still been alive? He was certain he'd throttled her thoroughly enough.

And of course no one believed his side of the story. It was all so damned unfair.

But that was before.

Now he knew that his life to date had been nothing but a dance through lilacs and butterflies. 'Butterflies,' he whispered aloud, deep within the empty guts of the *Tempest*, then giggled, and clamped a hand over his mouth.

Glancing about at the empty hold he raised his treasure in his hands. He brushed away the swarming roaches and weevils, took a nibble of what was left of the hardtack, then thrust it back into its filthy cloth wrapping and tucked it away in its hiding spot behind crates of rotted mouldy cloth.

He straightened from his knees and nearly toppled as a wave of darkness took him; he steadied himself at a timber. *Not eating well of late*, he thought, and giggled again. He made for the deck.

What new expanse of empty sea awaits!

He emerged beneath a clear, star-studded night-time sky when he climbed to the mid-deck. Peering about – squinting, as his vision was not what it used to be either – he found their tormentor near the bows. The daemon in man form, Kallor, stood with hands clasped behind his back, armoured as always, peering up at the stars. A faint wind brushed his wispy iron-grey hair and beard.

A mad urge to rush the man and thrust him over the side took hold of Lars, but he wept instead as he no longer had the strength even to throttle a child. Instead, he sidled up beside the monster and asked, 'Why read the stars, m'lord?'

The creature shot him a glance of disgust before returning to examining the night sky. 'Just dredging up an old memory, in truth.'

'Memory?'

'Yes.' Kallor turned to the stern, calling, 'A point north, steersman!'

Lars and he waited in silence for a time, until there came from the darkness a weak 'Aye'.

'Memory, m'lord?' Lars prompted, blinking, and though the sea was uncannily calm this night he steadied himself with a hand at the railing. How long had it been since he'd eaten real food? Not counting the blood he drank from that wounded fellow he'd found below . . .

The monster in human form nodded, smiling faintly, as if at an old memory. 'Yes. I came this way once before . . . long ago.'

Lars blinked again, peered uncomprehending at the great vastness of rolling waves surrounding them and the empty heavens coursing above, and could not contain the hilarity that came bubbling up from within. He laughed openly, giggling and guffawing. He swept an arm to the broad sea, sneering in open scorn. 'You came *this* way? In the trackless ocean? Are you a fool?'

Kallor glanced to him in revulsion, then raised an arm and swung it backhanded.

Stars exploded in Lars' vision. Stars that floated, dimming, like butterflies, until they faded and darkness took him.

He awoke to glaring sunshine and the thump of feet on the decking. Something crusted his mouth. He groaned, fumbled at the railing above him, and drew himself up. One of the last of their sailors came limping past, his head hanging, and Lars called to him, 'What is it? What's going on?'

The sailor pointed ahead. 'Land.'

Lars blinked. Land? Truly? He squinted to the western horizon – all he could make out was a dark blur far off atop the waves. Land? Really? Which could it be? Fabled Stratem? Rich Quon? Or perhaps the immense lands of the Seven Holy Cities? He staggered after his tormentor to the very bows. 'What land is this, m'lord?' he asked, and could not help but flinch away as the fiend turned to him.

This time, however, an indulgent smile crooked the monster's mouth, as if he were addressing a child, and he said, 'It is no land.'

Lars examined the broad thin smear. Not land? He blinked, nearly faint from lack of food, and decided that perhaps he could no longer trust his senses. How could this be?

But as the *Tempest* closed upon the dark blur it became more and more clear that the manifestation, whatever it was, certainly was *not* land. Land thickened as one neared from offshore; highlands and distant mountains resolved out of the blue haze, and clouds massed. Here, however, no such distant inland heights appeared; the darkness remained just that, a thin line floating barely above the waves.

It was not until they were almost within bowshot that Lars could make out exactly what they approached: a floating construct. Huge, immense, fully the size of a large fortress or city. He marvelled that such an artefact could exist – and that he, or anyone he knew, would have no knowledge of it. It astounded him that there could exist some whole new place in the world of which he had heard no hint whatsoever.

Enormous tree-trunk pillars supported piers that extended from its boardwalk wharves. Smoke and the stink of humanity now wafted over them; that and a delicious commingled mouth-watering scent of cookery that almost made him faint. Those among the crew of the *Tempest* who still had the strength to rise now struggled with lowering the sails and preparing lines.

As the *Tempest* neared a berth at the end of one such pier, Lars saw no other vessels of its size anywhere. All the rest were small single-masted open boats, or oared smacks or dories – none capable of any ocean crossing.

Lines were thrown, weakly, all falling short, but crew on shore used boathooks to catch them, drawing in the *Tempest* just as a double file of armoured men and women came marching down the pier. Each carried a large oval shield on their back, and held a wicked-looking crossbow. They lined up facing the *Tempest*, and on an order the front rank knelt and raised their weapons, while the second remained standing, also with weapons raised. All this Kallor took in while leaning on the side rail, an amused smile hovering at his lips.

A strange armoured figure then pushed through the double line to stand before it. Lars thought it a thin man in plate, but he appeared even too skinny for that. Yet he seemed to be encased in metal – rusted and dented bands gleamed here and there, and even his face was a contoured metallic mask. Twin wickedly curved blades hung at his hips. He raised an arm, pointing, and Lars was amazed to see that the hand too was metal, shaped from articulating metal segments.

'You,' came a screeching, scraping voice, as of metal snagging on metal, 'are known of old. You are not welcome here among the Meckros.'

The fiend merely shrugged his mail-encased shoulders. 'I am not here for trouble. I simply wish to trade.'

Lars frowned at that, thinking: *Trade?* So, this was not their destination after all? A terrible suspicion now dawned upon him and he thought, *So, we are to travel even further?*

Another figure pushed forward, this one a bearded old man, his thin hair tied in a long braid and a gold circlet of metal upon his head. 'You have nothing we want,' he shouted. 'Begone, or we will slay you all!'

'What of slaves?' Kallor answered. 'You may have four of my crew.'

Now Lars gaped in truth. *What? Slaves?*

The city elder looked over the crew now crowding the side, Lars included, and shook his head. 'They are too sickly. They would be of no use.'

Lars let out a breath of relief while the monster sighed deeply, as if disappointed. 'Very well. For a few barrels of food and water I trade you your continued miserable existence. A fair deal, I should think.'

The elder flinched as if struck; he choked, fury darkening his face. 'That is blackmail! We will not agree to that!'

'Think on my last visit,' Kallor reminded him mildly.

The fellow's hands clenched and unclenched. He cast quick calculating glances between the unnatural creature of metal at his side and the fiend on the ship. In the quiet, Lars became aware of a strange whirring sound wafting across the gap, as of gears spinning and ratchets softly clicking.

'Keng here may defeat you,' the old man finally pronounced.

Kallor pointed. 'That *thing* cannot slay me. You know this. Yet I have it within my power to sink your precious city. Think on that.'

The elder glowered, his mouth working. Finally, he spat through gritted teeth, 'Very well. A few barrels of dried fish, fruit, and water. And that is appropriate, as that is all you are worth.'

Kallor was grinning now, and he shook a warning finger. 'Careful, or I shall add one pickled head to my order.'

The city elder snarled, huffing, and pushed his way through the guards, disappearing from sight. The eerie creature, Keng, remained; immobile, watchful, its inner mechanisms whirring.

Kallor turned away from the *Tempest*'s side, chuckling. His grey, dead-eyed gaze swept Lars and he motioned to him. 'You should be pleased. Food is on the way.'

Lars swallowed to wet his parched throat, ventured warily, 'Then, m'lord, we are not to stay?'

The fiend appeared surprised. 'Stay? Here?' He laughed scornfully. 'There is nothing for me here in the middle of nowhere. No, we continue westward.'

'Westward, m'lord? May I ask where?' He flinched, anticipating a blow for his daring.

But Kallor merely peered in that direction, frowning in thought behind his iron-grey beard. 'Southern Quon Tali, I believe. I shall know as we draw closer.' His armoured boots thumped the decking as he stepped away. 'However,' and he turned back, a finger raised, 'if you are considering jumping ship and trying your luck among the Meckros, you will be disappointed. They are a ruthless and efficient people who cannot afford to feed anyone who cannot contribute. Sickly ones like all of you will simply be thrown into their pens of carnivorous fish.' The dead eyes scanned all on deck, including Lars, and the monster smiled without humour. 'Therefore, I suggest your chances remain better with me.' He bowed his head in withdrawal. 'If you need me, I shall be in my cabin.' And he clomped across the deck and slammed the cabin door behind him.

Lars wrapped his arms round his head and sank down to his haunches, shuddering with suppressed sobs. A nightmare! His life had become a living nightmare. Whatever did he do to deserve this?

It was all so completely unfair!

Chapter 13

OVER THE COURSE OF THEIR MARCH SOUTHWARD THROUGH the farms and grasslands of Itko Kan, Dassem and Shear sparred as often as her duties allowed. Apart from these practice sessions the journey was uneventful for Dassem; he cared for Nara, fed their horses, and kept watch at the rear of the caravan.

So regular became their evening bouts that when they returned to camp late at night Dassem began to notice some smirks and knowing looks directed their way from the guards. If such assumptions regarding them troubled Shear, she gave no hint.

Over the weeks he found he was coming to regard her as an extraordinary training partner. So skilled, in fact, that he now understood he'd become lax this last year in Heng; that he'd lost his fine edge in that city, lacking as he did any true competition.

Yet even while he warmed to her as an exceptionally skilled master of the sword, she seemed to grow ever more distant, formal, and withdrawn. It puzzled him at first, but then he decided that such behaviour must be due to the fact their time together would be soon coming to an end.

This evening, as they walked to an isolated spot for their sword practice, Shear was even more quiet and curt. He was not altogether surprised – in three days the caravan would reach Fedal, its destination in the southern confederacy of Itko Kan, and from there he planned to head onward to Horan on the coast to hire transport out to the isle of Malaz. It was probable that neither of them would ever find another training partner of such skill – at least not for some time – and he, too, regretted their parting for this very reason.

They came to the broad gravel shore of a creek low in its course. The pale water-worn stones shone silver in the moonlight and the creek chuckled and hissed just loudly enough to smother the incessant drone of the night insects. Bats flickered overhead targeting that chorus.

Shear faced him, her wooden bokken still pushed through her wide sash. Her painted mask was a dark oval against her face and her long black hair blew about unbound. She seemed to be regarding him with particular intensity this eve.

'This will be our last bout,' she announced.

'I am not leaving quite yet,' he answered. 'There still may be time.'

She shook her head. 'No. No more practice. We now recognize each other as plausible rivals. I am satisfied of this, as are you. Therefore, we must settle the matter.'

'What do you mean?'

'I mean that among my people, the Seguleh, hierarchy is everything. All know their place.' She motioned to indicate the two of them. 'We must now establish rank between us.'

He shook his head. 'Such things do not concern me.'

She slid one foot forward, her eyes within the mask narrowing. 'You must take this seriously.'

He peered round at the darkness as if helpless. 'Shear, I . . . very well.' He opened his arms. 'You win. I concede.'

She drew in a swift blur that cut the air. 'I warn you – I shall force you to defend yourself! Do not dare to dismiss me. Fight with all you have. Or I shall not relent.'

He still had not drawn his bokken. 'Shear, please . . . this is not necessary.'

'It is necessary to me,' she answered, and charged.

She came with bokken raised high, her sandalled feet shushing the gravel, and still he made no move. The wooden blade swept down in a savage stroke aimed at his neck only to clack against his blade at the very last instant.

He slid backwards, blade held readied; he was certain that cut would have broken his neck had he not caught it. 'Shear . . . please.'

She came on again, unhesitating, holding nothing back in her speed and power. Her assault drove him to yield ground, which he did, circling. Her skill astonished him; so far in his young career he'd faced no better – other than his teacher, of course. She'd obviously trained under the very best, and faced the strongest of opponents.

Yet after all these weeks of studying her technique – which was as close to flawless as he'd seen – it seemed to him that it possessed one weakness: a certain blindness to variety. Clearly she was extraordinarily well taught, yet that teaching had been limited within a single school of thought.

Whereas his training had involved exposure to countless.

And so he decided to defend for a time, letting her expend her first reserves. Though he did not fool himself into thinking she would weaken; her endurance was as formidable as her skill.

So they circled, feet shuffling among the gravel, swords clacking and grating. An onlooker could not have separated the intricacy of entwined feint, counter-feint, attack and riposte.

No prior true crossing of swords had ever lasted so long for Dassem. As veterans will say, most duels last only for one or two passes; superiority – or luck – usually reveals itself quickly.

She and he, however, had had time to become acquainted with one another's style and potential. This ruled out one of the main reasons behind the speed of most encounters: ignorance of the true ability of one's opponent. Their rigorous training also ruled out more commonplace explanations – overconfidence, impetuousness, and plain simple panic.

As Shear continued to push him it became clear that he would have to end this convincingly; no false yielding would satisfy her. So he gave veiled retreat while quickly changing angles before turning to the attack. Now she gave ground before him.

In mid-advance he suddenly switched to a new style that he had not yet used with her, a more raw brawling technique of the southern confederacy, and surprised her for an instant. This fraction of a second of advantage was all it bought him, yet it was enough to brush his blade across her forearm. She pulled back, disengaging, and stood openly breathing heavily, her chest rising and falling. She raised her bokken to her mask, acknowledging the touch, then sheathed it savagely through her sash. Both knew that in a bout as even as theirs such a wound – though certainly not fatal – would tip the scales in Dassem's favour. The match was over.

He sheathed his own bokken. 'An excellent fight,' he began,

but Shear simply turned and walked away into the moonlight. Frowning, he hurried after her. 'Please do not be upset. One of us had to win, the other not. You knew this.'

He was surprised to see her wiping at her face beneath her mask. 'You do not understand.'

'Will you not explain?'

She grasped her sash tightly. 'Among my people,' she began, clearing her throat, 'I held a certain rank among the most skilled. Now I must abandon that rank.'

'Because you lost to an outsider?'

'Because I lost.'

'Ah.' He walked silently with her for a time. The night wind was chill and he enjoyed the sensation as it crossed his sweaty face and cooled his sweat-soaked shirt. 'Do not be hard upon yourself. You should not take this defeat as meaning anything.'

'Oh? And why is that?'

'Because I am not like any other.'

Her lips quirked in amusement and she spared him one quick glance. 'Forgive me, but that sounds vain.'

'It is true. It was not a fair fight.'

'And why is that?'

'Because I am already dead.'

She halted amid the tall grass and, surprised, he halted as well. She studied him closely, then shook her head. 'Now you sound deluded, or insane.'

'No, it is true.' He invited her onward. 'Walk with me and I will tell you a story I have never told anyone else.'

Still she did not move. 'And what is this tale?'

'The story of my youth.'

She set a palm to the pommel of her bokken and peered round at the empty shadowed rustling grasslands; it was not yet midnight. Grinding out a breath, she walked on. 'If you must.'

He caught up, tucked his hands into his sash.

'I was born on the Dal Hon savanna. I never knew my father. Our village bordered a hilly region of dry caves, sinkholes and gorges. Here we children often went to play our games of brigands, raiders, and champions. And it was here that my journey began.

'One eve we played too long among the dusty gorges and ravines. Dusk came quickly, as it does in equatorial regions. Perceiving our negligence, and our danger, we ran for the village. I was among the youngest of the band, and the last straggler. That was when we heard the hunting growl of a leopard closer than we'd ever heard it before.

'We all screamed and ran in a blind panic, of course. We all knew the danger. These predators patrolled the boundaries of our village nightly, and we all knew someone – a cousin, or a neighbour's daughter – who had been taken over the years.'

Shear had her bokken out and was swishing it through the tall grass. 'Do not tell me you were eaten by a leopard.'

'No. Something even stranger. In the darkness and panic I fell into one of the many sinkholes and caves that pocketed the hills. Down I tumbled and struck my head.' He looked to the starred night sky, frowned in recollection. 'I arose – dazed from the blow to my head – and groped through the tunnels and caverns in a fog. How long I wandered I know not. All I know is that eventually I collapsed, perhaps from pain, or exhaustion, or even starvation.'

He glanced to Shear, awaiting another glib comment, but she was silent, evidently content to listen for the moment. He continued, 'I awoke to the light of a small fire, and I was not alone. Someone sat across the fire. At the time I thought him just a skinny old man, but later I realized that he was in fact a dried and desiccated corpse – perhaps the remains of another victim of the sinkholes. He told me that if I wished to escape the caves and return to my family I had to defeat him, and he tossed an old rusted hook-blade to me.'

'What did you do?' Shear asked, wonder now colouring her voice.

Dassem laughed. 'First I ran! I searched every foot of the caverns for escape. But there was none. The only way out was through him. And so I picked up the old blade and had at him.'

'And what happened?' Shear breathed.

He shrugged. 'He beat me down, of course. And when I straightened once more he corrected my grip. The next time he showed me a stance.' He let out a shaky breath then, as if reliving the terror of those lightless days. 'And so it went. On and on. Eventually I would become sleepy and lie down. When I awoke a small meal would be ready by the fire – a seared lizard or snake, a handful of old stale rice. And then we would fight again.

'As the days passed, I came to realize that I would never defeat this creature, whatever it was. So I threw down the blade. I told it I would not cooperate; that it had to let me pass.'

'And what happened?' Shear asked for a second time.

He shrugged again. 'It struck me down. When I awoke, I repeated my demand. And it struck me down once more. This kept on for some time, until, eventually, for some unknown reason, it relented and allowed me to pass.'

'I see,' Shear said quietly. 'So that is why you are different? Not like other swordmasters?'

They had stopped walking, as the camp was near. Its torches and lamps shone among the wagons and tents like a constellation brought to earth.

'That was only the beginning,' Dassem answered, and he let out a long steadying breath as if preparing himself for the memory to come. 'I returned to my village. It was dark outside beyond the caves, early evening. I ran straight to my family hut. There, as usual, was my mother preparing the evening meal at the stone hearth. I moved into the light at the open doorway and greeted her, my arms open.'

He paused, turning half away, and breathed harshly. 'My mother looked up. Her eyes widened in amazement. And then she screamed in complete horror. "*Begone, ghost!*" she howled at me. "Revenant! Fiend!" Nothing I said made any difference. She even threw stones at me. Then neighbours gathered and they too threw garbage and rocks. They drove me off from the village, calling me a ghost returned to torment them.'

He broke off, his voice choking, and he gripped the worn wood of the bokken, clenching his fingers until the knuckles whitened. Shear remained silent, watching, her eyes hidden behind her painted mask. After a time, he cleared his throat and continued, 'I learned afterwards that four months had passed. It had been assumed that the leopard had claimed me. There had even been a funeral. I have stood upon my own grave.'

He studied Shear, his lips quirking drolly. 'So you see. I am dead after all. There you are.' He sighed then, lifting his shoulders. 'Having nowhere else to go I returned to the caves and there found the ancient waiting for me at his small fire in the dark. I picked up the blade and returned to attempting to defeat him.'

'And what happened?' Shear asked for the third time, almost inaudibly.

He nodded, taking a deep breath to steady himself. 'I defeated him. It took twelve years. Twelve years of constant training and duelling under his tutelage. I did not remain hidden in the caverns all that time, of course . . . I went out for food and to seek company. But all had been warned against the ghost – the living man claimed by death – and so I was driven from every village. Eventually, I would reluctantly return to my harsh tutelage, and in the end I pushed him back and beat him down – or he deemed me skilled enough and allowed me to do so. In any case, of course, it was Hood himself possessing that body. And when I emerged once more into the sunlight I was his trained sword. The Mortal Sword of Hood. And so I have been – or was. But no longer.'

Shear was hugging herself, eyeing him in wonder, though it was difficult to see past her mask. 'That is not something one can just put down, I think, like an old coat, or a worn blade.'

He shrugged again. 'We shall see. In any case, I no longer answer to him.'

'Perhaps you do, though. Perhaps you cannot help but follow his path, as it is now part of you.'

He sighed, looking away to the distant fires of the camp. 'Yes. It may be that our choices are determined and limited by our character and learned preferences, that is true. However, it is still reassuring to hold on to the conceit of freedom, is it not?'

Shear smiled beneath her mask and reached out gently with one hand to caress his cheek; her hand was cold and hard against his face, but welcome. 'So, it is true,' she said, 'you *are* not like any other.'

Then she took his hand and led him aside to a meadow amid a copse of woods, and there she unbuckled her belt and let it fall into the tall grass, and he did as well. Tentatively, then, he reached up to her mask but gently she lowered his hand, saying, 'No. I have chosen to do it.'

So she lifted it from her face and stared up at him, bared perhaps for the first time with another. Her eyes were dark in the night and held his. He lowered his mouth to hers.

* * *

Tattersail pushed aside the open door to the main keep of the Hold and surveyed the damage. Her boots crunched on the litter of broken glass and pots. Mock entered behind her, his hands clasped behind his back, one dark brow arched in silent commentary.

255

A long table had been overturned. Kegs had been broached and left on their sides. Spilt wine stained the flags. Chairs lay every which way, and the stink of old meat and stale beer assailed her. Servants busy cleaning halted in their work and bowed, then returned to their duties.

Stooping, she picked up the broken stem of a slim wineglass. They'd even broken her finest crystal. 'Who was it?' she asked.

Mock gave an unconcerned wave then tried to pour a glass from a decanter but found it empty. 'The guards say it was Geffen come to try to take the Hold.'

'Send a crew to arrest him and confiscate all he has as payment.'

'Not necessary,' Mock answered, setting down the glass. 'He's dead.'

'Who did it?'

Mock swept his arms wide. 'Does it matter? I hear his lieutenant murdered him and decamped.' He stroked his chin. 'A wise woman, that.'

A guard wearing the gaudy purple colours of Mock's house guards – what Mock liked to call his 'Palace Guards' – approached and bowed. Tattersail didn't recognize the fellow. 'Hold secure, admiral.'

Mock acknowledged this then tilted his head thoughtfully. 'And where is Commander Durall?'

'Halfway to the Wickan Plains by now, I should think.'

Mock nodded. 'And you are . . . ?'

'Egil, sir.'

'Drew the short straw, did you?'

The man just shrugged in his leather hauberk. 'Next in command.'

'Perhaps I should have you thrown into a cell below, Egil.'

The guard's thin lips quirked up in a sort of sardonic comment. 'You're rather understaffed for that.'

Mock nodded sourly, his own expression mirroring the man's. 'Painfully true . . . commander.' And he dismissed him.

After Egil left – kicking through the wreckage as he went – Tattersail whispered, 'I don't trust that man.'

'I trust no one,' Mock answered, adding hastily, 'excepting you, of course.'

'So what do we do?'

He was systematically checking every keg and carafe for leavings. 'We wait, love. We wait and see.'

'See what?'

'Whether the captains agree on challenging me after this. My bet is that they won't.'

Tattersail crossed her arms tightly over her chest. *Good. That's one thing we don't need right now.* Across the hall, one surviving hanging caught her eye – Agayla's dark foreboding tapestry – and she winced. Stupid vandals! Of all the things to leave undamaged . . . then she shrugged. Perhaps some aura of that formidable woman imbued it. She knew she certainly didn't want to touch it. 'So they still agree you should be admiral.'

A burst of laughter answered her and she turned. Mock was shaking his head, a jug in his hand. 'You are so very charming, my dear.' He filled a glass from the jug, took an experimental sip, made a sour face, and continued drinking regardless. 'They *all* think they can do a better job than I . . . they just can't agree who should! And they all know I have one thing they do not.'

'Which is?'

The heels of his tall boots crackled over the litter as he approached, and he brushed the back of a hand across her cheek. 'You, my dear. They all saw who broke the Napan lines and who allowed them to escape – *you*, my dear.'

He opened his arms wide, jug in one hand, glass in the other, winking. 'I will check upstairs, love. I just pray no one vomited there.'

Watching him go, Tattersail shook her head. *Such a rogue!*

Footsteps at the entrance brought her round. A woman was standing in the threshold, peering about the reception hall. Tattersail had never seen her before, and from her plain homespun shirt and trousers and dirty bare feet, she thought her a servitor come to ask for work in the kitchens. She drew breath to shoo her out of the keep but in that instant she felt the woman's full presence, and the weight and power of her aura nearly thrust her back. *Ye gods! Who is this?*

Tattersail's hands jerked to raise her Warren as the woman came forward, kicking unconcerned through broken glass. One hand instead went to her throat and clutched there, as her breath would not come. 'Who are you?' she managed shakily.

The woman was short, like her, but willow thin. Her features were odd – perhaps of a people unknown to Tattersail: the face long and the eyes large. The mouth lipless.

'Call me Nightchill,' she answered.

'What do you want?'

'You.'

Tattersail clutched even tighter at her neck. She gasped, 'Why?'

'To meet you. I sensed your performance. It was impressive.'

The terrifying power of this woman's aura – the most potent she had ever sensed, far greater than the glimpses she had had of Agayla's – made Tattersail want to faint, but she dragged her hand from her throat and nodded, acknowledging the compliment, whispering, 'Well . . . thank you.'

'And to tell you that you are wasted here.'

Now Tattersail frowned. 'Did Agayla send you?'

An entirely humourless smile drew up one edge of the woman's slash of a mouth. 'No. Agayla did not send me. I am here to do you this one favour, and to warn you. There are powers circling this island that you are not ready for, child. They will annihilate you. Leave while you can.'

Now Tattersail found her teeth clenching and her legs steadying. This again! 'I can take care of myself and I'll leave when I damn well choose!'

The woman shrugged, untroubled. 'Very well. It is your choice. Do not say I did not warn you, however.' And she tipped her head in farewell and walked away.

Tattersail's gaze went to the midnight hanging once more and narrowed there. Damn her meddling! Then her brows clenched and she stared anew. Was that ugly portrait of the Hold even darker with swirling shadows now?

*

Nedurian stood at Malaz's harbour wharf and watched the beaten and bedraggled fleet of freebooters and would-be raiders come straggling in. Mock's *Insufferable* had been among the first, looking damaged from the engagement, but still seaworthy. The *Intolerant* and the *Intemperate* were missing, apparently casualties of the engagement. So too were so many of the freebooter fleet. More were limping in even as he watched, but it appeared as if fully half the assembled flotilla had failed to escape the ambush.

King Tarel had struck his piratical rivals a severe blow. It was

258

the talk of the waterfront, of course; the Napan betrayal. And thinking of his employers, Nedurian was worried. The townsfolk might want blood.

He pushed away from the wooden crates he was leaning against and headed to the row of waterfont dives that included the Hanged Man, and Smiley's.

He found the Napan crew closing up shop even though it was the evening, the best time for their trade. A small two-wheeled cart stood at the door. In it lay the body of Amiss, wrapped in canvas sail cloth and sewn tight.

'Come with us,' Surly said, sounding tired. Tocaras helped her up on to the cart, where she sat cradling her side with one arm. Urko took up the two poles of the cart and started pulling, and the rest of the Napans followed along.

It was to be a burial, obviously, and Nedurian didn't know whether to be honoured or resentful at being included; honoured, as the only non-Napan present, resentful because perhaps he wasn't trusted enough to be left behind.

Urko led them south to the very tip of the waterfront, where fishers pulled their tiny dories and dugouts from the surf. Coins changed hands with one such fellow and Urko gently carried the wrapped body to a dory and laid it within.

Surly waved Nedurian to join them. He sat at the bow, wrapped in a blanket against the unusual chill of the night. A lantern next to him lit the waves and the five Napans: Surly, Shrift and Tocaras at the canvas-wrapped body, Urko and Grinner at the oars.

Once they were far out beyond the harbour, Surly and lean Tocaras lifted the body to the gunwale. Surly said a few words in benediction, or farewell, and together they let slip the corpse into the dark water and watched it sink from sight.

After a long silence, empty but for the slap of the waves and the far-off crash of the surf into the cliffs north of the city, Urko and Shrift began to power the small dory back to the glow of the distant lanterns of Malaz harbour. Nedurian addressed Tocaras. 'So, a burial at sea . . .'

The tall, pole-slim fellow nodded sombrely. 'Yes. Always a sea burial for us Napans. It's a tradition.' And he added, more softly, 'But not for me.'

'No?'

'No.'

'May I ask why not?'

Looking out across the dark waters, the fellow grimaced as if in distaste. 'I hate it. The sea. It's taken too many from me.'

Nedurian thought of so many of his old friends, gone now, and he nodded. 'I can understand that.'

No more was said until they returned to Smiley's. Nedurian, Surly and Urko took up posts to keep watch. The mage sat at one of the narrow windows, an eye on the gleaming cobbles of the night-time street. Urko sat at the door, while Surly busied herself at the bar. A large fire cast an uneven amber glow over the common room.

Nedurian sipped his watered wine. He glanced about the quiet room, asked, 'What about your local hires? Where are they?'

'They'll drag their sorry arses back once they've run out of coin,' Surly said from behind the scarred wooden counter.

'And what about you lot?' he asked Urko, who sat on a tall stool with his hands and chin resting atop a short hardwood staff before him. His coarse features drew down in a scowl.

'What about us?'

'Why are you still here? Why not leave? You heard how King Tarel betrayed the fleet. Mock might order you arrested.'

Urko snorted his derision. 'He can try.'

'What I mean is, wouldn't it be safer to head to the mainland, hire out as crew?'

The giant fellow's gaze slid to Surly, his wide knotted hands clenched on the staff. 'Can't. We're—'

'That's enough,' Surly cut in. Her eyes were on Nedurian now, suspicious. 'You're asking a lot of questions.'

He raised his hands open in surrender. 'You're right. Never mind. None of my business. But I'll let you know . . . I really don't care if you're wanted on the mainland.'

Urko just eyed Surly, saying nothing.

'We'll leave,' Surly added, meditatively cleaning glasses, 'when the *Twisted* returns.'

'It's overdue,' Nedurian said, then wished he hadn't.

Now Urko lowered his gaze, frowning even more deeply, his hands clenching as he thumped the staff to the hardwood floor.

*

Three nights later, Jull Solman, a fisherman out of Malaz City, sat in the dugout that his father had sat in all his life, and set his lines.

His lantern wobbled and glowed in the night from its stand at the pointed bow.

Satisfied with his lines, he crouched and waited for the lantern to do its work of drawing the curious fish from the dark depths below. During these quiet moments he would think, and he reflected now that all his life he'd resented that he was still nothing more than a fisher like his father before him . . . while others, friends and cousins, had joined the raiders and become crew on Malazan freebooters.

That is, until this latest disastrous raid, what with near half the crews failing to return. Only now was he beginning to see the wisdom in his father's words, and his demands that he follow in his footsteps and remain a fisher.

Perhaps he hadn't been such a bitter, mean, stubborn, worthless old fool after all.

As to his father's other claims and wild talk . . . well, some things were just too foolish to believe. That these raiders and pirates were just recent arrivals to the island and that its true occupants were the fisher folk themselves? Jull could only shake his head. What of it if it were true?

And that the island's true guardian and protector was a common fisher just like them? He reached out and jiggled one of the lines. Nothing more than wishful thinking. Ridiculous old local legends and stories.

That hook, as the saying goes, was just too big to swallow.

It was then in his musings that he glimpsed a strange glow approaching from the south. Squinting, he sat up and stared, studying the eerie phenomenon. A patch of nightglow as can sometimes gyre atop the waves? A gathering of the bright deep-water fish? Or – and here the hair upon his neck stirred and prickled – the daemon Stormriders come to claim his spirit?

The glow thickened into a patch of mist and fog that closed upon him, and now, amid this freezing witch-gust of air, there emerged the tall prow of a vessel. Jull gaped up as it passed: a caravel, great tendrils and scarves of mist boiling from its hull; its sails hanging in torn ribbons; great sheaths of ice crackling and calving from its sides as it came. And there, in spidery silver upon its black hull as it loomed past, he read, emblazoned, the name *Twisted*.

Jull fell back into his dugout as it rocked gently from the ghostly passage. By the gods! The cursed witch-vessel itself. Everyone said it had sunk! Yet here it was, spat up from the very floor of the Abyss. Returned from the sunken paths of Ruse. Cursed from who knew what fiendish rendezvous? Perhaps a pact with the Riders themselves . . .

He shivered anew in the unearthly wind blowing off the daemon-vessel as he yanked up his lines. This tale would win him an entire night of free drinks at the Hanged Man. What a dreadful portent! The *Twisted* returned from its presumed end . . . he shook his head as he readied the oars. Escaped the ambush after all . . . well, who would even dare attack it anyway?

Dreadful times were coming with the return of such a harbinger, for sure.

Chapter 14

KORO ALIGHTED ON THE BLUNT STONE TIP OF A STANDING menhir and cocked his head, regarding with his black beady eyes the surrounding rocky dunes of what some named the Plains of Waste. Idly, he preened the bedraggled fur of his body and wondered anew what to do about these damned pesky meddlers in Shadow.

If Edgewalker refused to act – the obdurate fool! – then it must fall to him.

Yet how to be rid of them?

Had Koro still held human form he would have tapped his chin with a finger, but as it was he pecked at the gritty ancient stone of the menhir then squawked and flapped his membranous wings in alarm as a spark of power glowed to silver life and began rolling a turning route down the outside of the carved stone.

He alighted again, watching, intrigued, while the quicksilver flash spiralled like a bead of mercury down a curved runnel hacked in the face of the stone. Glyphs of power glowed to life as it descended.

Close to the base, the bead of silver was now a blazing fist of power spinning with dizzying speed.

Koro squawed anew, losing his perch, as the ball of sizzling might smashed into something at the base of the stone. Alighting once more, he turned first one black bead of an eye to the spot, then the other. A heap of wind-blown sand there was shifting, and a groan reached him.

A chitinous armoured head and shoulders emerged, shaking off the sands.

Koro now knew where he perched, and he looked to the pewter sky. Oh, *him*.

'Where am I?' the unfortunate below asked aloud.

'You are imprisoned,' Koro answered.

The alien angles of the daemon's armoured head lowered as it considered its buried torso. 'This I see.'

'I want to get rid of two meddling troublemakers,' Koro continued. 'Have you any ideas?'

'Troublemakers?' the entity echoed, sounding confused. 'What, pray tell, do you mean by that?'

'Oh, shut up!' Koro hissed, shifting from foot to foot.

'I once was powerful,' the daemon murmured, as if groping after something. 'I once was . . . someone . . .'

Koro rolled his pebble eyes to the sky once more. 'Oh, please! Well, now you're an imprisoned nobody.' Then he jumped, his tattered wings half-flapping, and he opened his beak in silent laughter. *Of course!*

'Do you know my name?' the creature below asked, almost plaintively.

'Shut up, fool – I am having an inspiration!'

'I think you know my name,' the daemon continued stubbornly.

Koro cursed, pecked the stone, then jumped into the air. 'Fool!'

A spark of silver glowed to life atop the menhir.

'I will remember you!' the daemon howled after him.

No you won't.

And he cawed his harsh laughter as he went.

*

The meagre fire cast further shifting shadows across the tall crumbling walls of the gulch surrounding them, and standing in the darkness Dancer wondered on the wisdom of such an . . . extravagance?

He glanced back to the fire, and the dark figure hunched there, staring into its depths, chin resting atop his walking stick. Clenching his teeth, he returned to stare down at Kellanved. After a moment, he let out a long-suffering breath and said once more, 'We really should return.'

The wizened black-skinned mage did not answer; he kept his gaze firm upon the fire. Wilfully so, it seemed to Dancer, who cleared his throat again. 'They'll catch us eventually – you must know this.'

The hunched Dal Hon shrugged, unconcerned. 'I will shift us again.'

'There were four last time.'

'I can now stay ahead of them.'

Dancer drew a quick breath, fought down his anger and grated, 'For the moment. But eventually . . .'

The little man's shoulders clenched higher and his lips tightened stubbornly.

Sighing, Dancer looked away to the weak shifting shadows. 'What is this thing you're trying to sense, anyway?'

'The node!' the young mage – who still appeared an ancient – exploded. 'The locus! The heart!'

Dancer eyed the surrounding slopes and eased the blades in their sheaths about his chest, thighs, and neck. 'And what does all that rubbish mean in plain language?'

The little man flapped his hands in mute frustration. Finally, he slammed his stick into the sands. 'You have heard, I hope, of the Throne of Night?'

'Yes. In songs and legends.'

'Well, exactly,' the mage announced, as if it were all common sense.

'Exactly what?'

The Dal Hon spluttered, flapping his hands. 'Well – Light and Night had thrones, yes?'

Dancer nodded. 'So they say.'

'Well . . . so too must Shadow, then!'

Dancer drew a blade, a razor stiletto, and thumbed its edge. 'I understand that's all more poetry than history.'

Kellanved examined his ebony walking stick, huffing. 'Well . . . yes. However, each must possess some centre of power. Some locus. Call it what you will. Control that, and one controls the entire Realm!'

Dancer pushed the blade home into the sheath at his left wrist, nodded thoughtfully. 'Our path is disputed.'

Kellanved now tapped his fingers upon the silver hound's head of the walking stick. 'Yes. Well. An inconvenience. Once we have—'

Dancer raised a finger. 'No. They must be handled first. And we cannot do that while on the run.'

Kellanved set his chin atop the stick as if pouting and stared into the guttering fire. After a time he sighed, resentfully, 'Oh . . . very well!'

Dancer eased his shoulders, and the joints cracked with the strain of his tension. Inwardly, he allowed himself a satisfied nod. *Very good.*

He sat across the fire to rest. 'You will keep watch?'

The mage nodded. 'Yes. I will keep watch.'

The next day – if the slight brightening of the monochromatic grey of Shadow could be called 'day' – Dancer became aware of the dot in the sky of the strange flying creature which, from time to time, seemed to have been trailing them.

'It's back,' he announced to Kellanved, who merely waved his stick, unimpressed.

This time, however, the shape flapped ever closer, becoming ever larger, until it plopped down ahead of them in a very ungainly fashion, raising dust as it paced about. Dancer thought it an ugly cross between a bat and a pelican. Kellanved, for his part, stopped before it and rested his hands atop his walking stick. Then he actually addressed it, saying invitingly, 'Yes?'

To Dancer's surprise, and profound unease, the creature drew itself up almost haughtily and cawed, 'Welcome to Shadow.'

Kellanved merely nodded, as if this were an everyday occurrence. 'Our thanks. Welcome indeed.'

The bat-thing now cast its tiny glistening black eyes about the desolate surroundings, then lowered its knife-like head to croak, 'I know what it is you seek.'

Kellanved glanced to Dancer, his brows raised. 'And that is . . . ?'

The beast actually looked to the sky as if exasperated. 'Shadow House, of course!' It bounced from one clawed foot to the other. 'Shadow House, you fool!'

Now Kellanved shot Dancer a rather bemused look. He gave an exaggerated knowing nod. 'Ahhhh! Shadow House. Of course!'

The creature calmed, bobbing its hatchet head. 'I will take you.'

'Why?' Dancer demanded.

The beast squawked, flapping its ragged wings of black skin. 'What? Why? I offer you the Realm and you ask *why*?'

Kellanved stilled. 'The Realm, you say?'

'Why?' Dancer asked again, his voice now hard. He glanced about, wondering whether this was a delaying tactic. Were enemies closing upon them even now?

'Tell me more about the Realm,' Kellanved invited.

'Why?' Dancer repeated, firmly, eyeing the horizons.

Kellanved sighed, his shoulders slumping. 'Very well. Why?'

The beast's gaze shifted right to left. 'Ah, well . . .' It rubbed its wings together and lowered its head even further. 'There are secrets within. Secrets that you must share with me!'

Kellanved turned to Dancer. 'There you are. Secrets.' He pointed his walking stick ahead. 'Do lead on.'

The creature bounced into the air, laughing a bird-like croak as it went. 'This way!'

Kellanved strolled onward. Dancer pressed a hand to his forehead, then reluctantly followed. 'I don't like it,' he complained.

The Dal Hon mage waved the stick about to indicate the leagues of empty rocky hillsides. 'Which of our many options would you prefer, then?'

Dancer gritted his teeth. 'Fine. We investigate then leave, yes?'

Ahead, Kellanved nodded absently, already humming to himself.

They travelled for what seemed to Dancer to be far too long; eventually the hounds would arrive, as they always did. And he saw no likely cave or retreat anywhere within reach. Once more they were gambling on Kellanved's being able to shift them elsewhere and Dancer did not like it. One failure and that would be it.

Ahead, a dark line appeared to be nearing – some sort of break in the monotonous rocky desert landscape of this region of Shadow. Dancer was now leading Kellanved, who limped, wincing in his tattered shoes, and so he paused, gesturing ahead. 'Our destination?'

Kellanved came alongside, winded and sweating. He shaded his gaze. 'Very possibly. There is something there. I sense . . .' He trailed off as above the dark shape of their guide was now stooping towards them, its thin wings flapping furiously.

As it passed overhead it squawked: '*Run!*'

Dancer caught his companion's eye. *Shit.*

They both ran.

Dancer, however, soon pulled ahead of the limping, huffing

mage and so he halted, kicking up dust and stones, cursing. He drew his heaviest blades, searched the hillsides behind for signs of movement.

Quiet this time. Getting smarter.

'Hurry,' he snapped at Kellanved, who'd halted with him.

'If I'd known we'd be tramping all over I'd have worn different shoes, I assure you.'

'Just run,' Dancer snapped, impatient.

But the mage merely shook his head, gesturing ahead, panting.

Reluctant, dreading what he knew he'd see, Dancer slowly turned about. Ahead, two shapes fully as large as colts had risen from among the rocks, each shaking sand from its back. One bore savage scars across its black muzzle, while the other's mismatched eyes blazed yellow and blue.

Hunting as a pack. Should've known.

He raised his twinned heavy parrying gauches while turning full circle. From each direction a hound now closed. He counted five.

Driven? Can we have been driven like rabbits into this ambush?

'Get us out of here,' he mouthed to Kellanved.

Overhead, their erstwhile guide had taken off, flying like an arrow for the dark line far off on the horizon. And Dancer wondered . . . could they have been following it? How smart were these things?

'How many are there of these beasts, do you imagine?' Kellanved asked.

'Just move us!'

'Yes, yes. No need to be snippy.'

Dancer turned another full circle to see that, indeed, the creatures were closing upon them from all sides. They were not of one singular hue, being tawny, or earthen brown, or mottled grey and black. Yet they were certainly alike in their titanic size, and the strange lustre, or luminosity, of their eyes. They stalked forward now, low on their forepaws, ears down, lips pulled back from canines the length of his fingers. Their low hunting growl shook the ground beneath his feet and vibrated in his chest.

'Now would be good,' he murmured to his companion.

But Kellanved did not have to respond. Tatters of darkness flitted across Dancer's vision, deepening and thickening like sifting shadows until he could see only dense murk, like a midnight under-water vision of the world.

A blasting howl of lustful frustration made him flinch, and then he hit the ground hard and rolled in dust.

He came up with weapons raised, circling, but they were alone. Kellanved sat hunched in the dust nearby; he appeared to be examining his feet. A forest's edge rose some leagues distant – their destination, Dancer assumed.

'Run,' he said.

The mage gestured to the flapping leather remnants of his shoes. 'I really do have a complaint for that cobbler.'

'Ignore them – just run!'

'I can't!'

A hound's deep rich baying sounded from the distance, closing.

Dancer yanked him to his feet and they ran, awkwardly, Kellanved hopping as he pulled at the tattered strips tied about his feet.

Dancer searched the edge for some path or route into the thick woods, but none was visible, so he headed straight for the nearest verge and ploughed in, pushing aside dry black branches, his feet sinking into a deep loose layer of rotting leaves and bracken. Only after pushing onward for some time, yanking Kellanved firmly along, did he pause, listening. He could hear the beast's howling still, but it sounded strangely distant, muted somehow.

A rustling in the branches above caused him to snatch up his throwing daggers. It was the black bat-like thing, hopping among the higher boughs. 'You see!' it croaked, triumphant.

'They are not following,' Kellanved observed, and he frowned in distaste at his bare feet. 'Why are they not following?'

The bat-thing cocked its head. Its black pebble eyes peered about. 'Well, uh . . . they are forbidden! Yes! They are forbidden from entering the forest.'

'Why?'

Koro hopped from foot to foot in frustration. 'Because they are! Because of the House – yes! The House is near!'

Dancer peered into the tangled depths of the woods. 'How near?'

'Near!' The creature flapped into the air, calling, 'This way!'

Kellanved was gingerly testing his feet on the cluttered ground. 'Perhaps you could—'

'No, I couldn't,' Dancer cut in, heading off to follow the beast.

'Just for a short while . . .'

269

'No.'

'Until we reach the House.'

'No.'

'You're not being cooperative at all,' the mage grumbled.

'I did not buy cheap shoes.'

Kellanved harrumphed. 'They were not cheap, I tell you that.'

'All the more reason—'

'Could you two possibly shut up!' came a call from above. Both Dancer and Kellanved peered upwards, blinking. Koro was above, bobbing its sharp, knife-like head. 'I'm trying to listen!'

Dancer stilled, listening as well.

'For what?' Kellanved asked, and Dancer shot him a glare.

Each of the creature's wide membranous wings held a tiny clawed hand and the beast pressed one now to its edged beak, hissing, 'Shh!'

Dancer listened, motionless. He heard only the creaking of the countless trees about them. Kellanved cleared his throat. 'Ah, there's something . . .'

'Quiet.'

'Something's got my—'

Dancer turned on him. 'Will you be quiet!'

The mage pointed to his feet, hidden in the deep loam. 'Something's grabbed my foot.'

Dancer cursed; he moved to draw a blade but found he couldn't – a vine had tightened itself about his forearm. 'What in the name of . . .'

Kellanved was suddenly yanked down into the loam up to his knees. Yet he did not appear panicked, only embarrassed. He observed, 'Well, this is depressingly familiar.'

Dancer tried to reach a blade with his other hand but found it too bound by vines. They pulled, yanking him tight up against a nearby tree trunk.

Above, the creature cawed its harsh laugh. 'Here they come – your panicked screams! Ha, ha, ha.'

'Are you panicked?' Dancer asked Kellanved.

The mage threw his walking stick at the beast, missing widely. 'Not yet.'

The creature paced back and forth on its high branch. 'Well, they're coming! I assure you! Once you find yourself— gahhh!'

The bat-thing now hung upside down, swinging wildly, one foot caught up by a vine. 'Help! It has me! Look what you've done! You fools!'

It flapped its wings furiously, pulling and pulling; then, with a parting snap, the vine broke and the beast ricocheted off, bouncing from tree to tree. 'You will scream!' it squawked as it flapped away. 'You'll see! Entombed for ever! Absorbed! Becoming one with Shadow! Ha, ha!'

Dancer watched it go, then settled his attention upon Kellanved. 'So. What now?'

The mage was tapping a free hand to his chin, his eyes narrowed. 'Could it really be that simple?' he mused aloud.

Thick woody limbs now closed upon Dancer's chest, tightening. 'Whatever it is you'd better hurry.'

A vine yanked Kellanved's hand away and he was pulled down to his waist. 'An idea,' he explained. 'All this time I've been trying to *force* Shadow. But perhaps that's wrong. Perhaps I should ease into it. Become one with it, as the creature said. Perhaps that's the secret.'

Dancer did not answer as he was holding his breath in outward pressure against the crushing embrace of the branches. He simply jerked a nod and fumed that he could no longer even curse the pontificating fool.

The mage was nodding as he slipped to his chest among the rotting leaves. 'Very well. I will give it a try – though it will be difficult and we are far from Malaz.'

Dancer smiled a rictus of encouragement, his lips clenched.

'So . . . here goes,' the mage said as his head disappeared down beneath the loamy steaming surface.

His vision darkening, Dancer looked to the pewter-grey sky through the closing branches. *Well . . . so much for that.* The limbs tightened, crushing his chest, and his breath burst from him. He fought to inhale again and again, until nothingness took him.

* * *

The day of his execution Tayschrenn wore the clean linen shirt and trousers provided for him. Stubble now roughened his skull and chin, and though he'd no polished bronze or silver mirror to see in he knew he'd lost weight and must appear rather haggard. As anyone who'd spent weeks contemplating one's imminent execution would. Especially when a fresh cup of poison is provided alongside each day's portion of water.

That day, two of the cult Fangs appeared at his cell as escort. When the thick wooden door was pulled open they'd seemed a touch surprised to find him within, and still alive. In the past, many so sentenced had preferred to take their own life rather than face the horror to come. Which was precisely why the priesthood had allowed him to sit so long in solitary reflection on that poison.

And which was precisely why he refused the option. No convenient hidden disappearance that could easily be swept aside and forgotten for him. No, he would go out in full public display and do his best to rub their faces in it.

And so he rose from his meditation, dressed in the clean new clothes, and exited calmly and quietly.

One factor did penetrate his calm, however. It was plain from his cell window that it was the dead of night. As he walked the empty halls, the uneasy suspicion came to him that perhaps they intended to throw him into the Pits unannounced, in the dark, without any witnesses.

The way one might dispose of an embarrassing piece of evidence.

High Priestess Salleen, after all, hadn't announced the exact *time* of his execution. Just the sort of oily bureaucratic solution a career functionary might favour.

The suspicion wormed through the wall of calm he'd so carefully built between his fears and his reason, and caused him to check his pace. *What then?*

One of the Fangs urged him onward and he resumed pacing, thinking, *Well, if they go that far then perhaps I need not co-operate after all . . .*

His fears, however, were put to rest when he was delivered to a holding cell at the Civic Pit. Here, he knew, he would sit and wait while the crowd gathered above. It now looked like a noon execution.

The morning's light grew slanting down in dust-filled rays from high narrow windows. The day's heat reached his cell. The muted din of conversation slowly swelled. It sounded like a packed crowd. Then came a quiet knock at his door and he cocked a brow. Really? A polite knock?

'Yes?'

A Fang of D'rek opened the door from without and a white-robed acolyte entered. She held in both hands a small earthenware cup full of a thick dark liquid.

Tayschrenn knew this: D'rek's Mercy – a numbing potion that would dull the pain to come. Unfortunately, it also numbed the mind. The young woman held out the cup, her head lowered.

He shook his head, then to his surprise found that he had to swallow to speak, and murmured, 'No.'

She bowed lower, saying, 'This is not about bravery, Tayschrenn.'

'I do not wish to go to D'rek with a clouded mind.'

The acolyte nodded. 'I understand.' She withdrew to the door, but paused there, trembling almost. 'I am sorry, Tayschrenn. Not all agree with this.'

He frowned at her. Agree with what? His execution? Tallow's rise?

One of the Fangs guarding the cell grabbed her arm and pulled her out, slamming the door shut.

He sat in silence, frowning still. Had there been a faction looking to him, after all? Had he, in his inaction, let them down? Yet he had not asked for any of this, nor did he want it.

So he sat while above roars and cheering came and went for the preliminary executions – petty criminals, minor cult offenders and the like – until a single voice, rendered unintelligible by the yards of stone between, spoke at length.

They were announcing him, listing his supposed crimes.

Sure enough, the door opened and the two Fangs of D'rek gestured him out. Rising, he was surprised again by how dry his mouth was and the heat and sweat of his hands. Just the flesh, he reminded himself, dreading impending dissolution. That is all.

He was led up a narrow passage of dressed stone blocks. Cells lining the way held the condemned, and the stink of human excrement, piss and stale sweat hung thick in the enclosed space. Tayschrenn merely noted all this in passing, without discomfort; he knew far worse was to come. In the half-light steaming down from a door ahead he noted messages scrawled upon the faces of the blocks: *Tell Herina I love her, Damn the bitch Salleen!* and *May D'rek forgive them.*

The Fang ahead at the door carried a red sash. She waved him closer. 'Turn round,' she ordered. Feeling oddly dazed, Tayschrenn complied. His hands were taken and the sash was cinched tight about his wrists.

He gave a light snort of appreciation of the gesture – Tallow, it would seem, was not without a poetic side.

The iron latch of the door clanged, the heavy stone barrier grated as it swung open, and Tayschrenn was pushed out on to the glaringly bright sands of the Civic Pit. He stood blinking for a time, unaccustomed to the light, and a huge roar arose from the stands, a punishing thunder of shouts, applause, catcalls, curses, and cheering.

Squinting around, he saw that the rising circular rings of the coliseum were very nearly full to capacity. A good turnout for Salleen and Tallow.

Dutifully, he walked out towards the centre of the broad circular pit. The dry husks of thousands of shed carapaces crackled beneath his sandalled feet as he went. The sunlight blasted down upon him and he couldn't even bring his hands out from behind his back to shield his gaze. He damned the heat; already his clothes hung heavy and damp.

Sweating, he noted, distantly and analytically. *I am sweating so much because I am . . . frightened. There. It's been said. I can admit it. The terror of the unknown. In that at least I share a commonality with the herd that surrounds me.*

More or less at the centre he halted and turned to face the main seating platform. In the glare he couldn't make out any one individual, just a sea of dark robes. Eventually, the roaring calls and jeers died down enough for a single voice to surface above the sullen grumbling.

'Tayschrenn!' the voice called – High Priestess Salleen.

He raised his chin with what he hoped signalled defiance and pride. Yet he was panting, his pulse racing in that damned unavoidable fleshly weakness. *Deep breaths*, he chided himself.

'Your crimes against the integrity of the cult have been enumerated and suitable punishment has been writ. You have been found guilty of putting your own benefit and selfish desires ahead of the good of the faith of D'rek. Have you any last words before judgement is enacted?'

Strange, he noted, standing before them, blinking, how power-hungry people tend to charge their opponents with the very sins that apply to them. He opened his mouth to speak but found he had no breath for speech. The sun's glare was making his eyes water – why else would wetness be cold on his cheeks? And the tightness in his chest choking off speech – appalled outrage, surely.

'No? Nothing?' Salleen prompted. 'Not even an appeal to D'rek for forgiveness?'

This announcement stung Tayschrenn like nothing else in the entire charade of the trial, the cowardly sentencing, and now this farcical perversion of mercy. '*Forgiveness?*' he shouted, hoarse, his voice near cracking. '*You* are the ones who will beg for forgiveness!' But Salleen had signalled the drummers and now their blasting cacophony robbed him of any hope of being heard. None the less, the dark bulk next to Salleen that was Tallow seemed to stir at his words, perhaps uneasy, perhaps worried that he would lash out now, at the end.

But he would give them no such satisfaction.

He would meet D'rek with more dignity and courage than any they could ever muster – though it annoyed him how his eyes did sting and water in the glare and he could not wipe them.

So he turned his back upon them to await the end. The thunder of the drums shook the sands beneath his feet, vibrating the ground, calling the denizens below. And there in the dark caverns and tunnels he knew they stirred, rising, heeding the summons. Soon they would be upon him, seething, pricking, filling his mouth and nose until he choked . . .

He blinked savagely, weaving upon his feet, suddenly unsteady.

The heat, he decided. *Must be this damned heat . . .*

The hissing of the horde's arrival assaulted him then. Louder, it seemed, even than the drums. All about him, closing. He blinked the tears from his eyes, fought the rabid urge to flee. *No*, he thought to himself . . . *Wait!*

A tickling wave of thousands surged across his feet like a surf. Countless probosces probed his flesh. A million feet climbed his ankles.

Wait . . . No! This is not . . . I want to . . .

A rising numbness in his feet and legs now made it difficult to stand. He fell to his knees, or thought he did. Was this tide of vermin rising upon him or was he sinking into it? He could no longer tell.

The numbness took his chest and for this he was thankful, as a writing layer of creatures now blanketed his clamped mouth and closed eyes. But he could not seal his nostrils and they entered there – the tiny silverfish and the smallest of the flesh-eating maggots. Then his breath exploded from him in a convulsive gasp and they foamed into his opened mouth as he inhaled.

He gagged and gagged, rolling and vomiting even as he fought to inhale. But no breath could breach the sea of writhing creatures choking him. He screamed mutely in an abhorrence and revulsion beyond any his mind could grasp, and, thankfully, it gave up. Darkness descended . . .

*

Though the Civic Pit lay far across the city, Silla could still hear the muted distant roar of the gathered crowd. Even in this court over-looking the sea from a far side chapel of the temple, even here she could not escape it.

As if she ever would for the rest of her life.

She wrung her cold hands together, pacing. Why was the fool still here! Wasn't enough enough? Must he go to the end to prove his point?

That thought froze her in her pacing.

Of course he would. He was right. He knew he was right. And he would go to the end to prove it.

But Tallow had promised her it would never come to this. That he would send him away to a new life on the mainland.

The Invigilator! She grasped the stone lip of the ledge over-looking the sea. Damn the man! Nothing but lies!

She stilled, watching the dizzying glimmer of the waves far below. But that wasn't true. He hadn't lied. He'd showed her concocted evidence and testimony that he could've used to condemn Tayschrenn to the death of the Fang that very day in court. Only her cooperation had saved his life. Only her testimony saved him from the poison that day.

Only today . . .

She jumped then as the reverberation of the drums struck her.

He's still there? *Why? Why won't he flee?*

She pressed her fists to her mouth. Damn him! Damn the stubborn fool! Would he really be *that* wilfully determined? To go to his death rather than yield to anyone?

She nodded then, a fist at her mouth, and sighed. *Yes . . . Yes, he would.*

The distant commingled awe and delight of thousands now swelled and she clutched at the ledge for support. *Great D'rek! He's being taken!* Taken!

And all because of her. No – she saved him! Saved his life that day. And Tallow assured her it wouldn't come to this . . .

Tallow! She straightened then, her breath easing from her in a hiss. From inside her robes she drew a small sheathed dagger and examined the wax seal at the lip of the bronze sheath.

This she had meant for herself. But another had earned its kiss far more than she. She would play the part of the beaten-down disciple for now. Until the moment came. Then he would pay for his lies. *He will pay.*

She pushed the sheathed blade back down within her robes, wiped the wetness from her face, and slipped back within the temple precincts.

Chapter 15

CARTHERON STOOD WITH CHOSS AND HAWL ON BOARD THE *Twisted*, awaiting Surly. It had been nearly a week since they'd limped into Malaz harbour, and now their commander wanted a detailed appraisal of the ship's condition.

The news was grim and Surly, he knew, would not be happy.

He watched from the railing as she marched out on to the pier, accompanied by Urko, Shrift, and ten or so local Malazan toughs – her bodyguard now that they'd hardened their control of the majority of the island's black market. Also trailing along was this new follower, Nedurian, old and scarred, in plain travel-stained leathers, looking more like a retired fisherman than a veteran mage. Cartheron had to say that he wasn't certain he trusted the fellow yet.

The toughs remained at the gangway while Surly, Urko, Shrift and the mage came stamping up. On deck, she crossed her arms and faced him; her habitual sour expression demanded, *Well?* He noticed she favoured her side, where, he understood, Geffen had cut her quite badly before she broke his neck. Local healers had done their work, but these things still smarted, he knew.

Cartheron cleared his throat, glanced to Choss and Hawl. Might as well jump into the depths, he reasoned. 'We recommend laying up the entire winter season for a proper refit.'

That he'd said the wrong thing was immediately evident in her flat side-to-side denial. 'Not what I want to hear, Crust. I want off this island.'

'We need the time,' Choss put in. 'We struck two ice floes.'

'Doesn't matter. I don't want to be here all winter.'

'She won't be ready,' Hawl said.

Shrift now waved her impatience, butting in. 'What's the problem? We just take another!' She motioned all about. 'There're plenty.'

'Not like this one,' Nedurian drawled from where he leaned against the railing outside their circle.

Shrift turned a sneer on the man. For some unknown reason the swordswoman had no time for the mage. 'Oh? How so?'

By way of answer, the fellow rested his lazy gaze on Hawl. 'Because she's ensorcelled. Isn't that so, Hawl?'

Hawl eyed him in turn, then nodded. 'Aye.'

'No other vessel could have made it out of the strait,' the mage continued. 'Isn't that true?'

'Possibly,' Hawl granted.

Cartheron was thinking of the *Just Cause*. They'd lost sight of it soon after entering the Strait of Storms, and after that they had all been too busy fighting the ice buildup and evading the floes to consider its fate. But he still couldn't let go of his worry – what if it had made it after all? Wouldn't it be prudent . . .

He cleared his throat again, saying, 'Surly might be right. Perhaps we should push off as soon as possible. Finish the repairs elsewhere.'

'And just where?' Hawl answered, exasperated. 'We can't show our faces anywhere on the mainland.'

'Kartool?' Choss offered.

Shrift shuddered and Urko's blunt face twisted in disgust. 'Gods, no,' he rumbled.

'Further afield,' Surly said, crossing her arms. 'We offer our services to one of the Seven Holy Cities. Aren, or Ubaryd.'

'Got no navies worth the name,' Urko offered, nodding and scratching his chin.

'We'd be facing the Falari,' Hawl warned.

Urko waved one great paw in dismissal. 'Faugh! We can take them.'

But Surly would not move her steady gaze from Cartheron. He tapped his fingers on the scarred railing. 'Heard troubling things about that sea cult of theirs. What is it? The . . . Jhistel? Blood sacrifices.'

Surly's gaze did not waver. 'We'll face that when we must. But right now we've hung about too long.'

Cartheron nodded his agreement. Yes. By now Tarel must know they were here, word from the *Just Cause* or not. He already seemed to have the island in his sights. 'Yes,' he agreed reluctantly. 'Minimal repairs. Just enough to get us to Seven Cities.'

Choss snorted, commenting under his breath, 'That's some journey, I'll have you know.'

'Regardless,' Surly said, and she uncrossed her arms. 'How long?' she asked Choss.

Their best boatwright twisted up his features, thinking. 'Two moons, soonest.'

'One.'

The man jerked his head as if pained. '*What?*'

'One,' she warned, pointing. 'We're done. Everyone help out on the repairs,' and she turned and headed down the gangway, followed by Urko, Shrift and the new mage.

Choss leaned against the railing and looked to Cartheron, shaking his head. 'Plenty of work ahead for all of us. So where's your new guy, Dujek, and his tag-along?'

'Out whipping our Malazan boys and girls into shape.'

Choss raised his chin to the pier. 'What do you think of the new mage?'

Cartheron considered, lifted his shoulders. 'Looks like a veteran.'

'He is,' Hawl said from behind. Cartheron turned to her; she was eyeing the retreating figures. 'He has ex-legionnaire written all over him.'

'Ex-legionnaire?' Cartheron echoed. 'As in the Talian iron legions?' He whistled. 'We could use him.'

'If we can trust him.'

'Trust him? What do you mean?'

But the heavy mage simply hugged her broad chest and tilted her head in thought. 'Don't know. Got a funny feeling on the ship just then with everyone . . . Keep an eye on him, Crust.'

Cartheron nodded his full agreement. 'If you say so, Hawl.'

* * *

The caravan was encamped a day's journey from Fedal, a southern Itko Kan city, and termination point of the main north–south overland trade route. At the sprawling caravanserai grounds – a broad meadow of trampled grass – fires were lit against the dark and animals were being brushed, fed, and cared for.

As was usual, Dassem went for a long walk through the night. This time, however, he was alone. Shear no longer even spoke to him, save to lower her masked head to him in passing as if she were his subordinate, which, he knew she now believed herself to be.

It was autumn; the grass was dry and brittle and snagged at his trousers. There was an early chill to the air; he'd overheard some merchants attribute this to the Sea of Storms just to their south.

He paused in the dark to look skyward. Old familiar stars glowed above the southern horizon. The constellations of his youth: the Spear, the Cart, the Sky Mother.

Tomorrow they would part. He would carry on to the coast to take a ship out to Malaz Island, which he'd heard described uninvitingly as cold, rainy, and dreary. While she, he understood, would return to her island home far away.

He ran a hand through the tall, sharp-edged grasses. Should he simply allow that to happen? Shouldn't he return, ask her to accompany him and Nara? Why not?

After standing silent for a time he let out a long slow breath. No; Hood had not taken his eye from him. He was certain of that. The Grey Walker held some special fate in store for him. Some stern lesson for his defiance.

He would not embroil her in that.

Yet shouldn't that be *her* choice? He could warn her of the dangers and let her choose . . .

He half turned back to the distant flickering fires of the encampment, then quickly sank to his haunches amid the tall sighing grasses.

Weapon oil and sweat.

Then, the brush of ring-mail, and the faint click of a crossbow setting.

He reached down to his waist only to remember that he'd left his sword behind.

And is Hood laughing now. Mortal Sword indeed! Ha!

He lay still, listening. From what he could piece together it sounded as if a wide, staggered picket line just passed his position, closing on the caravanserai. Crouched still, he padded along behind the nearest of the individuals. To his benefit it was a dark night, and none of the figures carried any source of light – no doubt being guided by the fires of the camp. He took the man from the rear, clamped his hands round his neck just long enough for unconsciousness, then lowered him into the grasses. What he found, a ragged patched hauberk over a stained old Kanian uniform, confirmed his suspicion: outlaws, or renegades.

Through this gap in the picket he hurried inward, still crouched for a time, and jogged for camp.

The main body of the outlaws entered the caravanserai even as he closed. Panicked shouts arose but thankfully no screams or clash of blades – yet.

He pushed through the milling families and groggy fretful merchants to a position across a fire from where Shear stood with Horst Grethall. The fat-bellied caravan-master had his arms in the air and was shouting for calm.

Shear, of course, spotted him amid the flickering shadows. In the firelight her mask seemed to swim with a kaleidoscope of rich colours. Her blade was not drawn, as yet. A hand low at her side gave a slight flat wave – *wait*.

'No need for any violence, Luel,' Horst was saying to one of the outlaws. 'You'll have your payment.'

'Tithe,' the man clarified, rather archly. He wore a faded officer's surcoat over a hauberk of scale. He was bearded, and his hair was long and bedraggled, suggesting he'd been camping in the field for a great many months. 'Our legal due for keeping the roads safe here, so close to the Dal Hon border.'

'Safe from whom?' Horst grumbled under his breath.

The former officer chose magnanimously to ignore the complaint. He gestured to his men and women, all probably his own troops, and they set to searching the wagons.

Dassem's hands clenched as bolts of cloth, blankets, baskets and cooking utensils came crashing out of the wagons amid protests and shouts.

'You are searching all the wagons and carts?' he called to the retired – or cashiered – officer.

Luel turned his way, searched the dim firelight. 'All must contribute to the tithe.' He squinted, frowning. 'And you are . . . ?'

Dassem started for his cart.

'Stop that man!' Luel bellowed.

Dassem threw down a number of the outlaw soldiers nearby but had to halt as numerous crossbows were levelled against him. He stood, waiting, while Luel marched up to study him closely.

Face to face, Luel said, 'You are in an awful hurry to reach your goods, my friend.'

Dassem said nothing, fists clenched. His gaze was fixed into the darkness where his cart lay.

'Forgot to hide something, perhaps? Some gold or silver maybe?' Luel looked him up and down. 'You don't look wealthy, but perhaps it's all hidden away in your wagon or among your rags, hey?'

Dassem studied the seven glinting crossbow quarrels arrayed before him, with more behind, no doubt. He damned this man for taking what looked like his entire command with him from the Kanian fold.

A bellow arose from the dark, a shout of open terror. '*Plague!*'

Dassem looked to the night sky and mouthed a silent curse.

One of the ex-soldiers came running to Luel, pointing a shaking finger back into the darkness. 'A cart,' he gasped, 'a girl – *plague!*'

'It is *not* plague,' Dassem announced to everyone.

Luel's gaze narrowed in suspicion. 'What's this? You bring a sick family member south with you?'

Horst now pushed forward, saying, outraged, 'You told me she was old and infirm!'

'She is not sick,' Dassem repeated, stubbornly, but sounding unconvincing even to himself.

'I've seen plague,' the outlaw told Luel, 'and she has it.' He slapped his hands to his mouth, saying, 'Gods! There must have been sickly vapours in there and they touched me!'

Luel nodded to the fellow. 'Burn it.'

'*No!*' Dassem lurched forward, then spun as a crossbow bolt gouged his left side, passing on into the darkness.

He stilled, hunched in pain, a hand pressed to his side, panting. Luel watched him warily, then waved his man onward. 'Go on. Burn it.'

Dassem reached out to Horst. 'Think, man. How could she be a carrier? Has anyone got sick? Have I?' But the fat caravan-master just backed away, shaking his head.

The outlaw jogged off. Dassem watched him disappear between the wagons, and steeled himself to follow though it meant a suicidal charge through a hail of crossbow bolts.

Even as he tensed for the leap, a great flash erupted from the nearby fire, blinding him and bringing cries of surprise and shock from everyone. A hand took his arm and he did not fight as he recognized the touch.

'This way,' Shear whispered, dragging him along by the elbow.

He wiped at his tearing eyes. 'What was that? Are you a mage?'

'No. It is a chemical made by a people north of my homeland. They trade small pinches of it.'

'That was a *pinch*?'

She pushed him up against a wagon. 'Do you begin all your fights unarmed?'

'Well – it was a spur of the moment thing.' He blinked repeatedly, struggling to regain his vision. 'Lead me to the northernmost part of the clearing.'

Shouts and panic now filled the air as the caravan merchants and families sought to flee. Luel's command-voice rose over the tumult: 'Find them and kill them!'

Shear took his arm and thrust a weapon into his hand. He hefted it and was appalled by its balance. 'What is *this*?'

She was pulling him along. 'A sword. I took it from one of the outlaws.'

'It is wretched.'

'So throw it away and request something more suitable.'

Shapes moved now in his vision; families dashing about in the dark. Shear moved suddenly and a body fell to the dirt, writhing and gurgling.

He wiped at his face. 'My apologies. It is a fine blade.'

They hurried onward; he could see almost well enough now to make his own way. 'You believe me, then?' he asked as they threaded between wagons. 'This isn't the plague.'

'If it was the plague, she'd be dead by now. As would you.'

'Exactly. Then why all this?'

'Fear is fear. It has no logic.'

He could make out the cart; men and women were gathered there, carrying torches. They'd pulled it clear and were throwing dry wood and brush up against its sides.

Despite the searing pain at his side, he clamped both hands on to the weapon, hissing, 'Hood witness,' and charged.

Together they cleared the area around the cart very quickly. Then by mutual nods they separated, he going to the left, she the right, and worked their way southward through the caravanserai slaying every outlaw they met.

After the fifteenth, he began to feel sorry for these common soldiers, renegade or not, and switched to incapacitating cuts across the face, weapon arm, side, or neck. Some of these would bleed out, he knew, but others would have the option of limping away.

He found Luel in the south-west corner, behind a semicircle of defending crossbowers, double-ranked. Some sort of word, or battle instinct, must have warned him of what was coming and he was retreating behind his surviving men and women. They were pacing backwards, kneeling, firing into the dark, switching ranks and reloading – all in sequence.

Crouched in the grasses, Dassem admired their precision and discipline.

Shear joined him and together they followed, hunched, parting the grass with their blades to study the formation for an opening.

'Perhaps we shall have to let them go,' Shear offered.

'We have to end this or they will return.' He peered back towards the camp, thinking. 'A moment,' he said, and jogged off.

In the camp he found what he sought: a family of Seti tribal descent, refugees of some feud or blood-crime. He approached the aged grandfather guarding their felt-covered cart and nodded a greeting. The man held a wicked recurve bow low before him, an arrow nocked. A tall spear, adorned with wolf-tails, leaned up against the cart next to him.

Dassem motioned to the weapon. 'May I borrow your fine spear?'

The fellow reached over and held it out. 'An honour, Sword of Death.'

Dassem shook his head. 'No longer.'

'I saw what I saw. And I heard the stories from Heng.'

Dassem merely held the weapon out, horizontal, and inclined his head in thanks. Then he jogged back westward to Shear's position in the dark.

He approached, hunched low, spear level with the ground. The

285

stamp of horses' hooves reached him, together with mild nickering and the jangle of tack. Shear was behind low brush and she gestured ahead. She whispered, 'They are collecting the horses.'

Dassem took a quick glance; the outlaws were gathering the beasts together, yet a solid picket of crossbowers still kept watch. Again Dassem regretted that such a competent commander should have left the Kanian fold.

He waited, crouched upon his haunches, weapon readied at his shoulder, for the moment he wanted, and eventually it came.

Luel appeared, swinging up on to his mount. He pointed about with his sword, giving orders. Dassem backed up three paces, then rose to his full height and extended his arm backwards. Shear opened her mouth to say something, but closed it without speaking, obviously not wishing to distract him.

He charged, thrusting his arm forward, hopping with the release. Shear rose to her feet, her masked face tracing the night sky as she followed the weapon's high arcing flight. Shouts arose in the camp – they'd been seen.

Atop his mount, Luel turned their way, pointing his sword.

As if by magic the spear sprouted from his lower torso and he grunted with the impact. The sword fell from his nerveless fingers. He clutched at the thick haft then slid backwards off the horse.

Alarm erupted in the camp. The crossbow ranks scattered, running to any nearby mounts, throwing themselves into the saddles, and kicking them into a gallop. In an instant all had fled the clearing. Shear and Dassem waited until the dust settled, then advanced.

They found the outlaw commander lying on his back, still alive and conscious, a bloodied hand on the haft standing straight above him. The man's dark eyes tracked Dassem as he closed to crouch next to him. Shear kept watch.

Luel licked his bloodied lips and whispered, 'Who *are* you?'

'I am Dassem Ultor.'

An explosion of laughter sprayed blood all over the man's beard and chest. He bared his reddened teeth in a grin. 'Should've guessed. I was at Heng. I heard Hood's Sword was there.'

Dassem nodded. 'I'm sorry.'

The commander gave a weak shrug. 'No matter. You now bring death to the south.'

'That is not my intent.'

The man's hand fell from the haft. 'Yet . . . it follows . . . you . . .'

Dassem closed the man's staring eyes, rose, and faced Shear. Blood spattered her trousers, shirt and mask from the battle.

'I am thinking you are no longer welcome among the caravan,' she said.

'And neither are you, no doubt. I am sorry.'

She waved that aside. 'No matter. I was planning to return to my people anyway.'

He nodded. 'I will collect our horses and go.'

'I will keep them all from bothering you in the meantime.'

'My thanks.' He reached out. 'Shear . . .'

She remained erect, hands at her sides. 'Yes?'

He let go a long breath, let the hand fall. 'Fare you well.'

She inclined her masked head slightly. 'You too, Sword of Hood.' She turned and jogged off.

He allowed her time to speak to Horst, then went to find his horses.

*　　*　　*

It was far from winter proper, yet a chill wind from the south sent shivers up Cartheron's back where he sat on a heap of rope inspecting the tackle of the running rigging taken from the mizzen mast. Most was far older and more worn than he would've liked; however, given the shortage of equipment, they had to make do.

They hadn't the time to haul the *Twisted* up so Choss was in charge of repairs and caulking below decks while he handled everything aloft. It was painful to him to have to pass sub-par blocks and frayed line, yet on Mock's orders no vendor on the island would sell them one nail or a single yard of canvas, even under the table. Still, they had managed to appropriate a few supplies.

It was dark, but they were working in shifts through the night by torch and lantern light, and had even taken to sleeping in the hammocks in the crew's quarters before the mast. They had to make do with what they could scrounge, or steal, and that was Grinner's area. Already he'd come through with some new line, lumber of questionable provenance, and fresh pitch.

Though they had been working like this for days, Cartheron still found it difficult to sleep given the occasional sightings of the ship's unofficial mascot, the strange nacht creature. That thing made him uneasy still, while Shift flatly refused to bed down on the vessel at all.

Surly, for her part, remained ensconced in Smiley's with her bodyguard, rarely showing herself. Running everything, collecting money, and no doubt impatiently awaiting the day of their departure.

He sat back and set his hands on his thighs, stretching his back and neck; but that was unfair. Her security was paramount to him as well, even though Geffen's organization, now under a lieutenant of his, was lying low, focused on regaining its strength. And as for Mock with his council of captains, the man had had no reported sober day in weeks. And the local merchants, wisely perhaps, took their lead from the council.

He stilled, then, noticing that the chill wind was no longer blowing in off the bay, but luffing his shirt from the front. He peered up, puzzled, and was surprised to see thick dark clouds massing over the island. A blaze of sheet lightning made him flinch and blink and he rose, peering to the south. The deep purple night sky was clear there, which was odd, given that most storms rolled over them out of the south.

A thick mist was now even rising off the icy waters and climbing the wharves. He backed away to the cargo hatch and called down, 'Hawl. Better get up here.'

Their mage was already on her way up the steep stairs. She went straight to the side and peered up the shore into town.

'What is it?' Cartheron asked.

She turned to him, frowning her worry. 'Shadow . . .'

'Truly?' He eyed the mist-shrouded streets. 'You think, maybe . . . it's our boy?'

A curse of alarm sounded from below and a short hairy shape burst from the companionway, swung over the side, and went loping up the pier to disappear into the swirling fog.

Hawl merely raised a brow in comment and Cartheron nodded. 'We have to warn Surly. I'll go.'

'Not alone.' Hawl leaned over the cargo hatch. 'Urko! You still down there?'

'Yeah?' came an answering bellow.

She pointed a warning finger at Cartheron. 'You take your brother.'

*

Grinner, Nedurian found, played a mean game of troughs. They sat before one of the two ground floor windows of Smiley's. Nedurian had played a lifetime, campaigning all across Quon east to west, and now in the unlikely figure of this burly, scarred knife-fighter he'd found a fellow adherent as steeped in the game's strategy as he.

He rolled again and considered his moves while Grinner chewed a thumbnail and eyed the board. When he hadn't moved for some time the Napan peered up at him, frowning. 'What is it?'

But Nedurian wasn't listening. For some time a vague worry had been tugging at him despite his submersion in the game, and only now had it finally surfaced in a prickling all up and down his arms and the stirring of the small hairs of his neck.

He rose from the table, jostling it and upsetting the stones. Grinner pulled away, his hands going to the yellowed horn knife grips standing from his vest. 'What is it?'

Mist shrouded the street outside beneath dark bunched clouds. Even as Nedurian watched, touching his Warren, shadows cast across the shrouds of fog seemed to shift and twist all of their own accord. He went for the door.

'What is it?' Grinner repeated.

Nedurian paused. 'Some sort of magery.' Pointing at Grinner, he warned him, 'Stay indoors!' and rushed out. He made for Agayla's; if anyone would be familiar with such a manifestation it would be she.

Oddly enough, though the woman's shop was only a few streets away, he almost became lost amid cobbled ways he didn't recognize. He stopped to strengthen his touch upon Rashan. Immediately, the town seemed to snap back into place all about him. He raced on.

Eventually, after a number of turns that proved inexplicably wrong, he stumbled upon her shop only to find her out in the street already, a silk shawl about her shoulders, glowering at the overcast night sky.

'Is it one of the island's Shadow Moons?' he asked, a touch out of breath.

289

'No. It resembles a Shadow Moon, but none has been presaged for years yet. This is worse. Some fool is opening a gateway between Shadow and here. And I think I know who.'

'Ah. Our peculiar visitor.'

'Yes. And he is a greater fool than I suspected. Doesn't he understand that *anything* can come through?'

This gave Nedurian pause. 'Anything?' he repeated, almost in disbelief.

She nodded, furious. 'Anything. We must be ready to defend the city.'

Nedurian ran a hand over his unshaven cheeks. Ye gods, this was not what he'd signed up for.

Civilians were crowding the street now, peering about in wonderment. Agayla waved them away. 'Hide indoors. It is a . . . a Shadow Storm. Lock your doors!' She imperiously waved him away as well. 'Send everyone indoors.'

He inclined his head in acquiescence – as one could only do when Agayla used that tone – and jogged off, shouting as he went, 'Lock your doors! A Shadow Storm!'

*

High above Malaz City, Tattersail sat at table with Mock and a few of his favourite captains. Untan distilled grain liquor had flowed freely and the captains were trading banter and jokes with the admiral while Tattersail played with her knife and napkin.

Mock laughed roguishly at the jokes, sending winks to her across the table, but she was not amused by what she saw as these followers' transparent efforts at ingratiation and toadying. Mock, of course, was enjoying all the attention.

'Still no word from your sources on Nap?' Captain Hess asked, hooking an arm over the back of his tall chair.

'None,' Mock answered. 'Do not worry. They were savaged just as badly.' He eyed Tattersail directly across the full length of the table. 'Some warn of a follow-up invasion or attack, but I discount it utterly.'

Tattersail looked away, her grip on the silver knife tightening.

'Who will be the new flank admiral, then, Mock?' another asked, rather drunkenly.

The admiral raised his brows in exaggeration. 'This is true. We've lost Casson, haven't we?'

'Who, then?' the captain, Renish, pressed on, and Tattersail saw in his narrowed gaze that perhaps the man was not so drunk as he pretended.

Mock just smiled in his carefree manner, and, leaning forward conspiratorially, answered, 'Oh, someone at this table, no doubt.'

The seven captains eyed one another then, leaning away from their neighbours and glowering into their cups. Tattersail looked to the soot-blackened rafters far above. Gods! So predictable. Mock playing them against each other. As he had for years.

Her gaze chanced upon Agayla's dark tapestry and she dropped her knife with a loud clang. *So dark!*

The captains all stopped talking, eyeing her. Mock lifted his brows. 'Are you all right, dearest? Too much to drink, perhaps?' He elbowed Hess on his right, and all seven captains chuckled on cue.

She passed a shaky hand across her face, swallowing to calm herself. 'I'm fine. Something . . . something has disagreed with me. I think I will take some air.'

Mock half rose from his seat, bowing. 'Of course, dearest. Do take care, though. It looks like rain.'

She stood from the table and all the captains rose as well, bowing. She returned the civility and made for the main terrace, where she slammed the heavy iron-bound door behind her and stared out over the city, a hand going to her throat. *Ancient Ones! No wonder I've been so jittery.*

There, low over the city, a massive cyclone of energy gyred amid churning midnight clouds and flitting shadows. *Meanas! But who? How?*

She ran for Rampart Way – the nearest route down to the city below. Soon, however, she had to hike up the long dress Mock had asked her to put on for dinner. She cursed it, finally tearing off its lowest section and continuing on.

The dry, dusty words of one of the texts on Warren magics regarding such manifestations marched through her mind as she went:

Clouds, mists, or storms are a common by-product of the massive differentials in pressures, humidities, and temperatures when sufficiently large portals or gates between Realms are generated. Should such a differential prove large enough, the energies generated may induce a storm as destructive as any legendary Maelstrom.

Agayla would know what to do.

*

She had spent her time on the south coast facing the cold grey waters of the Strait of Storms. These entities known as the Stormriders were an interesting phenomenon. One she'd never had the inclination or opportunity to investigate before. Clearly, they represented a lingering ancient intrusion into the region. But just from where, she couldn't say. It would take generations of observation to know for certain, of course, but it appeared to her that their presence was slowly fading upon the world, grafting of an alien order as it was.

The flash of sheet lightning from behind threw her shadow far out before her, and Sister of Cold Nights straightened, lifting her head. *Was that . . .*

She turned to regard a dense mass of clouds slowly building over the island north of her, and nodded. *At last. Perhaps my time here has not been wasted after all.*

She started for the city.

*

Cartheron set a hand on his brother's arm, holding him back from a side street. 'I'm not so sure.'

Urko shook off his hand. 'We just head up this way to the square. The one with the broken statue.'

Cartheron squinted into the dense banners of hanging mist. 'Like that last turn?'

Urko huffed, crossing his thick arms. 'Hunh! One mistake! I'm telling you – this town is not this big!'

'I agree.'

It was strange; the moment they'd left the waterfront behind and walked up between the warehouses it was as if they'd entered another city. The narrow meandering streets were *familiar*, but not quite right. Same with the shop-fronts.

His brother spun then, crouching. 'Did you hear that?'

Cartheron squinted into the miasma. 'What?'

'Sounded like . . . claws scratching over stone.'

292

'A lost dog?'

'Damned big one,' Urko muttered.

Indeed, a looming dark shadow was now moving behind the shifting curtains of mist. One impossibly large. *A trick of this strange light*, Cartheron told himself. No beast could be that large. Probably just as high as his knees – *not* damned near the size of a bull. Just a distorted shadow.

A low growling rumble reached them then, as of rocks being ground together. The very cobbles beneath their feet vibrated with it. The brothers shared a glance: run or freeze?

Cartheron slowly reached down and drew his boot knife. The tiny weapon looked comical compared to the monster that was edging in upon them. That was, if the shadows, and their fears, were not playing tricks upon them.

A long, broad muzzle parted the vapours. It was fully as tall as their own heads. Lips drew back snarling from wet gums, and slit eyes glared an eerie near-black before them. A heady waft of desert scent, like spice, nearly made Cartheron dizzy.

Before he could act, his brother leapt upon the beast, wrapping an arm about its neck, bellowing, '*Run!*'

But Cartheron did not run: he stared, frozen, while his brother tightened the crook of his elbow upon the beast's throat and its eyes widened in something almost like surprise – if such a creature could be capable of such an emotion.

It reared, snarling, and threw itself against the wall next to them. Both it and his brother gave animal grunts as bricks crunched and wood splintered. It staggered off, attempting to shake this impudent fool from its back, but Cartheron knew that nothing short of decapitation would ease his brother's arms once he'd clamped them round anything.

They disappeared into the mist, the hound rearing and snarling, Urko half hopping, half dragging his feet. Cartheron moved to follow, but stopped – there was no way he would ever find them. He swore then he would honour his brother's damned fool move by beating this confounding miasma. He would escape it. Standing there, his back pressed against chill damp stone, he decided that perhaps the way to beat it was to remain still; it may be that some logic or pattern would emerge amid the confusing chiaroscuro.

Just as at sea when caught amid thick fog. You didn't *look*, you listened. And so he closed his eyes, listening to the night.

Nedurian soon found that he no longer had to warn the citizens of Malaz against entering the streets. It appeared they were quite familiar with these uncanny happenings: doors were slammed and barred and heavy shutters banged shut over windows. In no time he was alone in a tiny mist-laden square, and only then did it occur to him that he had no idea exactly where he was.

A low rumbling reached him then, as of a beast the size of a bull exhaling, and he thought, *Well, perhaps not so alone . . .*

He raised his Rashan Warren to its sizzling heights about him and waited, motionless, in a pool of absolute dark. Whatever this was, it ought to pass him by.

Instead, however, twin pinpoints of a sullen bluish glow emerged from the dark, closing, growing in brilliance, and he realized with a renewed prickling of his skin that he was being stalked through the paths of his own Warren of Night.

He shifted, then, blindly – a very dangerous move as one cannot predict just where one might emerge – and found himself in a new, equally unfamiliar cobbled way. Quickly, he crossed the street to put his back to a stone wall and tried to still his hammering heart. He had never seen that before. Some creature able to follow spoors through Warrens? Gods! No one would ever be able to escape such a—

He stared with mounting panic at the spot where he had emerged, for there, from the shifting shadows, a monstrous paw and fore-limb was emerging, followed by a long greying muzzle and twin blazing sky-blue eyes that peered right and left, scanning the street.

Nedurian slowly reached over to a door next to him, offered up a silent prayer to Apsalar, Lady of Thieves, and tried to lift the latch – it rose, and he ducked into a shop-front stuffed with household goods manufactured of tin: a tinsmith's. From a rear workroom he heard someone weeping in terror.

It occurred to him then to wonder why the creature had singled him out, and he realized that it must be one, or both, of two factors: he had been outside, and he possessed a raised Warren. Reluctantly, he understood what he must do, though it scraped against the grain of decades of habit. He let his Warren fall away, then froze, almost not breathing, listening to the night.

Outside, claws grated against the stone cobbles of the narrow street. He swallowed and fought the mad urge to flee. *No running – they are hunters.*

A great bull-bellows of an exhalation rattled the door and sent up a massive cloud of dust from the gap beneath. The air became redolent with a sweet spicy scent, as of mace, or anise seed. The frantic need to run made his legs quiver, but he fought it, though he expected at any instant the beast to crash through the flimsy barrier.

A last reverberating snort and the claws grated once more, swiftly, as the monster ran off – called perhaps by some other scent or spoor.

He let out a long hard breath, sagging in exhaustion and relief. He reached clumsily for the door. *Ancient gods! I am definitely too old for this.*

*

Tattersail passed through the streets of the high manor district then descended into the thick fogs that cloaked Malaz City proper. The haze was so dense she had to raise her Thyr Warren to its highest extent just to penetrate the coils and hanging curtains.

In the apparent quiet she began to wonder what she was doing here and just what it was she hoped to accomplish. Clearly, some sort of manifestation was taking shape in the city, but what? And what could she hope to contribute?

Perhaps it was one of the legendary Shadow Moons, though she understood such arrivals were always known long beforehand. Agayla spoke of them as highly regulated and predictable, like eclipses.

She turned a corner in the merchants' quarter and came face to face with several men loading goods into a wagon drawn up before an open shop-front. She stared and they froze, arms full of bolts of cloth, baskets and kegs.

One tossed his armload into the wagon and turned to his fellows. 'Well, well, mates. Look what we have here.'

'What are you *doing* . . .' she breathed in complete disbelief.

The one who had spoken hiked up his trousers and gestured to her, grinning. 'Some sort of social affair, is it?'

Looking down, she realized how absurd she must appear wandering the streets in a full evening gown, and that tattered and torn. Then she blinked, frowning – what she looked like was completely irrelevant! 'Run, now,' she told them.

They chuckled together, two circling behind her. 'First give us a kiss, lass,' the spokesman urged. 'Just a kiss, Miss High-and-mighty . . .'

The two horses at the wagon nickered then and reared in alarm, their sides quivering. The fellow glanced at them, scowling. 'See what's spooked the damned horses, Gravin.'

One of the men crossed to the horses, but before he could grasp the throat-latch of the nearest the animals reared again, chuffing in open terror, and bolted down the street. Kegs and crates crashed to the cobbles from the open rear as the wagon clattered into the mist.

Their leader looked to the clouds. 'Oh, for the love of Oponn!' He waved his fellows away. 'Well? Go get it, dammit!'

They jogged off, leaving her alone with two; the leader and one other. They moved towards her and she retreated, coming up against a cold stone wall. Her Warren sizzled in her hands, yet she found she could do nothing; she realized that she'd never before tried to use it face to face against another human being.

'Don't make me hurt you . . .' she breathed, her voice tight with fear.

They laughed – either in ignorance of her powers, or lacking true insight into her character.

'Missy,' said the leader, all hungry smile, hands reaching, 'you ain't gonna hurt—'

Many things happened all at once, then. A monstrous shape pounced from the fog, teeth tore and ripped, the men screamed – or tried to; it was more like a bursting of fluids and gore from their mouths – and she screamed, her Warren burst to life in a colossal eruption of power and light, and she was flung backwards, smashing her head against stone in an even brighter flare of brilliance. She knew nothing more.

*

Eyes on the wet cobbles, Cartheron heard, and did his best to follow, reassuringly human footsteps. A couple, walking calmly and with purpose through this nightmare; who they were he had no idea, but at least they weren't afraid.

That, he realized, should either reassure him or terrify him.

Presently, the footsteps stopped. He went forward a few more paces then halted as well, and slowly raised his gaze to find two figures eyeing him from up a narrow alleyway. A pair as unalike as any two people could be: one scrawny, short, and greying; the other huge, almost impossibly massive, rather like a walking dolmen, and carrying a long-hafted halberd over one shoulder with a blade large enough to behead a horse.

The scrawny older one pointed a warning finger. 'You should not be out this night.'

Cartheron smiled mirthlessly. 'I cottoned on to that. So what're you two doing out?'

He had recognized them now. The oldster and his buddy were regulars at Coop's Hanged Man inn, though never had he seen them so . . . sober. Even now he could make out the sickeningly sweet fumes of absinthe wafting from one or both of them.

'We have an errand,' the scrawny one said.

'Yes? And you are?' Cartheron asked.

'Faro,' said the oldster, and he nodded to his towering companion, 'Trenech.'

Trenech, it seemed, was a man of few words. He remained silent, twisting his head, constantly searching the night.

'I'm—'

'We know who you are,' Faro cut in.

Cartheron blinked. 'Oh?'

'You work for the interloper.'

'The . . . interloper?'

'Your employer. This mage of Shadow.'

'Ah . . . yes.'

'He has meddled with the House already. I warn you – we will brook no more interference.'

Cartheron was frowning in such confusion he could feel his brows hurting. He cleared his throat, 'Ah . . . as you say . . .'

Faro grunted, somehow satisfied.

From the mid-distance a hound's great baying howl broke upon them. Cartheron flinched and spun to scan the obscuring murk and rippling shadows.

'Perhaps you'd best come with us,' Faro said. 'You should be safe. Perhaps you can talk some sense into your patron.'

Cartheron turned back, his brows now raised very high indeed. 'My patron? Talk to him?'

Faro and his companion set off once more and Cartheron followed. 'Yes,' Faro said. 'Because he is approaching. And we believe that his goal is the House.'

House? Cartheron asked himself as he followed along. *What in the name of Mael are they talking about?* He squinted into the murk. *And Urko – don't you get yourself killed, damn you!*

*

Nedurian slammed shut the door to Smiley's and leaned against it, panting his relief. Next to the entrance, Grinner relaxed down into his seat, easing his knives back into their leather sheaths.

He wiped the cold clammy mist from his face, and let out a long breath, his hands still shaking. *Too long since I've walked an open battlefield of magery – a damned free-for-all of colliding Warrens, Realms, and rampaging monsters.*

Surly came out from behind the bar. 'Well? What's going on?'

He motioned for a moment to catch his breath, then said, 'Looks like your employer is making a show.'

She sent a scowling glance to a darkened window. 'All this?'

'Yes.'

She nodded curtly. 'All right. Let's go.'

He gaped at her, let out a near-nervous laugh. 'You don't quite understand . . .'

She pulled on a jacket; Grinner stood, as did Tocaras and Shrift at their table. Nearer the back, the two local hires, Dujek and Jack, stood up as well.

Surly waved them down. 'You lot guard the place. Grinner, you're with me.' She motioned Nedurian onward. 'Let's go.'

He pulled a hand down his face, let out another long breath. *Well, in for a penny, in for a crown.*

*

Crossing a stone bridge over one of the channels of a thin sluggish river that ran through the city, Sister of Cold Nights was rather surprised to see a great hulking fellow dragging himself up the dressed stonework side of the channel. He was sodden, and chuffing and puffing to himself as he climbed. *On such a night as this?* Curious, she went down to see who it was.

He was quite astonished when she reached down and pulled him up with one hand. He straightened, wiped at his mud-smeared jerkin and trousers. He was obviously of Napan descent, with the blue tinge to his skin. 'Thankee, ma'am. Name's Urko.'

'Nightchill.' She walked on and he trailed along with her. 'Not a night to be out,' she continued. 'There are *things* in this storm.'

'I know.' He raised his wide knotted hands. 'I nearly had one. Another minute and I'd have throttled it, I'm sure. But we fell into the river and I had to let go.'

She eyed him. 'Really? You had to?'

He grimaced, ran a hand over his crew-cut pate. 'Can't swim.'

'Ah.' She wondered if he was referring to one of the hounds, or some other fiend out of Shadow. She knew it was possible to destroy them – if one were potent enough. It was rare these days that anything could impress her; yet this one's feat, if true, was worthy of it.

She crossed streets and squares, always directing herself towards the nexus of power manifesting in the town. Eventually, she reached it, or as close as she could come in the normal mundane world. She faced a small square, a crossroads, really, graced by a small stone drinking fountain, fed, no doubt, by spring water channelled in from higher on the island.

Facing the small square, one block over, as she suspected, squatted the structure the locals called the Deadhouse.

Here also were gathered the night's witnesses.

Seeing these people through the murk, Urko, at her side, grunted his recognition. He bowed his farewell to her, and jogged off to join a group of his fellow Napans, together with a mage she knew to be a compatriot of Agayla's.

And speaking of the servant of the Weaver and an eye of the Enchantress, she too stood to one side. She went to join her and nodded a greeting, to which Agayla merely scowled. 'What do you want here, Elder?'

'I am merely curious.'

Agayla snorted her scepticism.

'And our friend Obo?'

Agayla snorted once again. 'Only the submersion of the entire island would bring him out.'

While they watched, the churning and spinning tatters of murk and shadow coalesced, rather like a sort of funnel cloud, while two shapes took on solidity and form within. The display of power was of interest to Sister of Cold Nights, as she saw demonstrated a mastery of Meanas. But she sensed far more – something she hadn't witnessed in ages – the lineaments of an Elder Realm thought lost. Ancient Kurald Emurlahn.

This, itself, was of great note generally as well as to her personally, as it touched directly upon her purposes. Great interest generally, as was affirmed by another figure she glimpsed watching from Shadow itself – no doubt invisible to all else present. Lean and tall, in weathered time-gnawed armour, his face a dried leather mien of bared yellow teeth.

She quickly glanced away. Edgewalker, guardian of Shadow.

The gyre of raw potency tightened and darkened. Energies crackled and snapped about it. It looked as if it consisted of a great mass of shadows all flowing into it from every nook and cranny of the city, and, perhaps, even beyond; mayhap the entire island. Thus it deepened and intensified, until not even her senses could penetrate the dense liquid gloom of dusk at its centre.

The concentration of power amassed impressed even her.

Then, with a boom as of a release of tension, or energies, that struck everyone as a physical blow to the chest, the pressure and 'presence' of a gateway passed and the gusting contrary winds began to ease. The shadows drifted away, revealing two figures in the square who had not been present earlier, the two whom she knew from Heng: the short mage of Meanas, and the slim knife-fighter with whom she had spoken before.

Sister of Cold Nights glanced over to where Edgewalker had been watching, fully expecting to see him gone. But he was not; he remained still, and appeared even more intent as he stared across the square. He even carried his sheathed sword in his bony hands now, as if ready to draw. She followed his gaze and had to tense. Four creatures of ancient legend were now edging forward into the square, muzzles low, ears down, clearly stalking the two at the centre. The Hounds of Shadow.

Everyone gathered about the side streets and alleyways backed away as the creatures slid forward on their forepaws, while the slim one, Dancer, shifted to guard the mage's back, drawing his knives.

She applauded such bravery, but it was useless. There was nothing they could do, nor could, or would, anyone interfere; those beasts could tear anyone and anything apart. Even Azathani had died in their maws.

Agayla, she noticed, had edged closer to her side. Wisely, she had yet to raise her Warren.

'Can you dismiss them?' Agayla whispered.

She shook her head.

Agayla crossed her arms. 'The fools. All that effort just to be torn to bits like all the others before them.'

But Sister of Cold Nights glanced aside to where Edgewalker still watched, intent, almost . . . concerned? 'Perhaps not,' she answered.

The beasts closed from all sides. The largest was mostly grey, though with a white stomach. Female, her blue eyes shone like sapphires, and it appeared as if she limped from some battle. Another bore a darker grey pelt – an offspring? – and his eyes were mismatched, one being a similar blue, the other a golden yellow. The third's pelt was all a scarred and tangled dirty yellow, its eyes dark, near black, while the last was a black so dark as to appear blue. Its eyes shone a rather alarming blood red.

Dancer said something over his shoulder to his companion then, which Sister of Cold Nights made out as, 'Now would be a good time . . .'

She could not help but smile at this last bit of bravado before the end. At least these two wouldn't shame themselves before being torn in two.

And yet . . . she kept a sidelong eye on Edgewalker. The ancient – some said the creator of Shadow itself – watched intently, a hand on his weapon's grip, the other on the sheath, as if ready to draw and stride forward.

Strange, that. He'd never interfered before. Not once, when so many had fallen attempting to master Shadow.

A whisper came to her then. A story she'd heard long ago from a fellow Azathani. That Edgewalker had tired of his guardianship and had been searching for a worthy inheritor all this time.

She eyed the little mage now, wondering; could it really be?

The Dal Hon ancient – though not really an ancient, she saw, as her vision could penetrate his glamour – now fiddled with his fingers at his chest. It was as if he were playing a child's game of cat's cradle, but with nothing visible between his fingers save shadows. And to her increasing disbelief, ropes and tangled knots of said shadows now came slithering out of the deeper pools of murk about and lashed themselves tight round the legs of the four beasts.

She would have been dismissive of such efforts were they plain Meanas workings alone, but these carried the unmistakable essence of Elder Kurald Emurlahn; somehow, this mage has mastered both and now had at his command *two* sources of power to draw upon.

Yet even such unprecedented might was not enough. The eldritch beasts fought and yanked despite their countless bonds, still drawing ever closer to the two men. The potency being brought into existence in the square raised a pressure in the air, making it hard to draw breath. The very stones of the street cracked and burst, heaving and grinding. The rising intensity of the unveiling reminded her of exchanges she'd witnessed long ago, when Elders fought without any regard for the calamities they unleashed.

Even Agayla winced, a hand going to her chest as she panted for breath. Across the way, the old mage she'd met on the dock fainted but was held up by a Napan with him.

Still these ancient monsters could not be brought to the ground. Each struggled onward, wrapped in twisting cords of shadow, snarling and slathering, utterly intent upon tearing these two trespassers to bloody shreds. The little black-skinned mage at the centre of the storm now leaned forward, hands lowering, as if he were pushing something down into the ground before him, straining with redoubled effort.

A new, third source of power broke upon everyone like a striking waterfall and Agayla grunted at the shock of it. Sister of Cold Nights, however, recognized the source of this new puissance being drawn by the mage and was outraged.

She knew its colourings, its flavour – name it what you will – and she could not believe it. *How can he touch this?* She knew very well that that particular Wound had been sealed away. Forbidden. Unbroachable. She knew this because it was she and her brothers Draconus and K'rul who had sealed it away ages ago. All to heal the ancient crimes of the so-called High King. How could this one have possibly penetrated their wardings? Then she understood, and crossed her arms, almost snarling herself.

Shadow. Of course. Broken, it leaks everywhere and into everything. Is this your insight, little man?

Then she paused, wondering. Did you see this, K'rul? Is this why you sent me this way? Perhaps so. And so she eased her shoulders. It was not for her to interfere. Events must unfold. Only then, K'rul had warned, could she reach her goal.

The fearsome potency now bearing down upon the four hounds would have crushed buildings. Two collapsed amid their ropes and fetters of knotted shadow. The muzzles of these quickly became lashed in their magical bonds and they were yanked to their sides where they lay panting, eyes rolling.

As for the largest, the one mostly grey, with a white stomach, her eyes seemed to shine like blue stars now, and she stood quivering in a raging fury, upright, refusing to kneel. The mage's partner, the lean one who moved so gracefully, approached, and raised a knife for the kill.

Yet at the last moment the mage stayed his partner's arm. Instead, he brought his head next to the hound's, despite the snarling lips and gnashing fangs, and appeared to whisper something into the matriarch's ear. Those ears fell then, the muscular shoulders hunching. And the mage backed away, gesturing. The countless fetters and chains of twisted shadow fell away like smoke and the hounds rose.

The tall matriarch shook herself, chuffing; then, with window-rattling howls, the four bounded off in all directions, growling and snarling their enraged frustration.

Sister of Cold Nights let out her breath, whispering to herself, 'Not since Dissim'belackiss . . .'

'What was that?' Agayla asked from her side, glaring, and wiping blood dripping from her nose.

'Nothing. Interesting times, yes?'

'Who is that little shit?' she growled. 'That was far more than Warren magics.'

'Yes, it was. The Enchantress is sure to be interested.'

'She knows already,' Agayla answered, daubing at her nose.

Of course. T'riss watching through her eyes.

In the square, the pair now walked to the two guardians at the gate to the Deadhouse. The mage and the short guardian whom she knew as Faro spoke together. She ached to hear their conversation, but thought it unseemly go to running across the square. So she walked – determinedly. Agayla accompanied her.

By time they reached the gate, the pair had entered the grounds and were approaching the House. For an instant a terrifying dread clutched her chest – *Ancients, they are not going to assail the House?* The entire city could be in danger.

But no such confrontation arose. To her eyes the two merely seemed to dissolve into the shadows and disappear as they neared the threshold.

Agayla clutched at her sleeve. 'What was that? Did they enter? What did you see?'

'I know not.'

Agayla growled wordlessly, yanked her grip free. 'Don't play the enigmatic Elder with me! What did you see?'

'What you saw. They disappeared.' She nodded to the guardians who were standing before the small garden gate, barring their way. 'You allowed them entrance?'

Faro nodded while his fellow held his huge halberd at the ready. 'Indeed.'

'Why?' Agayla snapped.

'They correctly intuited the limits of our purpose.'

'Which is?'

To this Faro said nothing. Not used to such open defiance, Agayla actually growled just as the hounds had.

'You are unfamiliar with the House?' Sister of Cold Nights asked her.

'Yes,' she grunted, reluctant to admit her lack of knowledge. 'The Enchantress warned me to stay away from it.'

T'riss would know. 'Wise of her.' She gestured to the guardians. 'These two are charged not with keeping things *out* of the grounds. They are charged with keeping things *in*.'

Faro inclined his head in agreement.

'And did those two enter the House?'

To this Faro merely shrugged. 'I care not.'

Agayla snarled anew, but Sister of Cold Nights bowed her farewell. 'We will learn no more here.' She turned away; the Napans were retreating, the large one, Urko, carrying their unconscious mage.

'Interesting times,' she repeated to Agayla, and, inclining her head in farewell, walked off. She heard Agayla's heeled boots cracking against the cobbles as she stormed away in the other direction.

Lastly, she scanned the murk for any sign of the one some named the guardian of Shadow, Edgewalker. But he had departed as well.

Tattersail awoke to the splitting agony of a headache such as she'd never before experienced. Blinking, she peered about; she lay in the street, sodden from mist and dew, and no sign of the storm remained. It was just before the dawn.

Groaning, she pushed herself upright. Her glance happened to skitter across the gory wreckage of two bodies down the street – each now supporting several seabirds and stray dogs – and, gagging, she staggered off.

She touched the back of her head and felt a crust of dried blood there. Gods, she'd hit her head hard. What a headache! How many bricks had fallen on her, anyway? She even had dried scabs from a nosebleed.

Nursing her head, she carried on through the Manor House district and up Rampart Way to the Hold. Here, the sleepy pre-dawn guards let her in with a nod – as a mage she was expected to be coming and going at all hours.

She climbed the stairs to the top floor and eased open the bedroom door so as not to wake Mock. She pulled the ruined dress over her head and dropped it to the floor, then soaked a cloth in a basin of water and wiped the dried blood from her face. Mock, hidden beneath the thick blankets, stirred then. She crossed to the large four-poster and drew back the covers.

It was not Mock in the bed; it was her maidservant, Viv. And she was wearing only a thin singlet.

The girl blinked sleepily, stared, then gaped. Her face went as white as the sheets heaped about her.

She threw herself forward to wrap her arms round a stunned Tattersail, sobbing. 'Don't blast me into nothingness! He made me do it! Threatened to sell me into slavery to the Dal Hon if I didn't! *Please.*'

Tattersail pulled at the girl's arms, trying to extricate herself. All she could manage were single soothing words such as, 'Quiet. Yes. Fine.'

The side door to the wash chamber opened and Mock walked in, fiddling with his untucked shirtings. 'Get a move on . . .' he began, and then he looked up. His brows rose, then he suddenly, inexplicably, laughed. He waved to the bed. 'She was scared by the storm so I let her sleep here, that is all. Nothing more, dearest.'

Viv gaped anew, making choking noises. Her face blazed a red to match her hair. Tattersail gestured for her to leave, and after one look up at her mistress she gathered together a handful of the sheets and scuttled off.

Mock went to a sideboard and poured a glass of wine. 'Please, dearest. It looks bad, yes. But what would I want with another, really, when I have you?'

She just shook her head – her aching, pulsing, reverberating head. 'I've been a fool, Mock. But I'm not *that* much of one.'

He leaned back against the table, opened his arms. 'Please! That girl? A dalliance. Nothing more. Nothing *serious*. Really.' And he tossed back the wine, but she noticed his hand shaking.

She realized with a shock that right now he was very scared of her. She merely shook her head. She simply felt tired. So very tired of it all. 'I'm not going to do anything, Mock. We're just finished.'

She went to an armoire, dug around and found a travelling bag. Into this went shirts and trousers and skirts and her Deck of Dragons. While she packed Mock kept speaking, but she ignored him.

'What do you mean, *finished*?' he was saying. 'You would throw away being a marquessa for *this*? Show some judgement, child. Some sense of proportion. Really. I do think it is time that you grew up. We make a great team shipboard, we really do. But, fine, if we don't get along in private that need not be a problem. We need not share a room. You can have the pick of any you should choose – benefits of being a marquessa, yes? Or even a queen.'

She was pushing her toiletries into the bag when he made this last comment and she had to stop herself from raising her Warren to show him what she thought of that loathsome idea.

When she reached the door he finally lost his temper. 'Fine!' he yelled. 'You'll never be anyone! You lack the backbone. Go back to your farm or your fisher parents or whatever! You'll be a nobody!'

She paused at the door, eyed him, standing flushed and dishevelled. 'I'd rather be what you call a nobody than contaminated by this.'

Walking away, she heard the glass burst against the door.

*

306

Later, in town, she knocked on another door. A sturdy one of thick oaken blanks, a garland of rare herbs strung across its front, fragrant and colourful.

The door opened and she stared into the face of her old patron and teacher, Agayla. The woman looked to be sharing the same headache Tattersail still nursed. She appeared pale, her eyes red and sunken, her hair rather frazzled and unkempt. But she opened her arms wide and gave her visitor a warm hug, drawing her within.

The shop looked just as it had before. As if no time had passed at all, and Tattersail cleared her throat. 'I've been a—'

Agayla raised a hand for silence. 'No need,' she murmured. 'Would you like some tea?'

Tattersail felt as if an immense weight had been lifted from her and she dared an attempt at a smile. 'Thank you. That would be . . . yes. Thank you.'

Over tea – Agayla's wonderful reviving herbal tea – the older woman eyed her as if attempting to take her measure. 'What did you make of the storm?' she asked, perhaps trying for neutral conversation.

Tattersail laughed weakly. 'I was unconscious almost all night. I fell and hit my head.'

'Ah.' Agayla nodded. 'So what do you plan now? As I said, there are schools in Kan that would take you in an instant. I will write a letter.'

Tattersail shook her head. 'No.'

Agayla raised a brow. 'Really? No?'

'No. I was wondering about those old-style mage academies in Tali. Are any of those still taking students?'

Agayla sat back. She raised her gaze to the ceiling, which was cluttered with sheaves of hanging drying herbs and clusters of leaves and bundled desiccated flowers. 'Old imperial style battle-magics? Really? Obsolete, I should think.'

But Tattersail was nodding. 'That's the training I want.'

Her slim, bird-like mentor studied her tea. 'It just so happens that two such academies still exist. They are small, however. Without prestige among the courts . . .'

'I don't care about that. I want that training.'

Agayla finished the tea. 'Well, if that is what you want, I will write you a letter of introduction, of course. You can take the first ship out to the mainland.'

Tattersail fought to suppress a blush of shame. *After the things I said to this woman* . . . She felt her eyes becoming hot and tearing up. Nothing had worked out as she wished. Everything was so ruined . . .

Agayla watched her silently for a time, then said, gently, 'Sometimes it is okay just to cry.'

Chapter 16

LEE WAITED OUT THE STORM IN THE SPRAWLING COMBINATION tavern and gambling room ground main floor of the Golden Gyrfalcon. Her table was towards the rear, where she sat leaning her chair back against the wall. With her sat a lieutenant and some guards – a paltry few now that business had fallen off so dramatically.

In fact, all she could be said to control was Geffen's old place plus a few warehouses down at the waterfront. Support just kept dribbling away as talk spread of the deadly knifer heading the opposition. She was frankly thinking of getting out of the business altogether. Trying another line of work.

It was far into the night when the storm petered out. Some of the sailors and local patrons claimed they heard hounds howling through all the thunder and rattling of windows, and talk naturally turned to the island's legendary Shadow Moons.

Lee just rolled her eyes; of course all the damned dogs were out there howling at the banging shutters and claps of thunder. Natural, wasn't it? No need to reach for any supernatural explanation.

Stupid island hicks.

Gasps sounded then from the front and several of the late night crowd jumped to their feet. Lee motioned for one of her boys to take a look, but even as the guard rose to his feet the source of the commotion appeared pushing his way across the room to them.

It was their friend Cowl. And he looked in a bad way.

The gasps were for the bright blood that smeared the man's shirt front, hands and face. He pulled a chair to Lee's table and sat, daubing at his bloody nose.

Her remaining lieutenant, a young gal named Ivala whose

ruthlessness impressed even Lee, shot her a look that said, *Now's our chance to rid ourselves of this asshole.*

Lee gave a slight negative shake of her head.

'Get me a Hood-damned rag, would you,' Cowl croaked, his voice hoarse.

None of Lee's three guards, nor Ivala, nor Lee moved to get up.

The assassin cocked a brow to Lee, who sighed, and motioned to one of the staff. She called over, 'Bring a wet rag,' and the serving girl ran for the kitchens.

'What happened to you?' she asked. 'Get mugged?'

The young fellow – actually probably only slightly younger than she – shot her a warning glare, then glanced significantly to her guards.

Lee rolled her eyes again, but waved them away. 'Get some sleep, everyone,' she told them. They all got up to go, leaving the two of them alone.

The servitor came back with a wet cloth that Cowl used to clean his face and hands. Lee watched, her hands tucked up under her armpits, leaning back in her chair. It occurred to her that the man's nosebleed, or whatever it was, appeared far worse because of his near sickly paleness.

'Notice anything strange about the storm?' he finally asked, the cloth now pressed to his nose.

She shook her head. 'No.'

He snorted, then winced, cursing, and pressed harder on his face.

'Why?'

'Our friends are back.'

Lee poured herself a fresh glass of red wine. 'Really? You mean the two you've been waiting for?'

'Yeah. Them. Turns out that Dal Hon mage is the real thing. He's damned strong.' Cowl took the glass just as Lee finished filling it, and drank.

'Hey! That was mine.'

Cowl tossed the rest back.

Lee gestured impatiently for a servitor. 'So?'

'Looks like it's knife to knife for us. Him and me. Which is fine. I prefer it that way. No confusion as to the results, if you know what I mean.'

Lee took a fresh glass from the servitor and poured again. 'Whatever.' She eyed the fellow and hoped her disapproval was clear. 'Listen, them and me, we got an understanding. You go after that Dancer fellow and they'll think I'm behind it. I don't want that kind of trouble.'

The damned assassin laughed again – wincing once more and holding his head. Once he'd regained his composure he waved her off as if dismissing her. 'The only reason you're still here is you're too small to bother with. But . . .' and he raised a hand as if to forestall any umbrage from her, 'I take your point. I'll make it clear that it's personal and professional. Just between him and me.'

Lee was sceptical but let it lie. 'Fine.'

He stood, pushing back his chair. 'Thanks for the drink.'

She raised her glass to him. *Here's hoping you die, asshole.*

*

After helping Urko carry Nedurian to a room, Cartheron went to the bar and pulled a tankard of weak beer, then slumped into a chair. The rest of the crew did likewise. It was quiet now, the only noise being Urko talking at a table with all those who hadn't been outside, explaining, as best he could, what they'd seen.

'So . . . they're back?' Tocaras asked.

'Don't know,' Cartheron answered. He glanced to Surly at the bar. 'They disappeared again.' She stood leaning against the counter, arms crossed, glaring at the air ahead of her. 'So,' he prompted, 'what do we do?'

'Carry on with the repairs,' she said.

'Are we gonna go?' Urko asked. 'He won't want us takin' his ship.'

Surly cast him her searing glare. 'It's *our* ship.'

Urko shrugged. 'Yeah. But we promised to work for him.'

Surly's lips turned down even further. 'We'll work for him from far away. Anyway, he's gone again, isn't he? Disappeared. Maybe gone for ever. We have to just assume—'

Grinner came thumping down the stairs.

'How is he?' Cartheron asked.

He nodded his assurances to everyone. 'He'll live. Just some kind of shock. Our, ah, patron's magery doesn't agree with him, apparently.' He turned to Surly. 'May I?'

She gestured him off. 'Of course. Go ahead.'

He hurried out the door.

Of course, Cartheron thought, *he's worried about Hawl.*

Shrift rose and went to the door as well. 'I'll take watch,' she said, and stepped out.

'Crust,' Surly said from the bar.

'Yes?'

She was still staring off ahead of her. 'You have another moon.'

Cartheron nodded. Damned straight – after *that* display. Best to be careful. He shook his head. Who would've thought the little runt had that in him? Taming the Hounds of Shadow? He drank and shook his head again. *By all the ancient powers above and below . . . who would've thought?* 'How long this time, I wonder, hey?' he murmured aloud.

Surly just stared ahead, thinking furiously perhaps about what this latest revelation meant for her long-term plans.

'Don't know,' Urko answered. 'The locals say no one and nothing ever comes *out* of that place.'

Cartheron emptied his earthenware mug and sighed. Well, they had plenty of work to do, regardless.

*　*　*

Dancer found himself in darkness. Not the dark as of a moonless night, but a complete and utter black, as if he swam lost within a sea of elemental night.

'Where are we?' he asked of the blackness.

'I'm not sure,' Kellanved answered, sounding reassuringly close, but also completely spent and wrung out.

Understandably so. 'Can't you see?' he asked.

'No. Too dark.'

'Well – make some light. Do your hocus-pocus magery.'

'Can't. There are no shadows here.'

'You can't make us a plain light?' Dancer felt almost betrayed. 'What kind of a mage are you?'

'Not that kind. Ah!' Above, a door had opened casting weak watery light, as of a sickle moon, down a set of stone steps. The feeble light was occluded, however, by the lumbering gigantic shape of an armoured colossus who came thumping down the steps.

312

Dancer drew his heavy parrying gauche once more, thinking, *This is just not my night.*

'We are within,' Kellanved called out. 'Why dispute this now?'

The giant did not answer from within its obscuring full helm. It drew a blade fully as large as a two-handed sword, and held it in one gauntleted hand. It swung ponderously. Dancer and Kellanved evaded the blow. The blade rang on the stone-flagged floor.

'Do something,' Dancer hissed to his partner.

Kellanved held up his open hands. 'I have nothing left.'

Snarling his frustration, Dancer threw himself at the colossus, striking low, but his blade rebounded from the giant's mailed leggings. He evaded another sluggish blow and called, 'This is not my strong suit!'

'I have a plan,' Kellanved answered, throwing a finger in the air. Dodging a straight up and down cut, the clashing iron raising sparks from the stones, Kellanved ran for the stairs.

Dancer watched him go almost with disbelief. 'That's your plan? Run away?'

Topping the steps, Kellanved called down, 'A time-honoured tradition.'

Dancer easily evaded the ponderous guardian to follow his partner up the stairs. He found an empty hallway. From below came the heavy thumping of the giant, pursuing.

A panicked yell from Kellanved brought Dancer running up the hall to a small parlour, or salon, where flames crackled in a fireplace. Dim dirty windows hinted at early morning outside. Kellanved writhed on the floor, fighting something small and furry that was wrapped round his head yanking at his hair.

Dancer let his arms fall. 'It's that nacht thing. Your pet.'

Kellanved stopped wriggling. He struggled to his feet, dragged the thing round to study it. 'Demon! Bad Demon!'

The thing let out an enormous belch and Kellanved flinched.

Dancer looked to the thick, soot-blackened log rafters above. 'Change its damned name, would you?'

A crashing footfall announced the entry of the giant, blade readied. Kellanved froze, gaping up at it, as did the nacht in his hands, its arms wrapped round his neck. It seemed to Dancer that both wore the exact same expression of stunned consternation.

The armoured colossus lowered its blade, its shoulders falling, as if in disappointment, then it turned and trudged away down the hall.

Carefully extricating himself from the creature, losing little pawfuls of hair, Kellanved set the beast down on a nearby table. He brushed his hands together. 'There! Now that that's settled . . .'

Dancer threw out his arms. 'What? What's settled?'

The little mage just shrugged. 'I have no idea.' He peered about the room. 'Now let's have a look round.'

'We are in this house thing then?' Kellanved nodded absently. 'I thought it was supposed to be hard to enter.'

'Oh, it is, I assure you.'

'But we got in without much trouble.'

Kellanved made a tsking noise. 'Really? Not much trouble? I'll have you know the route I brought us on couldn't be duplicated by anyone alive. We sneaked in, my friend. If you try to force your way in, then yes, it is frankly impossible. But if you come sidling up through darkness and shadow, shift through a number of Warrens and Realms, edging up closer and closer each time, pretending to be part of the darkness, sorting and searching, until, finally, the planes overlap . . . so to speak . . .'

Dancer eyed him sidelong. 'If you say so.'

The mage fiddled with his newly reappeared walking stick, peering about, not meeting Dancer's steady gaze.

'Or . . . it just let us in.'

'That would rather take away from the magnificence of my achievement, don't you think?'

Dancer crossed his arms. 'What did you say to that hound, anyway?'

Kellanved sent him a look, one brow raised. 'What? Ah! I merely told her that if they cast their lots in with me they would see a great deal of action.' He waved Dancer onward. 'You see, it struck me that they must be truly bored sniffing among the sands and ruins and ghosts. With me they're sure to get out much more.'

Dancer let out a long breath, ruefully shaking his head. 'In other words, you cut a deal.'

The little mage's face twisted up, pained. 'Really, Dancer. Words do mean something, you know. You should take more care in your, ah, casting.'

But Dancer would not stop shaking his head. 'No. I'm spot on.

Don't you see it? We're the hounds in this scenario. The House cut *us* a deal.'

Kellanved had his arms out as if bewildered. 'I assure you I have no idea what you are talking about. It was only through my pure genius and profound insight into the mysteries of Warren manipulation that I was able to penetrate the hidden interstices, aporia, and lacunae of this structure's thaumaturgical defences.'

Dancer waved him silent and headed up the hall. 'Save it for the histories.'

Falling into step with him, Kellanved raised a finger into the air. 'Histories! Now *there's* an idea.'

* * *

Four days after the night of the Shadow Storm – as everyone was calling it – Tocaras waved Cartheron to the front door of Smiley's. He gestured outside. 'Someone here about hiring on.'

Cartheron nodded; he was about to set out for the waterfont anyway. He opened the door to see a tall and lean young Dal Hon lad standing before a small two-wheeled cart; the kind wharf stevedores use to haul awkward loads. It held what looked like a big roll of blankets.

The lad bowed from his waist with an odd sort of formality and stiffness. 'You work for a mage and his partner? The one who recently had dealings with the place called the Deadhouse?'

Cartheron nodded, rather intrigued. 'Yes?'

'I wish to offer my services – in return for a favour.'

'Well . . . they're not here right now . . .'

'They have entered that place, as some of the locals say?'

Cartheron nodded again. 'We think so . . .'

The lad gave a curt nod. 'Very well. I will wait. But first I have an errand to run. Is there by chance a temple to Hood within this town?'

Cartheron rubbed his chin, rather bemused. 'Well . . . there's a quarter where you can find all kindsa altars and such, down the way, but maybe not a *temple*.'

The lad peered down the street. 'Very good. My name is Dassem, by the way.'

'Cartheron Crust.'

The fellow took up the long handles of the two-wheeled cart

and headed on down the street. Cartheron watched him for a moment, rubbing his chin, still bemused.

The door opened behind him and Hawl peered out, blinking and wincing in the morning light – she still hadn't fully recovered from whatever trauma had been inflicted on her that night.

'Who was that?' she asked, a strange sort of urgency in her tone.

'Don't know. Some Dal Hon named Dassem who wants to talk to Kellanved.'

She stared after him, then turned back to the common room, calling, 'Grinner! Follow that Dal Hon with the cart.'

Grinner rose from his table and ducked out past them. 'Right.'

Cartheron nodded his farewell to Hawl and ambled off for another day's work refitting the *Twisted*.

That night, when Cartheron returned to Smiley's, he was rather surprised to find the Dal Hon fellow sitting at a table in the corner of the common room. He crossed over to where Shrift, Grinner and Nedurian held a table on the opposite side of the room. The rest of the place was empty but for three regulars – drunken sailors all.

He sat down and nodded over to their visitor. He asked, low, 'So what's the story on this guy?'

Grinner just shrugged. 'He pulls his cart over the altar quarters, talks to some people, then drags it to an old place built of field-stones on the edge of town. There, some old guy comes out and actually bows to our boy here! He puts his bundle inside, leaves his cart there, and comes back here. Been here all day.'

Cartheron grunted, losing interest.

'How're the repairs coming?' Shrift asked.

'Faster if you'd help out.'

The swordswoman shivered her revulsion. 'I ain't goin' near that thing.'

'You'll have to eventually.'

She looked away. 'I know, I know.'

'So what now?' Grinner asked, sending a meaningful glance to their guest.

Cartheron decided he had to eat, even if his brother was cooking. He stood, saying, 'Nothing. Just keep working,' and headed for the kitchen.

After searching the 'house' – which proved remarkably pedestrian in its empty dust-filled chambers and closets – Kellanved headed for the font door. Here, the giant set of oddly designed armour of interlocking iron plates, complete with full helm, stood in an alcove. Rather like a museum display.

Kellanved regarded the thing for some time, peering up, while Dancer waited, impatient. The mage reached out with his walking stick and tapped the battered chestplate. It did not ring hollow; rather, it thumped densely.

The giant's helm grated as it lowered its head to peer at him.

Kellanved hurriedly yanked away the walking stick. 'Your pardon.' He wriggled his fingers towards the front door. 'I was just wondering . . . if we leave . . . if we *can* leave . . . will we be able to return?'

The helm rose as the giant seemed to dismiss them.

Dancer and Kellanved exchanged glances and the mage shrugged. 'Well, only one way to find out, yes?'

Dancer raised a hand. 'Wait. Are you saying you brought us in here fully aware of the possibility that we may never – ever – leave again? Prisoners for the rest of our lives?'

Kellanved backed away towards the door. He fluttered his hands. 'Now, let's not get ahead of ourselves.'

Unbelievable! Dancer reached to catch the fellow by his wide collar, but at that moment Kellanved lifted the latch behind him, pushed open the door, and tumbled out on to the broad slate landing. Dancer strode forward, meaning to throttle him where he lay. One step took him across the threshold, and the door slammed shut behind his back, battering him on to his stomach. He scrambled quickly to his feet and stood over Kellanved, furious. 'You could've told me!'

The mage was peering up the walkway. He pointed. 'Not in front of the neighbours.'

Dancer looked up, blinking at the bright daylight: a few kids on the street stood frozen, gaping at them, as did pedestrians in the small crossroads further away. He pulled Kellanved to his feet. 'You're lucky.'

The mage straightened his worn and tattered shirt, vest, and jacket. 'There. You see? No problem at all.' And he started up the walkway, swinging his stick, and humming to himself.

Dancer could only shake his head. *Unbelievable. Completely unbelievable.*

When they entered Smiley's everyone jumped. The Napans, plus others who must be local hires, even exchanged nervous glances. Dancer peered round, a touch perplexed. 'What is it?'

Grinner, clearing his throat, was the first to sit down again. 'Nothing,' he said, but he kept eyeing them sidelong. An old veteran with him, possibly Talian by his greying straight black hair, approached and bowed to Kellanved.

'Magister, I am Nedurian – I have enlisted with your representative, Surly.'

Kellanved fluttered his fingers in response. 'Very good. We need more talents. Especially ex-legion.'

The fellow looked a touch startled, but bowed again, returning to his table.

Surly emerged from the kitchen. She stood regarding them for some time with her arms crossed, as if to say, *Well well, look who's come dragging themselves back.*

She approached, her lips twisted in disapproval, and Dancer almost felt contrite – as if he'd been out on a bender. She looked them up and down, said, 'Some show twelve days ago.'

Dancer's brows rose. *Twelve days? Ye gods. Much longer than I thought.*

'Thank you,' Kellanved said smugly, and Dancer wanted to hit him. The mage started for the stairs, walking stick tapping the stone floor. 'I'll be in my office if you wish to talk.'

Dancer watched him go. *Hiding in your office, you mean.* He faced Surly, but frowned then, and glanced to a figure sitting far to the back. Having his attention, the figure stood, and Dancer could not believe whom he was seeing.

The man approached and Dancer looked him up and down. 'What in the name of all the gods are *you* doing here?'

It was their righteous friend from Li Heng, Dassem, and he glanced to the stairs. 'I have business to discuss with your partner.'

'With *us*, you mean.'

The man took a steadying breath, and seeing that gesture Dancer understood just how extraordinarily important the business was to him. 'With the two of you, then. In private.'

Dancer nodded. 'Very well.' He gestured Dassem to the stairs. 'Let's talk.' He nodded to Surly, *Later*, but as she watched them go she was scowling her dissatisfaction even more.

When they entered the office, Kellanved was standing at the window, rocking back and forth on his heels. He turned when Dancer shut the door, and nodded to Dassem. 'What brings you to Malaz Island? Changed your mind?'

'In a way,' the man answered stiffly. 'A service for a service.'

'This being?'

The fellow was very uncomfortable. Obviously not used to explaining himself, he cleared his throat and said, 'I have something I wish to place in the Deadhouse.'

'It's not some kind of damned storage closet,' Dancer snorted, going to a small table to pour himself a glass of wine.

Kellanved was slowly shaking his head in thought. 'Well . . . it sort of is, actually. And in return?'

'In return I shall serve you.'

Dancer spluttered on his drink. He eyed the swordsman, wiping his shirt front. '*You*, serve *us*?'

Dassem's eyes narrowed, as if he'd detected some sort of insult. 'My word is good . . .'

Kellanved raised his hands placatingly. 'Please do not misunderstand. We do not doubt your word. It is just that . . . our goals may not be aligned.'

'I care nothing for your goals. I will serve you.'

Dancer eyed Kellanved, raising a brow.

The mage tapped his walking stick to the floorboards, rocked back and forth again. 'Well, this is all very hypothetical anyway. We may not even be able to re-enter the House.'

Dassem took hold of the door latch. 'Then let us see.'

Kellanved and Dancer exchanged glances once more and Dancer shrugged. The mage pointed his stick to the door. 'Very well . . .'

Dassem led them to the edge of town. Here, at an old dwelling constructed of flat fieldstones, he brought out a bundle and laid it in a cart. A bearded old man in rags lived in the shack, and kept bowing to Dassem the entire time.

When they left, Dassem pulling the cart, Dancer couldn't help glancing back. The oldster was on his knees in the dirt, hands raised in prayer.

'An adherent of Hood,' Dassem explained.

Kellanved led the way to the House. Dancer brought up the rear, behind the cart. His neck kept itching as it did when he was under observation and he turned his head to see a slim young lad in dark clothes following them at a distance. He frowned, but continued on, glancing back every so often to keep track of the young fellow. He didn't like the smug smile on his face – as if he were privy to some amusing secret known only to him.

At the House, Dassem gently picked up the fat roll of blankets and carried it in both arms. Kellanved opened the little iron gate. They walked up the stone path, Dancer in the rear. When Kellanved paused on the broad landing before the door, Dancer looked back and saw the pale lad at the fieldstone wall. The smile was gone. He appeared rather sour now.

As Kellanved hesitated, Dassem reached in past him and took the latch. To Dancer's great surprise it lifted, and the swordsman pushed open the door. Kellanved entered, while Dancer came in last. As he closed the door behind him, he glimpsed the pale lad's scowl.

Dassem gently laid the roll down in a side room just off the entrance hall. Dancer and Kellanved watched, curious. He drew back folds of the rolled blankets to reveal the head and face of a young Dal Hon girl, her eyes closed, her hair a sweaty mess, to all appearances asleep.

'What's this?' Dancer asked.

Dassem did not look up from the girl. 'Someone I swore I would protect.'

'She will be safe here,' said Kellanved, and Dancer was quite surprised by how serious the mage sounded.

With the back of his hand, Dassem eased the girl's sweaty hair from her face, nodding. 'So I was assured.'

Dancer was going to ask who in the Abyss had assured him of that when the mage brushed his hands together, announcing, 'Good. So, we have an accord?'

Kneeling next to the girl, the swordsman bowed his head. 'We have an accord.'

'Excellent. You will accompany us, then. We have an . . . errand, of a sort, to run.'

Dancer eyed his partner in open suspicion. 'What's this?'

Kellanved was grinning. 'You'll see . . .'

Shadows now came swirling up about them and Dancer raised a warning finger. 'I told you! No sudden damned—'

The three disappeared, leaving dust motes and a few dried leaves and needles to swirl about the sleeping girl. After a time, heavy footsteps sounded and the armoured colossus appeared in the arched entryway. The helmed head lowered as it regarded this strange new visitor.

* * *

The first thing Tayschrenn became aware of were his hands and feet – they prickled abominably. Next, his arms and legs registered their agonizing reawakening, and he groaned. Or thought he did.

His chest suddenly flinched and his back arched. The pain was transporting; every nerve in his body was aflame. Now he was certain that he screamed until his throat was raw.

Then he slept the sleep of tortured exhaustion.

Noise awoke him next; the heavy dragging and brushing as of something very large moving over stone and dirt. Whispering reached his ears and he strained anew, listening.

'He's awake,' a male voice said from the dark.

'Yes, yes,' a female voice answered, impatient and dismissive.

He decided to ask them what was happening. He drew a breath and exhaled, moving his tongue and trying to speak. All he heard was a dry rasping and animal-like growling.

'He's dying,' said the male voice. 'Isn't that him dying?'

'No, it's not,' answered the female voice. 'Water,' she commanded, 'water for our guest.'

A short time later water suddenly poured over his face from the total darkness and he gasped, spluttering, trying to swallow without drowning.

'Enough water!' the female voice commanded once more. 'I apologize,' she said. 'We get so few visitors down here.'

'Where,' he managed, croaking, 'where am I?'

'Far below your island, little man. Very far indeed.'

'Who . . . who are you?'

'What?' the man answered, incredulous and angered. 'Who among all the ancients do you think?'

'Now, now,' the woman said. 'He is disoriented after his ordeal.

321

Light, I think. Let light be our answer.' Multiple hands clapped, brusquely.

While Tayschrenn watched, straining his eyes in the absolute black, tiny pinpoints of a greenish-bluish light blossomed to a glow. Here and there, all about, they multiplied by the thousands and thousands, until he made out an immense cavern, vaulted far above and boasting many tunnel entrances, and facing him two giant snake-like entities, each emerging from a different tunnel, titanic, each as large in scale as the tower of a fortress to him. One bore the upper portions and features of a human male, the other a female.

And Tayschrenn, the sceptic and doubting scholar, forced his agonized and punished limbs to move, and he rose to his knees, bowing before the pair, murmuring in awed reverence, 'D'rek . . .'

'Well, I should think so,' huffed the male portion.

'Thank you,' said the female, and she clasped her tiny hands together. 'Now, our time is short. We spare you, Tayschrenn, as your sentence was unjust. We are not without mercy, as you see.'

He bowed again, touching his head to the floor before him, and discovering it to be a sea of writhing beetles, roaches, centipedes and silverfish.

He attempted to disguise his shudder of revulsion.

'We shall send you back to the temple,' said the male.

'Yes,' nodded the female. 'And we ask that you carry a message. A warning.' Her voice hardened as she continued, 'Elements within the priesthood are advocating new directions for the cult and we are not pleased – is that clear?'

Tayschrenn bowed once more. 'Quite. I am honoured by your trust, and—'

'Yes, yes,' the male cut in. Aside, to the female, he murmured, 'He cannot remain much longer.'

She nodded. 'Indeed. Tayschrenn, the chemicals injected into your system are abating and you must go. Frankly, the atmosphere here within this cavern is poisonous to you, and so we shall dismiss you. Farewell, and good luck.'

He struggled to his feet, his head bowed. 'My thanks, Great One.' Even as he spoke, a strong ammonia stink assaulted him as he inhaled, making him cough. This air, he realized, was that of underground caves where those who wandered within soon expired for lack of breathable gases.

Male and female entities waved their dismissal and his vision dimmed. As they disappeared it occurred to him that the female's lower quarters curved to the left as they disappeared into a tunnel, while the male's curved to the right. The two, it seemed, might be the oppposite ends of the same entity.

A great dislocation assaulted him as he moved through a Realm he did not recognize, which he realized must be that of Elder, and unavailable to him. The vastness and depth of puissance he glimpsed in passing was beyond his imaginings. Then it disappeared in a sudden, disrupting shear.

*

The cavern lay dark and empty but for the uncounted millions of squirming insects.

'There is a strength in him,' said the male voice into the darkness.

'There will have to be,' answered the female.

'K'rul seems to think he may be the one.'

'Yet another candidate,' murmured the female sadly.

'*Someone* will have to succeed.'

'Perhaps,' allowed the female. 'Perhaps not. Change comes to us all.'

'*I* will not just step aside,' affirmed the male.

'No,' agreed the female, her voice hardening. 'Neither will I.'

*

On his knees, hands pressed to his thighs, Tayschrenn raised his head to find himself in familiar surroundings. It was a private audience chamber off the side of the cult's main temple. Shelves of scrolls lined the wall, while the top of a central table was hidden beneath numerous open manuscripts of ongoing research projects.

He crossed to the door and listened: the massed whispering and brushing of robes betrayed a service in progress. D'rek's timing could not have been better – of course. He took hold of the latch then paused for a time, readying himself. He was terrified, he discovered; his hands shook, his stomach clenched and rebelled. Why so much more nervous now? And he knew, of course. Now was about so much more than merely him.

He yanked open the door and entered the temple. It was crowded

323

with the faithful, all in ranks before the raised altar at the front where the cult elders led the service. Tallow stood in the central place – the Demidrek's. He was in mid-sentence, exhorting the faithful.

Tayschrenn calmly strode towards the altar, passing through line after line of the massed acolytes and full priests. At first a silence grew behind him as he passed, then it filled with gasps and awed whisperings.

The hissed discordance grew in volume and reached the front ranks. Tallow faltered, losing his tempo. 'And so, my children,' he was saying, 'we must return to the proper path, for we have lost our way . . .' He paused, eyed the rear of the hall, frowning. 'We must . . .'

His gaze found the vector of the growing disturbance and his eyes widened in shock. Beside him, Salleen lurched to her feet, glaring.

Tallow pointed, bellowing, 'What impostor's game is this? Who are you?'

'I am Tayschrenn,' he answered, and was proud of the steadiness of his voice.

Tallow was shaking his head, 'No. That is impossible.' Beside him, Salleen turned sickly pale, almost staggering.

'Not impossible. I have been sent to carry a message for the—'

'*Seize him!*' Tallow roared. 'He has evaded D'rek's justice! He is a blasphemer! He has spurned D'rek!'

'*No!*' a new high voice shrieked, a young woman's. A slim figure fought its way forward to the altar, approached Tallow. Now Tayschrenn felt his legs weaken and his resolve faltering as he recognized a dishevelled Silla. 'He is innocent!' She clasped Tallow's sleeve. 'You promised me he would live and now look! *Look!*' And she laughed wildly.

He pushed her from him. 'You are ill, sister. Someone restrain this poor child.' He turned from her, yet even as he did so her face grew savage and she leapt forward, swinging an arm. Something glinted in her hand, striking Tallow in the back, and he bellowed, staggering.

A burst of power from him tossed her backwards into the stone wall behind the altar, where her head hit with a meaty crack. She slumped to the floor, motionless. Tallow swung back to the hall, a hand over one shoulder, pressed to his back. 'He has sent his assassin upon me! I see it now! He would suborn the cult to his own ends! Slay him!'

Those nearest Tayschrenn now closed on him, grasping his dirty robes. Almost as an afterthought he raised his Warren and flicked them away, for his gaze was fixed upon the motionless shape of Silla where she lay. *You promised . . .* So, she said those things to try to save his life – a bargain offered by *him.*

And now . . . now she was dead.

Slain by . . . *him.*

His gaze shifted to the man himself as he straightened, rolling his meaty shoulders as if throwing off whatever damage the wound might have inflicted. Tayschrenn saw in his churning Warren-aura that strange taint, or coloration, now even more potent than before. And now he recognized it – the stain of Chaos. He raised an arm, pointing, '*Who do you serve?*'

The Invigilator smiled. Then he swept his arms forward, motioning all the cult's highest ranked priests and priestesses into action. 'Destroy the apostate!'

The entire body of Kartool's High Temple of D'rek hurled themselves upon Tayschrenn.

He threw up his protective barriers and was bludgeoned and buffeted within. He could not bring himself to strike back, and so he shifted into the Warren of Thyr and fled. And the army of D'rek mage-priests, those who could, followed.

Chapter 17

THE COAST LOOKED WILD AND UNINHABITED TO LARS, YET Kallor remained locked within his cabin, so he and the other seven survivors of the great ocean crossing waited at anchor while white tendrils of noxious smoke came leaking round the door and through gaps in the planking of their master's cabin walls.

Finally, towards noon, the door opened, disgorging a massive cloud of evil-smelling smoke that quickly wafted away. Kallor strode out accoutred as usual in his full-length coat of mail, his weapon at his side. He carried a burning smudge-pot that he waved in front of him as he walked to the side.

Lars, weak and faint with starvation, limped to him. Taking a deep breath, he dared, 'M'lord . . . shall we . . . disembark?'

Kallor ignored him. He studied the shore as if as hungry as Lars. He waved more of the dense smoke across his face, and murmured, bizarrely, 'Try to smell me now, bitch.'

The smoke lashed then, fuming as if caught in a fierce wind, though no such gusting brushed Lars or the gentle waves about them.

Kallor raised a hand for silence and studied the smoke intently. After a time he nodded as if at some conclusion, then covered the pot with its lid. 'We wait,' he announced, not even turning to face Lars. 'Something strange is coming.'

Lars eyed the quiet coast, uninhabited but for a few modest fishers' huts. What could possibly be coming that this fiend would be wary of? Whatever it might be, Lars decided that *he* certainly wanted nothing to do with it. Still, land, animals, larders . . . 'But perhaps there is food,' he whined before realizing it, and he flinched, covering his head, ready for a kick or a blow.

Their tormentor turned to him, scowling his profound disgust. 'There are fish, aren't there?'

Lars glanced at the listless, huddled crew. *Fish! Of course!* 'But,' he ventured, bowing, 'what can we use as bait?'

Kallor had started back to his cabin, but he paused, glancing at Lars. His deeply lined mouth drew up in an evil one-sided smile. 'Those rotting bodies you have hidden below, I should think.' And he slammed the door shut.

Lars started guiltily. He eyed the ragged sailors, who stared back, blinking, almost uncomprehending. He pointed angrily. 'You've been nibbling too! I know it! Now get some lines over the side!'

The sailors shuffled to obey.

*   *   *

Dassem sat before a modest fire next to a small series of half-buried walls and toppled stone arches. It was not night, as he would understand it, though the mage Kellanved had called it that. It was more like an overcast dusk, the sky a dark iron, the shadows thick and heavy. Sighing his impatience, he made a show of warming his hands. In his opinion this was a stupid errand. They should be on the island; it was clear to him that the power base these two counted on was not secure. Enemies remained within striking distance and ought to be eliminated. Greater consolidation was necessary, yet here they were, wasting precious time.

A dark shape came looming out of the dusky sky. Its ragged membranous wings flapped loudly as it descended to alight on an arch of ancient stones across the fire from him and he sat back, studying the strange cross between a pelican and a bat.

At last, he thought.

The creature paced atop the stone ledge. 'A *fire?*' it cawed harshly. 'You sit here plain as day and light a *fire?* Don't you know where you *are?*' Dassem opened his mouth to answer but the beast cut in, 'Never mind! Who are you? What are you doing here? What do you want?'

He thought through the answers the mage had schooled him in and responded, casually, 'I just thought I'd take a stroll . . .'

The beast pressed the tiny hands on its wings to its head. 'A

327

stroll! Ancient ones! What have we come to?' It swept a wing to encompass the desolate surroundings. 'What does this look like? A garden pastoral? Have you no respect?'

'It seems quiet enough,' Dassem answered.

The thing cackled a cawed laugh. It shifted its tiny black pebble eyes left and right. 'You'll see. Soon enough.' It pressed a tiny hand to one earhole, head cocked. 'Any time now . . .'

Dassem peered round as well, as if curious.

'Yup. Any moment . . .' The creature dropped its little hand. 'They should be here by now.'

'What should?' Dassem asked.

'Shut up, fool.'

Dassem sat back, sighing. 'Please?' he called loudly.

The thing frowned its confusion at him. 'What's that? Please? Why?' It hopped then, startled, peering round at the ruins. 'Who's there? Gaahh!' It leapt into the sky but shadows came lashing about it like knotted ropes and it fell tumbling to the sands.

Dancer came charging out from among the fallen stones to stand over it. Kellanved strolled along behind.

'You!' the creature gaped, astonished. 'How did you . . . ?'

Kellanved shrugged modestly, waved his walking stick. 'Oh, it was nothing really. I just—'

'Enough,' Dancer cut in. To the beast: 'Who do you work for?'

'Go to the Abyss.'

Kellanved planted his stick into the sands and sighed his disappointment. 'You really should cooperate.'

'I will tell you nothing. *Nothing*.' It struggled to raise one little hand, thumb and finger pinched together. 'See this? You are this. Tiny. A flea. Nothing. Shadow will swallow you.'

'We shall see.' He nodded to Dassem and Dancer, and the two grasped the thing's feet and dragged it off.

'What are you doing?' it demanded. 'What's going on?'

Dancer directed Dassem to a dark hole exposed among flagstones in the middle of the ruined building. They held the bat-like creature at the hole's lip.

Coming along behind, Kellanved offered, 'One last chance. Who is in charge here?'

'Kiss my furry—'

Dassem and Dancer let it fall. They heard it thump to the floor far below.

'What's this?' it squawked. '*Bodies?* There are bodies down here!'

Kellanved nodded to the stone that had covered the hole and Dassem began edging it towards the space. 'Do you wish to talk now?' he called.

'Only if you join me!'

'Well, you have a think about it,' Kellanved suggested. 'We'll talk later. In a hundred years,' he added, mostly to himself, as the stone slotted neatly back into place. 'Disappointing,' he went on. 'I'd hoped to get something out of that creature.'

'The island?' Dassem reminded him. 'Their strategic position is weak.'

'Hmm? What's that?'

'The Napans.'

'Our friend is right,' Dancer added. 'We're supposed to be in charge, remember?'

Kellanved rolled his eyes. He threw his arms out wide as if to embrace their surroundings. 'But this is all so much more fascinating!'

'Later,' Dancer answered firmly, and Dassem nodded his support.

Kellanved let his arms fall. His lips tightened into a disappointed moue, so very put upon. 'Oh, very well! If you insist.'

*   *   *

It was late afternoon and Cartheron had the last of a pot of rendered glue heating over a fire on the pier next to the *Twisted* when Tocaras, up aloft among the standing rigging, called to him and pointed out to the bay. He stepped up on to a crate for a good look and as soon as he saw the vessel swinging in across the mouth of the harbour he knew with a sort of heavy weight of despair that they'd waited too long.

It was Tarel's flagship, the *Sapphire*.

Choss, Urko, Hawl and Tocaras all gathered round.

'Jammed with marines, no doubt,' Urko said with a curse.

'Why just the flagship?' Tocaras wondered.

'They're not here to fight the Malazans,' Hawl observed darkly.

Cartheron nodded his agreement. 'Grab your gear and let's go.'

He doused the fire, collected his tools, and jogged with the others for Smiley's.

Already a launch was being lowered over the *Sapphire*'s side. Cartheron's last glimpse of the harbour waters allowed him to see a white flag flapping above the crowded boat.

*

When word came of a large Napan man-o-war blockading the harbour mouth, Lee's brows rose. When further word came that it was no less than King Tarel's flagship, Lee decided to amble down to the waterfront to see how poor old Admiral Mock was going to handle *this* development.

The Malazan captains had the waterfront cordoned off by ranks of armed marines and sailors. A small contingent of Napans, an honour guard of some sort, together with one rather fat official, climbed up from a packed launch and approached along a jetty.

Mock was waiting with a handful of his captains. Lee pushed her way closer, thinking, *This really ought to be good.*

'Admiral Koreth,' Mock said, bowing. 'You are come for another visit?'

The Napan admiral returned the bow, if curtly. 'I am come at behest of King Tarel.'

Mock stroked his moustache, nodding. 'Ah, yes. My brother regent. How fares he?'

Koreth had drawn off leather gloves that he now slapped across one leg, impatient. 'The king is well. He is irked, however, by an oversight of yours. A mistake, no doubt, as I am certain you mean no insult.'

Mock peered about, eyeing the massed Malazan sailors and marines who held the waterfront and were glaring down at the admiral's elite Napan escort. 'Oh? An oversight, you say? And that is?'

'You have allowed wanted Napan criminals to reside on your island.'

Mock raised his face to a freshening wind coming in off the bay, nodding to himself. 'Ah . . . I see the way of your tack now, admiral.' He shrugged. 'Malaz is an open port. Any and all are welcome.'

Koreth was tapping his gloves against his thigh. 'I understand your pride in this. Malaz has traditionally been an open port. That is a shame.'

Mock lost his playful smile, eyed the man's small escort significantly. 'Have a care, admiral.'

Koreth raised his open hands. 'Oh, I do not mean for you or me. I meant for our prisoners.'

'Prisoners?'

'Yes. Captives from our recent . . . unpleasantness. Some four score Malazan crew, men and women.'

The Malazans assembled on the waterfront set to muttering among themselves. Lee had to shake her head in admiration. *Well played, Koreth.*

Mock could also see this news spreading among the crews, so he put on a stern face, shocked. 'And where are these prisoners?'

Koreth gestured lazily to his vessel. 'Why, on board the *Sapphire*, now.'

Mock set his hands on his hips, raising his voice. 'I demand you hand them over immediately!'

'In return for the Napan criminals in your midst, aye.'

'First bring them all ashore.'

'Half, first.'

'You fetch these Napans – I'll not lift a hand against any free resident.'

Koreth inclined his head, pleased. 'As it should be. Done.'

'Done!'

Koreth nodded to one of his escort, who began signalling the *Sapphire*. Mock turned to his captains. 'Give the Napans some help in bringing our lads and lasses ashore.' Hess, Guran and Renish set off down the pier, shouting orders.

Lee turned away. Everything seemed to be well in hand. Koreth's hands, that is. A straight exchange, and one Mock could not have dared turn down. Could those damned Napans really be out of her way? She paused as she pushed through the crowd, thinking that she should get over there herself with her boys and be ready to move in immediately.

A familiar face caught her attention among the press: that scarred old mage who now worked for the Napans. She gave him her best savage smile. *You, my friend, are about to be out of a job.*

But the mage wasn't even looking at her. His attention was focused to the north-east, far out to sea. The man's eyes grew huge and he went scrambling off, shoving men and women out of his way.

331

Lee peered out over the bay, frowning. Some sort of strange disturbance was headed their way. It looked like a waterspout, or one of those twisting, gyring winds that could whip up over the plains. What did they call them – wind-devils? Cyclones?

She shaded her gaze now from dust being thrown up by the gathering winds. What was so frightening about a little localized blow like this? And there wasn't even a cloud in the sky.

*

Cartheron came thumping down the stairs of Smiley's, kitbag on his shoulder, sword at his hip. He was rather surprised to find the whole crew gathered in the common room. 'We have to go now,' he said, a touch uncertain. But Urko, leaning against a wall, just pointed to Surly. She had her arms crossed and Cartheron thought, *Shit!*

'I'm not running,' she said. 'There's nowhere to run *to*.'

Urko nodded his fierce agreement.

'We can find a ship on the far side of the island . . .'

Choss snorted. 'A *ship*? Rowboat, you mean.'

'There's bound to be something.'

Surly shook her head. 'No. I'll not be run down like a rabbit. We meet them here.'

Urko smacked a fist into a palm with a resounding slap. 'About damned time.'

Cartheron motioned to the local hires watching the windows. 'And the locals?'

Surly eyed them as well, then raised her voice to address them. 'You're all free to go. I give you leave. This isn't your fight.'

Their unofficial leaders, the old veteran Dujek and his seeming adjutant Jack, shared a glance, then Dujek cleared his throat. 'If it's all right with all a' you, we'll stay.'

Surly nodded her gratitude. 'You're more than welcome.'

Two Malazan toughs watching the door shouted a warning, and yanked it open. In burst Hawl and Nedurian. 'I have an errand!' the old Talian mage shouted to Surly, then Hawl pushed him back towards the door and he was off.

Surly raised her hands to Hawl. 'It's okay, we know.'

Hawl shook her head, short of breath. 'No – you most certainly don't.'

Once again, Nedurian found Agayla out in the street before her shop. The cobbled way ran more or less east–west down to the waterfront and she was watching the waters of the bay in the darkening dusk. Barely visible far out across the waves rose a strange blur of a disturbance, and it looked to be headed straight for them.

'Impressive, yes?' he said to Agayla.

She nodded, her scowling face showing her habitual disapproval, together with a touch of apprehensiveness. 'I've not seen the like in a century. And it is still leagues off . . .'

'Who do you think it could be?'

She shook her head in a negative. 'I do not know . . . but there are few who are *that* powerful.'

He blinked in the gusting winds, blew on his fists to warm his hands. 'I'm not looking forward to this.'

She eyed him, frowned her confusion, then shook her head. 'We're not interfering. It's not our fight.'

'But the city . . .'

She continued shaking her head in a firm negative. 'Even so. Our duties lie elsewhere. Understood?'

'But escalation . . . what of the other? This Nightchill?'

'She has already moved out of the way. She's in the south. In fact,' and Agayla rubbed her arms as if chilled, 'we should join her. We will be lodestones to what is coming.'

He looked away, into town. 'I have other duties . . .'

'You will be a danger to everyone around you and they will be helpless before *this*.'

He risked another glance towards the disturbance and winced at the yammering lashing power at its heart. He'd seen such things before. Abyss, he'd been a participant.

A full-on to the death mage duel, Warren sizzling against Warren. He'd seen such things brush entire battalions aside. For now, whoever it was, they appeared entirely engrossed with one another. He dared not upset that balance.

He gave a curt bob of his head. 'Very well. Though it galls me to retreat like this.'

'With luck they will sweep right on across the island. Frankly, to them, it is as if we aren't even here.'

Kellanved shifted the three of them from Shadow and Dancer was relieved to find himself back within the House. *No surprises for once!* After brushing dust from his shirt and trousers, he led the way to the front door. As usual, the armoured giant stood resting in its alcove. Here, Dassem paused, eyeing the empty side room where they had left his friend.

'As I said,' Kellanved murmured in the silence, 'the House has moved her somewhere.'

'But where?' the Dal Hon swordsman answered, and Dancer could tell he was upset by the way his hands clenched.

Kellanved gave a small shrug. 'Perhaps somewhere less . . . busy.'

Dancer snorted his agreement. 'I'll say. It must seem like a major port now with us coming and going.' He pushed open the door and set out across the yard to the gate. It was evening, the stars emerging overhead. Kellanved followed, and Dassem came along behind.

The wind was high; some sort of blow was closing upon them from the east, which was surprising as most storms swept in from the south. Strange, given that it was a clear night. Not one cloud in the darkening sky.

Dancer glanced down the way to the waterfront and stopped, surprised. A damned huge man-o-war lay at anchor, effectively blockading the harbour. And though its sails were down for the blow, they were clearly a very dark blue.

He gestured towards the bay. 'What's this?'

'That is a Napan vessel,' Dassem answered.

Dancer looked to the sky. 'I can see that. I mean what's going on?'

Kellanved threw his arms out, aggrieved. 'For the love of Oponn. I leave on a short errand and everything goes to the Abyss!'

'And there's a windstorm blowing in over the island,' Dancer added.

Kellanved squinted east into the gathering murk. His shaggy greying brows rose and he actually straightened a touch, as if rising up on his toes. 'Oh, dear . . .'

'Oh dear what?' Dancer asked, knowing that tone.

The mage shooed him and Dassem away. 'Go and see if our friends need help. I'm going to be busy for a time.'

'Busy doing what?'

The little fellow waved them off. 'Go now. Run.'

Dancer backed away, unwilling to leave. Dassem was already jogging towards Smiley's.

The gyring winds struck them then, sweeping up the shore and over the city. It reminded Dancer of the dust storms that often came howling across the central Seti Plains. He raised a hand to shade his eyes against the gusting, stinging grit and dirt. Kellanved now stood at the middle of the street, arms out, as if he were beckoning to the winds.

Dancer took a step towards him. *What on earth . . .*

The heavens opened up in a white blinding blast that threw him backwards into a wall. Dazed, he staggered for the street. '*Kellanved!*'

A smoking hole in the cobbles was all that remained. The stones lay about, some glowing red, hissing and crackling. *All the gods . . . he couldn't possibly . . . really be . . .* Blinking, Dancer forced himself to look away, then ran for Smiley's.

He found the place preparing for a siege. Surly's people were out piling carts and barrels across the front of the bar. Within, an argument was raging.

Dujek and the youth, Jack, stood in the centre of a ring of yelling Napans. Arms open as if begging, Jack was insisting, 'Please, reconsider.'

'At least listen to him,' Dujek put in.

Spotting Dancer, Surly waved her brusque impatience at the two non-Napans. 'Order these two to stand down.'

Dassem, Dancer noted, stood to one side, listening.

'What's the problem?' Dancer asked Dujek.

Surly's jaws worked as she swallowed her anger. 'We don't have time to argue,' she snarled.

'We're wrong to dig in here,' Jack told Dancer. 'We have no avenue of retreat.' Dujek nodded his support.

'What would you have us do, then?'

Jack pointed outside. 'The bridges are natural chokepoints in this swamp of a city. The south channel has only three to speak of. If we barricade those we can hold them off. If they look like breaking through, we fall back to another bridge, and so on.'

Dancer raised a hand to forestall the barrage of objections from the Napan crew. 'Just how many soldiers are we talking here?'

'We're thinking about a hundred elites,' said Grinner. 'They're forming columns now. We have to act.'

'A hundred?' Dassem said suddenly. Dancer was quite startled; he'd almost forgotten about the Dal Hon.

'More or less,' Grinner answered, wondering where this was going.

'Which of the three bridges is the narrowest?' Dassem asked.

Jack answered, frowning, 'The one highest inland. Why?'

The swordsman strode for the door. 'Hold the other two bridges and send the Napans to me. I will meet them there.'

He was out the door before Dancer could object. Dujek and Jack stared at one another, quite startled, until Surly threw her arms out, demanding, 'Who in the name of the Abyss *is* that madman?'

'You wouldn't believe me if I told you,' Dancer answered.

Cartheron poked his head in the door, holding it open against a savagely gusting wind. 'Are we staying or going? We have to move – now!'

Dancer waved everyone out. 'Take all the carts and cargo and barricade the bridges.'

A brilliant flash burst upon them then, momentarily blinding them, and a blast rumbled across the city.

'Lightning strike,' Tocaras said as the echoes of the eruption died away.

'That was no lightning,' Dancer said.

*

Once most of them were on the way, plus some thirty local hires, Cartheron ducked back within Smiley's and shut the door against the raging winds. All that remained were Grinner, Hawl, Shrift, and a very angry Surly. 'Are you going to cooperate, Surly, or am I going to have to guard the door?'

She thrust an arm out, pointing. 'Get going! You're needed. We're too shorthanded to hold anyone back.'

'Except you,' he answered, firm. 'We can't let them see you.'

'I can fight!' she nearly yelled, almost stamping a foot.

Cartheron rubbed the stubble of his unshaven chin. 'Let's hope you don't have to,' he answered, 'because that would mean we're all dead.'

Surly straightened as if slapped. She wrapped her arms round herself in a hug and jerked a fierce nod. 'I'm sorry. Go. You're needed.'

He answered her nod. 'Good luck.' To Grinner, he ordered, 'Guard her.'

The burly fellow, their best fighter by far, waved him off.

He pushed open the door and leaned into the gusting, contrary wind. The streets were completely empty of anyone; the inhabitants of Malaz were more than familiar with stormy nights.

Urko and he had each been given charge of one of the lower bridges; what the Dal Hon swordsman intended at the third, he had no idea. He only knew that this Dancer character – who was no fool – had confidence in him. And in any case, he had enough to worry about at his own command. Jogging up to the bridge, he saw his troops still piling and lashing crates and cargo to carts that they'd turned on their sides. Young Jack was there, as well as Choss and Dancer, and some fifteen local Malazan hires, ex-raiders, toughs, and street-bravos all.

'Just in time,' Choss called, pointing past the barricade.

Cartheron nodded to him and climbed up on to a cart; a column of the Napan elites was on its way up the street.

The fierce wind buffeted him then, almost sending him head over heels, and he shielded his eyes, frowning into the winds. It was odd – there were no clouds at all.

'Something strange, Crust,' Choss called up. 'I seen a robed guy watching us. When I looked back, he was gone.'

'I believe it's a mage battle,' Dancer put in. 'Kellanved's . . . got involved.'

Cartheron grunted, unimpressed. What entirely engrossed him was the Napan officer leading the approaching column. He started down the opposite side of the barricade.

'*Crust!*' Choss bellowed, outraged.

'Keep building!' he shouted back. 'I'll buy us some time.' Jumping down to the worn timbers of the bridge, he walked forward, hands raised. 'Clementh!' he called. 'Is that you!'

The female officer raised a hand to call a halt and started forward alone. They met about a quarter of the way up the arch of the bridge. She wore a set of heavy leather armour, scaled in skirting down to her ankles, each scale intaglioed in swirls and edged in bronze. She pushed back her domed helm and unbuttoned its cheek-guards, then set her gauntleted fists at her hips.

'Cartheron Crust . . . it *is* you.'

'Clementh. Good to see you.' He gestured to her gear. 'Coming up in the world, I see.'

She inclined her head. 'Lieutenant in the Royal Guard.'

Cartheron nodded, impressed. 'So he sent the Royals, hey?'

'For his sister? Of course.'

He shook his head. 'She's dead. Took her own life.'

Clementh waved a hand, dismissive. 'Don't even try. We've had spies on the island for weeks. She's been identified.'

'Listen, Clementh. Why follow that fool? Look at the damage he's done to the fleets. Come over to us. You know Sureth is in the right.'

She lifted her shoulders in a shrug. 'Look what damage he's done to the Malazan fleets. At least he acts.'

'The right is hers.'

She lifted a hand to forestall anything more. 'Don't try to involve me in a political argument right now, Crust. What's done is done. Stand aside, or, unfortunately, I'll just have to kill you and feel bad about it afterwards.'

'You can try.'

She pulled down her helm. 'What? Fifty of the Royal Guard against your ragtag pirates? Don't be a fool, Crust.'

He was backing away. 'We'll see. Until then.' He saluted and jogged back to the barricade.

Climbing down, he noticed that the piled wood of the crates and carts was wet and slick with oil. Choss met him on the other side. 'Is that Clementh?' he asked.

'Yeah.'

'Damn. She's good.'

'I know.'

Choss handed him a spear and he took it, his brows rising. 'Good idea.'

'Jack's.'

Everyone, he saw, was armed with spears and other pole weapons, even Dancer. With luck, they'd be able to hold the Napans off. He nodded to everyone. 'Okay. Line up. Double ranks.' He looked at the spear in Dancer's hands. 'You okay with that?'

The assassin was peering off at the sky as if distracted, but he nodded. 'For now.'

'Good.' Marching boots shook the timbers of the bridge. 'Because here they come.'

*

Dancer did his best to push aside his worries regarding Kellanved – had he truly been blown to atoms? Really? Just like that? Could anything regarding him be *that* plain and simple?

But once the fighting started it was easy to set all that aside and slip into the focus of battle and instantly forget all else. He thrust as quickly as he could through gaps in the barricade, catching thighs, stomachs, and occasionally necks, then yanking the spear back before the blade could be shorn off. The young officer, Jack, was the best armoured of all of them, in a long mail hauberk; he held the top of the barricade, hammering down with his shield. Choss and Cartheron fought as if on board a ship, with twinned long-knives each, catching swords and counter-thrusting, while the Malazans brawled without any rules at all – stabbing feet, spitting in faces, thrusting into groins. It appeared to Dancer that these Royal Guards were rather at a disadvantage in the chaos of this street-fight.

Yet weight of numbers was slowly telling. Their barricade was beginning to teeter backwards on to them. Gaps were being hacked open by the Guards' heavy bastard-swords.

It was frankly looking bad for the defenders when Jack jumped down from a cart to snatch up a torch from its fitting on the bridge. He yelled to everyone: '*Burn it!*' and threw the torch on to the oil-soaked wood. It went up with a bursting whoosh of air. Screams reached them through the roar of flames; Dancer retreated, shielding his face from the heat of the inferno. He held a length of wood now no taller than him, the rest having been hacked away some time ago, but its cut end was sharp, and wet with blood.

So hot was the fire that even the timbers of the bridge caught, and it soon became obvious that the white-hot conflagration would eventually consume the entire bridge. The defenders retreated to the street.

In the light of the burning bridge Dancer could see that the Napans had retreated as well. He saw them marching away for the next bridge – Urko's command. After damning the noisome stinking swamp of a river all year, Dancer now blessed it; not one of those heavily armoured soldiers would dare wade into that quagmire.

He motioned to Cartheron. 'I'm going to help Dassem. You join Urko.'

Cartheron raised a hand. 'I'll check on Surly first.' He ordered everyone else to head for Urko.

Dancer started up the cobbled way that traced the channel. Cartheron struck off along an alleyway. Choss, who was wounded, was helped by Jack as the rest of the crew made their way to Urko's bridge.

Jogging along through the blustering, lashing winds, Dancer decided that he had to believe that Kellanved couldn't just have been blown up like that. After all the tricks he'd pulled? It must have been another of his diversions . . . mustn't it?

He slowed to a walk. Someone had stepped out on to the empty street in front of him. A slim fellow all in dark clothes. Pale, with short black hair, his hands loose at his sides and a mocking arrogant grin on his lips, the meaning of which Dancer knew all too well.

He felt his shoulders fall as he looked up at the night sky. *Oh, for the love of Burn . . . I do not have time for this.* He waved the fellow off. 'Not now. I'm damned busy.'

The lad laughed, high and sneering. '*Not now,*' he teased. 'Pathetic. You sound like a mark begging for his life. I expected better.'

Dancer pointed past him. 'Look. There's a man up there about to attempt the greatest feat of arms I've ever heard of, and he could use my help.'

The lad reached behind his back, and when he brought his hands out each held a very long and very slim blade. 'Do I look like I give a shit?'

Dancer drew his own blades from his chest baldrics. 'I don't give a shit about *this.*'

'That doesn't sound like the Dancer I'm after.'

'I guess I went and grew up.'

That pulled down the youth's thin lips. He struck a ready stance, blades straight forward. 'Just so you know – it's Cowl who is about to kill you.'

Dancer eased back into a bent knee stance. 'Spare me. I've heard it all before.'

The youth, Cowl, charged.

'What's he doin' just standin' there?' one of her boys complained.

Lee rolled her eyes. 'How in the Abyss should I know?'

'Let's rush 'im,' another suggested.

She and ten of her remaining toughs were crouched in the mouth of an alleyway eyeing Stonemason Bridge, where a solitary swordsman stood watch. 'Sure,' Lee hissed, 'your knife against his sword!'

'Well, how're we gonna get past?'

'I don't know!' she growled once more.

'Just shoot 'im,' another urged.

Lee hefted her crossbow. 'In this wind? Forget it. Have to get much closer.'

'Fine. Let's do it.'

'Wait!' another whispered. 'Someone's comin'.'

Marching feet approached up the channel road and a column of Napans emerged from the gloom. Grit and dirt blew about in lashing wind-devils as they closed on the bridge. Lee and her fellows eased further back into the alley.

At the base of the bridge, the swordsman drew his blade and threw the sheath out over the river. Lee watched it flash as it arced away. Something in that gesture made her lower her crossbow and gesture for her lads and lasses to stand down.

The dark fellow, a Dal Hon so she'd been told, struck a ready stance blocking the narrow stone bridge. The column of Napans paused briefly, as if dumbfounded, then an officer barked an order, and swords were drawn.

'He's not really goin' to . . .' one her lasses began before trailing off, almost in awe.

Lee found herself straightening for a better view. 'It damn well looks like it.'

The Napan soldiers, heavy infantry all, came on two at a time. They carried swords and shields. The Dal Hon held his blade two-handed.

They met with a crash of blade against shield and blade. The Malazan toughs swore as the first ranks of the Napans seemed to melt one blurred stroke at a time. They fell, limp, to the mortared stones or tumbled over the low guarding lip to splash on to the muddy shore below.

Their officer called another order and the next ranks came on crouched behind shields, obviously meaning to push the fellow back. The Dal Hon did give way, but only one pace as he somehow slashed round or above or behind to bring each shieldbearer down in a dance that Lee simply could not believe.

'What in the Abyss . . .' one of her lads breathed, hushed.

The remaining column lost patience with hiding behind their shields and now charged as if meaning to trample the swordsman. This massed rush did buy them another two paces of the bridge, but some eight fell to achieve that length. Still the rest pressed on, as if simple brutal repetition would somehow win them through.

Lee actually winced when two blurred strokes felled the last two of the column. Now the swordsman faced the officer across a length of stone bridge carpeted by the armoured corpses of his command.

The officer stood motionless for a time as he scanned the wreckage of his men and women, and then his head rose to study the agent of this destruction. He reached up and unbuttoned his helm and threw it aside, drew his sword, and carefully, gingerly, stepped between the fallen to close with the Dal Hon.

The swordsman awaited him, blade out before him, not even the slightest movement of his chest beneath a simple blood-spattered jerkin betraying any shortage of breath.

And Lee could not breathe either. All she could think was how this could not be and how never, ever, would she have believed such a thing.

The two met perhaps a quarter of the way up the arch of the bridge. They touched blades and immediately the officer drew his back, slashing. The swordsman slid the blow and countered, and the officer's head sailed through the air to fall with a splash into the Malaz river channel.

The swordsman cleaned his blade on the officer's surcoat, sheathed it, and resumed his patient watch.

'Hood's mercy,' another of her lads murmured.

'I believe so,' Lee said. 'Let's—'

Further marching boots rang in the night and a second column of Napan heavy infantry emerged through the wind-tossed dust and leaf litter.

Lee almost groaned in empathetic pain. *Gods, no . . .*

Dassem felt his shoulders fall ever so slightly as the second column of Napan soldiers came marching up the way. He did not know what he expected to come of pursuing his purpose here, but he hadn't anticipated sadness. It was all such a waste. A damned useless waste of life and potential.

Downstream, just visible, pulsed the glow of a fire where one of the other bridges burned. Whether it was stone or wood did not matter; just so long as they kept the fire going long enough to funnel all the Napans to him.

And these appeared to be the last, for tonight. At orders from their female officer they formed up, facing him just back from the base of the bridge. Then the officer came forward, sword sheathed, and picked her way through her fallen fellows to study him.

For a Napan, sharing their blue coloration, she appeared rather sickly pale, even ashen now. 'You did this?' she breathed in disbelief.

He pointed back the way they'd come. 'Turn round. Leave. No more need fall.'

She was shaking her head, studying the bodies. 'We too have our duty.'

He regarded the woman with new understanding. 'I see. Your name?'

'Clementh.'

'Dassem.'

'We must try . . .'

'Yes,' he said, when her words tailed off. 'I understand.'

She retreated to her command, and spoke to them for a time. Then, drawing, she came on, leading the attack. And Dassem winced inside: *She would make this as hard as she could, wouldn't she?*

They met, and he slashed her among the first. Her soldiers dragged her back while the front rank raised shields. Then they came on again, two by two. The narrow stone span forced them together, inhibiting them. Dassem retreated one pace to clear space for himself and met them two-handed, clashing swords aside and thrusting at legs, arms, and exposed necks. He found he had to retreat yet another step as the fallen piled over one another on the narrow bridge.

More fell and Dassem had to force back his regret for what he had to do. It was pitiful that these good men and women should have to lay themselves down. He longed, then, for the old days of champions.

A shout pulled them back a step, shields raised, watching him warily from beneath the lips of their inlaid iron and bronze helmets. Clementh pushed her way forward, a bloodied arm hanging limp.

Even more ashen now from loss of blood, she eyed him, panting with the effort of holding herself erect. Dassem remained at the ready, blood-splashed and aching, but ready. She turned to her command, ordered, 'Withdraw.'

They began backing away, stepping carefully over the fallen. A few stooped to pick up or drag wounded. Clementh struggled to sheathe her sword. 'Tarel will have my head for this,' she said.

'But your men and women will live,' Dassem finished for her.

She nodded, taking a deep breath. 'We will see to the fallen.'

He nodded as well. 'I will not interfere.'

'I thank you for that.'

Now he shook his head. 'No. I thank you. I did not enjoy this.'

She eyed him for a time, her gaze weighing. 'Good.'

*

Cartheron slammed open the door to Smiley's to find the common room empty. 'Lady Sureth!' he called, panicked for some reason.

'Yes?' she called, pushing open the kitchen door.

He swallowed his sudden dread. *Ah.* 'Where is everyone?'

'Upstairs.'

Shrift appeared on the stairs, peering down into the room, looking very surprised. 'Crust . . .' she said, almost stammering. 'What're . . . what're you doing here?'

'Where's Grinner?'

She gestured upstairs. 'With Hawl. She's sick or something. We're worried about her.'

He started up. 'I'll take a look.'

Shrift allowed him to pass with a help yourself gesture. She followed him up.

He opened the door to her room and stood frozen for a heartbeat, unable to comprehend what confronted him. Hawl lay on the bed, her chest a wet mess of blood; on the floor just at his feet lay Grinner, face down, stabbed in the back.

As he drew breath to shout a hand closed over his mouth from behind and searing pain lanced his back as a length of razor iron was pushed through his torso. He fell, stunned in agony. Only distantly did he register a boot on his back and the blade's being yanked free.

A woman's voice, Shrift, breathed close into his ear: 'Should've paid better, Crust.' Then footsteps thumped away down the stairs.

Distantly, from below, he heard Sureth ask, 'How is she?'

Some mumbled answer sounded, then a table crashed and feet stamped. Someone was cursing and he realized it was him. *Low*, he told himself, *she struck low*.

He started dragging his body towards the stairs.

*

They each fought with two knives. Their favourites, of course; preferred weight and lengths. Dancer lost count of the thin slashes he received on arms, sides and thighs as they ran, fought, twisted, jumped, swept and rolled. Conscious thought and planning were gone; all that remained was pure instinct and muscle reflex as attacks and blocks, feints and reverses flew past one another too fast for the mind to separate or even register.

His shirt hung in tatters, slashed from his arms, chest and back. The lad's own face, neck and chest were a smear of blood, and when they grappled, tiring now, their arms slipped and slid on the sweat and blood sheathing them as they each fought for advantage.

Even so, the lad Cowl's wide eyes blazed with a seemingly insane fury just a hand's breadth from Dancer's own, utterly untouched by the normal fear of mortality, and from this Dancer knew he was locked in potentially the most perilous duel of his life.

For no one was more dangerous than those who did not care if they lived or died.

So they fought on, crashing through doors, slamming into tables, slashing, neither quite able to land a stopping, definitive blow. A kick from Cowl sent him flying backwards into the road and the lad launched himself upon him and Dancer caught blade for blade. The lad head-butted him and though he'd turned his head aside stars still flashed in his vision and agony flamed from his thigh – he staggered off, clutching his leg.

Cowl followed, but slowly now, shifting his grips on his knives, rubbing a bloody forearm across his face but leaving even more of a smeared layer. His hair was a slick sweaty mess and he panted, favouring his own right leg as he tracked Dancer's movements.

Dancer limped to half fall against the stone lip of a river channel. He shook drops of sweat from his vision, or perhaps they were tears of pain. He managed to straighten, held out his weapons, ready.

The lad was nodding now as he came. He pointed one blood-smeared knife. 'You were good,' he panted. 'But now it ends as it always does.'

He edged up closer and closer, knives weaving in a dance of diversion and deceit, reversing, twisting, low and high, never stopping.

Dancer waited until just the right distance, then rushed him.

They grappled, arms twisting and sliding, neither releasing his blades. Their hot wet breath mixed as they turned round and round each other, grunting and hissing, legs kicking, searching for a hold.

Dancer realized his strength was leaving him in a steady stream out of the thrust through his leg. He had no more time.

He dipped his shoulder, which allowed Cowl to bring his knife up towards his chest. Immediately, the assassin abandoned his other weapon to clamp both hands to the slick grip to push. Dancer dropped his blades to wrap both hands round Cowl's and they stood rigid, straining, their breaths rasping from taut chests.

'It's all right,' Cowl whispered bare inches from his face, his eyes so eerie and wild. 'You did your best.' And he crooned as if to a child: 'No more worries now . . . hush now . . . It'll all be over soon . . .'

Dancer knew it had to be now. That this was in fact his last chance. He allowed a fraction of the true exhaustion that hung upon him to show, and the keen tip of Cowl's blade edged closer to his chest. The assassin leaned even more of his weight on the knife, straining.

Dancer threw both of them backwards over the stone lip.

In that instant of surprise he twisted the blade up towards Cowl's neck.

They hit the swampy mud and reeds and immediately sank. He lost track of the man as he flailed, coughing on a lungful of fetid slimy water. He drew two more blades, spinning, turning, searching, but no fiend came lunging from the weeds.

He lay still, worked on slowing his breath, and listened to the night.

The punishing winds lashed the tall weeds and rushes. Another brilliant burst flashed across the city and the report of the explosion rumbled and echoed over the rooftops. Slowly, so very weary, he pushed his way through the muck for the sloped stone wall of the channel.

Chapter 18

TAYSCHRENN SAT WITH HIS KNEES DRAWN UP TO HIS CHEST and his arms wrapped round them. He rocked, eyes closed, thinking, *Get up! Move!* But he could not. He was so tired. Just resting on land was privilege enough. The barrage was a constant background now; blasting attacks potent enough to have sprayed the consciousness of any other practitioner across the hillsides. Still they pursued; still they sought him.

Just go away!

But they would not, of course. They smelled blood now, so to speak. A day ago he simply ignored all their combined efforts as a nuisance to his flight. But not now. Now it was becoming increasingly difficult to maintain his defences. Eventually, they would crack beneath the relentless punishment.

He'd been so certain he could escape them! Yet, somehow, they had pursued him into the deepest lineaments of D'riss and found him there; somehow they had even tracked his essence into far hinterlands of the Warren of Thyr. He had even thrown what little bits and pieces of Mockra he'd picked up as false trails and delusions; yet they had seen through these and pushed on upon his trail. Only through the sheer might of his command did he now stave them off.

The priests of D'rek were utterly remorseless.

If he could just hold on – outlast them. Then, perhaps, he had a chance.

He blinked then, where he crouched in an alley of shingle-stone buildings in some cold city, and suddenly found himself somewhere else.

It was light now, a sort of dusk, and the ground was soft beneath him. He eased the clench of his arms and raised his head, cracking open his eyes. His essence, his kha, had been transported somewhere new.

A plain of ashen dust surrounded him; rounded hills rose in the distance. The sky was clear – oddly so. Stars ought to be visible in this seeming evening dusk.

A man stood in front of him, short, in fine dark clothes that appeared to have seen better days. He rocked back and forth on the heels of new shoes, a short walking stick planted before him. He was Dal Hon, and projected the appearance of a wizened oldster, but Tayschrenn could see through this affectation to the features of a young skinny lad.

He frowned, sensing around himself. 'Meanas?' he offered.

The Dal Hon lad waggled his head in an '*almost*' gesture. 'Close.'

'My body remains. This buys me no time.'

The lad tilted his head again, as if weighing the matter. 'Eventually. In the meantime . . . let's have a chat.'

Tayschrenn rose, stretching. He studied the fellow more closely, and the more he examined him, the more confused he became. The skein of his Warren manipulation was different from any he'd encountered before. Somehow . . . altered. It was as if the fellow was annealed with a multiplicity of commingled influences and sources of power. There was even a tinge of the Elder about him. It was clear to Tayschrenn that he had endured some sort of transformational experience.

'I know of all the High Sorcerers of our age,' he said, walking a circuit of the strange fellow. 'I have made it my research. The Ascendants, the Enchantress, the Tiste, and the Jaghut. But you . . . I do not know you.'

The little fellow looked very pleased. 'Good. Now, time is short . . .'

Tayschrenn shook his head. He looked away, studying his surroundings. 'No. There is nothing you can offer. There is nowhere to hide. Not even here. And this is new – not young, obviously. No, this shard, or fragment, is very old. Ancient, even. New to be accessed, I mean.'

The Dal Hon lad appeared vexed. 'Yes, yes. Fine. You are well versed in Warren thaumaturgy, I'm sure.' He drew a breath as if calming himself. 'Kellanved,' he said, tipping his head.

'Tayschrenn.'

'Good. Now,' and he raised his walking stick, brushed dirt from its silver-capped tip. 'What if I told you there was a place where you could hide from your pursuers?'

'As I said – there is no Warren or Realm that can escape D'rek.'

The Dal Hon mage raised a hand for silence. 'Indulge me. What choice do you have?'

Indeed. What choice did he have? He was quite certain he wouldn't last out the night. He sighed, still studying the plain of wind-blown ash. There was sadness here. Lingering ancient curses of inhuman power . . . Elders had forged this. He shook his head. 'What of it?'

'Do you vow to serve me?'

Tayschrenn turned to regard him directly. '*Serve?*'

The hunched mage, with his false projected thinning hair, fat little paunch, and age-twisted arms, shrugged, almost wincing. 'Well . . . work for me.'

'Work . . .' Tayschrenn nodded thoughtfully. Clearly, there were insights to be gained here. What lay behind this one's strange powers? Then he remembered his position and snorted. 'If you can save my life then I will work for you.'

'Very good. We have a deal. Now, the hard part is that you're rather far from where you have to be. You're going to have to move.'

'Move?' he echoed. 'I do not think I have the strength.'

'I will help.'

He looked the scrawny fellow up and down. 'Pardon my scepticism.'

'We shall just have to do our best, shan't we?'

Tayschrenn shrugged. He considered himself as good as dead anyway.

* * *

Cartheron became conscious at the base of the stairs. He flailed, coughing and wincing, and thought, *Shit, passed out. Must've been the slide down the stairs.*

He edged his elbows underneath him and pulled, one over the other, until his vision darkened and he had to take a breather . . . or two . . .

He next came to on the common room floor. The door to Smiley's was banging in the wind. Tables were overturned and broken glass and shards of stoneware littered the floor. Of Sureth or Shrift there was no sign.

He took another deep breath and started for the door. Somehow, though, he couldn't bring his elbows up underneath himself any more and so he clawed at the floorboards, pulling. He heaved until his vision darkened once more, then eased off. *No more strength. Gonna die on this damned beer-soaked floor. What a wretched comedown in the world. Always hoped to sink with my command in some damn-fool brave hopeless action.*

Footsteps sounded and he blinked, focusing his vision to see two bare feet before his face – Napan blue. *Bare?* He peered up at a bloodied Lady Sureth; the sleeve and flesh of one arm was slashed open, and another gash bled across her stomach.

She lifted one of his arms and picked him up. 'How . . . what . . . ?' he managed, sounding delirious to himself.

'Shrift was smart,' Sureth said as she half-dragged him out of the door. 'She was patient, wasn't she? She killed Amiss, she told me so. Amiss became suspicious of her so she staged her murder to start a blood-feud with Geffen – hoped to thin our numbers even more.'

Out on the street, Sureth dragged him to the nearest shop and banged on the door. 'But she made one mistake, yes, Cartheron? *Cartheron.*'

He blinked heavily, nodded, or lolled his head. 'Yes? A mistake?' he said – or thought he did. He couldn't be sure, there was such a loud roaring in his ears.

'That's right,' Sureth said. 'She was newest to my service, wasn't she? She thought I'd be the easiest part.'

At this Cartheron laughed. The pain was excruciating, but he laughed anyway. *Gods! Sureth easy? No, lass, you are the hardest of us all . . .*

And he heard talk then. Sureth demanding to see a healer, or medicer, or churgeon, and he sank into the roaring dark winds that had been pulling at him so insistently.

*

Nedurian watched the mage-battle raging just to the north over Malaz City and was awed by the scale of it. Astounding. At least a hundred versus one – and that one not even answering the constant

351

withering assault. He wondered what the man or woman could possibly have done. Spat on D'rek's altar? For he knew the identity of the attackers. All shared the same aspect: that of the priest-mages of D'rek.

Watching also were Agayla and the eerie Nightchill. None had raised their Warrens, or powers, or whatever it may be that they could call upon should they wish to. Even this far from the clash they did not wish to risk attracting any attention.

Behind him, the sea still surged against the rocks and the thin strand of the south coast. The sky was clear and full of stars and it was quite cold. It was as if nothing untoward at all were happening just leagues off.

He hugged himself against the chill. Neither of the sorceresses appeared to notice the wintry bite to the night air. Offshore, a vessel had dropped anchor in a nearby cove, perhaps putting in against the strange blow.

Agayla had assured him that this battle, or duel, would merely lash its way across the island and continue onward unmindful of its course. Yet none of this had happened. The quarry of the chase appeared to have gone to ground somewhere in the city itself. He was anxious about this, but at least the feud didn't appear to be spilling over into any actual physical damage to the city. If all went well, it would end soon enough, and the inhabitants of Malaz would open their shutters to tomorrow's dawn and marvel at the wrack left behind by the strange storm that had battered the island overnight.

And that would be that.

He rubbed his hands together and blew upon them. A fire would be a fine idea; he supposed it would be up to him to collect the firewood.

And why did he think of fire just now? He peered round, frowning, because he could've sworn he'd smelled smoke. But not just any smoke – a rare and strange scent. Like burned exotic herbs and woods. Like . . . incense?

*　　*　　*

Two fists yanked on Tayschrenn's shirt front and he peered up, blinking. It was the Dal Hon mage here with him in the narrow alleyway.

352

'Keep moving,' the mage of Meanas said.

'This is suicide, you realize,' Tayshcrenn told him. Nevertheless, he struggled to rise to his feet once more. Distantly, he marvelled at the survival imperative of mortal flesh.

Once he was on his feet the diminutive mage took part of his weight and guided him forward, saying, 'Good, good. Just walk. Ignore everything you might see.'

Tayshcrenn arched a brow, rather curious about that command despite his bleariness.

A storm of shadows enmeshed them. They churned and flowed, almost like a constant coursing waterfall, on and on. Within them Tayshcrenn glimpsed an almost infinite regression of himself and his guide all limping along – all in differing locales: following various streets, crossing various squares, and even tracing water-front wharves.

He turned an eye on his rescuer. 'Impressive . . .'

'Shh. That's just the opening.'

Their next steps yanked them into a narrow canyon of dry dusty slopes and he pressed a hand to his head, groaning at the searing pain grating there from the workings of this man's Warren, or altered aspect. As if peering through a kaleidoscope of possibilities he glimpsed himself cowering at the feet of a D'rek priest who laughed his victory; himself stepping through a Warren portal into a cityscape he did not know; himself fleeing onward across a broad savanna of windswept grasses; himself on board a small skiff sailing westward; himself dead in more ways than he would rather have seen or cared to consider.

And it all seemed so very *real* to him. The headache of it all was almost more than he could bear – he even began to worry for his sanity. The next moment he became almost certain of his insanity when their path among the canyons brought them right before the muzzles of two gigantic hounds who perked up as if startled, heads tilting in disbelief. He glanced back to see them now padding along behind, ears low, eyes narrowed, on the hunt.

'There's—'

'Shh,' came a tense warning from the mage. 'Almost there.'

All this time, the flurry and rush of D'rek probing had not relented. If anything, it seemed to be intensifying. 'They're coming,' he panted.

'You're too damned potent to disguise,' his guide complained.

A roar like that of a lion sounded then, followed by a scream and the crunch of bones and rending of flesh. Fearful, he tried to turn to look but the mage of Meanas urged him onward. He was, at that moment, experiencing a kind of sliding simultaneity of multiple selves that threatened to split his head in its impossibility. He felt as if his consciousness was being fragmented into pieces and was astounded that this odd little fellow could so easily endure such a storm of manipulation, let alone generate it.

Among these multiple concurrent possibilities was one strengthening version where they pushed through a tiny iron gate and up a narrow path of paving stones to tumble on to a broad slate landing before an iron-bound door.

The mage was yanking on his sweaty, dirt-smeared robes. 'Hurry!'

But he had to hold his head just to be sure that it was still whole. And he wondered, *Am I really here?*

'Run down at last!' a voice called, and Tayschrenn peered over see a coterie of D'rek priests and priestesses at the gate and low wall of the property.

The mage of Meanas was struggling with the door. 'Come on!'

He shook his head. 'It's no use . . .'

The D'rek adherents swung over the wall and came on across the wild unkempt garden.

The door swung open, almost brushing Tayschrenn aside. At that moment he became further certain of his insanity as the ground itself became alive with writhing vines and roots all lashing themselves about the priests and priestesses, who screamed their mortal terror. They cut and pulled and blasted at the bonds but to no benefit he could discern as each now began sinking, flailing and writhing in utter blind panic.

The few who won through – mostly on the narrow walkway, and each of them a Fang of D'rek – now drew daggers. Yet at that instant a towering presence brushed past Tayschrenn to take these in huge armoured fists and throw them aside on to the steaming ground, where the vines and roots quickly enmeshed them.

All this Tayschrenn took in almost as if dream-walking, or in a daze. He turned to the house and what he now saw there, and what he understood of it, froze him completely.

The spindly mage was pulling at him. 'Now! Come!'

He shook his head in mute denial. *No*, he mouthed, barely able to speak. 'Do you know what this *is*?'

'Yes, yes. Now move! More are coming!'

He gaped up at the armoured colossus as it thumped past, ignoring him completely, to re-enter the house. 'You would choose to be entombed for ever?'

The fellow waved his hands, a touch frantic. 'Not a bit of it! Now come!'

He shook his head. Better any fate than this mad desperate throw.

Strangely, instead of becoming angry or impatient, the little Dal Hon mage just shrugged and clasped his hands behind his back. 'Well, all right,' he said. 'But too bad for them.' And he rocked back and forth on his heels.

Tayschrenn eyed him narrowly. 'Who?'

The mage nodded to the street where Tayschrenn sensed a further mass of priests and priestesses rushing in upon them. 'Damn you . . .' he hissed.

The fellow shrugged innocently. 'Perhaps you ought to get rid of them.'

Tayschrenn shook his heavy head. 'I can't kill them. They're just being used.'

The wizened mage rolled his eyes to the sky. 'Oh, dear Ascendants. Just get rid of them! Push them away. Whatever.' He fluttered a hand to the door. 'Demonstrate to me that you are worthy to be shown the secrets within.'

Tayschrenn blinked blearily in his exhaustion, taking this in. *Of course I've driven them off before! Many times! But they'd just returned. Again and again. Like a stinging cloud of insects. Yet this mage claims this would be the last time . . . Very well. I'll drive them off all right!*

As more of the pursuers appeared, he drew down far into the depths of his Warren to summon every bare remaining scrap of power to thrust it outwards in one last great surge. He stored it momentarily, feeling it gnawing within at the lineaments of his flesh like a fire, then released it in a sudden surging blast of might that shot outwards like an eruption that seared across the Warrens.

He opened his eyes, blinking. The little mage now stood pressed up against the sturdy iron-bound door, a hand at his forehead.

'Well,' the fellow managed, his voice shaky and hoarse, 'that was something.' He waved to the sky. 'Behold.'

Tayschrenn glanced about; the skies were clear of pursuers. Like summoning a gale within the Warrens, he'd driven them away. Just how far, though, he couldn't say for certain. They may be gathering themselves to return this very moment – or perhaps not.

Kellanved gestured invitingly to the door. 'Impressive. You may pass within.'

He eyed him sharply. 'Not as a prisoner?'

'No. Not as a prisoner, I assure you.'

Somehow, he didn't think much of any assurance coming from this fellow, but he did burn with curiosity. The legendary Azath! What an opportunity! 'Very well.'

The supposed elderly mage opened the door and waved him in. He entered a touch tentatively, still wary despite his wonder. Kellanved pushed in behind him.

The door slammed shut of its own volition.

*　　*　　*

'The battle appears to be relenting,' Nedurian pronounced – purely for form's sake, as no doubt both Agayla and Nightchill had sensed this long before him. They nodded, kindly refraining from telling him to shut up.

The strange woman, Nightchill, whom Agayla had warned him to regard as pretty much an Ascendant, had been sitting atop a tall boulder, and she climbed down now, in a rather ungainly manner. This awkwardness suggested to Nedurian the suspicion that perhaps she was not entirely familiar, or at ease, with the form she currently possessed.

'Resolution has been reached,' she announced. 'Though what form this has taken I cannot say for certain. I suspect—'

Her words were cut off abruptly as a shape swiftly rounded the boulder and something punched into her body. Nedurian gaped, horrified to see the bloody length of an enormous sword blade standing from her chest.

From behind, a man peered over her shoulder, all iron-grey hair and beard, lined savage face and sneering lips. He pointed past Nightchill to Agayla, shouting, 'Make no move, witch! Or she

356

dies.' He spared a glance for Nedurian. 'Or you, legionnaire. This is between me and her.'

Horribly, the blade twisted then as he turned it within Nightchill, and the woman shuddered, still conscious, still standing. The man returned his attention to Agayla. 'Or your mistress!' he warned. 'I see her there, watching. Interfere, T'riss, and you are next! I, the High King, so swear!'

'High King no longer, Kallor,' Agayla grated, visibly shaking with rage.

Kallor barked a harsh laugh. 'What matter circumstances? We speak in timeless truths now.' He set his lips close to Nightchill's ear. 'Why not employ your witchery to blast me to cinders or crack me to shards? You are inestimably powerful. So very much more powerful than I. Why not?'

The blade twisted again and Nightchill gurgled her agony, rising up on to her toes. Blood marred her lips, bubbling. Nedurian cast a pleading look to Agayla but the sorceress shook her head.

'Why not?' Kallor raged. 'I will tell you why not! Because I have been preparing for this, Sister. Ages ago – ages and ages – I purchased a rare ore mined in a land far away. A kingdom's ransom it cost me. And I dusted it upon this blade just before I plunged it into you. A pinch. Just one tiny pinch. But it constrains you now, doesn't it? Now you will be the first to feel the full weight of my judgement. And your damned brothers will follow! Damn you for interfering with me! Damn you for ever!'

He grasped a handful of her hair then, yanking her head high and exposing her neck. 'Your kind are notorious for the difficulty of dispatching them – but I know of one sure way. A good clean beheading always does the trick.'

Nedurian lurched forward then, no matter Agayla's objections, but in an instant Kallor had yanked free the blade and set it to Nightchill's neck. 'Think again, legionnaire! I will free her head from her body.'

'You're going to anyway,' Nedurian growled.

'Yes. But do you want to be the immediate cause?' He backed away, half dragging the wounded Nightchill before him. 'By the sea, I think. And I shall cast your head to the fishes . . .'

A strange thing happened then: ropes, or lines, or tangled netting, leapt up and lashed themselves about Kallor's arm and neck to pull him backwards. He flailed, snarling, but the sea-wrack snatched him with a great yank and the heavy bastard-sword went flying from his grip. Nighchill collapsed and Nedurian and Agayla ran to her.

Nedurian cradled the poor woman's shoulders. Amazingly, she was still conscious, and she fought to turn her head – to turn it to the shore where this Kallor fiend now flailed amid a lashing mass of twisting seaweed-draped old fishing netting and ancient grey lines, perhaps old forgotten rope from centuries of fishing.

The netting was dragging him, bellowing and struggling, down the strand to where a small skiff waited, pulled up on the gravel. To one side stood what appeared to be an old fisherman in tattered worn canvas jerkin and trousers, pipe in mouth. He was gesturing with his hands, making weaving motions, even as Kallor flopped up over the side of the skiff.

'I will slay you too, you damned interfering old bastard!' Kallor was yelling now, hoarse. 'Sister!' he called, 'I will find you again! And when I do I will destroy you! I, Kallor, do so swear!'

The seamed, sun-darkened old fisherman pushed then, with his hands, and the skiff surged out into the surf, rising and falling as it crested waves, diminishing into the distance.

The fisherman took his pipe from his mouth. 'You are not welcome here, Kallor Eiderann Tes'thesula,' he called to the surf. 'Each time you rise so too shall you fall.' And he set the pipe back into his mouth, nodding to himself, and came up the shore to where Nightchill lay in Nedurian's arms.

All this was astounding enough to him, but to top it all off Agayla then knelt to one knee before the old man, saying, 'We are sorry, Fisher. We did not mean to disturb you.'

The old man waved her apology aside, his pale sky-blue eyes actually amused. 'It is an old feud. And a stubborn one.' He bent over Nightchill. 'Ach, Sister. You are gravely wounded. It will not heal, will it?'

Nightchill seemed to recognize him and she whispered, 'Fisher now, is it?'

He set a finger to her bloody lips. 'Hush. Lucky for you m'lady is with me. She'll sing you whole, she will.'

He picked her up quite easily for such an old fellow.

'I'm honoured,' she murmured.

'Think nothing of it,' he said, and headed off.

Nedurian moved to follow but Agayla held him back by gripping his arm. 'She is in good hands,' she said.

'Who was that?'

'Don't you think we ought to be heading back?' Agayla brushed her sleeves as if removing dust.

'Agayla . . . who?'

She motioned aside as if inviting him to walk with her. 'You're not going to leave me to go alone, are you?'

He rolled his eyes and started off. 'Fine. Don't tell me.'

'Some things,' she said, taking his arm, 'aren't meant to be known.'

'So I gather. But what about – what's his name – that Kallor?'

She shook her head, her thick mane of dark hair blowing in the gusting winds. 'I don't believe we'll be seeing him again.'

*

Dawn's pink and golden light came slanting across the town to limn the man still standing guard on Stonemason's Bridge. Lee also stood a vigil of a sort; leaning up against a wall, watching him. Half her lads and lasses had wandered off. A few lay in the alleyway, asleep.

But not Lee. She'd seen something she'd never ever expected to see in her lifetime. Perfection. Or at least the pursuit of it. None of this wretched slouching along she'd seen so much of everywhere. No, not that. Expertise. Mastery. And she recognized it as something she'd wanted and looked for all her life.

She peered down at a snoring Two-ton and kicked him awake. He snorted, fumbling, then blinked up at her. 'Wha'?'

'I'm quitting.'

He frowned, pulling a hand down his face. 'Wha'?'

'You boys and girls can decide who's in charge, okay?'

He smacked his lips, screwed up one eye. 'Quittin'? Really?'

'Yeah.'

He pushed himself up on to one elbow. 'Well . . . whatcha gonna do?'

She nodded towards the bridge. 'We'll see.'

He eyed the bridge. 'Gonna throw in with them?'

She lifted her shoulders. 'We'll see.'

He pushed himself up all the way, brushed dirt from his trousers. 'I'm with ya.'

She scowled up at him. 'No . . . you don't have to be.'

He crossed his arms, resolute. 'I'm with ya, lass.'

She pressed a hand to her forehead, shook her head. 'Gods. Fine! Whatever.' She waved to the others. 'Send them off.'

'Right.'

Two-ton urged the rest of the gang back to the Gyrfalcon, then they set out towards the bridge. The swordsman calmly watched their approach. The stone arch was clear now; a crew from the Napan ship had come and collected the wounded and all the bodies. All that was left was scattered broken equipment and a lot of drying blood and other fluids staining the cobbles. He stood at ease, his sword sheathed. Crusted blood splashed his tunic and trousers. His sleeves were fairly stiff with it. Stopping a short distance off, she regarded him in turn. Dark, he was, with the curly kinky hair that suggested Dal Hon blood. Tall and wiry, handsome in a lean and hungry sort of way. His eyes appeared dark blue and they held an eerie distance in them, almost a kind of sadness. How the girls must sigh at that melancholy gaze, she admitted. But not her. That was not what she wanted from him.

She knelt to one knee and bowed her head. Gathering her resolve, she said forcefully, 'I would serve . . . if you would have me.'

After a short silence, he said, 'Stand.' She rose. He regarded her, then his eyes switched to the lumbering Two-ton. She looked to him as well, a touch irked by his intrusion.

The giant of a fellow pushed a knuckle to his brow. 'Two-ton, sor,' he rumbled. 'In your service – if you please.'

The swordsman nodded. 'Dassem.' He peered past them, towards the waterfront. 'The Napan vessel?'

'Withdrawn,' Lee answered.

He raised a hand as if signalling a pause. 'I warn you, it is not to me you should swear allegiance. It is my . . .' He paused for some time, obviously searching for the correct term. Finally, he settled on 'employer'.

'The knifer Dancer?'

He inclined his head in assent. 'If that troubles you, you may go. I would quite understand.'

She shook her head. 'No. That doesn't bother me.'

The man raised a brow, obviously quite surprised. 'Very well. This way,' and he turned round and headed back over the bridge.

Dancer walked the streets in the early morning light; or, more accurately, he tottered, paused, staggered, and dragged himself along. Early risers out on the streets to inspect the damage from the overnight storm took one look at him, gaped, and ran in the opposite direction.

He found the door to Smiley's ajar, the common room a mess of overturned tables, chairs, and broken glassware. Surly sat on a tall stool at the bar, an old man bent at her bared arm, sewing up a long ugly-looking gash.

Seeing him, the Napan crew, Choss, Urko and Tocaras, all lurched to their feet, swearing, and came forward to help. He waved them off and eased himself down in a chair at a table next to the door. Choss came round with a tiny shot glass that he filled from some foreign-looking decanter. 'You look like you've been dragged behind horses.' He also draped a blanket over his shoulders.

'Feel like it too,' he answered, and tossed back the shot – only to hiss and wince when the alcohol stung his gashed lip. Blood now caked the glass from his smeared hands and he realized he badly needed to clean up.

'Who's after you?' he asked of Surly.

The churgeon peered over and looked him up and down. 'I'm good, but I'm not that good.'

'I'll take whatever you got,' Dancer answered. He looked to Choss. 'So. What happened?'

The burly mariner leaned forward on to his elbows, scowling. 'We lost Hawl and Grinner. Shrift tried to throw in for Tarel an' Crust is sore wounded.'

'What of the locals – what was his name . . . Dujek?'

Urko jerked a thumb to the kitchen. 'Him 'n' Jack are making breakfast. We sent the rest of the troops off to rest.'

Dancer nodded at that. 'Sounds good. I need that – and a bath.'

'Don't look at us,' Tocaras told him.

The old churgeon looked round again and pointed down the street. 'Try old lady Carragan. Runs a boarding house. She has a bath.'

Dancer tipped his head. 'Many thanks.' He tried to rise, then found he'd have to try harder if he wished to succeed.

The door opened and in strode a blood-splashed Dassem.

Everyone in the room stared for a time, silent. He answered their stares with a pinched brow.

'So . . .' Dancer finally said into the silence. 'You held them off.' The swordsman gave a curt assent. 'I, ah, apologize for not being there. I was on my way. But I was . . . sidetracked.'

Dassem looked him up and down. 'So I see.'

The door opened again and in walked their old enemy, Lee, and a huge street-tough.

Urko lurched to his feet, bellowing, 'What's this?'

Dassem raised his hands for calm. 'They're here to join.'

Urko fell back into his chair with a massive sigh. 'Thank the gods.'

The young woman, his opponent from prior encounters, looked Dancer up and down. With a sort of sideways smile she said, 'I see you met Cowl.' Dancer nodded. 'And I guess you won.'

'I guess so,' Dancer agreed. 'You are here to join, then?' Lee nodded. He pointed her to Surly. 'Talk to her.'

Dassem peered round the room, then asked, 'Where's the mage – Kellanved?'

Dancer felt his face stiffen and he looked away. 'Still . . . missing.'

A soft curse sounded from Surly at the bar. She poured herself a shot from the expensive foreign decanter and tossed it back. 'Why am I not surprised?'

'We need to organize,' Dassem answered. 'Mock may choose to strike against us now to gain favour—'

'Mock no longer,' Lee interjected.

Dassem looked at her. 'Oh?'

'One of the lasses let me know last night. He had an accident in the Hold. Fell off a parapet and over the cliff. A troika of captains rules now.'

'Ah. None the less. They may strike.'

'Let them,' Urko growled, leaning forward. 'We can take them!'

'Not if they can unite all the crews,' Surly warned.

Urko sank back into his chair. 'Dammit.'

Surly waved Lee to her and the two spoke for a time. Two-ton thumped down at a table and poured himself a flagon of beer.

Then Dassem spoke to the room, addressing everyone. 'My

strength is tactics, and I am new, so it is not for me to say. But what is our position?'

Everyone eyed Surly. She pointed Lee aside, murmuring something to her, then sent a hard look to Dancer. *Up to me, I guess*, he decided, and he rose, wincing and hissing as multiple cuts stretched and reopened. 'We rest up,' he announced. 'Keep a wary watch, of course. In a couple of days we'll have a council to decide.'

Everyone nodded.

Dancer answered the nods. 'Good. If anyone needs me I'll be getting cleaned up.' He walked stiff-legged out of the door, making for old lady Carragan's.

*

The swampy delta of a salt marsh extends out into the harbour where the main channel of the Malaz river empties into the bay. Here, at dawn, the seabirds erupted into the air, cawing their complaints as something moved within the muck and slime.

The tall reeds and cattails shook as a mud-caked shape pulled itself out of the silts and up the side of a sandbar. The man had one hand pressed to his neck where the mud glistened a deep red. His chest was shaking as if spasming and finally, reluctantly, a gurgling laugh burst forth from his smeared lips as he chuckled uncontrollably. Crimson bubbles foamed at the fingers pressed to his neck. Yet he laughed on, wheezing.

After a time, he gestured with his other hand in a sweeping motion and darkness swirled up about him. When it dispersed he was gone, and the spiralling seabirds descended to roost among the reeds once again.

Chapter 19

THE NEXT THING TAYSCHRENN WAS AWARE OF HE WAS OUTSIDE in sunlight leaning up against the gritty stone wall of the house while the short mock-elderly Kellanved had a hand on his shoulder and was peering up at him, looking quite concerned.

'You are all right?' he asked, frowning.

He blinked, thinking rather panickily, *Am I? Am I all right?* 'What . . . what happened?'

'You passed out immediately,' the wizened fellow said. 'Exhaustion, mental and physical, obviously.'

He straightened to eye the mage of Meanas just as narrowly. 'Obviously,' he echoed drily.

The Dal Hon mage brushed his hands together. 'Good. Well, that's that. They saw you enter the Azath House and so they think you entombed for ever. And so they have abandoned the chase, hmm? Just don't raise your Warren any time soon, yes?'

'Of course.'

The mage took a deep breath and his walking stick appeared in his hand. 'Well, then. Let us see how things have shaken out, yes?' and he started down the path.

Ahead, two figures roused themselves to stand barring the way: one short and wiry, the other massive and holding a tall halberd across the gate.

Leading the way, Kellanved paused. 'What is this?'

The short wiry one pointed a recriminating finger. 'You are abusing your position,' he accused. 'How much more of this coming and going must we endure?'

The mage of Meanas tapped his walking stick to his mouth,

striking an exaggerated thinking pose. 'Well . . . that depends entirely upon you, don't you think?'

The short elderly fellow flinched as if struck; clearly he was not used to being spoken to in this manner. 'Why, you little rat,' he spluttered. 'If you think we will tolerate these insults—'

Kellanved pushed ahead between the pair. 'You'll just have to, won't you? The House chooses, not you. So you'll just have to make the best of it.' He urged Tayschrenn onward. 'Come, come.'

Tayschrenn slid forward, uneasily, between the scowling short fellow and the big one whose hands gripped and regripped the long haft of his halberd.

They left them behind, staring after them, glowering pure anger.

'Who are they?' Tayschrenn asked.

Kellanved gave a dismissive wave of a hand. 'Oh, guardians set by Burn to watch over the House. Penance, no doubt, for some ancient crime. Or,' and he set the silver hound's head of the walking stick to his mouth, 'devotional acts, perhaps.'

Tayschrenn arched a brow as he regarded the diminutive mage scuttling along next to him. Clearly, this one had spent a great deal of time poking about into the hidden workings of the powers active in the world. Something he had sorely neglected.

The mage used his walking stick to push open the door to a bar whose hanging tile announced its name to be Smiley's.

Everyone within swore and jumped to their feet as they entered.

Kellanved bobbed his head. 'Nice to be appreciated. How long has it been?'

A lean Napan woman at the bar answered, 'Three days.'

'Dancer?' he asked.

'Recuperating.'

'Very good.' He motioned Tayschrenn forward. 'This way.' He paused. 'Ah! Surly, Tayschrenn.' He pointed about the broad room, picking people out. 'Urko, Choss, Tocaras, and, ah, others.'

Tayschrenn nodded a greeting, then Kellanved urged him up a stairway. 'My office,' he explained. Within, he gestured to a side table. 'Drink?'

Tayschrenn found a decanter of white wine and poured himself a touch. He crossed to the one window and peered out at grey slate roofs, a cloudy sky, and the iron-grey waters of the bay beyond. He sighed his . . . discouragement. 'So – I'm working for a petty criminal.'

Kellanved had eased himself down in a chair behind the expanse of a broad empty desk. His chin barely cleared it and he frowned, studying the bulky piece as if it had unaccountably risen. He raised a finger. 'Soon to be far less petty.'

A knock, and the door opened to reveal a tall lean fellow who moved stiffly as if feeling recent wounds. Kellanved stood. 'Ah, Dancer. This is Tayschrenn.' Dancer nodded and Tayschrenn studied him in turn. Deadly, he decided.

Another knock and in came a broad-shouldered curly-haired man who nodded to Dancer and Kellanved in turn. Kellanved made the introductions.

'So they were chasing you,' Dancer said. Tayschrenn inclined his head.

A third knock heralded the Napan woman, Surly. She studied everyone, then shut the door behind her. 'Thank you for helping,' she said.

Tayschrenn could read the pain the admission of such a need cost her.

Kellanved set his hands on the desk before him. 'Good. We are all here. What I want to know is why we are. We should be in the Hold by now.'

Everyone blinked at him, uncertain. The rather hard-bitten-looking woman, Surly, cleared her throat. 'I do not believe the captains would accept you.'

Kellanved shrugged. 'They will have no choice.'

'Good luck,' Surly answered. 'But we're leaving.'

The one called Dancer crossed his arms and leaned up against the desk. 'Why?'

She laughed. 'Why? They know we're here. They won't give up. We have to go.' She waved to Kellanved. 'You can keep the *Twisted*. It's more yours than ours. We'll take some smaller craft tonight and head out. We're thinking of going north. Serving with the Falari.'

'No,' Kellanved said.

She blinked, drawing herself up stiffly. 'You cannot stop us.'

Kellanved raised his open hands. 'I know. I cannot compel you. Nor would I want to. What I can do is offer something.'

She eyed him, openly suspicious. 'What?'

'Nap.'

Her look changed to one of sceptical evaluation. 'Really? You think you can offer Nap?'

He nodded, quite serious. The woman's gaze narrowed, and shifted to the one called Dancer. 'No one kills Tarel. I forbid it.'

Both Kellanved and Dancer nodded; and Tayschrenn found it humorous that they actually nodded in unison.

'Agreed,' said Kellanved.

'And just how will you perform this miracle?' Surly asked, cocking a brow.

The hunched little mage tapped his hands on the desk. 'Tonight we will take the Hold.'

Both her brows rose as she considered this. 'Ah. I see.'

*

Dancer wasn't ready for another fight so soon. He wasn't happy with Kellanved's announcement, but when everyone had been dismissed to organize the move the mage assured him that it wouldn't come to that.

Dancer took him at his word and went to prepare. He had discarded his old clothes, which had been hacked to rags, and selected a new shirt and trousers. He retied the bindings over the thrust through his thigh, feeling the stitches pulling, and dressed, then drew on his thin armoured vest, his shirt, his baldrics, and a brocaded felt vest over all.

When night came they set out, leaving a skeleton guard at Smiley's. Since Lee's defection to Dassem half her crew had come over as well, so they now effectively controlled the entire city. All that was left was the Hold, as Kellanved rightly saw.

All told, they mustered close to fifty foot-soldiers. Jack and Tocaras commanded a contingent of twenty, and Dujek and Choss another. Both of these had set out earlier, overland, to come to the Hold from the rear. The main party, Dassem, Dancer, Kellanved and the mage Tayschrenn, together with Surly, the Napans, and Lee, would climb the twisting Rampart Way. Cartheron alone remained behind, still gravely wounded, and guarded by four trusted local hires.

Dancer winced all the way, favouring his wounded leg. He hoped he wouldn't have to act later, and with that in mind he pushed ahead to where Dassem led.

367

'I'm wounded,' he whispered as they climbed the broad twisting stairs.

'I saw.'

'You'll have to cover for me.'

'Agreed.'

'Good.' He fell back to Kellanved's side. The mage was faring no better, puffing and sweating. 'No wonder the city and the Hold are so divided,' he huffed, wiping his face with a handkerchief.

'It's good for you to get out.'

'Says who?'

After much twisting and turning back and forth, they reached the top landing and the Hold walls. An arched tunnel led to the first bailey, past which lay an inner bailey and the keep itself. Entrance to the inner bailey was guarded by another stone archway, and here the gatekeeper sat. Torches hissed and snapped along the wall, while a lantern in a sconce next to him provided the only light in the archway.

Kellanved nodded to him. 'Lubben, I believe?'

The gatekeeper, a hunchback, grinned back. 'Been wondering when you'd turn up.'

'And?'

'And what?'

'Is there some secret password we should know? A key we need? Or perhaps you'd like a bag of coin?'

Though hunched from his twisted back, the fellow was quite sturdy and muscular-looking, with thick arms and thighs. Dancer thought he might prove a dangerous opponent. But he waved aside Kellanved's suggestions, saying, 'Nah. Go on through.'

Kellanved peered about, suspicious and rather taken aback. 'Just like that?'

'Yeah. Just like that.'

'Why?'

'Because I want to see what you're gonna do.'

Kellanved nodded now, in understanding. 'Ah! I see. You are a student of the circus of the world.'

The fellow gave a wink, took a silver flask from inside his shirt, and tossed back a mouthful. 'Good luck,' he offered.

Kellanved nodded his farewell and pushed open the iron-bound door. The inner bailey was unguarded. Oil lamps flickered next to the door to the main keep. Here, Dassem and Urko took the lead.

Dancer took up Kellanved's left side while Surly fell in behind.

Urko slammed open the door and they marched up the entranceway into the main reception hall. A huge fire burned in a large stone fireplace along the rear wall. Tables were crowded by crews who stared now, suddenly silent. At the high table sat three captains. These three now eyed them, surprised and rather annoyed.

'So, it is true,' Kellanved announced loudly. 'Mock no longer.'

The three captains shared dark knowing grins.

'Fell drunk from a parapet,' said one.

'Threw himself over pining for his sorceress lass,' said another.

'We haven't decided yet,' explained the third. Then he added, 'So, what are you doing here, mage? You have the city. The old rules as under Mock remain.'

Kellanved walked forward, out on to the open floor of the wide hall. He tapped the stones with his walking stick as he went, a finger raised as if about to question a point of procedure. 'Ah! The old rules . . . about them. I have a question. Is it not Malazan tradition that the strongest captain rules?'

'That is so,' answered the bearded one on the right. Renish, Dancer believed was his name. 'But you are no captain.'

Kellanved gave an exaggerated nod. 'Ah. But . . . you see, I believe I am. I have a vessel. The *Twisted*.'

The middle one laughed his scorn. He bore long moustaches after the style of Mock. Hess, Dancer knew. 'You may *own* that scow, but you are no seaman. No mariner!'

The gathered crews all joined in the laughter. Kellanved waited for the noise to die down, rocking back and forth on his heels, hands behind his back. He nodded again. 'True, true. I am no sailor. However, I do have sailors and captains who serve me. Skilled captains such as Urko, Choss, and Cartheron Crust.'

'Napans,' hissed the last captain at the table, scarred and sundarkened, wearing a sturdy leather jack, long-knives at his waist. Guran.

Kellanved raised his chin. 'Napan *renegades*. Wanted outlaws. Thus, dare I say, honorary Malazans?'

Arguments broke out among the company as the gathered raiders and marines set to talking all at once. Guran banged a pewter tankard on the table for silence. Once the babble had settled, he regarded Kellanved. 'Your point?' he demanded.

'Ah! My point. Yes. Well . . . seeing as I have as many as four or five captains in my service, I suppose that makes me an admiral.'

'What!' Guran exploded. The crews surged to their feet in an uproar. Hess and Renish gaped at the mage, astounded by his claim.

Dancer peered round at the chaos and struggled to suppress a smile. Whatever was going to transpire this night he was enjoying this. The odd little fellow nominating himself as admiral.

It took all three captains waving their arms and shouting and banging the table to restore order. Hess, at the centre, now spoke. 'You are standing for admiral of Malaz, are you?'

Kellanved inclined his head. 'I am.'

'You do realize that you must be ready to enforce this claim? That any challenge must be met in combat? Combat with knife or sword – no tricks or damned magery?'

'Yes.'

'Combat,' Hess added, 'to the death?'

Kellanved waved a hand dismissively. 'I do.'

The three captains exchanged triumphant glances. Guran stood.

Dancer felt a sudden sinking feeling, as if all their plans had just gone awry. How could the lad hope to fight any of these experienced raiders? Hadn't he foreseen a challenge?'

Kellanved raised a finger once more. Guran scowled, but nodded, 'What?'

'I understand I may nominate a champion – should you agree.'

Guran cast his brother captains another glance of triumph. 'Wrong.' He started down from the high table. '*If* you choose to hide behind a champion, then the challenger may select him from among your crew.'

The sturdy fellow rounded the table and set his fists to his waist. He studied all who had come with Kellanved. The crews had remained on their feet as well, and now they set to moving the tables and benches aside, clearing a space.

The captain took his time, eyeing every one of Kellanved's people. Most he dismissed immediately, such as Dassem and Urko. His gaze lingered for a time on Surly, before moving on to the last of them at the rear, the young woman, Lee.

Dancer snarled inwardly. Stupid traditions! They should just set to knifing everyone! To this end he caught Surly's eye, and was surprised to see there a similar opinion. But Kellanved obviously knew him too well, because he felt the lad's hand at his arm, pressing him back.

Guran gestured to Lee, inviting her forward. 'You, lass. You'll do. Will you fight for your admiral here?'

'No!' Dassem called, stepping up. 'Not her. I will fight.'

Guran waggled a finger at him. 'No, boyo. Not you.' He pointed to Lee. 'Her.'

Dassem faced her. 'You need not do this. None will hold you to it.'

Surprising Dancer, the lean young woman looked to Surly, as if seeking permission, and Surly nodded as if granting it. Smiling, she turned to Guran. 'I accept.'

A wide space had been cleared and everyone edged back towards the walls. Guran drew his long-knives while he started to circle. Dancer fumed inwardly at this development. The man was obviously a veteran of countless knife fights, on land and at sea. How could Kellanved have allowed his claim to come to this? Hadn't he anticipated such a possibility? Gods, from what he'd heard, Dassem on his own could slaughter everyone in this hall. But then they wouldn't have Malaz, would they? And they never would. It had to be won over, and that meant bowing to the Malazans' absurd way of handling command.

But if they failed here – as they did at Heng – he resolved never to let the pint-sized fakir forget it.

Lee circled as well, eyeing her opponent, and Dancer was not encouraged by what he saw. She wore plain loose pantaloons, gathered in at a wide sash, and a loose silk shirt. Guran, on the other hand, wore an armoured and layered leather jack over his shirt. Offhand, he didn't think much of her chances.

Still, she'd shown an inner steel in their dealings; as when she'd stood up to him. And she'd been hard enough to take over after Geffen died at Surly's hands.

Guran struck a ready position, both long-knives raised. Lee reached back to her collar with both hands and came away with twinned, extremely long and thin stilettos. Dancer's brows rose at that – she hadn't drawn those on him!

And rightly so, he reflected, as they hadn't been embroiled in a blood-feud at that time.

The circles the two traced tightened with every circuit. They held their blades extended, watching, gauging. Once they were near enough they began feinting and probing. Guran slashed with his heavier weapons and far greater strength; Lee slipped and dodged, never parrying square on, or meeting any attack directly.

Dancer urged her on, nodding. *Good! Yes. Keep your distance. Look out – yes.*

Guran pressed the attack, confident and dismissive – too much so, as Dancer clearly saw and hoped Lee did as well. Yet the man had survived countless such duels and showed a healthy respect for the woman's needle-like weapons.

Suddenly they were close; Lee had chosen her moment. Guran slashed and thrust yet she wove and slipped every attack though they now stood toe to toe. Then she spun aside, whipping in a reverse circle, and her blade darted out in a blur like a striking serpent to pass through the man's neck in a needle thrust. She landed on her knees even as he slashed in return, breaking one of her blades and leaving her open to a follow-up.

The second thrust never came. The man was blinking, a hand at his throat, tottering sideways and stumbling. He fell back against a table, his eyes wide and confused.

Dancer let out a long breath he hadn't been aware he'd been holding. Lee straightened and flicked the few drops of blood from her remaining stiletto. Guran dropped both his weapons to clutch at his neck. He was staring about wildly, his eyes almost pleading; then he fell to his knees and toppled forward, dead.

In the silence that followed Dancer noted how Lee inclined her head to Surly, and how Surly came out to take her hands and congratulate her.

Kellanved stepped to the centre of the cleared space. He planted his walking stick and regarded the other two captains. 'Do we have an accord?' he asked.

Hess and Renish glanced to the crews as if gauging their chances. Kellanved saw it, and he tapped his walking stick on the ground once more. The resounding echoes of that merest touch rattled the windows and forced groans from the blackened timber rafters far above. Dust came sifting down over everyone.

Both captains jerked an assent and Kellanved nodded loftily, satisfied. 'Excellent. Our business is done, then.' He waved to the crews. 'Return to the tables – I'll not interfere with the festivities.' He motioned to Hess. 'Just what is the occasion, anyway?'

Hess drew a shaky hand down his moustaches. He bowed his head. 'It is one of the festivals of Chem, ah, admiral, sir.'

'Ah yes! Of course.' He extended an arm to the stairs. 'Might we have a tour of the quarters?'

Hess bowed again, inviting him forward. 'Yes, admiral. This way.'

Kellanved motioned to Tayschrenn. 'Come. You may find this of interest.'

This new mage – a renegade from Kartool, Dancer understood – looked utterly disdainful, but steeled himself with a breath and followed.

Dancer went to Lee, who was pouring herself a glass of wine. He bowed his head in acknowledgement. 'Well done. Very impressive. I'm glad we never had to cross blades.'

She daubed a cloth to her face, nodding. 'Thank you.' Her glance, he noticed, was not upon him, but over his shoulder to – he looked – the swordsman Dassem, who had moved to put his back to a wall and was assessing the various exits and blind spots in the chamber.

'Have you seen *him* fight?' she asked.

Rather startled by the question, he frowned, shaking his head. 'No. Why?'

A secretive smile came to her lips and she gave him a strange look, as if to say, *You have no idea.*

He wondered, then, what he had missed in her exchanges with Dassem, and, it seemed, with Surly.

He watched Kellanved climbing the stairs with the Kartool mage, Tayschrenn, waving his hands and no doubt spouting the most absurd nonsense. It was no longer just the two of them. Things would be much more complicated now.

Epilogue

THEY WERE PACKING UP THEIR POSSESSIONS AT SMILEY'S FOR their move to the Hold when a cry of dismay and pain from Kellanved in his office brought Dancer running – him and several Napans, and the bodyguard Kellanved now trailed round after him; but Dancer was the first to arrive.

He found the mage on his hands and knees on the floor, his butt in the air, as he shuffled about running his hands over the dusty floorboards, moaning.

Dancer knelt beside him, taking his shoulder. 'What is it! Are you wounded?' Choss, Tocaras and Lee crowded the doorway together with several of the Malazan bodyguards.

The Dal Hon pressed his hands to his wrinkled forehead. 'Gone! It's gone! I've searched everywhere!'

Dancer scanned the dirty boards. 'What's gone? What is it?'

'My stone!'

Dancer flinched away. *Oh, for the love of Burn!* He pushed the lad over and crossed to the side table to pour himself a drink. Seeing everyone in the doorway, he waved them off. The Napans exchanged uncertain glances, but nodded, and headed back downstairs. Two of the bodyguards shut the door and waited outside.

Kellanved had dusted himself off and retreated to the broad empty expanse of his desk. 'Someone has taken it,' he announced, steepling his fingers, his gaze narrowing.

Dancer tossed back his drink. 'It's just a rock. Forget it.'

Kellanved shook his head. 'Oh no, my friend. There's more to it than that. I can sense it.' He tapped his fingertips together. 'I just can't parse its secret yet.'

A knock and the door opened to reveal Surly, Lee behind her. 'There a problem?'

'No—' Dancer began.

'Who's been in here?' Kellanved demanded.

Dancer looked to the ceiling in mute frustration. Surly shrugged. 'Just about everyone at one time or another.'

'The office was tossed, wasn't it – Lee?'

She nodded. 'Yes. Geffen's boys ran through everything looking for valuables.'

The shrivelled fellow, looking even more frail and tiny behind his huge desk, tapped his fingers to his lips. 'No . . . they wouldn't have touched it.'

'Touched what?' Lee asked.

Kellanved waved her away. 'Never mind!' To Surly, he said, 'Who cleaned up in here?'

Her mouth turned down as she considered. 'Urko did most of that.'

'Send him up.'

'Kellanved . . .' Dancer began, but the mage raised a hand to forestall him.

'Just a few questions.'

Dancer sighed, leaned back against the low table, stretched out his legs, and crossed his arms.

A while later Urko came stomping up the stairs. He wore a stained leather apron, his sleeves pushed up over his thick forearms.

Kellanved nodded to him. 'Ah, good, Urko. Have you seen a . . .' He looked him up and down. 'What *are* you doing?'

'Rendering.'

The mage blinked. 'Right. Rendering.' It was clear to Dancer from the way he said it that he had no idea what rendering was. He flapped a hand. 'Well. When you cleaned up here, did you find any curios, odd stones, bits and bobs, that sort of thing?'

The huge fellow tucked his ham hands up under his armpits, and cocked his head, thinking. He nodded, his head tilted. 'Yeah. I remember. Two of Burn's gifts: a stone shell and a stone animal tooth, and one of them worked pieces of flint that turn up all over.'

'Like an arrowhead?'

'Yeah. But 'tisn't. It's a broken tip from a spear. River-smoothed. Real glossy. From them old people from ages ago.'

Kellanved's shoulders eased and he nodded. 'Yes. That's it. It's one of my favourites. Do you still have it?'

He frowned then, almost wary. 'Yeah, I got it. It's in the kitchen. It's a nice piece.'

'May I have it back?'

'Back? I found it, y'know.'

'Found it? *I* found it, I'll have you know!'

Dancer pushed forward, hands raised. To Urko he said, 'What would you like – for it, I mean?'

The big fellow's hands were out now. He slammed one fist into a palm, considering. 'A ship,' he finally said. 'A captaincy.'

'A captaincy?' Kellanved protested in disbelief. 'For a rock?'

Urko threw a hand in the air, half turning away. 'Fine!'

'Okay!' Kellanved called, clutching the edge of the desk. 'Okay. Yes. You can have the *Twisted*.'

'Not *that* ship. Another.'

Kellanved raised his hands in surrender. 'Very well! Another. A ship. Yours.'

The fellow cheered up immensely, grinning. 'Good! A command. And before Cartheron.' He chortled all the way down the stairs.

Dancer examined the mage until he hunched his shoulders, demanding, 'What?'

Dancer pointed to the stairs. 'You're giving away captaincies for shiny rocks now?'

The little fellow flapped a hand. 'He was going to get one anyway, wasn't he?'

Dancer considered, scratched his brow, then shrugged. 'Hunh. I suppose so.'

'There you go.'

Lee entered, holding out a triangular brown stone. 'Urko told me to bring this up.'

Dancer held out a hand and she tossed it to him. He crossed the room and dropped it on to the empty desktop. It clattered there noisily and Dancer stood looking down at it for rather a long time. Then he picked it up again and dropped it once more.

Kellanved, who had been twiddling his thumbs, now looked up, puzzled.

Dancer pushed the rock with a finger and it spun lazily.

Lee cleared her throat. 'Ah . . . is that all?'

Both men were staring, fascinated, at the rock. Dancer looked over, distracted, and waved her out. She went, shaking her head at the craziness of her employers, and Dancer returned to studying the worked stone spear-tip. It occurred to him that he'd seen it fall to the ground many times. In Heng, now that he thought about it, it had always pointed west. Now, when he flicked it, it rocked and spun, yet always returned to point north.

Every time.

Kellanved was staring, his eyes huge. He pressed his fists to his chin, triumphant. '*Yes!* I knew it!'

'Knew what?'

'It points the way, Dancer.'

'The way? The way to what?'

Kellanved raised a finger into the air and whispered, his voice lowered, peering about as if someone were listening: 'To the grave-yard of the Army of Bone.'

Dancer flinching away, scowling. 'Children's bedtime stories.'

'No, true. An ancient army, cursed to search forever – so they say.'

'Search for what?'

The little fellow flicked his fingers, irritated. 'Well . . . for their enemy, I assume. What else does an army search for?'

'A tavern?'

Kellanved made a face. 'Very funny. No, this is very important. We'll have to leave right away.'

Dancer stared; then, seeing that the lad was serious, laughed his utter disbelief. 'Leave? In case you've forgotten, you promised these people you'd take Nap.'

Kellanved waved all that aside. 'Yes, yes. We'll manage that. But this . .'

Dancer eyed him. 'Look, I'm going to collect my kit, okay?' He pointed, glaring. 'No taking off without me, all right?' The little fellow's wrinkled chin was resting on his hands, flat on the desk, and he was staring at the rock, fascinated.

'All right?' Dancer repeated.

The mage blinked, glanced to him, flicked a hand. 'Yes, yes.'

'Good.' Dancer paused at the door to peer back. Kellanved was poking at the rock, making it spin. He shook his head and shut the door, thinking, *If he leaves without me, I'll kill him.*

When Lee returned downstairs Surly waved for her to join her in the kitchen. The Napan named Cartheron, she noticed, followed her in. Surly sent a glance to the giant fellow, Urko, who went to guard the rear door. The other brother, Cartheron, stood watch at the inner door – pale and sweaty from a serious wound, but standing just the same.

Surly eyed Lee up and down, and Lee, in turn, eyed Surly. Lean and hard was her evaluation; and she'd seen her in action, too, against Geffen. This one was no fool.

'There'll be fighting when we move against Nap,' Surly said, 'but you don't strike me as a sailor or a marine, isn't that so?'

Lee crossed her arms. 'I can fight.'

The Napan woman nodded. At some time, Lee noticed, she'd been hit very hard across the nose; it was flattened slightly. And she kept her hair short, just as Lee did. 'Yes,' she said. 'You gave us a very nice demonstration of that. Well done. But in the future don't advertise your skills, hey?'

Lee nodded, wondering where this was headed.

'You are no mage, are you?'

'No.'

Surly continued gauging her. 'So, you need work that will match your, ah, particular skill. I believe I have such work – if you are interested.'

Lee uncrossed her arms and clasped her hands behind her back; she was surprised to find them sweaty. She inclined her head: *I'm interested.*

'Very good. I have people on the island of Nap who work for me. They need to know our plans. None of us Napans can go – we'd be detained on sight. You, however, aren't Napan and aren't known. I want you to deliver a message for us. Will you do this?'

For some reason Lee found that she couldn't speak – yet inside all she was thinking was *Yes!* Real work! Not this wretched herding of street-toughs or intimidating shopkeepers. She nodded, fierce.

Surly inclined her head in answer. 'Good. You will take a trader to the mainland. From there you will take another vessel to Dariyal, the capital of Nap. There you will find an inn called the Pin and Strake. You should see a man at the rear using a knife to eat or

378

whittle. You will compliment him on the knife and you will ask him if it's Wickan. Have you got that?'

Lee nodded again. 'Yes. Wickan.'

'He will leave the inn later and you will follow him. He will lead you to another man, a very large Napan – fat rather than muscular, not like Urko – and you will say to him: "Your worst student sends her regards."' Surly studied her critically. 'Do you have that?'

'Yes. Worst student.'

'You understand that if you vary at all from these instructions you will be killed?'

Lee felt a fierce desire to leave at once – she could do this. *I can do this. This woman, Surly, will see.* She swallowed hard to say tautly, 'Yes.'

The Napan nodded again. 'Very good. He will ask if you have a message for him and you will say this: "We are proceeding by other means." Repeat that, please.'

Lee took a breath to steel herself, repeated, 'We are proceeding by other means.'

The woman smiled, faintly. Lee had the feeling that this was all the smile the woman would ever muster. 'Good. Now, do not worry. It's just a message. But your name is known, and I want you to change it. A new name for a new role. Can you think of one?'

She swallowed. 'I've always liked the name Opal.'

Surly inclined her head in assent, accepting it. 'Very good, Opal.' She took hold of her shoulders, looking her up and down. 'Give me those earrings,' she said. 'Too distinctive.'

Lee handed them over.

After examining them for a moment, Surly broke one in two and handed one of the pieces to her. 'Take this. You may have to send a message. Include your half to prove authenticity, yes?'

Lee squeezed the fragment in her hand. Surly looked to Urko, who peered out into the back alley then nodded the all clear. Surly handed Lee a small bag of coin and gestured her out. 'May Chem watch over you.'

Lee bowed to her and went to the door, but just outside she stopped and whispered low to the great hulking fellow, 'Who *is* she?'

'Someone worth following, lass – now go.' He pushed her on with one wide paw.

379

She went, and not running either, as that would attract attention. She walked down to the docks, where she'd get a room for the night before taking a day-trader across to the mainland tomorrow. Under a hanging street-lamp, she opened her hand to examine the fragment: it was half the hummingbird earring. Just the clasp that would pinch the ear: a silver three-toed bird's claw.

ABOUT THE AUTHOR

Born in Winnipeg, Ian Cameron Esslemont has studied and worked as an archaeologist, travelled extensively in South East Asia and lived in Thailand and Japan for several years. He now lives in Fairbanks, Alaska, with his wife and children. He has a creative writing degree and his novels are all set in the fantasy world of Malaz that he co-created with Steven Erikson. *Deadhouse Landing* follows *Dancer's Lament* and continues the story of the turbulent early history of one of the great imagined landscapes. To find out more, visit www.malazanempire.com / www.ian-esslemont.com